Lege et Lacrima

ALINA COMSA

BOOK 1 OF THE LOST HOPE SERIES

Lege et Lacrima, Book One of the Lost Hope Series

Lege et Lacrima is the first book in the Lost Hope series of interconnected standalone novels. It's a strangers-to-lovers romance with a pinch of suspense, complete with HEA, and the tiniest of cliffhangers. This book is intended for readers 18+, with explicit scenes, mature language, touching on sensitive topics, and more.

Published by: Malum Canticus Books

Editing by: Katelyn Smith

Cover design by: Siiri Becker (Ultrasonic Assets)

E-book ISBN: 978-1-7385278-0-9

Print ISBN: 978-1-7385278-1-6

Contents

Dedication

To my other half,

Thanks, love, for taking one for the team

doing all the dishes.

And to hazelnut lattes for keeping me awake.

To anyone ever forced to prove their worthiness

for a scrap of love and affection.

You are worthy. You are loved.

Blurb

My entire life I've been dismissed, cast aside, thrown away, whenever something better appeared on the horizon.

Finding my boyfriend in bed with another woman obliterates the last of my confidence, hopes, and dreams.

It's only fitting I end up in Lost Hope, a small town in the heart of snowy mountains and lush green forests.

My roots spring to life here, the first ones in years. They're as fragile as I am, anchoring deeper and deeper with every unexpected connection I forge, withering under the unknown threats looming over me.

I'm as hopeless as the town's name, until a snowstorm brings *HIM* to my doorstep.

Tall, dark, and impossibly protective, he's determined to be my knight in shining... tattoos.

My darkness doesn't deter him, and all my efforts to keep my distance are thwarted by his secret weapons of ice destruction: his ridiculously cute stepsisters. Between a preteen with a wit so sharp it slices clean through my steel walls, and a toddler determined to melt the ice caps around my heart, one snuggle at a time, there's no escape.

My instincts to run away fade into nothingness with every stolen kiss and possessive touch.

He may have traded the Marines for a guardianship, but his predatory instincts are alive and well.

And his ultimate mission is to slay my demons and make me **his**.

Welcome to Lost Hope

I've had tons of fun writing the first book in the town of Lost Hope. Tons of crying, too, but who's counting at this point?

I hope you enjoy reading Lalah's story as much as I enjoyed telling it. And I really hope you enjoy her knight in shinning... tattoos. :-)

For the best reading experience, it is recommended to start with Lege et Lacrima and continue with the order the books are released in. Each novel has the spotlight on a different couple, but the main story continues in subsequent books.

Latin words and their meaning in Lege et Lacrima:

- **Lege et Lacrima:** Read it and weep

- **Meus Bellator**: My Warrior

- **Astrum:** Star

- **Cedo:** To yield. **Used as:** Release. Give up and come sit next to me.

- **Introrsum:** Inward; Within. **Used as:** Get inside (house).

- **Obsideo:** To besiege; To blockade. **Used as:** Block.

- **Laxo:** To loosen; To relax. **Used as:** Released from all commands.

- **Spatior:** To walk; To stroll. **Used as:** Outside, bathroom.

You'll also find toddler talk. Because aren't they oh so adorable when they smile, bat their eyelashes, and say "pwease"?

And from toddlers we're moving on to some Irish curses... because the *accent*. Amirite or Amirite? :D

Now, before we delve any further, some sensible subjects are touched in the book. There's nothing graphic, and I've done my absolute best to treat them with the sensibility and care those mentions deserve.

Lege et Lacrima has the following mentions:

- Child abuse/neglect

- Sexual assault

- Death of a parent

- Drug use (with and without consent)

- Depression

- Car crash

- Cheating

- Bullying

Your mental health is a priority.

Playlist

♡ Gabby Barrett & Charlie Puth - I Hope

♡ Sam Smith & Normani - Dancing with a Stranger

♡ Disturbed - The Sound of Silence

♡ Bishop Briggs - River

♡ Imagine Dragons - Demons

♡ Sia - Unstoppable

♡ Evanescence - Bring Me to Life

♡ Maroon 5 - She Will Be Loved

♡ Modà - Sono Già Solo

♡ Imagine Dragons - Believer

♡ Hoobastank - The Reason

♡ Christina Aguilera & Alejandro Fernandez - Hoy Tengo Ganas De Ti

Prologue

I've never been lucky. Not one day in my life. If something goes well or my way, I always know to watch my back. The other shoe will soon drop. That's what I'm thinking as I stare at the lottery ticket. The damned, winning lottery ticket.

"Oh, boy," I mumble to myself, chewing on my bottom lip. "Lady Luck will definitely take a big bite out of my ass."

It's ironic, really. I've never bought a lottery ticket. I despise the sense of irrational hope while knowing there's so little chance of actually winning anything at all. I blame boredom and this never-ending work conference for creating the perfect recipe for disaster. Not only have I bought a lottery ticket but actually won the blasted thing.

All it took was dinner out with some industry peers. A few drinks too many and they felt it would be a great idea to recreate the lottery-playing episode from *Friends*. One would think quality assurance auditors are tamer than that. My refusal to participate fell on deaf ears. A day later, I was the unwilling winner of hundreds of millions of dollars. *What in the actual fuck?*

Placing the ticket neatly in my phone case, I hurry to board the plane taking me home. I guess daydreaming about all the ways Karma will club me in the head after all the millions she'll be dropping into my bank account makes time pass faster.

The four-hour flight from LaGuardia to St. Louis Lambert International Airport passes in the blink of an eye. Before I even realize what's happening, I'm waiting in the crowded pickup area for my boyfriend, Callum, to arrive.

I dropped him a message before boarding with my arrival time and pizza preference. I sent another text telling him I'd landed, but surprisingly, both showed unread.

My mind is still in a fog trying to process all the ways my life will change now... All I want is to get home, have a cup of steaming coffee and, I guess, inform my live-in boyfriend of eight years that we're multi-millionaires.

How is this my life?

After twenty minutes of pacing back and forth in the pickup area, twirling a minty vape around my fingers, my frustration increases with every second Callum doesn't show up. My anxiety is through the roof, and I can't douse it. Not even the rumble of planes taking off or the familiar sights of my city can distract me from the doom I cloaked myself in.

After ten more minutes, Callum is still nowhere to be seen, so I call him. A couple of rings sound in my ear, and his voicemail kicks in.

"Fucking great," I mumble to myself.

I hit the rideshare app, booking one to take me home. If Callum didn't read the messages, there's no chance in hell he's on his way.

Kudos to the driver for reading my mood correctly and allowing me to stew in my misery. I spend the entire ride back home worrying about breaking the news to Callum and how this is going to affect our lives.

Growing up, my family was always about money. Not necessarily in a materialistic kind of way, but more in constantly excusing shitty behavior by blaming the lack of money.

Daddy Dearest was in a bad mood?

That's because I was always in need of a schoolbook or new clothes. Or because I wasn't careful enough, and I damaged the soles of my shoes after wearing them for more than a year. Or because my mother kept nagging about new kitchen appliances.

All I heard all day, every day, was how hard he worked for the money we so carelessly spent. His bad moods always meant new bruises on me, a slap to my face, the sharp sting of a belt on my bottom, a ruler splicing open my palms.

When money was not an excuse for anger, it was used to control. As long as Daddy Dearest was the provider, I wasn't entitled to a voice, to opinions nor to protect myself when he laid his hands and feet on me.

The ironic thing was we were never really without. Daddy Dearest held a good enough job that we easily classified as upper-middle class, but my family life always orbited around money. With them, you were only worth as much as the zeroes in your bank account.

So it worries me tremendously how this will impact my relationship.

Callum had big dreams of us moving to Chicago, but I love our little city of East St. Louis. I love that in certain areas of the city you have one foot in Missouri, and the other in Illinois, essentially being in two places at once.

With its steel arches and age-weathered stone piers, the Eads Bridge was and continues to be my safe place, my beacon of freedom. A physical parallel to my life. My feet on different sides of an imaginary border.

On the left, standing five feet six inches tall, long hair in the wind, is Lalah the Wild. Lalah the Traveler, who only knows safety, love, and care. Lalah the Dauntless, nurtured and protected.

On the right, barely standing up, shoulders hunched under the weight of her hurt, downcast eyes, is Alana the Unworthy. Alana the Inconvenience, an anxious mess of fuck-ups and neediness, and all she knows is pain and soul-deep terror.

Even with all the downs of my upbringing, this city is also where I met Callum. Where we fell in love, and he helped me build a safe space for myself. I'm worried he'll push now for a move to Chicago since we can afford it.

Well, I can afford it.

I know, I know, I should be ecstatic. My financial troubles will soon be gone. But then again, I don't have any financial troubles. Fair, I don't live lavishly, but I earn enough to put a roof over my head, food on my table, more books than I can read in a lifetime, and even a splurge here and there on my favorite perfume.

I don't have to overthink where my next meal will come from. I don't have to worry about not being able to pay my bills. I have enough. *Had* enough, I guess.

Now I have enough to feed and clothe a small country. So I'm not ecstatic.

In fact, I'm freefalling as I stand with my key poised to my apartment's door, and the landing makes for an agonizing pit in my stomach threatening to consume me.

Some people say they can sense just moments before disaster strikes. I believe them because I am one of those people. Growing up in the home I did, I learned how to feel the tension around me; how to interpret the mood of the adults who were supposed to love and protect me.

This saved me most of the time from any new bruises I'd have to explain in school the next day.

I sensed, minutes before Daddy Dearest got home, the mood he was in. If I had a pit in my stomach, it meant I needed to be as quiet as possible, make myself as small as possible, and hide.

So it makes no sense why, as I push open the door and enter my apartment, my stomach is churning and I feel like throwing up. Callum Greyson is not a violent man. I *never* have to fear that from him. He never raises his voice or his hands at me. He's soft, dependable – despite not picking me up from the airport earlier – caring, if with a slightly traditional view on relationship dynamics.

The hallway light is turned off, and the apartment is quiet, making for an eerie feeling. *Where on Earth is he?* Usually, by 8 pm, he'd be on the sofa watching a movie or binging one of his superhero series.

A soft thumping comes from the walls. I curse my neighbors mentally while imagining a herd of baby elephants marching around in the apartment next to ours. The thumping is followed by a guttural moan. This time coming from our bedroom. My heart seizes, and then I giggle under my breath.

Was the asshole watching porn this whole time, and that's why he missed my calls and texts?

I leave my carry-on in the hallway, dump my flats and softly pad toward our bedroom. I guess a nice quickie before sharing life-altering news wouldn't be the worst thing in the world. I missed the nerdy lump of a man the entire week I was away.

I laugh again under my breath, thinking of how embarrassed he'll be when I open our bedroom door, catching him with his hand down his boxers, and the pit in my stomach is all but forgotten.

Twisting the knob slowly, I push open the door with care so I don't startle him. I peek at our bed with the biggest smile on my face. The soft thumping is washed out by the sound of my heart breaking, a rhythmic knife-stab straight to my chest. My body grows numb and cold, the pit in my stomach returning with a vengeance, threatening to freeze me in place.

In MY bedroom, on MY favorite space sheets, the asshole jackhammers relentlessly into another woman. I'm hypnotized by the sight of his ass vigorously pumping into her, moving up and down like a pocket watch trying to get into the depths of my shattered soul.

They are so enthralled in each other that they haven't noticed me gaping like a fucking fish in the doorway.

I clear my throat to get their attention. That's when the asshole halts mid-thrust and, like in *The Exorcist*, slowly rotates his red neck to face me. *What the fuck? Is that a smirk on his face?* I don't waste time analyzing his reaction, as everything in me turns to stone.

"Once you're done, pack your shit and get the fuck out. Leave your keys on the nightstand. I'll let you know when to come back for your crap. You have one hour," I say in an ice-cold voice.

No trace of hurt leaks out of me, *you bag of dicks*, even if inside I'm collapsing atom by atom.

With that, I quietly close the bedroom door, the door to my heart and the door to all my hopes and dreams, put my flats back on, and march my ass to the nearest coffee shop.

I have indeed never been lucky. Not a day in my life. And even though my ex-live-in boyfriend of eight years enjoys fucking someone else, Lady Luck sure enjoys fucking me.

Can you see me waving all the way from my bent-over position?

Chapter One

Lalah

Maevis Barlowe smiles softly at me. With her long braid tied loosely over her shoulder and brown doe eyes, she reminds me of a dark-haired Tinker Bell, both in her youthful appearance and her petite frame.

The rocking chair she sits in is strategically placed to offer the best view of the mountains surrounding us. And what a wonderful view it is. Tall, snowy peaks glow in the distance, a mantle of evergreens embracing the mountains and clear, blue skies as far as the eye can see.

"I know a three-month contract isn't ideal for long-term rentals," I tell her, "but I appreciate you giving me a tour of your lovely home, anyway." Returning her smile, I'm deciding how much to disclose.

After spending no more than three months in each of the places I fancied on stopping, now that I'm on the verge of hitting my thirties, I long for a home. A place of my own where I can exist, and breathe, and read, and not be constantly on the move.

I'd done nothing wrong, yet I was the one fleeing the only home I've ever known four years ago. I'm the one running away at the first sight of a tiny root trying to anchor itself into the ground.

I take a deep breath, and the pit in my stomach grows smaller. It shrinks with every step I take toward healing and every stitch I so painfully apply to my still-mending heart.

I swore to myself if a man ever cheated on me, like Daddy Dearest had on my mom, I wouldn't blame myself or my actions. I wouldn't overthink my behavior in a fruitless quest to understand if something I said, did, or maybe my looks, pushed a man who swore up and down how much he loved me, into the arms and between the legs of another woman.

Logically, I know that even if he was unhappy with me, he could've chosen to discuss his unhappiness, so we'd try to fix the issues. He could've chosen to break up with me, instead of disrespecting me by fucking another woman on my favorite sheets.

Emotionally, I know nothing. The darkness inside me keeps repeating how unlovable I am. How unworthy of attention and affection I am. I shut down the negative voice in my head with a sigh and force my attention back to Maevis.

"I'm willing to pay six months' worth of rent, if it helps you. My house is not ready yet, although I was promised it would be by the end of May. Now, I'm told the soonest move-in date is the middle of August because of the abnormal rain in April. It was impossible for the crew to get the supplies to the construction site," I explain.

I'm crossing my fingers and toes my offer appeals to her. I need to rent her family home for the following summer months.

"It's your house being built just outside town in the forest?" Maevis asks, her smile not faltering despite the tiny frown creasing her forehead. "The townsfolk were concerned, thinking a big conglomerate bought that parcel of land and we'll find ourselves with buildings of condos and city dwellers' holiday homes. The Mayor has been secretive when asked about it."

"No condos!" I laugh, thinking the Mayor has good reasons for keeping her mouth shut. "No city dwellers, either. Just me. I like to keep to myself, while not being too far away from town."

Her smile grows bigger, and she pushes to her feet with a dainty hand stretched toward me.

"You don't need to pay me for six months. I'm happy to open my home to you, Alana, for as long as you need it."

I wince at hearing my oh-so-formal first name. "Call me Lalah, please. You're doing me a huge favor after all."

She gestures at the rental agreement on the coffee table, and I waste no time picking up the pen and signing on the dotted line. Maevis takes the paperwork, leaving me with a copy and the keys to the house.

"I'll see you around, Lalah. Call me if you have any issues, and come visit me at Suga'High on Main Street."

Waving at her, I debate spending the night here and collecting my things from the hotel tomorrow, or driving to Billings now and returning to my temporary home the following day.

"Best get going!" I mumble and, slipping inside my car, I call my right-hand man, Marcus Reyes.

"Boss lady, what can I do you for this fine day?" His cheerful voice comes from my Bluetooth speaker and I sputter a laugh at his inappropriate greeting.

I knew from the first online meeting we had he was my kind of person. I guess I could also call him the only friend I have at the moment.

"Hello to you too, Marcus! Please transfer the deposit and three months' rent to Maevis Barlowe for the rental in Lost Hope, and place an on-hold transfer for an additional six months, to be cleared on the last day of my stay."

His long and deep sigh sounds in the quietness of my car.

"Lost Hope, Lalah? Are you for real? I still can't believe you are so determined to move in the middle of nowhere. Come to New York, babe. Live a little," he repeats the same things he's been telling me with every phone call.

Yeah, right. It'll be a cold day in Hell when I step another foot in New York again. Or East St. Louis. Or the state of Illinois, for that matter.

"I guess the town has a fitting name, a beacon to the lost souls such as mine." I smile, practically hearing his eyes rolling.

"What's with the extra generosity? I thought you've agreed to six months overall," he responds, thankfully dropping the New York spiel.

"We've agreed to three, actually. And you know why the extra generosity. Thanks for the help, M. I've got to drive back to Billings now." I hang up the phone and it's my turn to roll my eyes, even if he can't see me.

He knows I don't like being questioned once I'm set on a path. I'm done with anyone telling me what to do or controlling me. I'm my own woman and I make my own goddamned decisions.

He also knows why I'm so generous with Maevis since he compiled the thick dossier of information on Lost Hope.

I'm not just moving into a town because its name resonates with how I feel inside. Once the longing in my soul urged me to set up roots, I've started doing my homework.

A small town works best for me to feel safe. My searches on the main residents may be a bit of an overreaction, but I learned the hard way that safety is a luxury not all can afford.

I almost never felt safe as a child. As an adult, it became my primary goal. When I met Callum in my senior year of high school, I thought he'd be my beacon of safety. And he was, for eight blissful years.

Until Lady Luck decided to fatten up my bank account and rip my heart out of my chest, all in the span of twenty-four hours.

When you are cheated on, it doesn't only make you question your worthiness. It also makes you question your safety and your ability to trust your own judgment.

So invading the privacy of a handful of town people doesn't make me feel guilty. I've done what was needed to soothe myself and build the foundation to my safe place.

And by invading that privacy, I found out Maevis owns a bakery in town and rents her family home. All to pay off the debts of her asshole ex-husband and her father's care facility where he ended up after a devastating stroke.

Maevis is one of the good ones, and while I'll always keep my net worth hidden since my bank account doesn't define me, nor makes it easier for me to trust people, I still am in a position to help her.

Come evening, I find myself pacing the hotel room, restless and unsettled. Maybe it's just my nerves getting the best of me because of my upcoming move and planting roots somewhere, but I just can't calm myself down.

I grab my keycard and leave the hotel. Having dinner at the bar across the street is better than eating alone in my room wearing down the already threadbare carpet.

The bar is not too busy for a Friday evening, but the night is young. The air is thick with the aromas of food being cooked and the bitter scent of beer. I choose a seat at the most secluded available table and place my order of a burger and fries, then start people watching.

I've always loved people watching and making up stories about their lives and adventures. But lately this hobby is just one more thing that drains me. It intensifies the loneliness I've surrounded myself with. Instead of feeling it like a protective cloak, it's turning into the heaviest of boulders pressing down my chest.

Tonight is no exception. I quickly avert my eyes and pick up my phone, scrolling through social media. When Callum and I ended, I was quick to delete any trace of him from my accounts. I blocked him and all our friends since they were so very happy to side with him in our parting.

But as Lady Luck will have it, after four years of blissful ignorance, today she remembers me. It may be the fact I actually bothered to put on lipstick and feel pretty, but the next picture on my feed makes my stomach turn and recoil like I took a direct hit to my abdomen.

It looks like I missed removing one of those best friends I had, as Mr. and Mrs. Greyson are smiling at me from my phone screen. Callum in a three-piece suit, his hair styled within an inch of its life, has his arms wrapped around the woman I'd last seen on her back, moaning on my fucking space sheets. She's all dolled up in a princess style wedding dress.

If I was, at any point, confused about what the joyous occasion is, my friend's *oh so helpful* caption clarifies things extra fast for me.

Celebrating these two crazy kids finally tying the knot!
And on the same day marking their fifth year of being together!
So romantic!
                    #ProudestMaidOfHonor #CoupleGoals

FIFTH FUCKING YEAR?

Chapter Two

Lalah

With the same pit in my stomach, I walk inside the apartment I used to call home just last night. The only difference is I'm not expecting the other shoe to drop now. It already dropped yesterday, all the way to the pits of cheating hell.

I was numb when I walked to the coffee shop. On the way there, I believed I had the strength to return to the apartment and live there without him. Five minutes with a cup of hazelnut latte and a chance to process the events of that last hour showed me otherwise.

My apartment was no longer my safe space. I didn't know if this was a one-off or a full-blown affair. How could I when I gave all my trust to a man who threw it away like a week's old trash?

I didn't know how much of my apartment, of my personal things had been tainted by his betrayal. Just the thought of returning there made every cell in me rebel in revulsion. So with that in mind, I realized I was the one who needed to go.

Giving myself a break, I booked a night at a nearby hotel. After a night of tossing and turning, and feeling cold to the very bottom of my soul, I'm now back in the place where my heart was ripped out of my chest less than twelve hours ago. Same as yesterday, the apartment is quiet.

"One foot in front of the other. Just breathe. One step, and then another, and then another," I whisper to myself.

On shaky legs, I enter what used to be our bedroom, pull a suitcase from my closet, and start throwing in the clothes I may need for work and sleep. I also take small keepsakes from the life I lived before him.

When I look at my bookcase, I want to scream and rage. I came completely unprepared to pack my life away. I want to rage at Callum for forcing me into this situation because he can't keep his limp dick in his pants.

Google proves to be my savior and, after a hefty fee, I have a moving company booked, due to arrive in the next half hour. They'll pack the things I still consider mine and shove them into a storage space until my mind clears of the fog choking it and I decide what my next steps are.

"Who the fuck are all these people?" Callum shouts from the hallway. I stand from my kneeled position where I was placing the last of my precious books in a box and move toward him.

"Keep your fucking voice down, you inconsiderate prick. They're helping me move," I say to him, in the same cold, impersonal voice matching the harsh lines of my face.

His golden-brown eyes find me and I can practically see the cogs in his head moving. His skin crinkles at the corner of his eyes, trying to look apologetic, but I see through his façade now. He is most definitely not sorry for hurting me. He's not even sorry he's been caught.

Clarity hits me with the strength of a freight train, forcing me to take a step back, away from him. He knew I was coming home yesterday. He wanted to be caught because the spineless bastard didn't have balls big enough to end our relationship face to face like a man.

"Where do you think you're going?" he lifts a condescending eyebrow at me.

"I don't see how that is any of your business. We should be done packing in the next hour or so. I've moved all the bills from my accounts to yours and called the landlord to explain I'm leaving and I'd like to be removed from the contract. He's expecting your call."

He opens his mouth to interrupt me, but I lift my palm to stop him.

"Now is not the time to run your mouth. It's the time to keep quiet and listen. You don't want to live here, you deal with the landlord. You knew what you were doing yesterday and were well aware of what I was walking into. Deal with the fucking consequences like an adult. I'm taking my books and some personal stuff. You're free to keep all the things you tainted like an asshole. MY FUCKING SPACE SHEETS, CALLUM!?"

"Of course, that's what you care about. Your books and the bedsheets," he scoffs at me. "Don't sit there and act all hurt, Alana. Aren't you the one who doesn't need anyone? Eight years we've been together and eight years you refused to marry me, refused to have my children. For eight years at your side, I felt less than a man," he spits through clenched teeth.

"That so? I guess fucking other women behind my back got you that man card you're craving so much. You're throwing marriage and kids in my face like that was a decision I made on my own." My arms fly wide, gesturing between the two of us. "What kids do you want, Callum, when you can't even take care of yourself? And you know well enough there are no children in my future. YOU WERE FUCKING THERE." I draw a deep breath, gripping my hair in frustration.

"Marriage? When have you ever proposed or even hinted at wanting to get married? You speak of marriage as if you weren't balls deep in another woman just last night."

"You're right. I didn't want to get married," he says, a hint of laughter in his words. "To you," Callum clarifies, his mouth twisting in a cruel smirk. Who even is this person? *"Who the fuck would want to tie their life to a soul-sucking bitch like you?" he throws over his shoulder, as he leaves the apartment.*

"Fifth fucking year!" I exclaim on a shuddered breath, looking around for a waitress. A tall redhead wearing a stained apron, holding a tray with her forearm, starts my way.

"What can I get you, hun?" she shouts, trying to drown out the increasingly loud noises in the bar.

"Two shots of whiskey. Top shelf," I tell her.

I haven't had a hint of alcohol in the past four years, but this night calls for a celebration of truth.

It's not like I still have feelings for him. Whatever love I carried died a quick death the minute my brain came online and processed what I saw in my bed that night.

But, the betrayal still cuts deep.

I'm not one to put all men in the same box. I don't think all men are scoundrels and spineless assholes, but I do believe the men destined to be in my life are exactly that.

The first shot of whiskey incinerates all the revulsion in me, but I don't feel the burn as it hits my tongue. I pick up the second shot and down it like there's no tomorrow. The second one relaxes my body, warming me from the inside out.

With my food forgotten, I move toward the dance floor on the opposite side of the bar. Sam Smith's "Dancing with a Stranger" is blasting through the speakers and I start moving to the beat. I feel the lyrics in my soul, and my body is quick to follow suit.

My shoulders shimmy and my hips undulate when a pair of big hands enclose my waist. The warmth of thick thighs at the back of mine hugs me, his hips rotating in rhythm with mine. His breath tickles my earlobe when he rasps the chorus in my ear.

I turn around, ready to give him a piece of my mind, but I'm stopped short at the sight of him. Ice-blue eyes watching me playfully from under hooded lids, a firm jaw with just the right amount of scruff supports a sexy smirk, and fucking dimples flash at me.

I'm done for.

My hands touch the steel chest underneath the soft pale cotton of his T-shirt and intertwine at his nape. His palm meets my lower back, and he pushes my body flush to his, his knee parting my thighs.

The touch of his jeans-clad leg against my core sends electric shocks through my body and wetness dampens my panties. My fingers clamp in his silky light-brown hair and I pull myself even closer to him when his erection rubs against my belly.

I don't think about how the last hands to touch me were Callum's cheating ones. I don't think of the picture on my social media feed. All I think is this man looks like a goddamned great mistake and I am due a couple of hours of fun.

I smirk back at him, and his full-blown smile lights up his face deepening those sexy as fuck dimples.

"Wanna get out of here?" he rasps.

I lift on my tippy-toes and purr in his ear, "I thought you'd never ask."

He grins at me, his full, plump lips lifting at one corner as his palm drags across my back and waist, before firmly clasping my fingers with his.

"I've a hotel room across the road," he says, leading me out of the crowded bar and into the crisp night. Goosebumps sprout on my arms, a mixture of anticipation for what is to come and the chill in the air.

I pay no attention to the hotel reception or the brief lift ride to his floor. My mind is blissfully quiet. No rage thrumming in my veins, no loneliness suffocating me.

The whiskey didn't get me drunk enough to lose my awareness, just buzzed enough to have fire running through my veins. My feet glide down the hallway of the same hotel I'm staying in.

As soon as the door closes shut with a soft click, he pounces. His palms cup my face, his fingers deep in my hair, his mouth drinking in my ragged breaths and the moans I can't contain in my throat. My back hits the wall with a thump and his body molds to mine, pinning me in place.

My brain logs off at the first swipe of his tongue against mine, tasting like mint and the smoky undertones of aged whiskey. My hands are greedy in getting him undressed. I'm desperate to feel his warmth over me. I'm desperate for this stranger to chase away the ice in my veins.

A faint alarm rings in the back of my mind because doing something like this is so out of character for me, but I'm quick to shut it down while basking in the affection he is so generously showing my body.

"Name's Maddox," his lips grit against the sensitive skin of my neck. "So now you know what you'll be screaming tonight."

I wake up thirsty as fuck, cursing myself for forgetting that alcohol dehy-drates me. The only cure for my scorching thirst is a can of ice-cold Coke Zero. My skin crawls as the walls of the softly lit room start to close in.

As I'm taking stock of my body, a strong arm tightens around my waist, and I find its owner sleeping deeply at my back.

I extract myself from the cage of his grip as slowly as possible to not wake him up. I don't regret him or what we shared last night. If anything, I feel lighter than I've felt in a long time.

No longer belonging to Callum, just to me.

But I don't need the awkward morning after with a stranger. He might have intimate knowledge of my body, but he still doesn't know my name. Maddox was the best kind of distraction when I desired it most. He needs to remain just that.

I waste no time throwing my clothes back on, double checking I still have my hotel room keycard in the back pocket of my jeans alongside my phone. Talk about awkward. Imagine having to return and wake the man up with the excuse of searching for them.

Looking over my shoulder at his sleeping form in the rumpled sheets, I smile and whisper softly, "Thanks for making me scream, Maddox," then close the door behind me and make my way to my room.

The short ride of shame in the elevator passes in the blink of an eye, and as soon as I get to my room, I hit the shower, scrubbing Maddox from my skin, and Callum from my mind for the last time.

Changed into my preferred uniform of leggings and sweatshirt, I drop my suitcase into the trunk of my car, and set the GPS on my phone for directions to my new temporary home in Lost Hope.

Chapter Three

Lalah

My temporary home is a quaint, three bedroom, ranch-style house, with the most magnificent porch in the history of all porches. Spread throughout the entire front of the house, with a two-seater swing and two rocking chairs, its open concept makes me feel right in the heart of the mountains looming tall and proud wherever I look.

I can see myself enjoying my morning coffee here with a soft blanket and a book to lose myself in. For the first time in years, I look forward to just live and enjoy every day.

It's difficult to switch from survival mode to actually living. I'm getting to a place where I am happy with myself once again; where my confidence doesn't feel as fragile as the wing of a butterfly.

When I found myself minus a boyfriend but with too much money in my bank account, I divided the money into three equal lumps: a chunk for me, a chunk for investments, and a chunk for becoming an angel investor.

Marcus is both my advisor and my assistant, putting up with my newly multi-millionaire ass with zero financial clue. The company he works for manages my investments and he looks for small businesses needing funds, researching the owners. If they tick all the boxes in my extensive list of "must haves", he'll send their business plans to me.

I temporarily move to the area where the business of interest is located. An assessment takes place until I grow restless with the need to leave, and then I decide whether or not to invest.

The profit I make is close to nothing because my goal is not financial gain, but to help people out. I invest in dreams, kindness, and sincerity.

Marcus is the face of *Lege et Lacrima*, I'm merely the pockets. And these particular pockets are really fucking fond of their privacy.

When I founded Lege et Lacrima, I pondered a suitable name for my company, and the best I came up with was "Read It and Weep".

A tribute to my love of reading. Especially in recent times, when I've been so afraid of connecting with other people, reading was my escape, my safe place, my protective cocoon.

And the "weep", well, that's my *fuck you* to all those trying to dim my light and stuff me in a box. Lege et Lacrima's only purpose is to realize people's dreams. To save their dreams, when mine were shattered and discarded.

The Latin name honors my love of Ancient Italy – my fervent desire to walk the Roman cobbled streets, eating my weight in pizza and pasta, and drowning myself in a sea of gelato.

When I became restless in the last town I visited, plagued with the urge to move on, I began researching charities. That's how I found Hope Haven in Lost Hope, Montana; a non-profit shelter for domestic violence survivors, renting the biggest commercial building in town.

Their dedication and passion to support victims of domestic violence, helping them not just heal, but thrive and spread their light to the world again, was the catalyst for my move.

The minute I stepped foot in town, not only did I fall in love, but felt like I could take a full breath of air for the first time in years. A deep sense of belonging settled into my soul and hope resonated within me.

I cannot for the life of me say exactly what gave me that feeling.

Maybe it was the gigantic looming mountains clad in evergreens; the sharp, stony tops towering around me like silent guardians, or the winding roads passing over crystal clear streams.

Everything about Lost Hope screamed *home* to me.

Marcus's research told tales in numbers and graphs of the five thousand people living here and their small businesses. But it didn't show me how close knit the community is. How warmth radiates from every brick and wooden plank, despite the freezing wintery air.

And it definitely didn't tell me I'd come for a short visit and I'd end up planting the first of my roots here. In the frozen ground of Lost Hope, I left a seed and actually wanted to nurture it and let it grow.

On my second visit, I met Mayor Brown. A tall, blonde, no-nonsense woman, Mayor Brown won me over with her love and loyalty for her town. Over delicious coffee and the most decadent of pastries, we struck a deal.

I will assess all businesses in town for three months. Lege et Lacrima will invest in the ones that most qualify. And all Mrs. Mayor has to do is keep quiet about our deal.

My assessment was planned for selfish reasons, too.

I wanted to see if the feeling of belonging and home would remain after a brief stay here.

But my impulsiveness won.

Before I knew it, I was the proud owner of forty acres of forest outside Lost Hope's borders, with the most beautiful clearing in the center of all that land.

And soon after, the construction of my forever home began.

With my meager belongings packed and tucked into the guest bedroom of Maevis's home, I decide a grocery run takes priority.

Lost Hope's Main Street looks as if plucked directly from a fairytale. With wooden plank sidewalks bordered by knee high shrubbery and cobble-stoned roads, it gives the feeling of blending in with nature.

Artistically carved wooden benches, with curved armrests and engraved delicate patterns, are peppered along the sidewalk on both sides of the street.

I imagine myself sitting here, enjoying a breezy summer day, hazelnut latte in hand, mind lost in a book, letting the hustle and bustle of the townsfolk engulf me.

With the sun shining, making the vibrant green of the forest feel alive, I stop at the Mom and Pop grocery shop at the end of Main Street, choosing a cart from the front of the store.

The trill of the wind chime announces my entrance. A sturdy man in his sixties smiles at me from the cashier stand. His salt and pepper hair and long beard give him a grandfatherly look, and his presence puts me at ease.

I wave at him and make my way through the aisles packed with goodies, taking my time selecting fresh fruits and vegetables. My nose is in seventh heaven with the strawberry scent floating around the aisle. Once I'm certain I have everything I need for the next three or four days, I push my cart toward the cashier stand.

"Welcome to Lucy's Market. I'm Pete, but everyone around these parts calls me GrandPa," he tells me with a kind smile.

I smile in return and offer, "I'm Lalah. So very nice to meet you, GrandPa. The veggies here are a thing of beauty."

His crinkled eyes shine with pride. "My wife, Lucy, grows all the vegetables in our gardens, so you'll see a lot of seasonal products here," he explains, then looks curiously at me. "You're new in town. What brings you to our side of the mountain?"

Bless the curiosity of small towns. By dinner time, everyone will know of my arrival. I maintain my smile, although some of my feathers are ruffled.

"You're a lucky man. Lucy most definitely has talented green thumbs," I respond while packing the groceries he has scanned. "Home, I suppose, brought me here. I fell in love with Lost Hope during an earlier visit. The mountains, the view, the air, the people, all called on me to settle here."

His gaze bores into mine, his silvery orbs assessing the sincerity of my words. It seems he finds what he seeks, as he rewards me with another kind, full smile.

"Welcome home, Lalah! You have yourself a great day!"

I huff and puff on my way out of the store, cursing internally for not parking closer, as my bags are full to the brim. Paying more attention not to drop any of my bags, I bump into someone. The sound of a cup hitting the sidewalk makes me lift my head only to find a furious blonde throwing daggers at me from narrowed eyes.

"Watch where you walk," she hisses.

"I'm sorry. I really didn't mean to bump into you," I tell her honestly.

"And I really don't care what you meant. You spilled my coffee and ruined my top. Do you have any idea how much this top cost me?" She looks at me, popping a perfectly arched eyebrow high on her forehead.

For fuck's sake. Of all the people on this fucking sidewalk, I bump into the fucking prom queen.

"Happy to reimburse the cost of dry cleaning or the cost of the top," I deadpan. As sorry as I am for bumping into her, I can't stand the entitlement wafting off her.

She rolls her eyes at me and huffs, "As if you could afford it. Based on the clothes you're wearing, the best you could do is a Target gift card. Just watch where you walk."

What the hell is wrong with what I'm wearing? I feel like an extra from *Mean Girls* right now instead of a nearly thirty years old woman. I squint my eyes at her, rearrange the bags in my hands, and turn around toward my car.

"Just leave a total with GrandPa. Wouldn't want you living without your expensive top," I throw over my shoulder as I leave.

Chapter Four

Lalah

I drop my bags into the trunk of my car and wiggle my numb arms around. It needs to be a lesson for me — my eyes are bigger than my arms — and next time I decide to buy half the store to park my car directly at the entrance.

I replayed the encounter with the blonde bitch in my head the entire drive home and through the unpacking of my groceries. I wholeheartedly despise bullies. I grew up with one, and I know how to stand my ground when face to face with them.

Pain and misery will either make you lose your way, or force you to grow up and build a thick skin. My skin is bulletproof at this point. I make a mental note to pay attention if she comes up in my assessment. If that's the way she treats people, then I want no part in it.

To distract myself from the sour encounter with the blonde bitch, I pick up my phone and call Matt, the owner of the construction company building my home.

He answers three rings in, and before I even get a chance to greet him, he starts apologizing.

"I'm sorry, Lalah. We really didn't expect so many delays. We have the last of the supplies on site. If the weather holds steady for the next couple of months, we'll be able to finish earlier than Mid August."

I roll my eyes at my phone. As much as I like the place I'm renting now, I'm eager to move into my forever home. I'm eager to see my dream before my eyes.

"I get it, Matt. You can't control the weather. Is the road completed at least?"

With the house being built in a clearing in the middle of the forest, only a beaten path connects it to the main road. The architect anticipated this would be a problem in the rainy season or during wintertime when snow engulfs everything around. To save me a headache, he designed a custom heated road, so I'm not left stranded with no access to food or amenities.

"The road is done. You'll love it. Be it winter or summer, the trees on each side form an arch overhead. It's straight out of one of those fantasy books you got my wife addicted to."

A genuine laugh escapes my lips. Matthew's wife, Beth, is a nurse at the General Hospital in Forrest Falls. I was fortunate enough to get to know her during many of the video calls he and I had.

"Oh, that sounds dreamy. When can I visit?"

"From this point on, whenever you like. The sooner, the better. We can sit down and go over the interior finishes. We're nearly there, kid. As much as I hate delaying you so, those special requirements of yours took a long time to complete," he explains, drawing a big breath.

"When we start moving the furniture, the security company will come and install your security system and automate the shutters."

"Thanks, Matt. I'll let you know when I'm able to come visit. Take care for now," I say, ending the call.

Excitement is bubbling in my soul. As much as I understand some delays can't be helped, time seems to crawl the closer we get to move-in day.

I've been living in Lost Hope for a month now, and apart from the nasty encounter with the wannabe-Regina, everyone around town seems welcoming and friendly.

Deciding the excellent progress of my home is worth a celebration, I jump into my car and head toward Suga'High.

In all my treks through town, I haven't stopped at Maevis's bakery. I spent most of my time finding my way around and assessing the other businesses on Main Street.

The aroma of baked goods makes my mouth water as soon as I exit my car. I make my way to the entrance and my face lights up with a smile when I see Maevis behind the counter.

A big glass shelf filled with all sorts of sugary goodies dominates the far wall. There are also two tables in front of each window for people to sit and enjoy her baked treats.

The bakery is inviting and warm but strangely bare for such a large space.

"Well hello, stranger!" Her joyful smile greets me. "Long time no see."

I rush to the glass display, eyes big as saucers, trying and failing to decide which work of art to sink my teeth in first.

"Happy to be here, Maevis. My god, I'll never leave this bakery. If these taste half as good as they smell, you might as well name a table after me and put a sleeping bag under it."

She blushes shyly, and I find it endearing she is so modest when her creations speak for themselves.

"I just got a batch of hazelnut and chocolate chip cookies out of the oven. If you can't decide, start with those," she advises.

"Now we're talking. It's like you have a direct line to my stomach."

She makes her way back into the kitchen, through the door behind the cash register. Seconds later, she returns with a plate full of steaming, oven-warm cookies.

I wipe my mouth with the back of my hand, pretty sure I'd find drool on my chin. Her dark caramel eyes sparkle with laughter at my antics. I greedily snatch a cookie off the plate, wasting no time in taking a huge bite.

No manners from this *lady* when sugary treats are involved.

Although it's one of my greatest pet-peeves when people talk with their mouths full or chew loudly, I can't help the moan of pleasure escaping my throat. Praise, too, is quick to find the way out of my brain and into the world.

"Mother of all mouth-watering cookies. This is the best thing I've ever tasted."

Maevis laughs at my garbled words, but her laughter is drowned by the high-pitched wail of an alarm.

We hasten to exit the bakery, and I look around, realizing it's *my* car screaming bloody murder on the otherwise tranquil street. I hurry toward the parking lot and nearly drop the half cookie I'm still clinging to when I take in the damage.

All four tires are slashed and deflated with a "LEAVE" scratched on the hood.

"Oh my God!" Maevis whispers, horrified. "Who would do that?"

I narrow my eyes, looking up and down the street. I have a pretty good idea *who* would do this, but didn't realize the dumb bitch would take it as far as damaging my car.

I returned to Lucy's Market to replenish my groceries three days after I bumped into her. Pete gave me an unopened envelope she had left with him. Instead of a dry cleaning bill, it contained the nicest of notes.

> *"Desperate bitches have no chance with him. Move along."*

It left me confused who the "him" she referred to was, but I chalked it up to her seeing me around Main Street talking to different business owners and employees, and the object of her fancy must have been one of them.

I did find the name of the raging bitch from Pete. *Maddison Brown*. Much to my utter shock, the daughter of Mayor Brown. I struggled to understand how such a malevolent person is the daughter of a woman I grew to like and respect, although her sense of entitlement made sense.

I guess being the daughter of the Mayor without notable accomplishments of your own comes with a sense of superiority. It's for sure going to make an interesting conversation with Gretchen once I complete my assessments.

It was then I connected the dots. Mrs. Mayor spoke fondly of her daughter and her high-end salon. Confessed to me her motherly worries when Maddison struggled to graduate high school. How relieved she felt when she enrolled in a cosmetology program at the community college in Billings and earned her license.

She went on and on explaining she was aware her Maddy always seemed to be just on the right side of vain, and wanted more for her daughter than being seen as a pretty girl. At the time, I felt for them both. I considered her daughter to be a determined and clever woman.

Book smarts do not always equal cleverness and fortitude, and I was looking forward to getting to know her and investing in her business. Well, technically Mrs. Brown's business since she is the one fronting the deposit and signing as collateral for the loan Maddison is still paying.

After our first encounter, I was willing to give her a second chance. I had time to calm down during the three days between my trips to Lucy's Market and was willing to believe her bitchy attitude came from the upset and adrenaline overload.

But the minute I read her note, I realized Maddison may be beautiful on the outside, but she was fucking rotten inside. *And now to go as far as destroying personal property?*

I don't believe in retaliation or vengeance.

If I did, Callum would've crawled on his knees begging for mercy by the time I was done with him. But I am not a pushover either, and Maddison Brown is starting to piss me off.

"You should call the police and report this. Chief Deputy Lawson takes these incidents seriously." Maevis's voice gets me out of my head.

"Is the police station close by?"

I figure the walk there would help settle my rage some. It's just a car, but the thought of someone taking liberties to destroy something of mine just for the sake of pettiness makes my blood boil.

"Right by the Town Hall. Are you ok? Do you want me to come with you?"

"That's alright. I appreciate you offering, but I could use the walk alone to process all this." She frowns as soon as I decline, so I'm quick to assure her. "I'm fine, really. I'm sure it's just a prank. Hazing the newcomer. Nothing to worry about."

"Let me know if you need a ride home. I'm closing in half an hour and I'm happy to drive you."

I'm humbled by her kindness, but apart from reporting this, I don't plan on interacting with anyone else today. I'm angry and drained, and all I want is to curl up on the swing with a good book and let the back-and-forth movement soothe my ruffled feathers.

I wave her goodbye and make my way to the station. As Maevis said, I find it in a two story building, just by the Town Hall. The building looks old, but well maintained, and the AC chilled air cools my rage too as soon as I step into the reception.

"I'm sure she's following you, Madd. No one knows her around here. Don't you think it's strange you met her one night, and soon after she moved here?" A feminine voice whispers.

As I clear the hallway, I notice a woman, her blonde hair up in a slick ponytail, lithe body cladded in a flowy mid-thigh summer dress. Her back is to me, and she's facing a tall, well-built man. As soon as I take a good look at his face, I swallow down an incredulous snort.

What a small world.

Make me scream, Maddox is a police officer in Lost Hope.

I didn't have any expectations, apart from great sex, from our encounter a month ago. Hence why I left without a goodbye or leaving a note. But it is nice to see a familiar face in these circumstances and, from what I remember, he's a friendly, good-time sort of guy.

I open my mouth to announce my presence and catch his eyes floating past the woman, meeting mine, and the mother of all scowls appears on his face.

"What the fuck are you doing here? Are you following me?" he thunders, none of the good guy to be seen.

Well, fuck.

Chapter Five

L'alah

I glance over my shoulder just in case someone else is behind me he could be pissed at, because surely his nasty scowl is not meant for me.

But nope, no one is trailing me.

Alrighty then, if this is the kind of asshole he plans to be...

"Following you?" I scowl right back at him.

Make me scream, Maddox indeed, just not in the way I experienced when I met him.

"How on earth could I have known who you are or where you work? We didn't exactly exchange business cards the last time we met," I tell him in a tone so cold I'm surprised he doesn't morph into a block of ice.

Would serve the bastard right for being a conceited asshole and thinking my being in Lost Hope has anything to do with him.

An indignant scoff comes from the blonde woman who is now facing me too, a gleam of pure victory in her blue eyes.

I return the look, making sure my resting bitch face is at an all time best. *This explains so much*, I think to myself.

Our adult Regina here has her sights set on Maddox and she's trying to run off the competition: Little Ol' Me.

I would laugh, and tell her she is welcome to keep him bow, bells, and whistles, but the psychotic bitch fucked with my car, and his behaviour right now shows me he's not even worth the effort to be passed over.

He steps in front of her, as if protecting Maddison from me. *What the fuck?!*

"You need to stop following me and leave. Right now! I don't do seconds, *sweetheart*," he quips condescendingly.

You sure know how to pick 'em, Lalah, I mentally roll my eyes to myself.

"That's all nice and well, Officer…" I try, but he interrupts, correcting me.

"Chief Deputy." Of fucking course. Queue the second mental eye roll in a matter of seconds, and I'm starting to get dizzy.

"As I was saying, *Chief*," I emphasize his title in a heady dose of sarcasm, "I came here to report my car being vandalized. This is a police station after all, not the final scene of the *Bachelor*."

He is clearly displeased with my words, but I can see by his creased forehead and the downturned twitch of his mouth that he starts doubting I'm here for him.

At the same time, Maddison too observes the brief confusion wash over his face, and screeches, "Oh my God! You really are delusional. You'd damage your own car just to seek him out?!"

Aaaand for five hundred bucks, Alex, this man just ate up a steaming pile of bullshit. I register the moment shutters slam back over his icy eyes, realizing nothing I'll say will reach him.

His over-inflated ego won't let him see past the bullshit. The mighty scowl returns with a vengeance, and Maddox lifts an arm pointing his finger to the exit.

"Leave! No one can help you with your problem here. A therapist, sure, but not the police. If you seek me out again, I'll have you arrested for stalking."

That's a sure way of getting me to burn this town to the ground, I think to myself. But then I remember Maevis, and Pete, and all the other wonderful people I got to meet here in the past month.

I won't allow a jealous bitch and a cocky asshole run me off simply because they can't see past their own narcissism.

"Noted," I acknowledge his threat and spin on my heel, power-marching toward my car.

Taking my phone out of my pockets, I take pictures of the damage before typing a text to Marcus, requesting a rental car and a mechanic to help with this mess.

I'm not about to let Maddox's unwillingness to help go, though. He's not doing much police work, really. All he had to do was find out where I live and when the rental agreement was signed, and he would've known I moved to Lost Hope *hours* before I met him.

With trembling hands betraying the fury I'm struggling to contain inside of me at the unfairness of this mess, I dial the number of the only person I think could help.

"Afternoon, Lalah! Have you finally decided to come and visit the house?" Matt greets me.

"Not yet, Matty! I found myself in a bit of a pickle. Do you happen to have a phone number for the county sheriff's office?"

"What the hell happened, Lalah? Are you OK? Lost Hope's police station is closer to you." His concerned voice fires question after question at me.

His care makes me smile. When I met Matt, I didn't really know what to make of him. I had just recently purchased my land and was looking to hire a construction company to work with the architect Marcus recommended.

I wanted to hire local companies for as much of the work as possible. By the time I met with Matt, I'd already interviewed four other companies and was feeling rather dejected.

The men I met tried to take advantage of my lack of knowledge, beefing up the price and giving unacceptable timelines. They straight up laughed in my face when they saw the construction plans, questioning if daddy will pay for all the work or if I plan on doing it on my back with my legs spread open.

To say I was apprehensive was an understatement. I promised myself he was my last try at outsourcing locally, and if it didn't work out, Marcus would hire a big-city company instead.

Like with the others, we met in the clearing that would house my home. When my eyes took in the flannel-wearing, bearded giant walking toward me, I realized it might not have been smart meeting people alone in the fucking forest. Hindsight *is* twenty-twenty and, at the time, I was not just impulsive, but downright reckless.

Which is ironic considering my home-to-be had the safety features of a fortress.

As it turns out, the bearded Paul Bunyan look-alike is also a giant teddy bear. I found out that afternoon he's in his mid forties and married his high school sweetheart, Beth, after their graduation. They've been both blessed and cursed, depending on the day you're asking, with fifteen-year-old twin terrors.

He started working for his father's construction company as a teen, and eventually took over when he retired. He lives and breathes construction, the passion for his trade clear as day as we poured over designs and material lists.

By the end of the first meeting, I had myself a construction company and put Matt in touch with Marcus so they could deal with payments, permits and the likes; I was thoroughly chastised by both men for being alone in the forest, and found myself adopted by Matt with an open invitation for Sunday family dinners.

"I'm fine," I try to appease his worries. "My car, not so much. Looks like someone took a dislike to my tires and tried to give 'em a trim."

"Jesus fuck, now's not the time for jokes, kid."

"I know. I'm fine, really. As for the proximity issue, it's not really something I want to get into right now. Small town ears and all that."

The last thing I need is for the good folks of Lost Hope to believe I have my heart set on the assholeish *chief deputy*. Although, I'm sure Maddison will drag my name through the mud until not even industrial bleach will clear it ever again.

"Tell you what, I'll come pick you up, take that car of yours to a mechanic, then bring you to dinner so Beth can see for herself you're in one piece. I'll have the sheriff join us and you can talk to him in person."

"So can I have the car moved then? Someone is coming to pick it up."

"Yeah, kid. Beth's on the phone with Sheriff Richards. Take pictures of the damage and have the mechanic give it a good, thorough check to ensure nothing else's been messed with. What time do you want me to pick you up? Dinner's in two hours."

"I'll drive myself, thank you. Marcus arranged a rental for me. Thanks, Matty, really. You're my guardian angel. I'll see you guys soon."

A recovery pickup truck, with a faded logo of a wrench dripping oil advertising Tate's Shop, stops next to me. The driver's door opens to reveal a GQ Magazine model of a man. Seriously, what do they feed these men here?

He unfolds himself from the truck's cab and straightens to his full height. I'm not what people would call petite, nor am I particularly tall. Just tall enough to reach that cup in the middle of the top shelf without having to climb three tables and an oak tree.

He must be around six feet or taller. His coverall's sleeves are tied around his trim waist and his upper body is covered in a sleeveless black T-shirt that looks painted on him.

His sandy blonde hair is tied haphazardly in a man-bun atop of his head, and, surprise-surprise, his cornflower blue eyes are glaring at me from under hooded eyelids.

"Take a picture, will ya? It'll last longer," he tells me in a gravelly voice.

Oh, I like this dude, grumpiness and glaring included. And since I'm nothing but an obedient good girl, I raise my phone in his direction and give him my most sunshiny smile.

"Strike a pose and say *Cheese*! Make it good if it's a one and done kind of deal."

He looks at me incredulously for a second, the blue sky of his eyes widening in disbelief. His mouth opens, probably to rebuff me, but reconsiders, his sharp jaw snapping closed.

My serious face shows him I'm not seconds away from jumping his bones while planning our June wedding. His features relax and he drops the glare. *Much. Better.*

"I'm Lalah, and this old lady's crying out for a full set of new wheels, red soles and all." I jerk my thumb over my shoulder, pointing at my injured little Audi, then extend my hand toward him, initiating a handshake.

His right arm stretches to reciprocate, bringing into focus his tattooed skin. From wrist to shoulder, his tattoos are a work of art with swirly dark patterns and cursive numbers woven in the intricate design. In my gawking, I miss that he doesn't touch me before withdrawing his hand.

"Shit, sorry." He wipes his palm on his coveralls. "I was in a hurry, at your friend's insistence, to get your car and didn't wash my hands as thoroughly. Still have some grease marks. I'm Tatum, and own Tate's Shop," he rambles. The pink twinge of his cheeks underneath his light scruff is endearing.

For some very strange reason, although I was greeted with a grumpy glare, Tatum's presence really puts me at ease. It feels like I'm meeting an old friend after years of no contact and picking right up where we left off.

So I take a step forward, clasp his rough palm in mine and shake it, grease marks be damned. He almost smiles at me, which I take as a win.

Something tells me it takes a lot to get this man to smile.

"Let's take a look at this Lady and see how I can right her wrongs."

He fusses for two minutes around my car, checking up and down, left and right, and finally comes upon the friendly message scratched on top of the hood. I don't miss his questioning look and lift my shoulders in a what-can-you-do gesture.

"Have you reported this?" he questions.

"I tried.' My shoulder lifts in a minuscule shrug. "I'd rather not get into it here," I say, twirling my pointer finger around because, by this time, several people are gawking at us from the sidewalk. Whether it is the GQ Mechanic Model or the state of my car attracting their attention, I couldn't tell.

"We can have it moved and worked on tho'. But, fair warning, you may have Sheriff Richards come to your shop and ask some questions. I've been advised to request a full inspection, to ensure all else is in working order."

He nods in my direction and ushers me toward the passenger seat of his truck, helping me climb the tall monstrosity. I can reach the middle top shelf, but can't climb a skyscraper on my own.

Fifteen minutes later, he has my car loaded onto the platform at the back of his truck.

"I can replace the tires as soon as I get it to the shop, but can't do anything about the paintwork or inspection until tomorrow."

"That's all fine. Take your time. I'm renting a car until you're done."

"I'll drop you home then. Leave your phone number so I can notify you when the car's ready, unless you'd prefer I let your friend know."

I pluck his phone from the cupholder in response and add my contact details. I may be getting ahead of myself, but I think I found a kindred spirit in Tatum.

Chapter Six

Lalah

The rental car is parked in front of the house with the keys locked in the mailbox. Hot damn, Marcus works fast. I need to consider a big, fat bonus for the man, because he's never failed me, not once in the four years I've known him.

I waste no time in taking a quick shower and getting dressed in my signature black leggings and hoodie. Tonight's hoodie sports an *I'm sorry I'm late. I didn't want to come* print, which I think Beth will appreciate.

"*She'll be late to her own funeral,*" Matt affectionately says every time we've had to wait for her.

I make a quick call to the grocery store and, hope beyond hope, GrandPa will help me out.

"Lucy's Market, Lucy speaking. How may I help?" a cheery voice greets me.

"H-hello," I mumble, gulping, and have half a mind to just hang up.

As much as I love her homegrown vegetables and fruits, and often send praise her way through her husband, I feel silly to ask a favor from someone I haven't actually met.

"This is Lalah McAdams. I'm sorry for such a last-minute request, but unforeseen circumstances made me late to a dinner party and I'm without a gift for my hosts. My momma would tan my hide if I showed up empty-handed. Uhm, because of the same circumstances, I'm reluctant leaving my car unattended, even if it's just to pop in and do a quick shop." I rush out.

"My husband can't shut up about you, Lalah. Don't worry, I've got you. Tell me what you have in mind, I'll pick it up, and bring 'em to your car. I heard about your tires, so I don't blame you, not one bit, for being cautious. I'm sorry for what happened to you. I swear this town is friendlier than this." She's quick to assure me, and the indignation in her voice on my behalf makes me smile.

"Thank you, Lucy. You're amazing. My hosts love GrandPa's red grape homemade wine, so a bottle of that, and maybe one of your beautiful bouquets of flowers, please?"

"You got it. I'll see you soon, Lalah," Lucy quips, and I haul ass to the store.

As I near Lucy's Market, a woman with honey colored, shoulder-length hair, dressed in a flowery summer dress, is waiting at the entrance of the store, arms full of a gorgeous arrangement of wildflowers.

My car slows to a stop in front of her, and she doesn't hesitate in opening the back door to drop the gifts inside. Once she's happy both are secured, she closes the door and comes next to my rolled-down window.

Friendly, familiar ice-blue eyes take me in, and I'm taken aback at the sense of déjà vu. *Of course, Chief Asshole is their son.*

I truly hope they're not as quick to jump to conclusions as him, otherwise I'll have to do my grocery run in Forrest Falls. It'd be a crying shame to miss out on Lucy's goodies.

What's truly upsetting for me is I have zero interest in Maddox.

He *is* a gorgeous man.

I'd have to be dead or blind not to see it.

But my heart is not healed enough for me to even consider dating. As much fun as I've had with him, I don't want a repeat performance.

So I keep my toes crossed Lucy doesn't jump to the same conclusion as him, and I don't have to avoid the grocery shop, too.

This mess is why I should've controlled my impulsiveness, and spent more time getting to know the town instead. Too late for that now.

"Thank you, again," I say, sincerity coating my words. "I'm truly grateful." I hand her five twenty-dollar bills to cover my goodies and a tip for her going the extra mile for me.

"My pleasure. You're one of us now. Drive safely." She waves me off.

During the drive to Matt and Beth's home in Forrest Falls, I think of Lucy's Market. Their business is on my short-list for approval. The plan is to pay off their mortgage and fund state-of-the-art greenhouses for their fruit and vegetable gardens.

I would also set a contract with Matt's company for building and maintaining the greenhouses indefinitely. But all this will go on hold until I see their reaction to the bullshit situation Maddox and Maddison created.

From what I can tell, Lucy's not yet aware of my dealings with her son. If I'm treated unfairly once she and her husband find out, I'll have to drop them off my list, unfortunately.

Assessing the morality of people isn't an objective way of determining where my investments go, but it is my money and I use it in the way I please and see fit.

Matt and Beth greet me with warm hugs as soon as I get out of my car and thank me profusely for the gifts.

Sheriff Richards is already seated in one of the recliners in their living room. A tall man, about the same age as Matt, the sheriff has a kind face and tiny wrinkles at the corners of his eyes, a sign he laughs often and freely, placing me at ease.

I'm feeling guilty toward Lucy and Pete because, essentially, I'm ratting their son out to his superior. My knees threaten to give up as I realize I'm forming attachments to people and feeling loyalty toward them.

Despite my newfound knowledge, the truth is, Maddison's actions worry me, and Maddox's refusal to hear me out leaves me with no other choice.

Before I left for Forrest Falls, Tatum sent me the videos he downloaded from my 360 angle dash cams. The videos show a fifteen-year-old circling my car and kneeling or crouching close to all my tires.

The angle is not wide enough to show him actually slashing through them, only scratching "LEAVE" on top of the hood. So it's not far-fetched to believe he's also the one messing with the tires.

Beth brings out coffees and then leaves me to discuss privately with Sheriff Richards.

I explain to him what brought me to Lost Hope and stress how important it is I remain anonymous in the assessments I'm completing.

He rightfully questions if this is not a result of my job, but I'm firm that the only person in the know is Mrs. Brown, and she signed a contract and more NDAs than she can read in her lifetime.

I then tell him the entire story, from buying the land outside Lost Hope, to the debacle with Maddison, showing him the note she left for me.

I tell him all about this afternoon, from how Maevis and I found my car damaged, to Maddox's refusal to help.

"Tatum followed-up the video with details about the boy, Andrew Taylor. The fifteen-year-old lives in the trailer park at the edge of Lost Hope, and is the son of a single mom, Renee, a waitress at the local diner, *Dine&Dash*," I explain, showing him the text message I received from Tate.

"I went over all the people I've spoken to this past month," I continue, "Andrew and Renee are not amongst them. It makes me believe he may have inflicted the damage, but he wasn't the brains behind the plan."

There's simply no reason for him to do it, unless forced or paid.

The Sheriff's eyebrows crease and his warm, brown eyes narrow. He clears his throat before sitting up straight in the recliner. "No, but he will tell us who made him do it."

"I understand you have to talk to the kid, but I want it made clear that I'm not pressing charges against him. I'm reporting this, because I have a feeling deep-down the instigator won't stop until I pack my bags and leave. And since I have no intention of leaving, there's a chance of this happening again or escalating. Or I'm simply being paranoid. Regardless, I'd like this on record," I sigh in my hands.

"Your concerns are justified, Lalah. I'll have this logged and will start an investigation. I will have to inform Chief Deputy Lawson of it, but he will not be privy to any details since he is part of the investigation."

"This is not a complaint against him. I am simply worried." I draw a deep breath before continuing, "Not being able to rely on his help just increases that concern." I'm quick to defend the jerk even if he doesn't deserve it, but I believe in fairness.

"Be that as it may, I still need to remind Lawson he's sworn to protect every citizen in Lost Hope. It's not a pick-and-choose kind of situation, regardless of his personal feelings. Unless, of course, there's a conflict of interest. He should've logged your report and investigated."

"Thank you, Sheriff. You taking my concerns seriously and accommodating my privacy really helps ease my worries."

He stands and hands me a business card. "Of course. I'll let you know what I find. In the meantime, if anything happens at all, please call me directly. You have my work cell number here and my office number, as well."

With that taken care of, I spend the rest of the evening with the Andersons, enjoying Beth's delicious fried chicken. I explain to them, as much as I can, what brought us here since they are both aware I am an assessor for Lege et Lacrima.

What they don't know is that I *am* Lege et Lacrima.

And, as much as I'm considering them family, they'll never know.

No one will.

Chapter Seven

Lalah

I'm enjoying a large cup of mid-morning joe, breathing in the scent of bitter goodness, swinging back and forth out on the porch. I went through yesterday's events maybe a thousand times in my head.

I hate that I'm feeling unsafe once again.

Not enough to make me pack up and leave – I have too much on my plate to uproot myself – but just enough to feel unsettled and constantly looking over my shoulder.

I decided regardless of what Tatum's inspection will find, I'm getting another car. A sturdier vehicle, able to cope with the treacherous mountain roads and the heavy snowfalls since I'll be living in my home in the forest come winter time.

As soon as I woke up this morning, I emailed Marcus a mile-long list of requirements for a new car. It will take two weeks to have it delivered to a dealership in Billings. The dealership has also agreed to a trade-in, so I'll drop my Audi there and come back with my new Subaru Solterra.

I'm trying not to be frivolous with my money, but this felt necessary. The safety features will include all angles dash cams and interior cameras. And of course, the comfort features of remote starting my car and the heated seats. I love those the most.

It will also be loaded with every piece of technology available, so if anyone comes close to it, I'll be able to see them from my phone.

Deep inside, I'm certain it's Maddison's work, but I won't throw any accusations, nor will I point any fingers until Sheriff Richards completes his investigation.

Until then, I won't be letting my guard down.

My phone ringing brings me out of my head.

"Morning, Lalah. Sorry to call so early, but I haven't heard from you since yesterday afternoon. I was driving myself crazy with worry," Maevis greets me. A wave of guilt hits me suddenly. She offered to drive me home yesterday, but I never got back to her.

"Morning, Maevis. I'm already on my second coffee. No harm, no foul. I'm sorry I worried you. Yesterday was a strange experience for me. Tatum picked up my car and gave me a ride home," I rush out an explanation.

"Tatum?" she asks in a high-pitched voice. *Curious. Is that interest I detect?*

"Uhm, yeah. My assistant called his garage. Do you know him?" I stupidly ask, as if they haven't both grown up in Lost Hope. *Smooth, Lalah.*

Fishing was never my thing, so better quit while I'm ahead.

"Yeah, I know him. I'm happy to hear you are well and things are resolved. Listen, I've got to go. I'll talk to you later," she hangs up abruptly.

Well, this is unexpected.

Both Maevis's interest in Tatum and the guilt I'm feeling for being a shit friend. The truth is, I'm fearful. When Callum and I broke up, all my so-called friends remained my friends enough to get the story out of me, and then threw me to the curb, one by one. My sense of trust in myself and others was completely shattered.

I am slowly, slowly learning to trust myself again and have confidence in my decisions, in reading other people and their intentions, but I always keep myself just far enough away from forming a connection.

Maevis is such a beautiful, kind person. I would be lucky to call her my friend and to be her friend myself. But I don't know how to take that extra step, that leap of faith in opening myself toward someone else, and give them the power to hurt me by making myself vulnerable to them.

I realize there is something brewing or something has already happened between her and Tatum. As much information as I have on paper about her, it doesn't really tell me the inner workings of who she is as a person.

All I know is she was married for five years and divorced just before her father's stroke, about two years ago. Her divorce was filed under "irreconcilable differences", which can be anything, really.

I don't know what led to her divorce, although the amount of debt her ex-husband accrued because of his gambling addiction makes me believe that's the main reason.

I may not know how to take the extra step in building a friendship with her, but if I read her interest correctly, I can at least put her mind at ease with anything she may have imagined around Tatum and I.

Sure, Tatum is out-of-this-world handsome, but there was no spark or butterflies on my part when we met, and, unless I read Tate completely wrong, he wasn't interested in me either.

With that in mind, I hurry through a shower, and dress in my normal leggings and hoodie attire, skipping the bra.

Bras are the devil's work, and if I can get away with not wearing one, I'll always skip the boobie trap. My B – sometimes C – cup breasts are small and perky enough they don't need the extra support. *Thank fuck for small mercies.*

Today's hoodie proudly states *Free Hugs. Just kidding. Do NOT touch me.*

I forego the car and walk to town. It's a beautiful enough day, with the sun shining high in the sky, doing its best to warm everything up, but so far the morning chill seems to be winning.

June may be close to ending, but this high in the mountains, it's unlikely we'll ever have too much heat. I can see myself wearing hoodies through most of the summer since I naturally run on the cold side.

The walk into town is refreshing, even with my eyes and ears peeled and on high alert.

Soon, I find myself in front of Dine&Dash, walking in with coffee in mind for myself, since I don't really know what Maevis prefers.

There's a welcoming air in the diner, the mouth-watering scent of fried bacon making my stomach growl. As I clear the door, a counter with eight stools, a couple of feet apart from each other, most likely for people who prefer to eat on their own, or just for people to have a place to sit while waiting for their to-go food reigns over the checkered floor.

I already know Dine&Dash has both eat-in and takeaway services from the folder Marcus put together for me. The diner is one of the businesses I am considering investing in.

The counter separates the dining area in half. To my right are six booths with four seats each, spread along the large front windows. A small path leads to bathrooms and a glass wall shows the inner works of the kitchen. To my left are eight tables, each with a different seat capacity, and, in the corner, a small rack filled with children's books, and a box full to the brim with toys.

The walls are painted a soft peach color, but there are areas where the paint is slightly cracked or peeling. Nothing seems outright damaged or neglected, but wear and tear marks are clear at a closer look.

Dine&Dash is a family business, where the owners have passed the mantle to a family member once they've reached retirement age. It's currently owned by sixty-year-old Ruth Lawson, Pete's sister.

Of course, the mess yesterday created another problem for me, with small town family relationships being so intertwined. Unlike Lucy's Market, Dine&Dash is not on my shortlist, so I can at least assess it as I normally would.

"Morning, hun. Can I help you?" a feminine voice with a hint of rasp addresses me.

My eyes widen in surprise when I take in the faded golden nametag of the person greeting me.

Renee Taylor.

And she does so with a wide smile and kind eyes. Renee doesn't watch me like she knows me, much less like she resents me in any shape or form.

I marginally relax and respond in kind.

"Good morning. I'd like a hazelnut latte to go, please. Actually, I'm on my way to visit Maevis Barlowe at Suga'High. You wouldn't know what's her poison of choice in the morning?" I ask, a cheeky grin tugging at my lips.

"You're new," she points out. "Everyone loves Maevis around these parts. If you're friends with her, you're good in my book. She always goes for the banana and strawberry milkshake. Mae says that with her always munching on a sweet pastry or another, she can at least pretend the bananas and strawberries are part of her five a day." She winks at me.

Renee is a gorgeous woman, although good looking seems to be a requirement for living in this town.

In the month I've been here, I have not seen one person looking anything less than beautiful, regardless of their age.

She's a petite woman, around Maevis's height, with a flawless mocha colored skin, mesmerizing dark-green eyes and bow-shaped lips. Even in her waitress uniform, I can tell she is fit, most likely from being on her feet all day long running around the diner. I can, however, see the tiredness she tried to hide with her makeup.

"I prefer to be called Lalah. Nice to meet you, Renee" I laugh and extend my hand to shake hers. "And you are right. Maevis is the best of us."

"Have a seat at the counter and I'll get those drinks ready for you in a jiff."

I sit patiently for the five minutes it takes her to prepare the drinks and thank her gratefully once she passes them over to me. I take a long sip of the hazelnut latte, nearly moaning out loud at the richness of the coffee.

God, they must lace these lattes with magic, because the taste is out of this world. It's no wonder people here are so against big name corporations in their town, when everything they have is so much better.

Leaving enough money on the counter to cover my drinks and a hefty tip, then make my way to Suga'High.

Chapter Eight

Lalah

There's a line, five people deep, at the counter, and I take my place in the queue. I'll let Maevis know I'm here, give her the drink and get one of those addictive cookies for a redo. Once she has a breather, I can talk to her about Tatum.

She notices me in line and smiles brightly at me, her dark amber eyes sparkling. "Lalah, I didn't expect you here this morning. I set aside some cookies for you yesterday. If you give me ten, I'll be right with you."

God, this woman slays me with her goodness. I have to figure out a way to get over myself and over my fear of being hurt emotionally, because it'll be a damned tragedy not to have her as a friend.

I lift her milkshake higher so she can see it, and wave it around. "And I brought a bribe for the cookies," I say, making my way toward the empty table. I peek at the queue, to make sure no one else claims it, and take my seat.

My phone chimes with a message, and a quick tap on the screen brings up Tatum's name.

> Morning, Lalah. I've replaced your tires and started on the inspection. So far, everything checks out. I had the hood polished, but I'll need to spray paint it, too. Luckily, your car's black. I'll have it done as soon as I finish the inspection. You can pick it up around 6 pm if that works for you.

Tatum Carter

> Morning, Tatum. That's fast work you've done there for me. I appreciate you. Good to know there's no further damage. See you at six.

Me

The sweet smell of vanilla hits my nose before a plate of cookies is placed in front of me, and I lift my eyes to see Maevis look at my phone with trepidation, her teeth nibbling at her bottom lip. I decide to just bite the bullet and get everything out. A quick scan of the bakery assures me we're safe to talk openly.

"Look, we, obviously, don't know each other, but I want to start by saying there's nothing going on between Tatum and I. We met yesterday when he came to pick up my car, and he was kind enough to drop me off at the rental. He seems like a solid person, and he might even become a great friend, but that's about all there is to it."

"Uhm, th-there's nothing between T-Tate and I," she stammers, but despite her words, the mother of all blushes paints her face. "And you don't owe me any explanations. Really, I'm sorry I reacted weirdly."

"There's nothing to it, Mae." I steel myself, my spine straightening on the chair. "I'm emotionally stunted. I'm not good at this shit, managing feelings, making and keeping friends..." I trail off when my own skin flushes red with embarrassment.

"You only really know I'm moving nearby soon. Truth is, this town is the first place in ages to make me want to stay. About four years ago, I came home from a conference to find my boyfriend in bed with another woman." I stop at her sharp gasp and put up my hand, palm facing her.

"No. This is not a tale of woe-is-me. Please, let me get it all out, so you'll know a bit of my past and get some clarity on where I'm standing. Being cheated on is one of the worst things that could've been done to me. When I saw him fucking her on my favourite sheets..." My lips twist in a wry smirk. "Can you tell I'm still bitter about the sheets?"

She laughs, and I feel better about getting into the nitty gritty of it.

"Yeah, something broke in me then. I grew numb and cold instantly. I've been cold forever, and can't warm up regardless of what I do." I take a quick look at her, ready to shut down at any crumb of pity in her eyes.

Pity feels like a merciful feeling, but for the person on the receiving end, it's more like salt thrown into a fresh wound. Pity is an empathetic confirmation you had it coming. It validates all the dark whispers in your mind trying to convince you of your unworthiness.

To my relief, she's watching me with sympathy, and I think I read a hint of understanding on her face, like she knows exactly where I'm coming from because she's unwillingly visited that place, too.

Taking a sip of my latte for some much needed warmth, I summarize for her the adventures of Lalah in Lost Hope.

"I can't believe Maddox was such an ass," she gasps, eyes rounded in shock. "You don't need to worry about his parents, not even about his auntie Ruth, though. They're the kind of people who like to form their own opinions and they definitely don't judge anyone based on empty talk."

My whole body braces as her words hit my ears. I made no mention of my worries to her, because it hits too close to my work, which is not something I think I'll ever be willing to talk about.

If the subject ever comes out in conversation with people, I usually just say *corporate* and scrunch my face, so to say it's so boring, not worth mentioning. Then add *working from home, making my own hours* with a shrug for good measure.

This way, I'm not questioned when I'm seen walking around *doing nothing* during those hours when most people are working.

It's just on the right side of truth, instead of an outright lie, as vague as that truth is.

"You *do* have a direct line to my brain," I choose to say instead. I would be an asshole not to acknowledge how easily she reads me. "Tell me the truth, do you also read palms, or keep it simple to minds only?"

She laughs at me again, then her face suddenly turns fierce, her pink lips thinning in a straight line. "I'm going to rip him a new one as soon as he steps in here. Where is he coming from thinking he's God's gift to women?"

"NO!" I shout. As much as I appreciate her open show of support, the last thing I need is to attract more attention and have a wildfire on my hands from a barely there spark.

"Sorry. Let me rephrase that." Clearing my throat, I soften my voice and say, "Please don't. I'm sure he'll get over it once he realizes I'm not interested in anything to do with him. In the meantime, I'm happy with the sheriff's help, and since my home will be in Forrest Falls, I'm not Maddox's concern."

"If you're sure…" she trails off, uncertainty shining in her round eyes.

Mae lifts her hand to her mouth, her fingers pressed together, and mimics a zipper being closed.

The front door opens, and none other than Chief Asshole enters the bakery. I glance at Maevis, hoping she will keep quiet while in the back of my mind, Lady Luck is dancing around, waving a strip of condoms at me, prancing around with a neon sign saying *Fucked over. Coming soon.*

"Morning, Mae-Rae. How are you today?" he says, completely ignoring my existence, icy eyes passing over me like I'm completely invisible.

I guess that's better than being glared at and threatened with jail time.

"Just here to pick up the croissants and danishes for the station."

Maevis frowns and looks at me for directions on how to act. My eyes beg her to just go with it, and not make a big deal out of this very awkward moment.

"Morning, Madd. I'll have them packed for you in a second."

She stands from her seat and makes her way to the counter. More people are coming in through the door, and before I blink once, there's a queue of ten.

I get up too and pick up my coffee. From her place behind the cash register, Mae turns to me, "I'll come see you tonight?"

"Uhm, I have... an... appointment tonight." I wince when she connects the dots and realizes my appointment this evening is with Tatum. There's a flash of pain on her face, there and gone the next second.

I can't fucking win today. I'm only picking up my car, not getting on my knees in front of him.

I'll need to do better at reassuring her, and I make a mental note to call her as soon as I'm leaving Tate's Shop.

Chapter Nine

Lalah

With a six-pack of non-alcoholic beers in my left hand and a meat lover's pizza in my right, I make my way on foot toward Tate's Shop since it's only two blocks away from Main Street.

I'm balancing the hell out of that pizza box since it carries not only my favorite form of sustenance, but also the leftover cookies I snatched from Maevis this morning.

I'm surprised to see a massive red-brick warehouse with five garage doors. They're all open wide, the bays occupied with cars in various states of disassembly.

A familiar drumming sound hits my ears, and my head involuntarily starts bopping on the catchy beats of "Down With the Sickness". I always had a soft spot for Disturbed.

My eyes take in the large parking lot next to the building, showing me Tatum doesn't hurt for business. It makes a lot of sense now why his garage was not on the list Marcus put together for me.

As soon as I enter the reception, a plump woman in her sixties, with a wavy chin-length bob, greets me from behind the tire shaped counter.

"Why, hello there. I'm Sarah. How can I help you?" She smiles at me warmly, eyes twinkling.

Seriously, everyone in this town is so welcoming and nice. And not a fake-polite cheeriness, but genuine niceness and warmth.

"Hello. I'm Lalah, nice to meet you. I'm looking for Tatum so I can pick up my car," I say, but it comes off as more of a question.

"Yes, of course. I'm Tate's mom. It's so very nice to meet you," she quips with a look on her face I'm not trying very hard to decipher, since I have a feeling it will scare the pizza out of me.

"For god's sake, mother! Quit planning our fucking wedding in your head!" Tatum's pained groan sounds from the gray sliding door connecting the garage to the reception.

Yup, I read *that* correctly, alright. Gulp.

I turn to him with a sheepish look, because I know I must've given her the wrong impression with the beer-pizza-cookies triple threat. *I really can't get things right today.*

"Language, Tate. You'll never be old enough for me not to shove soap down your throat," she threatens, but with a mischievous sparkle in her navy-blue eyes, so I know she's not offended by his cursing. "I'll leave you kids to it." She winks at me, before disappearing through the same door her son came in.

"Have a good day, ma'am," I say with an awkward wave, heat blazing through my cheeks.

Tatum rolls his eyes and gives me a half smirk from beneath his scruff.

"Sorry! I came bearing gifts. I can see how this would've sent the wrong message," I plead with him.

Dropping the pizza box on the tire counter, I pick up a beer that's thankfully still cold and pass it over to him.

"This better be a peace offering since she'll be pestering me for the next month," he pops an eyebrow at me.

"*Non-alcoholic* peace offering," I clarify, rolling my lips in a grimace. "Didn't know what time your day finished, so I figured best be safe than sorry. And a thank you for dealing with my car as fast as you did. I know what a massive favor it is, by the look of your full parking lot."

"Are those cookies from Suga'High?" he asks, snatching the pretty pink paper bag for himself. His face remains impassive, but if my ears are not deceiving me, there was a slight hitch in his voice when he said the bakery's name. *Looks like Mae's not the only one interested.*

"Those were supposed to be my treats, but whatever helps get over my faux-pass. I heard it's bad form to piss off the dude fixin' your car. Just doing my due diligence."

"Peace offering accepted, and I'm keeping the cookies. I figured it was best for you to know sooner rather than later what you're dealing with," he mumbles under his breath.

His sky-blue eyes pin me, an eyebrow popping on his sweaty forehead. "Had a call from Sheriff Richards, too. Thankfully, nothing else was damaged. *Why* am I getting a call from the sheriff and not a visit from Lawson, Lalah?"

I poke my tongue out at him and quip, "And men say women like to gossip. You're getting a call from Sheriff Richards because I technically live in Forrest Falls."

Those pretty blue eyes roll once again at me, his lips in a thin line, chin up in the air. His entire face calls me on my bullshit.

"You technically live in Mae's family home. Last I checked, which was just yesterday when I dropped you off, that's still in Lost Hope."

"Mae, huh?" I wiggle my eyebrows up and down, trying to deflect. His glare sharpens and I lock my knees together, because damn, the man is intense.

Too bad his pretty-boy intimidation doesn't work on me. This gal's made of sterner stuff.

"Ok, smartass. I live in Forrest Falls. My house isn't very livable at the moment and so, *temporarily*, I'm staying at Mae's. And there might have been an itty bitty misunderstanding on the chief's part, so he's not all that willing to help. Maddison Brown may have helped convince him," I add for good measure since I'm all about being open and up-front today with the people I'm going to be best friends with.

"What did Maddison do now? That woman's a menace," he spits, eyes suddenly widening as his jaw clenches. "She's done that to your car?"

I look at him through narrowed eyes. "What makes you think that? You saw the video from my dash cams."

He lifts his arms at chest level, palms facing me, as if to appear non-threatening to a pissed off bear. I guess I'm the bear here.

"I don't know the details of your dealings with Lawson and her. But you just told me her influence made him not help. I know how she operates better than most since she's been best friends with my ex-wife her whole life. It's not difficult to assume she thinks you're encroaching on her territory, Lalah. Maddison's been after him for the better part of this decade, in one form or another. And seriously, Lawson?" he mocks me, his full lips puckering as if he ate something sour.

"There's so much to unpack in that one sentence," I huff while marching to the pizza box and grabbing a slice.

Since he's such a chatterbox this evening, I already decided to adopt him as my big brother. Having another someone in my corner is better than having no one, but I'll be damned if I'm airing my dirty laundry on an empty stomach.

After chewing the life out of one pizza bite, I tell him, "There's nothing between me and Maddox. I have no interest in him whatsoever. When we met, I was having an existential crisis, and he was there, available, and willing."

He scoffs and throws me a look of pure disbelief.

"Don't you give me that fucking look, Tatum. Women are perfectly capable of having one-night stands with no feelings involved, and they don't need to be shamed for it," I scold him.

"Whoa, whoa," he defends, calloused palms once again facing me. "No. I'm sorry. I wasn't shaming you. *Your* body, *your* responsibility, *your* choice to do as you please. No judgment here. It's just..." he pauses, taking a deep breath.

"You don't look the type." His eyes widen in utter horror when his words hit his ears. "Shit. No. That came out wrong."

He releases a long exhale and looks me dead in the eyes. His mouth opens, then he seems to think better of whatever he wanted to say, as he shakes his head, before continuing, "I shouldn't say anything. I don't want you to think I'm a weirdo. Let me give you your invoice."

"Stop!" I demand. "Tell me. I want to hear what you have to say."

"Ah, hell," he groans, lifting his hands to mess with his bun, untying it and tying it back again, while pacing back and forth. I just follow him with my eyes and let him find his words.

After a couple more seconds of pacing, he settles on one of the chairs in the waiting area, legs spread, elbows on his knees, hands dangling between them, and once again looking directly into my eyes.

"I feel a kinship to you. It's unnerving. We met a day ago. *One* fucking day. But it lives deep in my gut, and my gut's never led me astray. I see the pain you're trying so fucking hard to hide. I also see your fear. And it's because of that fear, I say you don't look the type to sleep with someone you've just met."

I involuntarily take a step back, as if to put distance between him and me.

First Maevis, and now Tatum.

How are these people reading me so easily? I thought I had mastered hiding my feelings. I buried my pain so deep inside, it shouldn't be as obvious as it clearly is for the two of them to see it.

He stands then, arm extended in my direction before letting it fall back at his side. "Don't do that. I can read you because, for years, reading people has kept me alive. I'm sorry I freaked you out. That's why I didn't want to say anything."

"What do you mean reading people has kept you alive?" I ask, trying to stop myself from spiraling out by shifting the focus on him, and away from me.

"I served in the Marine Corps for eight years. You learn to adapt or you die. It's as simple as that, Lalah," he sighs.

You wouldn't know by watching me interact with others that I don't like people touching me. I don't, but I've learned to hide the cringe on my face when greeted with a hug, or a comforting hand in conversations. I've had this issue for most of my life.

My whole childhood touch was used to punish me and normalize the abuse by calling it *discipline,* or used to manipulate me. If I was a good, obedient girl, I would get hugs and the oh-so-craved forehead kisses. And if not, I would watch my brother drown in my parents' affection while I received disappointed, contemptuous looks at best.

At worst... *Cut it out, Lalah. Woman up!*

After Callum's affair came to light, I started hating touch even more. Every time someone lays a hand on me, regardless of how gentle or caring, my skin crawls with a thousand ants and my stomach revolts.

Even with all that, I still approach Tatum and circle my hands around his waist, laying my head on his chest. My heart hurts thinking that for eight years, there were at least 2920 opportunities where this man could've been killed or seriously hurt, and the world would've been deprived of all the goodness that is him.

For eight years, he fought bravely for us to live in peace, for us to lay our heads down at night without worry.

I squeeze him tighter.

"Thank you for your service. And thank you for not dying," I whisper, my face buried in the soft cotton of his T-shirt.

His arms come around my shoulders and he returns my squeeze, bending down at the knees and kissing the top of my head. "So you feel it too, then? It's why you're hugging me even though you don't like to be touched."

I release him then and take a step back, my red fingernail poking into his hard chest.

"Get out of my fucking head, man. What the fuck, seriously?" I spit, but there's no fire in my words.

My skin didn't crawl, and my legs weren't begging me to run away from him when I hugged him.

If anything, my mind is screaming in relief *Safe! Safe!*

"When I went to shake your hand yesterday, you briefly flinched away from me. I thought, at first, it was because I still had some grease on it, but then you centered yourself and shook my hand, anyway. You flinched again, twice - minimally, I'll give you that, barely there and gone - when I helped you climb in the truck."

I glare at him, but nod my head in acceptance of his words, confirming his assessment of me is spot on. I guess there's comfort in knowing someone in my life truly sees me and, although he may not know the cause, not judging me for it.

I also realize that I've been here for an hour, and during that time, never once has he initiated any kind of touch until *I* hugged him. Even when I passed him the beer bottle, he was careful taking it from me.

My eyes are getting wet, and I rapidly blink damp lashes, not allowing my tears to escape.

They're not bad tears.

Immense gratitude floods my veins for being right here, right now, and being lucky enough to have met this man. It's no wonder Maevis is so infatuated with him.

I'll take whatever Lady Luck will dish me in retaliation, but I think even she is impressed with him.

"I do." I admit, because he deserves it to be said out loud. "It's a strange feeling, not bad strange, mind you, but like my soul recognised a piece of itself in you. Not in a soulmate kind of way, so don't buy any engagement rings, but in a *You're family* kind of way," I tell him softly.

He *is* a ridiculously attractive man, but there is no chemistry between us, not the combustible kind, anyway.

I know it.

He knows it, too.

The corners of his eyes crinkle as his sharp chin tips in a nod.

"Exactly that. Like you are one of my sisters, I just didn't get to grow up with you. Which is for the best, for all intents and purposes. You three would've driven me mad long before now," he deadpans, biting the corner of his lip to stop a smile.

I burst into laughter, the sound of my giggles bouncing on the faded blue coloured walls.

"See, that right there. It's making me dizzy how I feel like I've known you forever, but then realize I don't even know you have sisters. Or that you've been married before. Don't think '*my ex-wife*' escaped my notice."

Chapter Ten

L'alah

"**M**ust we touch that subject?" he groans. I only lift an eyebrow in response.

"Fine. Let's make this quick, because *Lucy,* you still have some 'splainin to do. Two younger sisters; Sawyer, you'll surely get to meet. She's a teacher at the Daycare Center and the youngest. Selena lives in Chicago, and has lived there since college. Has no interest in coming back home, apart from quick visits for holidays," he pauses, running his fingers through his messy hair.

"Now, my sham of a marriage. We were what people call high school sweethearts and got married straight out of school. I enlisted, she followed me. Grew bored with living on base one year in, and said she wanted to go to college. I had no problem with that since I was deployed more than at home. Years flew by, she finished college, and rented an apartment in Billings, claiming she was still bored on base and didn't want to live with my parents. The stupid in me, of course, agreed to this, too."

His long caramel eyelashes lower and the look of dejection on his face tells me everything I need to know.

His story doesn't end well, and my stomach tightens in knots anticipating the blow I sense will come next.

"Came to see her on one of my weeks off between deployments, and found her engaged to someone else while still married to me. Filed for divorce and got deployed again. My mind wasn't in the game, so I ended up getting a bullet in my thigh for my efforts. Got discharged medically, and nine years later, here we are."

He scoffs, and his eyes look at me now, a veil of shame dulling their brightness. "I don't like talking about her because I'm still bitter about being distracted. I've put not just my life in danger, but the life of my team too," he ends with an anguished exhale.

My heart is hammering in my chest, bleeding painfully for him and everything he's gone through.

"Got it. Thank you for sharing with me..." I trail off. I know he doesn't want to dwell on our conversation, and nothing I say will bring him the absolution he so obviously craves.

If he's brave enough to tell his life story to a complete stranger, I too can share my latest mistake. So, for the second time today, I spill my story.

With every word out of my mouth, the betrayal stings a bit less; my lungs inflate a tad more; I stand just a little taller.

"So I got good and angry again." I walk him through that ill-fated night I met Maddox. "Threw some whiskey at my anger, and before that vein in your forehead explodes, no, I wasn't drunk. But it gave my recklessness a boost." I shrug, my shoulders lifting and dropping with the self-deprecating smile on my lips.

"I had a handsome man dancing with *me*, wanting *me*, and I went with it. I needed not to be alone, and I needed a distraction. I needed to feel I was enough. Woke up the next morning, no regrets and no yearning for more, sneaked out of his hotel room and went on my merry way."

"She knows," he rasps with an oh-shit-look on his face.

"Uhm, what?" I ask confused.

"Maddison. She knows. I was at JC's Pour that night, a bar just outside Lost Hope. Maddox, Maddison, Drake, his wife, and a bunch of others were there, too. I overheard them saying they were going to Billings. I'm sure she saw you leaving together."

"Oh, fuck." I facepalm as a lightbulb turns on in my head. "She hated me on sight. We bumped into each other the very next day at the grocery store. Maddison must have thought I went there looking for him. She already knew who I was," I conclude.

"She has him convinced I followed him here, and that I damaged my car myself so I'll have a reason to seek him out. Hence his refusal to help. Even threatened to arrest me."

Tatum throws his head back and laughs out loud, and I freeze, watching him in all his glory.

What a fucking sight.

We may have sibling chemistry, but I can damn sure appreciate the absolute male power Tatum is.

His wide shoulders are shaking and the amused look on his face lights up the entire room.

His laugh is deep and raspy, like he doesn't do it often, and his throat doesn't know how to work it correctly.

I can't help but laugh myself, feeling a weight lifting off my chest. Tatum is extremely good for my soul.

"That fucking ego of his will get him in trouble. I respect the work he does. Being chief deputy is not an easy job, not even in a small town such as ours. Especially when you have half the people you're trying to keep in line remind you they changed your diaper as a kid. Humbles a man, truly. But that ego has always been his downfall."

"You know what they say, pain is temporary, pride is forever. This also applies to me. I tried to explain to him once, but I won't do it a second time." I brush away all talk of Maddox with a wave of my hand.

My eyes lift to the round clock above the counter and I rush to say goodbye when I realize how much of his time I took.

"I better get out of your hair. Thank you for listening to me. I'm so thrilled I met you, Tatum."

"Likewise. Thanks for dinner, Lalah."

I pay my invoice and Tatum leads me to my newly painted car. It feels weird to drive it. Like it's not mine anymore. I hate that the temper tantrum of a spoiled woman has left me feeling so violated.

Connecting my headphones before driving away, I call Maevis.

"Hi, Lalah. I didn't expect your call."

"I know. I didn't like how our conversation ended, and also didn't want you to feel like I was pushing you away when I left."

"That's alright. You had an appointment," she says in a broken voice.

"Come on, Mae. Don't play clueless with me. I know you saw the message from Tatum. Just left his garage. Went there to pick up my car and bought him a pizza as a thank you, which we ended up sharing over conversation. I told you, we're not interested in each other that way.."

"Neither am I," she quickly interjects.

"Right. And I'm next in line for England's throne."

"Seriously. I'm not."

"Methinks the lady doth protest too much."

"Fine. I'm only agreeing because I don't want you to keep misquoting Shakespeare. I may have a tiny, teensy, barely there, crush on him. You know, like a proper thirty-three-year-old woman," she deadpans.

I can't help but laugh. "Well, do you want to have that crush turn into something more?"

"I'm not there yet," she whispers and then remains quiet. I get it. Oh, how I get it.

"Ok, then. You'll get there at your own pace. But, hear me out when I say, Tatum and I are just friends. We actually had a conversation about that just now. He sees me as one of his sisters. I'm simply the less annoying one. I'm taking that win and making myself a first place ribbon, duh. But there will be instances where I will hang out with him. I don't want you to make yourself sick thinking something more's going on."

"Thank you," she sighs, her relief palpable even through my headphones. "I know it's irrational. I'm not willing to do anything about my feelings, but I also don't want to see him with someone else, especially someone I consider my friend, too."

"You're all good. I've got your back. And you know what I've been through. I'll never do *that* to anyone, much less a friend. Anyway, I'm glad we cleared the air. I just got home and I'm ready to face plant and sleep for a week." I huff a laugh.

"I'm there with you, girl. Talk to you later. Good night."

I collect my phone from the cupholder and slam the door closed behind me. As I near the rental, I notice an envelope trapped between the windshield and the wiper. My blood runs cold and I immediately go on alert, circling the car, looking for any damage.

After ten minutes of searching every visible inch of the car, I settle, understanding that nothing seems wrong with it, and open the envelope. Inside there's a single piece of paper.

> *I'm so sorry for the damage. I had no choice.*
> *Watch your back with her.*

I take a picture of the note and send it to the Sheriff.

> Good evening, Sheriff Richards. I received this note today. Well, it was left in the windshield of my rental while I wasn't at home. I take it you talked to Andrew?

Me

> Evening, Lalah. I haven't, yet. Which goes a long way for him to apologize on his own, even if it's just an unsigned note. It also shows there was someone else involved, too. Check the dashcam and send me the video. Bring the note to the station when you make your way into Forrest Falls.

Sheriff Richards

> Yes, it was the same kid as in the other video. Thank you, Sheriff. Good night.

Me

Chapter Eleven

L'alah

It's been two calm and peaceful weeks without any vandalism or anonymous notes, and today it's finally time for me to pick up my Solterra. I'm excited to have the smell of a new car surround me. It's a weirdly pleasant and comforting scent.

Apart from no incidents, these past couple of weeks have been productive. Of course, people have heard of the chief's refusal to help, but no one has treated me any different. There's been no backlash, and I'm hopeful nothing will change.

I met Maevis for coffee and milkshakes nearly every day. I think it's safe to say she is now one of my best friends, on equal footing with Tatum. I also met him a few times for pizza and beers since the man is a machine himself and works crazy hours.

I'm just happy he spends a part of the little free time he has with me. I start to recognize that most of the relationships I had before were toxic. No one has ever made time for me. All the outings with my so-called friends were done on their terms.

Not if I needed to see them. Not if I needed a shoulder to cry on. And with my abandonment issues, I held on tight to every sliver of attention thrown my way.

A call comes through the speakers of my Audi and, with a press of a button in my wheel, Marcus's voice fills my car, dispelling all thoughts of my past.

"Are you on your way to Billings?"

"I am," I reply, checking my side mirrors before merging onto the interstate. "Had to take an hour detour outside of Lost Hope to see the shelves for the library since they'll be delivered to the house soon. They're freaking gorgeous!" I squeal excited.

"Might as well sign Lege over to me since you won't come up for air in the next five years once the library is done," he laughs.

"Damn straight I won't." I grin like a lunatic, thinking of all the books I get to have in my brand new library.

"Well, then let's get down to business and go through the list, so I can get all the contracts prepared. Suga'High?" he starts.

"Approved. You know good and well it was my first choice."

"Just confirming, boss lady. Don't get your beautiful tits in a twist. Lucy's Market?"

"Approved. Dine&Dash, too, before you ask. I swear to God, all the food in my fridge has gone to waste. I can't stop eating there. Their food is out of this world, bursting with flavor, and the service? Second to none. It feels like going to Grandma's," I gush, mouth watering as the memory of the lasagna I had last night pops in my head.

"That's because you refuse to come to New York. We have the best Italian restaurants."

"I'll take your word for it since you're my trusted advisor. What's next?"

"To be Read Cafe."

"That's... Annalise Barlowe, right? Maevis's sister-in-law?" I check.

"That's her. Currently a nurse aid for Forrest Falls Care Home. Quite a change in career," he trails off and I hear the disapproval in his tone.

"Not everyone enjoys corporate life, M. And I think a bookstore and coffee shop is a wonderful idea."

"Of course, you would. It has two of your favorites, all for the price of one. And you don't need to worry. Investing in a start-up is no different than what you've done with established businesses so far, maybe just forking out a bit of extra cash to avoid her taking business loans."

"And I have you to advise me at every step."

"You better believe it, darling. You turned this fancy boy into a posh man. My Armani loafers thank you."

I sputter a laugh at his silliness and continue going with him through our list. So far, in this first wave, I've approved about forty-five percent of all businesses in town.

The more time I spend here and get to know the people of Lost Hope, the more I want to contribute to the community.

"What about GlamUp?" He questions, a hint of cautiousness in his voice. He's well aware of my dealings with the owner.

"Yeah, that's a firm no. It's not like I was able to assess it. In her eyes, I'm persona non-grata. And even if I somehow managed to step foot into her salon, I don't trust Maddison with my hair. Hard pass."

I'm as vain as the next girl, and my hair is one of the things I love most about me. It's long to my waist, shiny and sleek. Although I am a natural brunette, I keep my hair dyed a midnight-black color that gives it just the right shade of blue in direct sunlight. I'm also currently sporting several blue highlights because I always liked my hair in more than one color.

So yeah, I take pride in my hair, and wouldn't trust Maddison holding a pair of scissors around it. She's most likely to stab me in the neck with them, anyway.

"You know damn well I don't reward destructive behavior, and one of the morality clauses for a contract with Lege et Lacrima is to not harm or bully others."

"You know it, boss lady. Off the list she goes. Mix'n'Match, the boutique clothing store? Didn't you say a couple of weeks ago they had a halter top you wanted?"

"It's off the list, too," I snap. "My favorite resident was there when I convinced myself to go and buy it. She was kind enough to inform the owner I won't be able to afford anything in the store and, unless she wanted to find herself with missing clothing I'll be later seen wearing, I should be asked to leave."

"It's like living in a soap opera. Maybe I *should* come and visit."

"God, you're a nuisance. Anyway, she kicked me out, no questions asked. Judging someone by what they're wearing and accusing them of thievery for no reason, it's a no-no with our morality clause."

"Alright, before your doom and gloom returns, let's move on to donations. Just keep thinking of your fancy new car. Keep with the positives."

I bark a laugh at his stilted comforting before urging him to carry on.

I end up approving a donation for the Fire Department to have their equipment replaced, as well as the mattresses for the firefighters that are on shift and have to sleep at the station.

These brave women and men risk their lives every day to protect and rescue us. They deserve to have a restful sleep when they can and new equipment to keep them protected.

Donations are also going to the elementary school, and will cover the cost of lunch for all children enrolled from kindergarten to fifth grade.

The middle and high schools will receive a grant allowing them to buy new laptops for all their students.

The last donation in Lost Hope is made toward Hope Haven, with a mandatory specification of buying the building outright, instead of having it rented or mortgaged. There should be enough left over for any necessary upgrades.

Because I'm a bleeding heart, I've also made a donation, this time from my personal accounts, to Forrest Falls Care Home, to pay off the care of Maevis's father, Ronald Barlowe.

"Thanks, boss lady. Call me once you have your new wheels and tell me how much you love me for my excellent taste in cars," Marcus says once we're done with the long, long list of donations.

I'm all kinds of excited. The list is done, so I can relax for a while before we start with wave two. In less than two hours, I'm going to drive back with my new car, and, hopefully, this feeling of being unsafe will be gone with the Audi.

I'm bouncing around in my seat as Ciara sings to Enrique Iglesias how she's not attached to material, when the hairs at the back of my neck stand-up straight.

The highway is fairly empty, with barely any traffic. I check my mirrors to ensure I'm not missing anything, and there's nothing to be seen.

Except, I can't shake the feeling that something is not quite right. The pit in my stomach makes itself known, the emptiness inside of me growing with each passing second.

I continue on my way, frequently checking my mirrors, but it isn't until I reach a part of the road with only one lane of traffic each-way that I notice a massive truck speeding up behind me.

I can't speed away from it since I'm already driving the limit, and I don't understand why they won't just overtake me already. The road is clear and they seem to be in a hurry, but prefer to stay nearly bumper to bumper with me.

On the next bend, I'm hit from behind and my wheel forces a sharp left. My heart speeds up and my hands start shaking, but I somehow maintain control of the car and straighten it back on the road. My adrenaline is through the roof, and I'm not sure how much longer I can continue like this.

I'm hoping there'll be a rest stop soon, so that I can pull over and let the maniac go on their merry way, but I can't get distracted looking at the GPS route with the road-raging asshole behind me. I mentally debate calling the sheriff, but I can do that as soon as I reach the next stop.

I'm pretty sure the dash camera at the back of the car would've caught their license plate already, and I can report the maniac endangering people later on.

I don't have time to brace or curse before I'm once again hit from behind. This time with enough force my car is shoved off the road. With the speed I am traveling and the uneven terrain, my car flips once and my breath freezes in my lungs.

On the second flip, my forehead hits the wheel, sparks of pain exploding behind my eyelids, and I'm then forced head first into the window.

On the third flip, I watch in horror at the massive evergreen that's going to stop my car from flipping further.

Time stands still for a second in the middle of the fourth flip, like I'm in an elevator suspended in descent before a hard stop. There's no cushioning between me and the hard tree trunk, just terrifyingly screeching metal and – *Oh, fuck, no airbag*. I brace my right hand on the wheel to try and protect my head – no time to move my left.

In the next second, time rushes and everything happens at once; the car slams into the tree, my head slams into the door, fiery pain engulfs my left arm, and everything turns black around me.

Chapter Twelve

L'alah

I come to with a pained groan. Everything hurts. My head is throbbing with every beat of my heart, my breath is shaky and shuddered, and sharp slashes of pain roll across my left arm. Only my right eye opens, with my other swollen shut.

I try to look around while moving my head as little as possible. I'm pretty sure I have a monster concussion and most definitely my left arm is broken.

The rest of my body feels like one giant bruise, so I'm uncertain if anything else is broken too, and I know I need to take care of my neck due to the risk of whiplash.

I don't know how long I've been out. I left for Billings just after lunch, and was on the highway for less than fifteen minutes when I was ran off the road. I should still be in or close to Forrest Falls.

The sun is now close to setting, so I think I've been unconscious for at least five or six hours. I was meant to pick up my car and drive it to Tatum's so he can give it a proper check. I thought better safe than sorry even with a new car, but it looks like I was never safe to begin with.

I can't start thinking about what caused this, if the hit was intentional or something as simple as road rage.

Trying to wiggle my right arm and, when it doesn't feel broken or more injured than simple bruises, I move it toward the release of my seatbelt.

The car's flipping was stopped by the tree with the wheels to the ground, so at least I'm not hanging upside down. Much to my surprise the seatbelt releases with a click, and I gently take my left arm from inside it, biting down a scream when the pain radiating through it increases tenfold.

Feeling lightheaded and extremely tired, I know that despite my injuries, I need to move fast and call for help before nightfall or I'm done for.

The roof of the car is bashed in, and the driver's door is completely wrapped around the tree. I'm not sure how I'm not dead. The windshield and the windows are all shattered, with tiny crystals of tempered glass everywhere around me.

I slowly take my phone from my jeans' pocket. I normally use Google Maps when driving, but today, for some strange reason, I went with the car's GPS. And thank fuck I did, otherwise my phone would've been lost or destroyed.

I unlock the screen and immediately wince in pain. The light from the phone is trying to stab its way into my brain. I decrease the luminosity as fast as my shaky fingers allow, and call the Fire Department in Lost Hope.

My brain is not fully online at the moment and my self-preservation instinct pushes me to get help as soon as possible.

"Lost Hope's Fire Department. Barlowe speaking. How may I help?" a deep voice greets me.

"H-hello," I try to say, although my voice comes out hoarse and strained. My throat is dry and hurting with every breath.

I must've screamed during the crash for it to be this sore, but I cannot focus enough to try and remember.

"I need help!" I croak. "My c-car... I c-crashed, I think, somewhere in Forrest Falls."

"Ok, darling. Stay calm. What's your name?" His serene voice and gentle demeanor are slowly soothing my fear.

"L-Lalah. Lalah McAdams," I force out in a stronger voice.

"Lalah McAdams, you said?" he repeats, a hint of ice in his tone.

"Y-yes."

"This is not the time for prank calls, Lalah. Seriously. Who are you trying to get the attention of now? Leave this line clear for actual emergencies.

How incredibly selfish of you," he spits out, not letting me get a word in edgewise, and hangs up.

"Fuck," I exhale out a sob.

This has gone too far. No one has treated me differently in town, but this is the second time I was refused help when really needed it, and now I need it more than ever.

I don't think anyone could get me out of this wrangled box of metal without the help of the Fire Department, and if they're not willing to come...

I don't even want to consider the consequences.

Lifting a shaky hand to my forehead, I push my hair behind my ear since it's sweaty and itchy where it stuck to my skin, but when I remove my hand, my fingers are painted in red.

I gulp down the need to vomit, and that's when my brain kicks in and remembers Beth works as a nurse in Forrest Falls. Surely someone there can help.

The call goes straight to voicemail when I try to call Beth. With trembling hands and dimming hopes, I hang up and dial Matt's number next.

"Lalah, thank God. Where are you? We were waiting for you at the house for hours, and you never got there."

"M-Matt... help!" I whisper brokenly, while tears of pain and relief are pouring down my battered face.

"WHERE ARE YOU?! WHAT HAPPENED TO YOU?!" Matt shouts, and I can feel his concern for me down to my marrow.

"C-car crash. I'll send you my phone's location. Matt, I can't get out," I sob, defeated.

"Baby girl, you stay put right there and I'll come and get you. Don't you dare hang up. You stay with me on the phone. Do you understand?"

"Yeah," I wheeze and put my phone on speaker, so I can send him my live location via text.

"Okay, kid. I got it. I'm going to put you on hold now, and call Richards and 911. One minute. Don't hang up," he orders me.

"Yeah, t-thank you, Matt," I whisper hoarsely as my throat is so sore and dry I can't even swallow.

I'm not sure how much time passes until I hear Matt's voice again. The world around me once more tints with blackness at the periphery of my vision, and I know it's only a matter of time until I pass out again.

"Ok, baby girl. I'm in my car on the way to you. Twenty minutes away, no more. The sheriff and fire department should be there much faster. Where are you hurt?"

"I'm not sure. My head and left arm for certain. Everything hurts; it flipped a couple of times; hit a tree," I stop when my throat won't work with me any longer.

"Fucking, blasted hell," he swears under his breath. "Ok, baby girl. You hang on tight. We'll be with you shortly."

In the distance, alarm sounds are coming closer and closer. My head starts throbbing like my brain is close to exploding, trying to block the offending sounds out.

I can faintly hear Matt calling my name, but I have no more strength to talk, so I just focus on breathing.

Screeching sounds of metal are all around me, but I'm so tired, I can't even open my eyes. Something tight is squeezing my neck, and then I'm airborne.

"How is she still alive?" A man says somewhere near me. "That car is mangled to pieces. She even managed to call for help."

A warm hand holds my right, rubbing soothing circles on my wrist.

"You'll be fine. You just relax and focus on healing. I'm so sorry, Lalah. I'm so, so incredibly fucking sorry. I've got you. Just relax and focus on healing."

A cool liquid is dripping in my veins and, once again, the world fades into nothingness.

A beeping sound arouses me from my sleep. I try to open my eyes, but one feels sewn shut, and the other eyelid weighs ten tons of heavy. My brain assaults me with the events of... *Today? Yesterday?* I'm not sure how much time has passed since they've found me, but it feels like I've been sleeping for at least a day.

I take stock of my body. Everything hurts as much as yesterday, although my head feels clearer, my thoughts less muddled. I can't move my left arm, but that doesn't tell me much, since my body refuses to respond to most of my commands.

I focus on trying to open my eyes, and after some excruciating minutes, my right eyelid lifts. The white light of the hospital room sends sharp pain through my temples. I notice I'm laid out in a bed, my lower body and torso covered in a scratchy, gray blanket.

A pair of amber eyes come into my field of vision, the dark-haired man watching me with a smile, "You're awake. I'm Drake. Drake Barlowe."

Barlowe? Isn't that the name of the person who hung up on me when I called the fire station? *What the fuck is he doing here? Is he trying to hurt me now?*

My blood pressure rises and the machine's beeping increases to match my racing heartbeat.

"Lalah, you're safe. Please, you need to calm down. You're safe. You're at the hospital in Forrest Falls."

I open my mouth to scream at him to get out, but nothing comes up. My throat feels torched. I'll try harder until I either force a scream out of my damned lungs or the blasted alarm connected to my heart makes enough noise to get someone here.

"G-get o-out!" I whisper-shout at him.

He looks at me like I've slapped him across the face. *How dare he?*

"G-get o-out!" I repeat and pray to whoever is listening that he does my bidding. He left me for dead yesterday, and now *what? Wants to sit at my bedside and sing Kumbaya?*

He looks at me, all saddened and dejected, but really, I think I'm excused in this situation for only being concerned with myself, and much to my relief, he leaves.

Soon after, Beth's worried face fills my view, accompanied by the neutral face of who I think it's my doctor.

"Miss McAdams, I'm Doctor Richards. I'm happy to see you back with us. How are you feeling? You took quite the tumble yesterday and, by the looks of that car, you're definitely lucky to be here with us."

Lucky. Yeah, if chased off a road and left for dead is what people these days qualify as lucky, I'm the luckiest.

I try to answer her, but my throat once more gives out on me, gravel coating my vocal cords. She seems to understand what the problem is immediately. "Would you like some water first?"

I nod my head as best as I can, and she pushes a straw between my lips. "Small sips. You don't want to make yourself sick."

The first sip of cool water burns my throat. I try for a second one, and this goes down slightly easier, but not without pain.

I take a third, and now that my vocal cords are gravel-free, good and lubricated, I manage a humming noise. The doctor takes that as my being done with the water and removes the straw.

"I guess I am as good as I can be. What's the damage?" I whisper hoarsely to her.

"You hit your head quite badly. Once on your forehead, and once on the side, on, my guess is the window, by the quantity of tempered glass we've removed from your hair. All in all, you have about twenty-five stitches, all hidden in your hairline, so if there's any scarring, it won't be visible. All these hits led to a grade III concussion," she informs me.

I know she's not done, so I internally brace for more bad news.

"You have fractured your radius. That's your forearm bone." She points at my casted arm. "We've managed to set the bone without surgery, but you'll have to wear a cast for three months, and will need physical therapy. You have some seatbelt burns, but those will heal within two weeks. The rest is just cuts and bruises. No more stitching needed, but you will be sore and in pain for quite some time," she trails off.

I close my eyes, trying to stop the tears from falling. I'm all alone, broken and bent, in a cold, sterile room.

The doctor must sense I'm nearing a mental breakdown as she hurries her next words.

"We will keep you under observation for the next twenty-four hours to see how that concussion of yours progresses. We've done a CT scan, and miraculously there is no brain injury. So unless your symptoms worsen during this time, you'll be free to go. You'll need to take it slow and rest adequately until you feel better. Only resume your normal routine once the lightheadedness and headaches are gone."

"Thank you, Doctor. I'll be sure to follow everything to a T," I whisper, my voice rough with sadness and heartbreak.

Someone ran me off the road. Drake left me basically for dead when I asked for help. *Selfish, selfish, selfish,* runs through my head in Drake's voice.

"You can have some more water, but only small sips. If you keep it down in the next four hours, we can upgrade you to soup." She smiles kindly at me and leaves, the door closing behind her with a soft thud.

I don't have time to wallow in misery as someone else takes a seat on the lone plastic chair next to my bed.

"My goodness, Lalah. You scared us half to death," Beth whispers next to me and takes my right hand in hers.

"I'm sorry," I say to her. What else can I say?

"Sheriff Richards wants to see you and ask some questions. You also have quite a welcome party from Lost Hope eager to see you, including the nice fireman who got you out of your car yesterday."

I stiffen at her words, my whole body freezing. They can't be near me. I'm too vulnerable. I can't protect myself. I have no idea what happened yesterday, but I know with certainty I've once again been refused help, and this time it nearly cost me my life.

"Sheriff Richards can come in. No one from Lost Hope is allowed in this room or near me. Beth, promise me, no one from Lost Hope is coming anywhere near me," I nearly shout, my heart hammering like crazy again.

She looks at me with wide eyes, but doesn't press the issue. "I'll get them to leave, baby girl. Relax, please, just calm down."

Chapter Thirteen

Lalah

I wake up to a sleeping Beth, her auburn, curly hair sprawled next to my arm on the bed, her soft hand holding mine tightly. I try to move as little as possible, mindful not to wake her up, but I need to use the bathroom. With how my bladder is screaming, I don't think I can hold it in much longer.

Slowly extracting my palm from her grip, I inch my way off the bed. Everything in me is hurting. My muscles are sore, my head throbbing, even my hair feels like it has sprouted pain centers in my sleep. Even though I try to contain them, whimpers escape my tightly closed lips.

"Where do you think you're going, Missy? Are you trying to give yourself another concussion?"

I try to give her a smile over my shoulder, although I'm certain it comes across as more of a grimace, what with my every cell screaming in pain.

"Bathroom," I whisper sheepishly.

"I'll come around and help you. Stay put."

She slowly eases me out of bed, and we take small steps toward the bathroom attached to the room.

"Your friend Marcus kept calling your phone, and I answered. He was crazy worried about you. I told him what happened. He's having the Solterra delivered to Lost Hope and arranged the private room for you at the hospital."

"No. I'm not going back to Lost Hope. I meant to talk to Matt, but I fell asleep again. I know they are about two weeks away from completion, but when I'm leaving this hospital, I'm going directly to *my* home. All security systems have been installed. The bedrooms are fully furnished. They just need to work on the library, the garage, and the shed outside. I can live there now."

"Lalah, what happened?" she asks me in a small, sad voice.

My head shakes back and forth as tears once again spill down my face. I hate crying. I hate feeling so weak and vulnerable, I can't even use the bathroom without help.

I won't let myself return to the place where someone is hell bent on harming me to this degree. I could've died, and all for what?

She helps seat me on the toilet and then leaves the room, giving me privacy. I go about my business and then support myself on the sink to get up and wash my hands.

My eyes move to the square mirror above the sink and I make the mistake of looking at my reflection.

My forehead is one giant, purple and black bruise, extending to my left eye, that is still so swollen it's shut tight. A line of stitches pepper my hairline.

While the right side of my face looks untouched, my bottom lip is busted, and there are blood streaks on my cheeks and chin.

I slowly wash my hands as best as I can with my left arm enclosed in a cast, then use my right to gently wipe the blood off my face.

I'm forcing my mind to think of the library, my future happy place, so it stops replaying the film of the car flipping, the icy coldness of fear crawling along my spine when I thought no help was coming, my shaky, bloodied fingers as I waited for Matt to get there.

My fingers brush through the dead-racoon-in-a-bird-nest that is my hair, but most likely I just made things worse. A hot, cleansing shower would make me feel better, but I don't think one's allowed at this point. I make a mental note to ask the good doctor about it before being discharged.

On the positive side, my brain feels fully functional and engaged now, and the headache has diminished considerably. The despair I felt when I first woke up also seems to be gone now.

My feet drag in slow motion on the white tiles, and I exit the bathroom with Beth waiting for me at the door. "You should've called for me, silly girl," she gently admonishes me. I give her a tight-lipped smile in return, but choose to remain silent.

She slowly guides me to the bed, and by the time I'm lying back down, I'm so tired, my lungs are working overtime like I just finished climbing three mountains.

As my breathing gets back to normal, a straw is once again placed against my busted lip. I help myself to three more sips.

"Are you ready for the sheriff now?"

"Yes, please. The sooner I get this over with, the sooner I can put it behind me."

She takes her phone out of her pocket and quickly taps on the screen. A minute later, Sheriff Richards makes his way into the room.

He looks just as concerned for me as Beth does. My heart softens a bit, as I realize there are still people out there who care for me and don't wish to see me harmed.

"Hi Lalah. I'm glad to see you up and awake. I've asked doctor Richards if you are taking any kind of pain medication that may impair your ability to consent, and she has assured me you're on nothing that can interfere. If you are willing and able, I'd like to take your statement now," he says, his honey glazed eyes softening as they trail over me.

"Thank you for being here," I rasp. "I'm ready to answer anything I can."

His dimpled chin tilts in acceptance as he continues, "Please know that pictures were taken of your injuries when you were brought in, but the extent of the damage, along with the pictures, will not be shared with the police until you consent. For that consent, doctor Richards needs to be present."

I nod in agreement, and one quick message later from the sheriff has the doctor walking into the room soon after. With both of them sitting side by side, identical dimpled chins and warm-brown eyes, I can tell they are related. It's clear they don't just share a last name.

The sheriff sees me assessing them and smiles, "Yes, doctor Richards is my sister. And she is still bound by HIPAA."

"I'm not concerned. I'm sure you are both extremely professional and take your oaths seriously. Doctor Richards, the sheriff explained my consent is required for the police to have access to my medical files and the pictures that were taken of my injuries. They can have access to anything pertinent to the investigation."

"Thank you, Lalah. I'll see that they receive anything they need. I'll leave you guys to it."

Sheriff Richards comes closer as soon as the door closes with a soft click behind her.

"Would you like to tell me what happened yesterday?"

I give him a step-by-step summary of my day from the moment I left home until I woke up the first time and realized I was in the hospital. I mention my airbag not deploying, and ask if any of the dash cams were saved. My hope is they can get the license plate number of the car that ran me off the road.

"That boy, Tatum, went and retrieved the car, but it's going nowhere unless the destination is a junkyard. The dash cams were destroyed, but we've been able to save the memory cards. I've submitted them and we're waiting now for my colleagues in Evidence to check the videos."

I sigh in relief. At least there is something that may help with this mystery.

"He's still here, you know. Flat out refused to leave, and said even if you don't want to see him, he'll stay at the hospital or wait out front until he can see with his own eyes that you're in one piece. Want me to remove him?"

My heart seizes in my chest. Relief and guilt are battling inside of me, my eyes itching with the urge to spill tears.

"No. He can stay. And he can come in, too. Regardless of what you find in the videos, I know what you *won't* find, and that's him. If I trust anything, I trust he'll never hurt me. We can also ask if he checked the airbags on the last inspection."

He nods at me and leaves, just to return a minute later with Tatum. I can feel the exhaustion and concern around him. The bags under his eyes have bags of their own, he is so tired. He's watching me as intently as I watch him, and to my complete shock, there are tears falling down his cheeks.

This mountain of a man, a former Marine, the bravest of the brave, he's crying for me, and my heart breaks a little.

"Goddammit Lalah, when I put my hands on who did this to you, I'm going to wring their neck," he rasps and hurries to my side, gently taking my hand into his.

I let his warmth seep into me for a good minute. Not saying anything, just looking into those bloodshot topaz eyes of his, basking in the care and affection swimming in them, all for me. *Family.*

I really must have banged my head extra hard if I thought for even one second someone I came to love as a brother could've ever harmed me. He is too much of a protector, much too honorable to have done something heinous like that.

"You may not want to say that in front of the Sheriff," I quip, to let him know I'm still me. A bit banged around, and a lot fearful, but still me.

The sheriff gives him, and then me, a long, hard look and retorts, "Hell, I'll help," shocking the life out of me. "But back to the matter at hand. Tatum, when you did the inspection, have you checked the airbags?"

"I did, yes. There was no damage to them, no sign of foul play. When the car left my garage two weeks ago, the airbags were in working order. Even took a video of the full inspection, so there's documented evidence of everything I checked, in case you ever needed it."

"Please, have it forwarded to me. I'll leave you guys be. Make sure you get plenty of rest, Lalah, and I hope you have a speedy recovery."

"Thank you, Sheriff."

Not two seconds after Richards disappeared, Tatum's thunderous face scowls at me. His tattooed, thick arms cross in front of his chest, straining the seams of his T-shirt.

My brain decides this is a perfect moment for me to be shocked at seeing him out of his usual coveralls and into dark ripped jeans that look painted on him.

A brief twinkle of amusement flashes in his eyes at my perusal, before the thunder wins over.

"I'm not even going to get into how you wouldn't let me see you, let me see for myself you're alive. I lost ten fucking years of my life when I found out about the car crash, Lalah. What the fuck happened?"

"I can't get into it again right now, Tatum." I croak, trying to force my tear ducts closed. "I'm sorry. I simply don't have it in me to relive it again. Richards has my permission to share the details with you, if you wish and he's able, but right now, I just can't."

He bends at the waist and carefully kisses my forehead, his fingers squeezing mine in comfort. "You're right. I'm sorry. Try to get some sleep. I promise I'll be here when you wake up. There's plenty of time for us to talk once you return to Lost Hope."

"Tatum, I'm not going back."

"What do you mean you're not going back?" His face frozen in shock and disappointment bears down on me, his lips nearly white with how tightly he's clenching his jaw.

"I mean exactly what I said. I'm not returning. As soon as I'm discharged, I'm moving into my home. I can't step foot in Lost Hope. Not right now, not for a long time. This has gone too far, and not just the accident," I sigh deeply and regret when the burns on my chest pull at my skin.

"When I woke up in the car, I called the fire department. As soon as I told them my name, I was told off for wasting their time; they called me selfish for not leaving the line clear for people with actual emergencies. I'm not safe in Lost Hope, Tatum."

"Who did you speak to?" He cuts my rambling off in a voice so dark and cold, I'm almost afraid to answer.

"Drake Barlowe..." I whisper, swallowing down the ball of nerves in my throat.

"That motherfucker!" He roars so fiercely even the mattress underneath me shakes. "I'm going to fucking kill him with my bare hands."

His rage is the catalyst for the anguished sobs wrecking my chest, from both physical and emotional pain. My shoulders shake and my tears flow freely down my face.

What a freaking mess.

Chapter Fourteen

Lalah

Matt huffed, puffed, grumbled, and complained, but I didn't budge, not even a fraction of an inch. And here we are, parked in front of my beautiful new home.

I hate that I am in so much pain I can't even stop to admire it properly.

The road leading to the house is just as beautiful as Matt said it was. Arched trees meet their branches above the road, creating a tunnel of green and sparks of light where the sun filters through the lush, dense canopy.

A gated entrance greets us about thirty yards away from the front of the house. The architect wanted me to put the gate and fence all around the borders of my private property, but I disagreed.

I want only the perimeter around the clearing to be protected, including the space reserved for a backyard and a potential vegetable garden, but keeping the rest of my land open and untouched.

The forest is much too beautiful to deny anyone access to it or to cut into it more than strictly necessary.

I had it all planned; I wanted to grow a tall green fence, made of plants and trees that would not interfere or harm the ecosystem of the forest, marking the entire perimeter of the land I own.

Now, I don't know.

I'm much too scared right now to make any kind of sane decisions. I'm just happy to know that inside my gate no one will ever be able to enter without my permission.

The house is magnificent.

Built entirely from one-way, polycarbonate glass, dark steel beams and slated roofs, I finally have my very own fortress of safety. On the outside, it looks like the house is built of mirrors reflecting the sky and trees around it.

From the inside, I'll be able to see the entire clearing, with a panoramic view of the dark forest and snow-peaked mountains.

I'm also able to activate thick metal shutters that would lower and cover the entire house, essentially transforming it into that impenetrable fortress I so badly need to feel safe.

I'm struggling up the stairs leading into the house, even though Tatum is at my side holding most of my weight. He huffs in annoyance, and before I know it, I'm airborne and cradled to his chest.

"Put me down, you ogre." I weakly slap at his arm.

"Yeah, abso-fucking-lutely not. I can't stand to look at the pain you're in. You're trembling like a leaf with the effort of just walking. So sit tight and I'll take you to your bedroom," he grumbles.

"Nooo..." I whine, as he stops right in front of the sleek, obsidian-black entrance door. "I want to see my home. No one is taking that away from me. I want to see my home for the first time. No concussion, no broken bones, and definitely no overprotective cavemen are going to take my first time away from me."

His neck cranes as his cornflower blue eyes bore into mine. Reading and cataloging all the pain and daze in my eyes. The stubbornness, too. If I have to crawl on this tour, I will.

"Fine. But you're not walking, so settle down for the free ride. And it's non-negotiable, so don't bother arguing. At the first sign of a headache, you're going straight to bed," he orders.

I can't fight him on this. He's right, even if I don't want to admit it. I'm okay now walking on my own to the bathroom and back, but, as soon as I'm done, I need to nap for an hour to replenish my energy.

Pressing my palm to the panel, the lock disengages with a soft click. I sneak my arm around his neck so I can turn my head and take in the foyer.

Two black glass walls, one sleek and shiny and the other matte, about seven feet apart, greet us from each side. Beyond the matte wall is where my library, spanning two floors and half of the house, is concealed. A twinge of anticipation and joy rushes through me knowing Matt's guys are hard at work putting my happy place together.

The foyer is empty, except for the closet door housing coats and shoes to my right, on the sleek glass wall. Shorter than its companion to the left, the end of the wall opening to the living room is cut in an L shape, allowing a glimpse of the dark mahogany velvet of the sofa pushed against it.

Tatum kicks his Converse off, his socked feet thumping on the plush dark carpet as he takes long strides toward the living room.

A whistle shrieks out of his lips as he looks at what I'm sure will be one of my favorite places to laze.

"Damn, girl. This is one big ass room," he comments, his eyes crinkling in amusement.

"The biggest on the first floor," I explain, embarrassment heating my cheeks.

"I know where I'll spend football season," he laughs, his chin pointing at the huge TV mounted above my equally large electric fireplace.

"Claiming your territory?"

"Damn right. VIP seats right here. Half the Main Street could fit on this U shaped sofa of yours."

"I like the coffee table best, so no stinky feet on it," I threaten.

He moves me closer to the wood and epoxy, knee height table, where the Andromeda galaxy shines proudly at me.

"Closeted nerd?" He wiggles his eyebrows up and down, teasing me.

"Very much in the open, thanks. There's something humbling when I look through the lenses of a telescope and see Jupiter in all his glory, bands of tempest and the Great Red Spot, surrounded by his bravest moons in an otherwise pitch black sky. Makes me realize how small I am in the grand scheme of things." I blink at him through wet lashes.

This blasted concussion is messing with my emotions.

I turn away from the table and take in the built-in window seat adorned with a rainbow of cushions, my eyes following the lines of floating racks framing three of the windowed walls. An array of colorful book spines reign over us.

"Up the stairs," Tate asks, his chin now pointing behind me, "or straight ahead?"

"Let's finish the floor first, please."

We move past my office door and I don't ask to step inside. It has the most security of the entire house because everything pertinent to Lege et Lacrima will be stored there.

The dining room comes next, open to the designer kitchen I longed for. Both rooms have dark marble floors since I figured this would be easiest to clean. I barely glance at the table, before he stops in the middle of the kitchen.

On the far wall, there are gleaming new cabinets in a dark cherry color, with the island housing the oversized farm sink and a baking station. Shiny appliances in a myriad of bright colors are spread all over the kitchen and my eyes go straight to my fancy La Spaziale coffee machine.

My mouth waters at the thought of making my own hazelnut lattes, but I am banned from coffee for a little while, so I can't try it's prowess just yet.

A breakfast nook with six stools, three on each side, is tucked close to the darkened window, an enclosed pantry hidden by the wooden wall behind the nook.

"Seriously, what are you doing with all this space?" Tatum asks, his chest shaking under me as he chuckles.

"I don't know. I wanted something smaller, but when the architect came with the plans..." I lift a shoulder in a small shrug, "I fell in love, I guess. Every room, all the little nooks and crannies, just screamed my name, so I went for it."

"You have a beautiful home, Lalah." His lips lift at the corners in a small smile, and I get the feeling he is not judging me for my over-the-top choice in house. "What's through the other two doors?"

"Directly behind you is the door to the basement. There's a laundry room there." My nose scrunches since it's not something I particularly long to see. "And a gym. More like a dance studio. Dancing's the only time you'll see me exercise unless something's chasing me. There's also a bathroom through there." I wave my hand to point at the door behind me.

He walks me to the sliding door and we both look through the see-through window at the enclosed porch that's still a work in progress.

"This is going to look great come winter. Lazing on a sofa, snow all around me, a cup of steaming coffee and a good book." I can't contain the sigh escaping my chest. "Yeah, as close to heaven as I'll ever get."

"You really made sure there's as little need as possible for you to interact with others," he mumbles under his breath.

"Can you blame me?" I ask, a hint of annoyance in my tone.

"I won't let you hide. Not from me. You like it or not, we have each other, and I think you never considered making new friends."

"I didn't." I lift my head off his shoulder to look at him directly. There's no sign of strain on his face from carting me around on this impromptu tour of my house, and I'm a big girl. Just goes to show how much strength this man has. "Somewhere deep inside I hoped, though. Guess I hoped a bit too much since now I'm stuck with your caveman ways."

He scoffs at me, but doesn't dignify me with a response as he makes his way back to the stairs and starts climbing two at the time. His arms tighten around me, keeping me as still as possible against his chest.

As much as I grumble, I'm extremely grateful for his thoughtfulness. My arm and my head don't need much stimulation to hurt.

"Four bedrooms?" A dark-blond eyebrow touching his hairline questions me.

"The one on the left is the master," I say instead of answering.

Yeah, so maybe I went a bit overboard.

Although it's only me living in the house, the little spark of hope inside my soul, somehow surviving through all my disappointments, urged me to have four bedrooms instead of just one.

Just in case I open myself again to other people and will have friends over.

Just in case I open my heart and meet someone to share my life with.

"Here we go," he says, entering the master and gently lowering me to the bed.

Beth, the angel that she is, made sure my bed has the fluffiest of pillows and blankets, so I am as comfortable as possible.

She also took it upon herself to talk to Forrest Falls Care Home and organize a nurse aide to come every day and help me with basics, such as showering and caring for my stitches until I am able to function on my own.

I'm still on bed rest and banned from watching TV, reading, or using my phone too much until my concussion clears.

"I've dimmed the windows, so it's nice and dark for you here," Tatum says as he pulls the blanket over me, tucking me in. "Your friend Marcus keeps calling. He's not very happy he can't get in touch with you. Even threatened to fly his ass here."

I snort and a stabbing pain shoots through my still swollen eye.

"I'll pay good money to see Mister Armani-Suits-and-Italian-loafers in the great outdoors of Montana. Hell might freeze over before that happens."

"God help us all. He flirted with me for over thirty minutes over the phone. He's something else." He laughs, but then quickly sobers up.

"I'm going to go to Lost Hope, pack your things from Maevis's house and bring them here for you. I'm also packing a duffel bag for myself and taking one of your guest bedrooms until you get stronger."

My eyes roll so hard at this, they wave hello to my concussed brain. And if my heart soars with gratitude at the extent of his care and loyalty, well, that's between me and my heart.

"You don't need to babysit me." I protest. As grateful as I feel, I don't want to be a burden to anyone. It's the surest way to make people abandon me.

Whenever I needed someone most, that was the precise moment they left me.

"I don't need to. I want to. You're my friend, Lalah. This is what friends do for each other. Are you going to be OK on your own for a couple of hours?"

"I'm not too happy being around other people... not knowing who is coming and going at all hours of the day. I guess I can make an exception for you." I stick my tongue out at him. I'd wink, but my face muscles are not very cooperative at the moment.

"Do you want me to wait until Matt's crew leaves?"

"Nah. I'll be fine. I've had temporary passes issued to the guys. Those will allow them entrance only in the areas they absolutely need to be. Matt said work will be completed on August first. The passes expire exactly then."

"Alright, baby girl. Get some sleep and I'll wake you up for dinner when I'm back."

He is a true brother to me, and this makes me feel guilty. I do have a younger brother, but we haven't spoken in four years, and even before I left, our talks were few and far between.

Maybe I could have tried harder to keep a hold of him when he started distancing himself from me, but I figured, if someone wants to be in my life, they'll be there without me having to force the issue.

Tatum's phone rings from his jeans pocket. He pulls it out and answers softly, but makes no move to leave the room, or leave at all, like he said he would. I try to keep my eyes averted and focus on something else, so I don't intrude into his private matters.

"Hi babe. I'm good, thanks. Yeah, we just got to the house and she's in bed, resting now," he pauses, listening to whoever is on the other side of the call, and slowly drags his palm over his face. "I don't know if that's such a good idea. I don't think she's up for any visitors."

That catches my attention. I worm my working hand out from under the blankets he cocooned me in and wiggle my fingers to catch his eye.

"I'm right here, dude. You can ask me directly, instead of deciding for me." He glares at me, but then covers the mic of his phone with a hand and addresses me directly.

"It's Maevis. She wants to come and see you. She's worried." I wince in pain. I don't know how to feel about Maevis right now.

It was her brother hanging up on me when I was still trapped in the car. I try not to think of all that happened and instead focus on feeling better and healing physically, then sort out my feelings and emotions about that day. I'm well aware I will need the help of a therapist because I refuse to regress and live my life in constant fear, but one step at a time.

"See? That right there." He points an accusatory finger at me. "That's why I'm making this decision for you."

I have seconds to decide how this is going to go. And with the firm belief that I won't regress, I immediately understand that Maevis isn't accountable for the actions of others, regardless of their relationship. I haven't met her brother before I first saw him yesterday in the hospital, and they are both adults, living their own lives.

My friendship with Maevis might not have come yet into their conversations. I'm not self-involved to the degree where I think any or all conversations may be about me.

"Put the phone on speaker." He rewards me with a big toothy smile, like he is proud of the decision I made. He does as directed and places the phone in my hand with the screen blackened to protect my eyes. "Hi, Mae," I say to her.

Her sharp inhale of air comes through the speaker, followed shortly by a sob bubbling out of her chest.

"Hush," I continue. "I'm here. Please, don't make me bawl again. I feel like I've been crying for years, and it's only really been two days."

"God, Lalah. It's so good to hear your voice. I want to come and see you, please. How are you? What happened? What can I do for you? Please, please, I just need to see you."

"I'm fine, really. My body feels like it's been tossed around in a car, which it was, so no surprise there, but I'm fine. I just need to sleep for a week or so, and I'll be right as rain. I'm happy for you to come and see me. Just... not today."

"Please..." she interrupts me.

"Mae, I'm exhausted. I'm sorry. I don't want to cause you any concern or worry. I'm just so tired and don't have it in me to dissect the whole story again. And I'm happy for Tate to pass any details on, but I won't go over it again. I can't."

I can feel her anguished sigh deep in my chest. "Tomorrow? Can we meet tomorrow? Drake wants to be there, too."

"NO!" My shout is firm. "You can come. Drake is not welcome here. I know why he wants to visit, but his apology will only make him feel better, not me. And right now, as much as I know this causes you pain because you're in the middle between me and your brother, right now, I need to be selfish and think only of me, so that I get better and back on my feet. I hate to say it Mae, but if you show up with him tomorrow, you won't be welcomed in."

"I get it. I'm so sorry, Lalah. I should've spoken to Maddox when you first told me how the two of you met. Maybe this wouldn't have happened."

"This is not on you, Mae. This is on whoever decided to run me off the road. I'm not even going to hold your brother's loyalty to Maddox against him, but I'm not ready to give him absolution for his choices, either. And I most definitely do not hold you accountable for the choices of others."

"I'm just happy you are alive, and as well as you can be in this situation. I'll see you tomorrow."

"You will. Just call Tatum when you get here, and he'll be able to let you in. Thanks for calling, Mae, and thanks for caring."

"Always."

Chapter Fifteen

Lalah

Tatum enters my bedroom with a silver tray in his hand and a smile on his face. He places the tray with a flourish on my nightstand and helps me sit higher on the headrest.

"Your breakfast is served, my lady."

"Get out of here, you goof. Don't you have work to do?" I tell him with a laugh.

"Not today. Not until I meet this nurse aide coming to look after you and I can see for myself you'll be ok with just her while I'm at the garage."

"Tatum..." My voice breaks, my eyes already filling with tears.

Fucking hell, what's with all the waterworks?

"No. Stop that right there. I told you, you're my sister. If anything like this were to happen – knock on wood – to Selena or Sawyer, I'll be there the same as I'm here. Mae's on her way, so you better eat those yummy banana-oatmeals Beth left for you," he says sarcastically, giving me no incentive to touch them, "so you have the energy to entertain."

"You sayin' my face isn't entertaining enough right now?"

"Purple and yellow are definitely not your colors," Tatum teases, a tiny grin tugging at his lips before turning serious. "Eat up. Fast like!" He snaps his fingers at me like an asshole.

I gobble up my breakfast, daydreaming about the coffee I'm still not allowed to have – at least not until my headaches go away completely. Then Tatum helps me walk to the bathroom to wash up as best as I can.

Luckily, Beth helped me wash my hair yesterday, so at least it's not caked in blood anymore. I throw it into a loose ponytail so that it doesn't pull at my stitches, and change into a fresh pair of PJs.

Tatum cut off the sleeve of one of my fluffy bathrobes and now it easily slides over the bulky cast that doesn't allow tight sleeves.

We make our way to the completed half of the back porch, and he leaves me sitting on the swing while he goes to let Maevis in. Shortly, both of them make their way to me.

Chocolaty-amber eyes take me in and redden before tears spill down her cheeks. I'm sure I must be a sight. The bruises on my face are slowly changing their blacks and dark purples to yellow, green and blue.

My face is an entire season change, but while trees changing the color of their leaves make for the dreamiest of sights, I make for one directly from the set of *The Walking Dead*.

"Good God, Lalah," she breathes and runs to give me a hug.

"Don't..." Tatum tries to warn her not to touch me, well versed in my aversion, especially now, but I stop him with a sharp look. I don't have a problem with Mae hugging me if it's for a short time, and she needs the reassurance that I'm still here.

She lets go of me after a few seconds and takes a seat next to me. We get to catching up, ignoring the purple elephant in the room, and she chatters away about all the happenings in Lost Hope. It's bittersweet for me at this point; I truly love the town, but I don't see myself stepping foot there anytime soon.

We're interrupted when my phone alerts me of someone being at the front gate. I frown at the screen, and Tatum snatches my phone from the coffee table, watching the video feed.

"Are we expecting anyone?" I ask.

"Oh, I think this may be the nurse aide from Forrest Falls," he clarifies, eyes still trained on my phone.

"Would you let her in for me, please? If it's anyone else, then I'm not interested in visitors."

He nods and gets up from the recliner he is sprawled in. They both return soon after. Tatum is wearing a bigger frown than I did earlier.

Next to him is a woman around my age and about the same height. She wears a soft smile on her face, not appearing to be shocked or disgusted at the sight of me. Her blonde highlighted caramel hair is bound in a ponytail swishing back and forth at her scrubs cladded back with every step she takes toward us.

"Annalise?" Maevis gasps. *Annalise? As in Annalise Barlowe, Drake's wife and Maevis' sister-in-law? What the hell?* I throw a glare in Tatum's direction, but then I remember Annalise works as a nurse aide at the Forrest Falls Care Home.

What on earth was Beth thinking?

She said she personally selected her for me. She was there when I flat-out refused to see anyone from Lost Hope back in the hospital, and it was Beth who made Drake leave.

"I know what you think," Annalise says in a no-nonsense tone before I open my mouth and ask her to leave.

"I'm not here for him. I'm here because Beth is an amazing woman and when she explained your situation, I was happy she trusted me to look after you. I'm not going to pretend to understand how you must be feeling about Drake right now, and if my being here harms you more than it helps you, then I'll leave and have her look for someone else." She pauses allowing me to make my decision, but when I remain quiet, she carries on.

"I'm not here to speak on his behalf. Drake knows how I feel about the stunt he pulled. Until he removes his head from his ass, I've advised him to sleep on Maddox's couch since he can't think for himself."

Maevis is nodding next to me, as if she is not surprised by her words. Annalise looks like a bit of a spitfire. My lips curve in a smile of their own accord. I think I'm going to like this woman. Not because she put her husband in time out, essentially choosing the side of a person she's never met over his. Simply because she comes across as a person who knows her own mind and is not afraid to stand up for what she believes in.

"Thank you," I say to her. "It's nice to meet you. I've heard wonderful things about you from Maevis here. You don't need to leave. I hate that I'm the cause of a wedge between you and your husband. If you decide to help me in the following weeks... I have to tell you, he is a hard limit for me. Maevis knows as much. I'm not ready to talk to him or of him."

"I get that. I truly do. And you're not the cause of anything. What's a little disagreement between spouses?" She lifts a shoulder in a half there shrug, a mischievous grin on her pink lips. "Makes for great makeup sex." Annalise winks as she takes a seat on one of the free recliners.

"Gag!" Maevis makes a sound of revulsion as her face scrunches in disgust, and I burst into laughter. I definitely like this woman. "That's my brother you're talking about. No, just no. Stop, please! Have mercy. I shared a womb with the man."

Tatum's phone interrupts our laughter. He looks at the screen with wide eyes, his lips parting in a shocked O, then gets up from his seat and steps away. His voice still carries to where we're sitting.

"Cap! To what do I owe the honor of this call? WHAT?!" His shout makes all three of us look at him and keeps us silent at the same time.

"That's horrible news, man. I can't imagine what you are going through. I'm so sorry for your loss," he murmurs somberly.

"Yes. Yes, of course. When?" He pauses, listening to the person talking on the other end. "That's fast-moving. No, I understand. I'll be there. Of course, I'll be there. See you soon, brother. Just wish it were under better circumstances."

Tatum turns our way and looks at me as if split between what he needs to do, a sad frown marring his features.

"That was my former Captain from the Corps," he tells me in the same somber voice he used earlier on the phone. "His mother and her husband died last night in a car crash," he whispers, giving me a serious look full of sadness and relief. Like it hit him my car crash just days before could've easily had the same outcome. "He is moving fast with the funeral, and he wanted to know if I'll be there."

"Of course, you'll be there. Your friend needs you right now."

"You need me, too," he counters.

"He needs you more. I'm still here, Tate. Battered but still kicking. He needs you *more*. Be there for him. I have Annalise here, and I have Maevis, Matt, and Beth. I have a fucking village supporting me."

His eyes close, head tipped back, as he considers my words. "I'm a terrible friend," he huffs before running a hand over his face, frustrated and so clearly torn between staying with me or supporting his Captain.

"You're not. You're the best of them. Go and get him through this horrible time. And let me know if any of you need anything. I'm happy to help in whatever manner I can."

He comes closer to me and kisses the top of my head. I don't miss Maevis' sigh, and I know she'd love to be at the receiving end of one of those top of the head kisses.

Maybe it's the hours I spent thinking I was going to die, but it frustrates me to no end she is denying herself the possibility of love with him.

"You'll message me every day. You'll tell me if you are not feeling well. And you'll take the utmost care of yourself," he orders me.

"Yes, *Daddy*," I say and give him my most saccharine smile.

"Ugh, no. Just NO. Thanks for ruining that particular fantasy for me, brat." His face pales, and his eyes widen in horror.

My evil cackle of laughter accompanies him all the way to the front gate.

"It's the town hall meeting today." Maevis' voice sounds from my phone. "I wonder what the Mayor wants to tell us. She invited the whole freaking town, but made it mandatory for anyone with a business. I wish you and Tatum could be here."

"I'm sure it will be fine," I tell her. "I don't live in town, and I don't have a business in town, so there's no reason for me to be there. And I think Tatum Sr. will be at the meeting. Tate is returning in a couple of days. His friend is going through a hard time, and he wanted to support him the best he could."

"I know. I'm just anxious." She exhales heavily as if expelling all her nerves with one breath.

"What for, Mae? I'm told these town meetings happen occasionally. Why are you worried?" The hypocrisy is very much alive in me. I mean, I'm well aware of what this town meeting is for.

I submitted my report and list of approved businesses to Mayor Brown just half an hour ago, followed by a twenty-minute phone conversation with her. To say she was appalled to learn of how I've been treated is an understatement. She even went as far as asking me if I'm sure I still want to donate money to the Fire Department.

I must confess that during the early days after my accident, I honestly wanted to pull the plug on the whole thing, but it would be unfair to punish an entire town for the actions of a few individuals.

Maevis and Annalise have been my rocks during the past few weeks, as well as Tatum, who made sure to call twice a day to check on me.

The Mayor also understood why I refused to invest in her daughter. She wished for a different outcome but didn't pressure me or try to change my mind. All in all, this town meeting will be a cause for celebration for Lost Hope.

"You're right. I'm just making things up in my mind. I'll call you after and let you know what went down."

"Yeah, babe. You do that. Go make yourself look pretty, and I look forward to you telling me all about it."

I push the swing back and forth with the tip of my toes and take in the beauty of my backyard. The house is finally ready. Matt's guys collected their tools and cleaned up the leftover materials earlier today. I gave them a nice bonus, because they've done an exquisite job in building the house of my dreams.

They'll have to return come spring, once the snow clears, to work on building floating planters for my vegetable garden, but that's the least of my worries now.

The backyard has a nice man-made pond where I can sit during hot summer days, or I can skate during winter. Close to the tall, black fence enclosing my little clearing in the woods, there's a shed full of gardening tools and chopped wood for bonfires.

In between the shed and the house, they've built me a little observatory for my telescope, which I'm extremely excited to use. The skies here are incredibly clear, and I've been able to see so many more constellations than when I lived in big cities. There are particular nights where one of the Milky Way's arms is visible to the naked eye.

Regardless of all the ugliness of the past weeks, I'm so happy to be living here.

Maevis took it upon herself to arrange regular grocery deliveries from Lucy's Market, which Pete does himself. He is not impressed with the state of me, and constantly fusses over me. Although most of the people who know me are aware I've been in a car crash, they don't know the details of all that went down.

I've urged the people who do know not to advertise the details. What's done is done. Besides, the more information that spills, the more difficult it'll be for Sheriff Richards to do his investigation.

He has got the license plate, but it was a rental car from a shady agency that doesn't do a great job at keeping records, so he's trying to slowly, slowly piece everything together. Of course, not knowing if I've intentionally been run off the road or not puts my paranoia at an all-time high.

No one has permission to come and go as they please. Every time someone shows up around the fence, one of the many cameras on the property sends a video feed to my phone. People walking through the woods have come close, but no one tried anything.

They couldn't even if they wanted to.

The fence is sixteen feet tall, so anyone will have a hard time climbing it. I'll know before they even try anyway, and I'll be able to shut down the house in a matter of seconds.

Nothing I don't want around can reach me here.

The best part, the fence doesn't take away from the view, as the house is quite tall, and it's seated on a taller inclination on the ground around the center of the clearing.

The greatest addition to the house is Astrum, a retired German Shepherd K9. Annalise noted I wasn't sleeping well, partly because of nightmares, reliving the crash in my dreams over and over again, and partly due to the crippling fear of being on my own during the night. I didn't realize what great comfort having Tatum stay here was until he was gone.

So she forced my ass into my new Solterra's passenger seat and drove me to an adoption center in Billings. The adoption center houses dogs that were part of the police force and either had to be retired or they lost their assigned handlers and couldn't be used anymore because they refused to bond with another.

Astrum is a lively three-year-old bundle of, I'd like to say fluffiness and joy; considering he's taller than me when standing on his hind legs and reaches my hips when on all fours, I'll go with a bundle of muscles and face kisses. He had to be retired after his handler was forced to give him up when his newborn turned out to be allergic to dogs.

The stubborn mutt refused to bond with anyone else, and so he was dropped to the K9 adoption center, where out of everyone, he chose me and made me immensely happy.

The drive back from the center was a lot smoother than the drive there, with Astrum refusing to sit anywhere but in my lap and distracting me from the fear and anxiety threatening to consume me.

My phone rings once again, and I'm surprised to see two hours have passed with me lost in thought.

"OH MY GOD, LALAH!" Annalise's excited voice blasts through my speaker.

"What happened?"

"I'm finally going to open my books and coffee shop. OH MY GOD!!! THIS IS A DREAM COME TRUE!"

A pleased smile graces my face at her words. It seems like the town meeting ended and everyone got the good news.

"Congratulations! I'm so happy for you. I look forward to being your first customer."

"GOD, I have so much to do, so much to plan for." Her voice takes a panicky edge.

"Breathe," I laugh. "It'll be great. I'm happy to sit with you, if you want, and help plan."

"Really? You'd do that for me?"

"Of course, I will. You're no longer my nurse aide. Never were, really. You know I consider you a friend, and what are friends for, if not for supporting each other?"

"Thank you! Seriously, thank you! I'm excited to get started. I'll let you go now. Good night, Lalah."

"Night."

As soon as she hangs up, Maevis's name shows on my phone. Looks like I'm due more good news.

"OH MY GOD, LALAH," she cries excitedly. I laugh at receiving the same greeting in the span of two minutes from two different people.

"I take it the meeting went well?" I quip like a smartass.

"It did. The Mayor called the meeting to let us know we've had an angel investor called Lege et Lacrima assess the businesses in our town, and they invested in a bunch of us, me included. I can't believe it. We even had their CFO, Marcus Reyes, join us via video call. They selected me too, Lalah," she shrieks. Her joy is palpable even through my phone and my soul settles. THIS is why I do what I do.

"My mortgage is paid off. My father's care is paid off through a different donation for Forrest Falls Care Home. I have enough money left over to do some upgrades to the kitchen in the bakery, and with the money I'm still not happy you paid for renting my house, I erased my ex-asshole's debts. You can't imagine the freedom I'm feeling right now. For the first time in over two years, I can finally take a full breath. My lungs don't know how to inflate that much anymore."

"Well deserved, hun. It was absolutely well deserved. Couldn't have happened to a better person."

"God, I won't be able to sleep tonight because of all the excitement. Celebratory cakes in the morning?"

"You betcha'. I look forward to tasting what you come up with."

I hang up the phone and look lovingly at Astrum. It seems like everything is returning to normal, and the people I care for the most are happy and healthy. There's one last thing I need to do, and that is finally talking to Drake.

I love Maevis like a sister, and in the past two weeks, I've come to see Annalise as a sister, too. The three of us have vastly different personalities, but for some reason, we just click, and I don't want my avoidance of Drake to ruin these friendships.

If he feels the same loyalty toward Maddox I feel for Maevis and Annalise, then I can see why he was quick to trust his friend's judgments of me, and I can't hold that against him.

Besides, he is Maevis' brother and Annalise's husband, so there's no way he really is a terrible or evil person. Not while he has two of the best people I've ever had the honor of meeting in his life.

Chapter Sixteen

Cole

I squint my eyes at the clear blue sky and blinding sunshine. They're mocking me. Mocking all four of us as we stand still like statues watching the coffins being lowered into the ground.

Clara whimpers, a pitiful mourning sound, hiding her face in the crook of my neck. Eliza's arms go around my thighs, her tiny body shaking under the weight of our collective sadness. My palm cradles the back of her head, smoothing her hair.

I suck in a breath, my mind spinning and sputtering, like an engine drowning in the wrong gear. I'm the one everyone counts on to come up with a plan even in the most dire of situations.

I'm the one pulling rabbits out of his fucking ass and carrying my team back home whenever we tethered between life and death during deployments.

And right now, there's nothing I can do to take away the pain my stepsisters are feeling. I can't bring their father back. I can't breathe life into my mother either.

A hand claps my back, before my brother's arm sneaks around me. That's it. My entire family.

And I'm the one responsible for them now.

My eyes burn as tears form behind my eyelids. I'm not too proud of a man to keep them at bay. My mother deserves every single last tear I have in my body. But my family needs me to be strong.

These two little souls that are now entirely in my care need me to be strong for them. Need me to carry their pain so they can heal.

As one, we take a step forward, and then another until we're face to face with the three graves. In nearly thirty-five years of life, I've lost three parents. To the left, the oldest headstone, weathered and chipped here and there, looms over the two newer ones. *Colton Hayes, beloved husband and father. Semper Fidelis.*

My mom's is front and center, her ivory headstone gleaming in the sunshine. A massive arrangement of pure-white lilies keeps vigil in front of the cold marble. My heart skips a beat at the sight of them. A spark of hope in all the darkness.

The flowers arrived this morning at the funeral home, an unsigned card attached to them.

> You're not alone, *Cap*.
> My heart breaks for you and your family.
> Draw strength from your loved ones.
> Lean on them and allow them to lean on you.
>
> My heartfelt condolences,
> A. M. (Lost Hope)

I shake my head, clearing all thoughts of the stranger who's done us a kindness. There'd be time later to ask Carter about them.

Kneeling in front of my mom's grave, my arm bands around Clara, who's still holding on to me like I'm her last hope. My hand buries in the freshly dug soil, gathering a handful in my fist before letting it scatter over the glossy cream casket.

"Rest well, Mom. Between Dad and Alecs, you'll be spoiled and protected for eternity." My voice cracks as I say a final goodbye to the incredible woman I had the honor of calling *my mother.*

Climbing to my feet, I move to the third and final grave. *Alecsander Hart.*

"Daddy!" Eliza's pained wail nearly brings me back to my knees.

"I've got her," Tatum assures me, scooping my sister up and in his arms. I've never been more grateful for my best friend. We're all a little lost right now, and having him here to hold the fort down until I get my bearings and wrap my head around our new reality is God sent.

I watch as he whispers in her ear, her tiny body fighting the comfort he brings. My eyes dart back to the slick, black stone, the same shade as the coffin rained down with earth and flowers.

My hand squeezes the edge of the slab. "I'm glad I got to meet you, Alecs. And I'm damned glad Blake got to know his father. Don't know what you and Mom were thinking, choosing me to look after your girls, but I promise you they'll want for nothing. Watch over us, will you? And don't laugh too hard when I stumble here and there. You were a great man, and I'll spend every day trying to live up to your example."

I turn around, only to come face to face with Blake. My brother is almost as tall as I am, even if there are thirteen years between the two of us. His silver eyes, red-rimmed with unshed tears, assess me, and his fingers clamp on my shoulder.

"They thought you've done a great fucking job raising me. They thought there isn't a man on this Earth with a heart bigger than yours or more responsible than you. We'll keep them safe and happy, brother," he chokes, his voice gritty and raw.

My forehead touches his, as finally the tears I was holding myself spill down my face. Yes, I need to be strong for what is left of my family, but I can be strong tomorrow.

The house is eerily quiet. There's no laughter in the living room. No *Modern Talking* blasting from Alecs's office.

Clara fell asleep on the way home from the cemetery, and Eliza locked herself in her room. Blake sits on the worn armchair, his eyes glazed over, looking at absolutely nothing.

I finally shed the stifling black suit and shoved it at the bottom of my closet. Making my way to the kitchen, I crack open a beer. I want nothing more than to get blackout drunk and wake up tomorrow still on base, ready to sign my life away for another four years with the Marine Corps.

But that's not my reality. Not anymore.

"Got another one of those?" Tatum asks from somewhere behind me.

I shove my hand into the fridge and toss him a cold bottle.

"Called your girlfriend?" I smirk at him, or attempt to anyway. Feels like more of a grimace.

He got here five days ago, after I called to let him know of the tragedy that shook my family to the core, and he flew to Richmond the very same day. Since he's been here, like clockwork, he called his friend every morning and evening.

"Not my girlfriend." He pops an eyebrow at me, beer bottle tilted to his lips. "But yeah, I called my *friend.*"

Before I can point out we're friends and he is not calling me twice a day, the doorbell rings. I swear under my breath, praying Clara doesn't wake up. This last week has been stressful enough, with today being its own special brand of hell. She needs to rest.

I really hope there aren't any more well-meaning neighbors with another fucking casserole. I'm grateful for all the support, I truly am, but if I don't see or smell another crockpot dinner for the rest of my life, I'll die a happy man.

"Evening," a pimpled face greets me. "Delivery from *Serendipità.*" My eyebrows shoot up my forehead at the name of the fanciest Italian restaurant in Richmond.

"Got the wrong address, kid. We didn't order anything."

The boy, no older than eighteen, scrunches his face, and his lips purse as he checks the ticket stapled to the overflowing bag.

"Are you not Cap or Tatum Carter?" he asks.

Huh. Looks like I'm not the only one sick of casseroles. I turn my head inside the door, eyes searching for Tate. "Yo, Carter. Did you order dinner?"

"My friend did," his voice comes from the kitchen.

Friend my ass. A strange rush flushes through me, a scowl rising on my face. *What the fuck? Is that jealousy?*

I shove my hand in my pocket, retrieving my wallet to tip the kid, but he pushes the bag in my arms, and with a wave over his shoulder he's jogging down the steps leading to the porch.

"Thanks man, but the lady tipped us a crazy amount. Enjoy your dinner," he hollers before jumping in his car and disappearing from sight.

The smell of tomato sauce and garlic hits my nostrils and my stomach makes an unholy noise, trying to eat its way through my abdomen to get to whatever delicious food is hidden in my arms.

"Thank fuck." Blake appears right in front of me, hunger clearly written on his face, unwrapping the food with his eyes. "I was prepared to let myself starve than eat any more funeral food..." he trails off, snatching the black paper bag from me and running to the living room.

"Set the table, you heathen. I'll go get Eliza."

The old stairs creak and groan under my feet, and I make a mental note to have them looked at. The list grows longer and longer with each passing day, and it's only been a week.

I reach my sister's bedroom door and tap softly with my fingers against the pink-painted wood.

"Eliza?" No response, but faint sniffles come from the other side of the wall. "Baby girl, come have dinner with us," I plead.

"I'm not hungry. Go away!" The sound of her tiny feet stomping lifts the corners of my mouth. She may be sad, but my little sister is a firecracker, and she'll get through to the other side.

"Sounds good to the angry monster in my stomach. More spaghetti and meatballs for me. Alright, squirt. I'll go tell Blake the excellent news."

It takes less than two seconds for her door to open, just a smidge, but enough to know she took the bait. Her blotched face and sunken eyes peer at me, half hidden by the wall. Breath is trapped inside my lungs, chained with her sadness.

I clear my throat so it doesn't betray my concern, and shrug as if I don't have a care in the world.

"What kind of spaghetti?" she whispers, her gray eyes – so similar to my brother's – gleaming with hope.

"Hmm…" I tap my finger to my chin. "Farfalle. Those yummy, yummy butterflies in sweet tomato sauce and crunchy garlic bread…" I trail off and, just in time, my stomach groans another loud protest.

Eliza's lips curve in a barely there smile, but it's more than I've seen from her all week.

"That's not spaghetti, silly," she huffs.

I let my mouth slack open, rounding my eyes until they're about to pop out of their sockets, and clasp my palms to my scruffed jaw. *I'm a goddamned emoji.*

"It's not?" I suck in an incredulous breath. "What is it then?"

"Pasta, Coley. What do they teach you in the military, if you don't know the difference between spaghetti and pasta?" She rolls her pretty eyes at me. *There she is, my strong-willed, sharp-shooting sister.*

"That's why I have you, baby girl. How about you come save me from making a fool out of myself in front of Blake, and I'll see about sharing my chocolate crostata with you?"

I know she can't resist a good dessert. A full-on smile tugs at my lips as she slips her tiny hand inside of my large one and leads me to the dining room.

Dinner is a quiet affair. This past week was loud with planning, neighbors coming to check-in on us, emergency appointments with a judge and Social Services. The quiet feels so wrong, so out of place in a home that was always filled with noise and laughter.

I shovel the last of the crostata in my mouth, leaning my back on the backrest of the chair, my legs extending under the table, crossed at the ankles.

My elbow nudges Eliza's arm, and when her head turns to me, I give her a cheeky grin. "You're gonna have to roll me to the couch, squirt. I'm too full to move," I groan, rubbing my abdomen. "If you do that, you earn yourself thirty extra minutes of TV tonight."

She pouts at me, and I choke on a laugh at the challenge brimming in her eyes. Her tiny palms plant on my shoulder, and she pushes with all her might. Not even a hair on me budges out of place. She lifts to her knees on the cushion of her seat, hands fisting. The more she pushes, the redder her face becomes, until she puffs an exasperated breath and plops back on her chair, arms folded at her chest.

"It's not fair. You're too big," she cries. "Why can't Blake and Tatum help? They're just sitting there, doing nothing," she points an accusatory finger across the table.

"Hey!" Blake protests. "My food baby needs a nap before I'm asked to roll boulders around," he defends, narrowing his eyes at me. "Maybe you should eat less and work out more, old man."

"Fuck off, fetus," I grumble in good humor.

"Swear jar," exclaim in unison both Eliza and Blake. "Five crisp dollars," says my sister, her palm up, fingers wiggling.

"Dammit," I mumble under my breath. I lost nearly two hundred dollars to the fucking swear jar these past seven days.

"It's ten now," she informs me primly.

"Fifteen, and you take a bath and go to sleep," I counter.

"Deal." Eliza rubs her hands together excitedly, dashing up the stairs to the bedroom.

Tatum and I push back from the table, cleaning containers, boxing left-overs and throwing them in the fridge. Soon enough, the house is once again drowning in silence.

"Get a beer and meet me on the porch," I ask him. "I'll say goodnight to Eliza and meet you there."

He pats my shoulder, and we each go about our business. I stop in my bedroom, checking on Clara, who is still sound asleep in her toddler crib. She didn't have any dinner, and went to sleep quite early too. It only means I'll have an ungodly wake up call in the middle of the night, but today has been devastatingly hard on all of us.

It will take a while to find our footing and get into a new routine.

"Eli's in bed, ready for you. I'm going out," Blake tells me, decked in a black button down and ripped white jeans.

My eyebrows shoot up in disbelief. "Don't go reckless on me, brother. Not today."

He scowls, but shakes his head before his mouth gets the better of him. "I'm not. I just need to... I don't even fucking know. Not be here for a second."

"Alright. Call me if you need me."

With a jerk of his chin, he disappears down the stairs and the soft click of the front door closing behind him reaches me.

Blake was always the easy going brother; life of the party, the jokester to my seriousness. I can't even begin to understand how he feels now, after losing Mom and Alecs. We all have a lot of healing to do, a lot to overcome.

I knock softly on Eliza's door before pushing it open, trying to be considerate of her privacy and her space. In a few short years, she'll be a teenager, a woman in the making. She needs to know her privacy will always be respected. And I need to start building a relationship of trust between us.

I'm not just her older stepbrother. I'm the brother who was almost never home. In the years since my mom and Alecs reconnected, I haven't been home much, except for the little free time I had between deployments.

The girls don't know me like they know Blake. So I need to put a lot of patience, understanding, and love on the table.

"Ready for bed, squirt?" I check with her before sitting down at the edge of her bed. She shuffles over to me, underneath her *Beauty and the Beast* cover, settling her head on my thigh.

My fingers automatically start smoothing her blonde, curly hair, brushing it off her eyes and forehead.

"I'm sad, Coley. I miss them so much," Eliza sighs. "Do you think they miss me?"

"I know they do, baby girl. And I miss them too. It's okay to be sad. It's okay to cry, too. You are entitled to feel however you are feeling. Just know that I'm here for you."

"Do you promise to never leave me?"

My heart jolts painfully in my chest at the sorrow in her voice. I'd do just about anything to bring her parents back to her, to have her return to the happy little girl she was just last week. So I make the one promise I cannot guarantee I can keep.

"I promise, baby girl. You'll always have me in your corner." Bending at the waist, I kiss her forehead. "Sleep now, squirt. I'll see you in the morning. Good night."

"Night, Coley. I love you." She snuggles down under her blankets and her eyelids flutter closed.

Making sure her night light is on, I jog down the stairs and meet Tatum out on the porch. He's seated on the bottom step, beer bottle dangling in between his knees. I collapse next to him, exhaling a heavy breath. He picks up an unopened beer and shoves it my way.

"How you holdin' up, man?"

I run a hand over my face, trying to clear off the misery of today before twisting the cap, twirling the cold metal between my fingers.

"Been better," I scoff derisively. "I'm trying to find my footing in this new reality I'm living now. Fuck!" Frustration courses through me, my fist clenching around the neck of the bottle. "Who am I, Carter? Who am I outside the Marines? I knew since the very first year I was going to be a lifer. I made my peace with not having a family of my own. How the fuck am I going to be a civilian and a father to them?"

I jump to my feet, unable to sit still for a moment longer, and pace the bottom of the stairs.

"Cole," Tatum's low, gravel-like voice reaches me, but I continue, cutting him off.

"How am I going to help them navigate through their grief? I can't even let myself grieve. It's fucking ironic. I don't fear death. Every fucking deployment we knew chances were high we may not make it back. I never for a second considered *their* death. Not now. Not like this. Not when she was finally happy."

Tears burn the back of my eyelids, the unfairness and injustice of lives cut way too short raging in me.

"Cap, sit the fuck down," he orders me. "Sit down!" He repeats, both his hands pressing down my shoulders, and my knees buckle under the weight of the day and all the drastic turns my life took.

He gets right in my face, crouched in front of me. His freakishly blue eyes laser-focus onto mine. This is no longer my friend, Tatum Carter. This is Second Lieutenant Marine Officer Tatum Carter. And he's about to rip into me.

"Listen up! You just lost your mother. Cry if you need to cry. Rage if you need to rage. But keep in mind, up there," he points to the bedroom window on the second floor, "two little girls went to sleep sad, but safe. Because they know you have their back. They'll be sad for a while. Hell, they may be sad forever when they think of Romina and Alecs, but they'll grow up knowing what it means to be loved and protected by a good man."

His fingers clamp down on my shoulders, the pressure centering my spiraling thoughts.

"You take one day at a time. They're no different than our team. And you fucking led us to hell and back in one piece. I get it, I really do. In my mind, I was a lifer, too. Until I wasn't." His voice cracks on the last words, breaking the tough lieutenant persona, but he powers through his own pain.

"Find yourself a goddamned therapist and one hour a week cry in your fucking combat boots. Then come home and be the best goddamned father figure and the best fucking man those girls are ever gonna meet in their lives."

So I let myself feel. The cold empty place in my heart where my mom, the strongest woman I've ever met, occupied. I allow the emptiness to wash over me once, then twice. My eyes scrunch-shut, my lungs heave with the burn of every breath.

"All you have to do is show up, Cap. It's in your blood. You're Cole motherfucking Hayes. Today, grieve. Tomorrow, do what you do best, and show up."

Chapter Seventeen

Lalah

I've heeded Tatum's advice to wait for his return before meeting with Drake. I didn't feel it would be a confrontation, but Tatum's words make sense. Annalise and Maevis would be there, of course, but even unintentionally, their allegiance would be with Drake, as silly as that sounds, so it makes sense that I have an ally of my own.

Someone concerned only with *my* well-being.

I also know that's not entirely true. I haven't missed the way Tatum watches Maevis, or the way he always makes a point of asking about her every time he calls. *Twice* a day. I'm really rooting for them, and wish they'd both remove their heads from their asses and take a chance on each other.

I'm once again sitting in the passenger seat of my car. Astrum is scrunched down at my feet with his head on my lap. My seat is pushed as far back as it will go to accommodate the furry giant.

For a beast as big as he is, I swear he thinks he is a lap dog. But I also know why he's all up in my business. He can feel the anxiety and fear rolling in waves off of me and lets me pet his head so that I can keep control of my feelings.

I haven't attempted getting behind the wheel and won't be doing so until my cast comes off, anyway. I already got in touch with a therapist, and I'm talking to her three times a week.

I don't feel like I've made much progress mentally, but I guess these kinds of things take time.

Today's the day I'm meeting with Drake.

Maevis has closed the bakery this morning so we can all meet there. As willing as I am to hear him out, I'm uncomfortable having him at my house. I don't like it much when people, especially people I don't know, encroach on my space.

In the last three weeks, my house has truly become my safe space and, with Astrum as my guardian, I'm feeling the most relaxed I've ever felt given the circumstances.

A stranger in my house will just ruin that peace for me. And as uncomfortable as it may be to return to Lost Hope, I know nothing's going to happen to me with Astrum and Tatum there.

Astrum may be a big teddy bear to me, but he is a vicious beast to his core. He nearly jumped at Tate's throat when he returned and let himself in with his access code.

"How's your friend?" I ask Tate. He only returned last night, and came directly to my house from the airport. He was dead on his feet, tired after the long flight from the East Coast, so I haven't had a chance to talk to him.

It felt insensitive to ask too many questions during his stay there. I sent a massive arrangement of flowers for the funeral, with a card expressing my condolences, and arranged dinner for them to be delivered after the service. I'm sure they had plenty of casseroles in their freezer, as it is after all funerals, but I had a weird pushing inside of me to do something, to offer some comfort.

"Hanging in there, I guess. He was named guardian of his younger step-sisters when his mom married their dad, and he wasn't aware of that. He has his hands full, that's for sure. The man may be an excellent leader when commanding a team of soldiers to their potential death, but I doubt the same tactics would work on the girls," he tells me with a sad smile.

"You'll tell me if there's anything I can do to help," I command, my heart jolting painfully in my chest.

I'm feeling weirdly protective of these people I've never met in my life, and most likely never will. My palm presses just above my heart, rubbing circles over the emptiness that appears there every time I think of his friend.

He nods, a sharp up and down movement of his head, in response.

"Your face is looking better," Tatum quips after a moment while we're stopped at one of the three traffic lights in Lost Hope.

"Thanks, I think?" I laugh.

"Ohh, quit it. You can open both eyes now, and most of the swelling has gone down. The bruises are mostly faded, too. With the stitches gone, once the redness of your eye recedes, you'll look as good as new. I'm pissed he doesn't get to see you as you were fresh from the hospital so that the image of you all battered and bruised will haunt him forever," he mumbles.

"But he did," I remind him gently. "He was the one pulling me out of the car. He was also there in my hospital room when I woke up."

He hums in response, not willing to cut Drake even a bit of slack, checking the side mirrors before parking directly in front of the bakery.

I think he's looking for a fight. It's a no-parking zone, but by leaving the car here, he knows there's a high chance of one of the deputies or even Maddox himself coming and asking us to move the car or slapping a fine on me.

He's unhappy that not much progress has been made to identify the person who ran me off the road that day, and he's shifted the blame on Maddox and Drake.

He comes around my side of the car, picks me up, and places me on my feet on the sidewalk. *Fucking caveman,* I think to myself. Astrum joins me, and by the raised hackles at his neck, he'd switched on his *predatory* mode.

I'm not concerned.

I know he will not attack anyone unless I'm attacked or I give him the command. I may have only had him for ten days, but we've bonded so completely during these ten days that it feels like I've always had him.

Tate opens the door to the bakery for me, and, with a hand at my back, he ushers me inside. Drake is already here, seated next to Annalise. The tables have been pushed together so we can all be in the same space.

Astrum growls low in his throat at Drake but doesn't make a move to leave my side.

I walk toward the table, and Drake stands in greeting. Much to my surprise, both Annalise and Maevis drag their chairs to sit at my side.

Tatum refuses to sit and leans on the closest wall, arms folded close to his chest, resting one ankle on top of the other, glaring daggers at Drake's head. Yikes. If looks could kill.

I take Drake in for the first time. He's taller than Tatum, with the same strong, muscular build. Seriously, what do they feed these men? He has the same chocolaty-amber eyes as Maevis and the same dark brown hair, although his is cut short and has more waviness to it.

As if commanded, all four of us drop to our seats. Drake just looks at me, not saying anything, and Maevis starts fussing over us. "I have some brownies for us, and I got you your hazelnut latte, Lalah."

I squeeze her arm to stop her. "There's no need to be anxious, hun. I think we all have the same intentions here," I offer.

"If the intention is cold-blooded murder, then sure," Tatum retorts from his self-appointed sentinel position. I roll my eyes at him, then look at Drake.

He doesn't shy away from my perusal, and, if anything, he tries to open his facial expressions more to me, so I can see all his feelings; the remorse in the thinning of his lips, the regret in his bloodshot eyes, and the guilt in his lowered lashes, all suffocating him.

"I can't express how sorry I am for hanging up on you, Lalah. My apology doesn't help you now and didn't help you then. I am selfish for even asking you to be here so I can beg for your forgiveness." His baritone voice crackles in the empty bakery. His amber gaze bores into mine, bleeding sincerity.

"It means the world you have agreed to see me. It keeps me awake at night thinking what could have happened to you if the sheriff didn't call as soon as he did. We could have been there earlier for you. I'm so, so sorry," he apologizes in a soft, honest voice.

It's clear as day he is sorry. For such a large man, he seems somehow small, dimmed, and I hurt on his behalf.

I hurt for Annalise and Maevis too, as it couldn't have been easy to see him like this for weeks.

"Why did you think my call for help wasn't genuine? This is what I questioned most. We never met. You were concerned and willing to help until you heard my name."

Astrum moves in between Annalise and me and lowers his head on my knees, sensing my anxiety. My fingers sink into his silky, black fur, thanking him silently for grounding me.

"It's so ridiculous, now that I think about it. The night you met him, a couple of us were at that bar. Me, Annalise, Maddox, and some other high school friends, Maddison included. Although she's a couple of years younger than us, she gravitates to where Maddox is. He noticed you dancing and went to you as soon as we got there. She was pissy the whole night and the whole drive back," he explains.

"I thought little of it. Much to my shame, I didn't connect the dots since this is the kind of thing Maddox does." He stops then, his gaze searching my face, trying to gauge what my reaction is to hearing Maddox is a man-whore.

There's no reaction because what Maddox does or how he spends his nights is no concern of mine. I nod to let him know he's good to carry on.

"Anyway, about a month later, he came to my house, all pissed and angry, and told me about your encounter at the police station. Saying that just before you went there, Maddison was telling him about seeing you around town, spending a lot of time at Lucy's Market, asking about him, and she swore up and down that you were following him." He gives me a pointed look, but I just cock an eyebrow in return.

"He was confused. Madd noticed you were genuinely surprised to see him there, but then Maddison accused you of damaging your own car, and he went with it. You left, but she kept telling him how he needs to be careful and then pressed the button that gets Maddox nuclear." He pauses, drawing a big breath.

"She told him you might try to use the people around him to get his attention, and you may try to engage Ryker. When it comes to him, Maddox doesn't see reason."

"Ryker?" I ask.

"His son. You didn't know about him?"

"I didn't. I don't discuss Maddox, Drake." I barely keep my eyes from rolling into the back of my head. It's getting frustrating how many times I have to repeat myself.

"I truly have no interest in him. If there was an inkling before he threatened to arrest me, it was purely because we're both living in the same town, so we could be neighborly," I clarify, and he nods as if expecting the exact answer I gave.

"Anyway, that's when he urged me to be wary of you, telling me about the stunt he thought you pulled with the car."

"I didn't," I interrupt.

"I know. I know *now*. Maevis ripped me a couple of new holes. Not that there was much left of me once Annalise finished telling me exactly what she thought of my behavior. And during all of that, she told me your side of the story. Three weeks ago when you called, I heeded his warning. I didn't think much of it. I don't have an excuse, Lalah. He's my best friend," he pleads with me before continuing, his fingers crushing one of the cookies, brushing and spreading the crumbs on the tabletop.

"I grew up with him, and he is a brother to me. I'm his son's godfather, so when he told me that someone was following him, that he was concerned for his son, and you were playing games trying to get his attention, I believed him. It has happened before. I'd do anything to keep Ryker safe." His chocolate eyes bore into mine, convincing me of his honesty.

"I was wrong about you. Hell, we both were, and it brings me immense joy to see you are not holding my mistakes against my wife or my sister. If it's any consolation, I am paying for my mistake. And not just by drowning in guilt and by having Annalise and Maevis disappointed in me. I was also suspended for a month for not responding to a call and for letting my personal feelings interfere with someone's safety."

His words sink inside of me. Drake is not a bad person. Misguided, in this situation, sure, but not bad. His mistake was not coming to my aid.

But he didn't cause the crash, and he did come through for me by getting me out of the car and safely to the hospital. I also know as disappointed as he is being over suspended, he's more upset with himself for not doing better.

"Thank you. I don't want you blaming yourself. And I hope there was something to be learned from all of this. I accept your apology."

Tatum scoffs at my words, and my eyes jump to him, blazing with reprimand. He's fine, he'll get over it.

The front door suddenly opens with a soft thud. "We're closed," says Maevis from next to me in a fake cheerful voice.

"What's going on?" a deep voice asks, and I turn toward it. Well, talk of the devil and he shall appear. His ice-blue eyes widen while taking me in. His face morphs from surprise to guilt and then anger as he looks at my still-healing face.

I guess he had his come-to-Jesus moment sometime in the past three weeks. My blood still boils at him being here, interrupting this private moment of healing.

I stand and notice from the corner of my eye Tatum has straightened too from his slump against the wall. Astrum takes an attack position, growling with all his might.

Maddox seems undeterred despite the hostility in the air and takes a few steps closer to me, his eyes apologetic.

"I'm so sor..." he starts, but I'm having none of it.

"Are you here as Chief Deputy Lawson or as Maddox, resident of Lost Hope?" I interrupt. He blinks at me in confusion.

"It's my day off," he cautiously says.

"Good!" I cock back my cast-enclosed arm as far as it goes and punch him straight in the nose. Pain radiates up and down my arm, and I try to shake it down. *Huh, who knew?* I guess I too am blaming Maddox.

"Fuuuuuuuuuck," he groans painfully, immediately holding his hand to his bleeding nose.

The room is dead silent, but at his exhale, everyone talks at the same time.

"Oh my God!" exclaims Maevis.

"Didn't know you had it in you," laughs Annalise.

Drake seems to be frozen in his seat looking at me with wide eyes and parted lips, while Tatum cackles like a madman, clapping my shoulder. "That's my girl!"

Maevis hands Maddox a couple of tissues so he can try to stop the blood from flowing down his chin.

I honestly didn't think I hit him *that* hard. First, it was my left hand that's been in a cast for three weeks now, and second, I'm more the type to hurt someone with my words, rather than my fists. I don't really condone violence.

But judging by the crimson rivulets staining his pale-blue button-down, I must have done some damage.

"I guess I deserve that," he tells me, but he's not mad at me. He took me punching him more like an acceptance of his interrupted apology. I nod my head at him, a smirk playing at the corners of my lips.

"I guess you did."

Two months of healing. Two months of unlearning things that have been beaten into me in my childhood.

I grew up thinking I wasn't good enough to be shown love, affection, or care. I was starved for it. Then I met Callum and felt like he showered me with everything I was deprived of. I hung on to him as tightly as possible. Because surely even a little bit was better than nothing.

What Callum gave me was actually crumbs, and since I didn't know any better, I confused his kind of love with the real deal.

I may not have found romantic love, and I may never find it, but that doesn't mean I'm not loved. Even if that's hard to believe with all the side-eye I'm getting right now.

"Stop looking at me like that," I grump at Tatum. "I'd rather eat dark chocolate with ninety percent cocoa for the rest of my life than admit you were right."

"You said dark chocolate makes you sad, and your sadness disqualifies it as chocolate since its only purpose is to make people happy." He throws my words in my face like the asshole he is.

"Well, I'd rather be sad than admit you are right. I told you before, pain is temporary, pride is forever."

"Spoken like a true smartass," he retorts.

"Seriously, Tate? *Steel Magnolias*?" I laugh because out of all the movies he could've quoted at me, I never would have pegged him as a magnolian.

"What? It's a good fucking movie, Lalah! Don't be such a snob." His outraged voice thunders in my car.

"My apologies. Fine. Just because you make me proud by quoting *Steel Magnolias*. Are you sitting comfortably? Do you need to pull over?"

"What for? Are you ok? Is your arm hurting?"

"For this..." I turn to watch him in the driver's seat, so he can see how serious I am. My chest rises with a long inhale as I say, "You were right, Tatum. There will be a snowstorm."

"Fuuuuuck yeaaaaaaah," he shouts, slapping both palms on the steering wheel and earning an indignant bark from Astrum.

"I hope it doesn't get any worse and they cancel your flight," I tell him, watching the snowflakes dance around us.

"Nah, I think the worst will hit tomorrow evening. Today's not cold enough for the flurries to stick, although you can never tell with snowstorms." He takes a quick look at me from the corner of his eye as he chews on the inside of his cheek.

"Do you have everything you need? You might be snowed-in for a couple of days, and even if you have the snowmobile, that left arm of yours has been in a cast for the past three months. It may be healed now but remains vulnerable, so you shouldn't force it by driving."

"I'm fine, Tate. It doesn't hurt, but honestly, I can't wait to get in the shower and shave the damn thing. I can't even see my tattoos for all the fur." I get an eye roll for that. Fair enough.

"I do have everything I need. Hell, I have everything half of Lost Hope may need. Ruth sent me a couple of trays with lasagna and baked mac & cheese." I count on the fingers of one hand.

"Maevis filled my freezer with cookie dough and my pantry with all sorts of baked treats." Second finger goes up.

"Pete filled my fridge with more fruits and vegetables than I ever had, even during summer days." Third finger pops next to the others. "You enjoy your time with Selena, and don't worry about me." I wiggle my fingers in front of his face before continuing.

"I'm actually excited to have two fully functional arms, and I'm excited for the snow, having the electric fireplace on, me sprawling out on the window seat with a hot chocolate, watching the snow fall."

"Why don't you ask Maevis to stay with you, at least until I come back?"

"I really should start charging you rent, what with you being at my place more than yours."

"Can't help it if you have a fancier barbeque than mine. And the big ass TV in the living room; I can watch all the football I please and feel like I'm at the stadium." He winks cheekily. "But seriously, ask her."

"Yeah, yeah. Mi casa es su casa and all that. And you bought that barbeque for my birthday. Maevis needs to be at the bakery. With it closed while the renovations were completed, she's afraid of falling behind."

"It won't happen," Tatum grits with conviction.

"*We* know that. Hell, even she knows it, but she's worried, and re-opening the bakery keeps her sane. I like her sane, so she's staying put."

"Pain in my ass," he mutters under his breath while stopping the car in front of the palm reader panel and entering the code to unlock the gates.

He parks my car inside the garage and I follow him out to his. "Thanks for driving me to the doctor's. I'm so happy to be without a cast I may throw myself a party tonight."

Stepping next to him, I engulf him in a hug that's quickly joined by Astrum. I plant my face in his chest and inhale deeply, his comforting scent of pine with a hint of motor oil filling my lungs.

Tatum gives the best hugs.

"Drive safely and message me when you land. I hope you have the best time with Selena." I break away from the hug and shove my hand in my handbag.

Reaching for the *Happy Birthday* card I bought for her with a five hundred dollar gift card for one of her favorite spas inside, I hand it to him.

"For the birthday gal." Selena has not been to Lost Hope since I moved here, but with Tatum spending a lot of time at my place, we have spoken via video call. We even exchanged numbers and social media details, so now we can talk without a growling Tatum around.

"Thanks, trouble. I'm sure she'll love it. Alright, best be on my way. Look after yourself. You better answer that fucking phone when I call, so I rest assured you're not buried under ten feet of snow with poor Astrum freezing his balls off trying to dig you out."

I'm still cackling with laughter, picturing exactly that as I make my way inside.

I'm really looking forward to having a weekend just to myself. As much as I love my friends, I get drained quite easily. That's unfortunately the curse of an introvert.

So, being snowed in doesn't sound too bad.

I can use this time to recharge, so when the snow clears, I'll be able to give them a hundred percent of me.

Chapter Eighteen

Cole

It's just our fucking luck it started snowing as soon as we crossed the state border into Montana. Snow was to be expected in these parts, so I made sure to have adequate tires fitted to my truck, as well as chains, but when I checked the weather before leaving Richmond two days ago, there were zero snow predictions, and it's just the middle of October.

What started with small flurries as we left Wyoming turned into a full-blown snowstorm the farther we traveled up US 212 on our way to Lost Hope.

I should pull over and wait for it to pass, but I'm driving precious cargo, and I don't think the snow will let up soon. Easing my foot from the accelerator, I squint through the windshield, trying to make the road out in front of me.

The GPS on the dash of my truck tells me we should be in Lost Hope in twenty minutes. There's no point in pulling over now and risk being buried in snow by morning.

Slow and steady wins the race.

I don't know what I was thinking, packing everything we owned in the back of my truck and leaving for Lost Hope.

The girls have been miserable since the funeral, Eliza more so than Clara. Clara doesn't really understand what happened, she just sees Eliza is sad, and it makes her sad too.

I throw a quick look in the mirror at both of them in the backseat. Eliza's curled up in her booster seat, her mouth slack with sleep, while Clara's sprawled out in her car seat, her tiny feet swinging into the back of mine. Even in her sleep, this kid can't stop moving.

They've been real troopers through the entire journey, hardly complaining. But if the drive has been tiring for me, I can't even imagine how tiring it was for two kids.

When I sat them all down and explained this harebrained plan of mine, they all agreed to the move. I think we were all happy to be out of the house they shared with their father and my mom.

"Watch out!" Blake shouts from the passenger seat when a fox cuts across the road and scurries in front of our car into the woods.

Like an idiot, I foot the brake hard. The back of the truck skids back and forth, like a fishtail, and the car moves closer and closer to the edge of the road.

I'm holding on to the wheel with all my might, trying to correct its course through the engine's brake.

It's no fucking use.

I braked too damn hard the first time, and now the car's going to go where it's going to go. We hit a snowdrift when the truck skids completely off the road and thankfully comes to a sputtering stop.

Clara starts crying and Eliza looks at me with round, wide, sleepy eyes.

"Shh, it's ok. It's ok." I soothe them in a low voice. "The car wanted to go skating in the snow. That's it." I try to explain, while attempting to lower my heart rate at the same time.

Fuck, that was too close. Blake huffs at my explanation, and Eliza glares at me like I'm the biggest dork on the face of the Earth. *I'm with you, kid.*

"Ok. Sit tight, and I'll try to get us out of this. Just twenty more minutes and we'll be there." I reassure myself and them.

Where there is, I have no idea. I'm hoping Tatum can accommodate all of us until I find a house to rent.

Harebrained plan, indeed.

But I couldn't bear the sadness and heartbreak in my mom's house for a second longer. Nor Clara's constant search for her parents or Eliza's sorrow. Blake and I are hurting too, but we are both adults with a different understanding of what loss means.

Selfishly, it's also easier for me to focus on the girls rather than on my mom dying and my forced retirement from the Marine Corps.

I hit reverse, but try as I may, there's no traction under the tires, so there's no getting us back on the road. Eliza looks at me with wide gray eyes in a *What'cha gonna do now?* kind of way that doesn't show any hope in me being able to figure it out. Blake is shaking in his seat, trying to contain his laughter.

For fuck's sake, I served in the Marines for seventeen years; brought myself and my team home safe, reasonably in one piece each and every time. I'll figure this out, too.

I open the truck's door and haul myself out. The snow and wind hit me in the face, trying to knock me off my feet. It's freezing balls out here. Despite the terrible weather, it feels damn good being on my feet and stretching my legs.

I blow a breath into my cupped palms, trying to keep them warm, and look around the truck's tires to see if there's any hope of getting us out of here and on our merry way.

I don't want to think about what will happen if I fail.

There hasn't been another car on the road for at least the last hour of our journey, and with the way it is snowing, I don't think the road will be plowed until it stops.

We can sit in the car for a while and let the engine run to keep us warm, but eventually it'll run out of gas; or battery; or both. *Staying put is not an option.*

With the temperatures dropping below freezing point, we'll be frozen solid by morning. Blake and I would most likely be ok, but I have a two-year-old and a ten-year-old with me, and they may not fare as well as us.

I walk to Blake's window and tap on it to get his attention. He lowers it and smirks at me. "Look girls, it's Father Frost."

"Knock that off, asshole, and pass me my coat and phone."

"Swear jar." Comes from the back of the truck from Eliza.

She's bound to have enough in that jar to pay for her college tuition, with all the swearing I've been doing since I got home.

I'm trying to cut the curses out of my vocabulary, but it's difficult after seventeen years with the Marines where I didn't really have to watch my mouth.

I take the coat and put it on, but it doesn't do much to alleviate the cold. With stiff hands, I unlock my phone and look on Google Maps, trying to find a house or shop nearby where I could walk and get some help. The screen shows some sort of structure less than two miles away with a path through the woods.

There's no information on what the structure is, but even if it's an abandoned cabin of sorts, I can get everyone there safely and light a fire. Quickly deciding to go and check it out for myself, and if I find it usable, I'll come back for my crew of misfits.

Best-case scenario it's not an abandoned building, and I can use their phone to call for help.

I downloaded the map on my phone at our last rest stop, and good thing I did since there's no reception here. I'm not sure if it's because of the weather, or because the area is so remote there aren't any cell towers around.

"I think I found somewhere to ask for help," I tell Blake. "Shouldn't be gone for more than an hour. Leave the engine running until then. We can't risk not being able to start the car if we have help coming."

"Are you sure, man? It's getting so dark out there. Maybe it's best we just sit here and wait."

"And risk getting completely snowed in? There's been no one on the road for the past hour. I'll be fine. Look after the girls and sit tight."

Turning my back to him, I walk close to the edge of the road, looking for a gap in the treeline that will lead me to the building shown on the map. I'm barely fifty feet away from the truck when the sound of steps crunching the snow and crying hits me.

I turn around just in time for Eliza to launch herself in my arms.

"Please, Cole, pleeease don't leave me. Please!" She sobs, and I hug her tightly to my chest.

"Baby girl, you need to go back to the car. I'm not leaving. I'm just going to check out this building very quickly and come back to you," I explain, but she's having none of it. Big, fat tears are rolling down her rosy cheeks, each one of them slaying my heart.

"PLEASE, COLE, take me with you," she sobs even harder, squeezing my neck.

I catch Blake's eyes through the windshield and he returns a helpless look. He wants to come and get her, but that would mean leaving Clara alone in the car.

"It's freezing and snowing, baby girl. You won't be comfortable walking, even if it's a small distance. I can't carry you. There's ice forming on the ground, and I might slip and hurt us both."

"I'll walk," she promises. "I'll walk, I won't be uncomfortable. Please, Cole, just don't leave me."

I know where her fear is coming from. Alecs and Mom left for a date night, promising they'd see her in the morning, only they never came back after a drunk driver T-boned their car.

I think quickly. The walk won't be more than twenty-five minutes, even at a slow pace to accommodate her speed. She's all bundled up, and if worse comes to worse, I will carry her even if I have to crawl to ensure she's safe.

There may also be wolves or bears in the woods, but from what I know of the state, they mostly live in Western Montana, although you never know what you may come across.

My gun's stashed in the pocket of my coat, so I can use it to scare any animals away. What I can't do is waste any more time debating.

It's almost completely dark outside.

Eliza slides down on her feet and I take her hand as we make our way slowly to the path. Much to my surprise, after ten minutes, we come across a road that's completely cleared of any snow, apart from a wide strip on the left, separating the road from the trees. I pull at her hand to stop. There's no reason for her to walk if the road is clear.

There are no signs of ice either, so I drop to my haunches, and she jumps on my back. With her arms banded around my neck and legs circling my waist, I make sure she's secure, then lift myself back up and start walking faster.

The snow continues to fall heavily, impeding my ability to see more than five feet in front of me. I do notice that whenever the snow touches the road's surface, it melts. Which means the road is heated, not recently plowed and salted as I initially thought.

Hope blossoms inside me that the building is actually lived in. No one invests in heated roads in the middle of the woods for shits and giggles.

Another ten minutes on this road led us directly to a tall fence. I can't see much beyond the fence because of the snow furiously falling from the dark skies, but there are some lights in the distance. Clearly, someone either lives or works here.

"I'm going to put you down now and look for a doorbell or some-thing," I tell Eliza. "Stay behind me, just in case."

I make my way to the gate, and sure enough, there's an intercom. I press the doorbell button for a long minute, but nothing happens.

Frustrated, I repeat the action five more times. At this point, I'm willing to test the definition of insanity for myself.

"I think there's no one home," whispers Eliza.

My fists bang on the gate, hoping to find a weak point or maybe make enough noise that whoever is there comes to investigate.

It takes me by surprise when my fist connects with metal for the millionth time, and the gate swishes open.

There's no time to react before I find myself sprawled on my back, with a massive beast of a dog growling in my face, pressing down on my chest with his massive paws.

I try to move, but the beast lowers its snout into my neck, so I still my movements. Eliza is screaming bloody murder next to us, and I will her silently to keep quiet so the beast doesn't focus on her.

"Who are you and what do you want?" A sharp feminine voice comes from near the gate.

I open my mouth to respond, but the beast growls louder.

"I'm going to call Astrum back to me. If you try to attack me, he'll rip you to shreds, and I'll let him. So if I were you, I wouldn't try anything stupid," she tells me in a calm and collected voice, and I believe her.

As if in slow motion, I watch Eliza start into a run and plow directly into the woman, with both of them falling into a heaping pile of limbs and snow.

My heart seizes in my chest, expecting the beast to jump off me and eat Eliza up in one bite. My muscles flex, ready to strike if he so much as twitches.

"Nooo. Leave my brother alone," she screams at the woman.

She puts her palms on Eliza's shoulders, not in a violent or threatening way, but to keep her still so she doesn't hurt herself on the ground, and looks my way.

"Astrum, cedo!" She commands in a voice so dominant I want to stand at attention like I used to back in the Corps.

The beast immediately releases me and runs to her side, taking a seat at her feet and swishing his tail back and forth like he wasn't seconds away from ripping out my throat just now.

She focuses her attention back on Eliza. "Astrum won't hurt either of you as long as no one hurts me. Let's help your brother up, and then you can tell me what brought you here," she tells my sister in a calm, soothing tone. The second Eliza starts to trust her hits me, because she's slipping her tiny palm into the woman's hand and holds on tight as they make their way to me.

Her features become more visible as she gets closer. She must be freezing because she's only wearing a too-large-for-her-frame black hoodie with *Yes.*

I'm cold. Me 24:7 printed in big white letters on her chest and a pair of leggings.

Fuck me, she's the most beautiful woman I've ever seen in my life.

She watches me with round eyes I can't see the color of, and that frustrates me to no end. She's not smiling. Her bow-shaped lips are tipped slightly down, as if she's unhappy. Her unhappiness doesn't sit right with me, and the urge to get those lips to smile at me hits my chest full force.

She extends a dainty hand to me, and my eyes are drawn to the long red nails I wouldn't mind feeling deep in my back. Even though I can help myself off the ground, I don't miss the opportunity to touch her. With her palm firmly enclosed in mine, I get back up to my feet, towering over her.

She's a slip of a thing, her eyes level with my chest. My skin tingles everywhere we touch. She immediately releases my hand, and takes a few steps back, the beast constantly near her, moving with her as if rehearsed.

Eliza remains quiet and looks between the two of us, torn, deciding whose side she should stay on.

"Start explaining. I'm freezing," she barks. This woman has balls, I'll give her that. And by the feel of what's happening below my belt, she has mine right now. Fuck me, I can't believe I was nearly mauled by a dog on the frozen ground, and I'm sitting here perving at a woman I don't even know, with my kid sister by my side.

Rock, meet bottom.

Chapter Nineteen

Cole

"**W**e were on our way to Lost Hope when a fox ran in front of the car. I braked too hard and drove the truck into a snowdrift. I couldn't get it out, so I came looking for help. My brother and baby sister are still there. This munchkin here insisted she come with me to keep me safe," I tell her with a self-deprecating smile. "As you can see, I needed it."

I extend my hand to her again, hoping she'll take it, just so I can feel the warm, soft skin of her palm against mine. "I'm Cole. Cole Hayes."

"Lalah McAdams." Much to my happiness, she does take it. Her touch is brief, seconds if that, before she retracts her hand, but long enough for me to feel a bolt of electricity hit me as soon as she touched me again.

"And I'm Eliza Hart. I'm ten," my sister tells her very matter-of-factly, going for a handshake like she's an adult, not a preteen.

Lalah's pillowy lips smile at her, not condescendingly, but with pride, shaking her hand for far longer than she did mine.

Aaaand now I'm jealous of my sister. Fucking great.

"What can I do for you, Eliza Hart and Cole Hayes?" She watches me when she asks as if she's still unsure we can be trusted.

I do understand her concern. She's a woman alone in the middle of the woods, and a man with a kid is trying to gain entry into her home to use her phone. The two of us having different surnames doesn't help our cause either.

"Is your cell phone working?" I ask, showing her my phone, "Mine isn't getting any signal and hasn't for a while now," I clarify, unlocking the screen so she'll see for herself I'm not trying to lie my way into her home.

"Not working." She shakes her head. "It's 'cause of the snowstorm. Where are your other brother and sister exactly?"

"Still in the car, down this road, then about five hundred yards east-bound."

She stays quiet for half a minute, looking at me intensely. She seems to have reached a conclusion when she nods her head, more to herself than for my benefit, and exhales sharply.

"Alright. Here's how it's going to be. You'll both come into the house. Cole, you're not allowed more than one foot past the entry," she speaks again in her commanding voice, and my cock goes half-mast into my jeans.

Goddammit, Hayes. Get it together.

"Eliza will come inside and sit in the living room with a hot chocolate to get warmed up. I'll get my snowsuit, and you and I, Cole, are going to take my snowmobile to your car and use it to try and get you back on the road. You can then pick up Eliza and be on your merry way."

She turns toward my sister, who, much to my horror, is petting the beast's head like he's the sweetest puppy to walk the earth, and ushers her to her home.

"Sounds like a good plan," I accept. I'm at the mercy of this woman, so what she wants, she gets. I am also hoping she keeps saying my name because I love the way it rolls out of her mouth.

Yes, I heard that, and yes, if I could facepalm myself without coming across as clinically insane, I would.

We follow her up the steps to the entrance, and I walk in but stop there. She leads Eliza to the sofa, and my sister throws herself into the pillows like she's right at home, with the beast quickly following her.

Lalah walks into her kitchen, and my eyes follow her ass, sashaying left and right, like the obedient puppy I turned into when I met her less than ten minutes ago.

There are no lights on inside the house, but the living room is encased in a warm shimmering glow, most likely from a fireplace.

I don't know who this woman is or what she's doing in the middle of the woods by herself, but from what I see from my place at the entrance, her home is a thing of beauty.

Lalah returns from the back of the house with a steaming cup of what I can only assume is the hot chocolate she promised my sister. She places it on a coffee table next to the sofa and confirms with Eliza she's fine to be on her own for a little while. She points at a TV remote on the table and tells my sister she's free to watch TV while waiting for our return.

She then walks toward me and unlocks the door to my left by pressing her hand to a palm reader. *What the fuck? Who the fuck is this woman?* She sees my surprised look but doesn't offer me any explanation. And why would she?

This is her home, and we're the intruders. She takes out a snowsuit, making quick work of pulling it up her body, followed by a pair of snow boots, and a snow mask. She takes another mask and a backpack, pushing them my way.

"Put them on and follow me." And I once again find myself obeying her like her wish is my command.

Might as well take one of Astrum's leashes and wrap it around my neck, handing it to her since it seems I'd willingly follow Lalah to the deepest pits of hell if only she asked.

She leads us to an attached garage that opens much the same way as the door inside. There's only one car in there, as well as a bike and a snowmobile.

She jumps on the snowmobile and reverses it outside, then throws me a saucy look over her shoulder before lowering her snow mask over her face.

"You coming or what?"

Just about.

Mentally slapping myself out of my pervy thoughts, I throw a leg over the leather seat, caging her between my thighs, circling my arms tightly around her waist, and pressing my chest to her back.

Her stomach is quivering under my palms, and I smile to myself, knowing I'm not the only one affected by this sudden attraction.

I can only pray she doesn't feel my cock saluting her from beneath my fly, and shoves me off the fucking snowmobile.

She makes quick work of starting it, and soon we're on our way back to Blake and Clara. The wide strip of snowy road makes more sense now as she speeds, and before I know it she's on the 212 flying toward my stranded truck.

She comes to a stop in front of my car, and I take a second to dismount because I don't want to let her go. I'm also in need of a minute to calm down the situation in my jeans, but I'm forced to get away from her when a car door forcefully swings open.

"You're back. And with help. Where's Eliza?" Blake asks.

Lalah remains seated on the snowmobile but turns to Blake and waves at him.

"Blake, this is Lalah McAdams. Lalah, this is my brother, Blake Hayes." I make the necessary introductions and smile to myself like a fucking toad when she doesn't dismount to shake his hand.

"There's a rope in that backpack. Take it out and tie the truck to the snowmobile. There are also four planks in it. Place one plank underneath each tire. That should be enough for you to gain traction, and with a little pull from me, I'll get you on the road. Once there, we'll stop so that we can untie the snowmobile." Her eyes find mine, a cocky smirk curving her plump lips. "I trust you know how to find your way back to mine?"

God, this fucking woman and her orders. It makes me want to take her in my arms and run in the woods, never letting her go or be seen ever again.

I complete her instructions quickly, and soon enough we're on our way to her place. Blake keeps throwing me knowing looks, and I barely resist the urge to slap the back of his head. I guess it takes one horn dog to know another, and it's most likely written on my damn forehead that I have the hots for this woman.

It's not just that she's beautiful, but the way she took control of the situation makes her one hundred percent hotter in my eyes. The *damsel in distress* kind was never appealing to me. Nothing wrong with them, just not my cup of tea.

By the time I park my car in front of her garage, Blake is slack-jawed at the sight of her house.

"Who is this woman?" he whispers in awe. I shrug, knowing nothing more than he does.

She taps her leather-clad fingers on my window. Clara takes this opportunity to wake up and whimper. Lalah looks at her through the back passenger window and her face changes from a hard-ass woman to pure awe.

That's Clara's power. The kid is the cutest girl to walk the Earth, able to win the hearts of the most hardened of men. Thank fuck Lalah's a woman.

"Come on, boys. Get the little girl inside and get warm. We can have dinner, and then you can go wherever it is you're going," she says and starts for the entrance.

I hurriedly unbuckle Clara from her car seat and cradle her to my chest. She's been quiet so far, but I know she'll turn into a screeching banshee once she gets hungry.

The three of us follow Lalah into the house, and finally, I'm allowed to step past her entrance. I take off my boots using only my feet so I don't disturb my baby sister, and move toward the living room where I left Eliza.

I find her sleeping on the sofa, cuddling with the beast. Astrum opens one eye and glares at me, warning me to keep quiet and let her sleep. I heed his threat, because the memory of his razor-sharp canines at my throat is still very much fresh in my mind.

"Whoa!" whispers Blake close to me, taking in the living room and the German Shepherd snuggling with our sister.

"Whoa indeed."

Lalah waves us into the dining room, where she has already set the table with a tray of lasagna towering in the middle.

As we take our seats, I remove Clara's pink winter jacket and sit her on my lap. It'll be easier to feed her this way. If I left her to her own devices, Lalah would still be cleaning tomato sauce off her floors come spring.

"You said you were going to Lost Hope. Visiting anyone in particular?" she asks, softly massaging her left arm.

She lives close to Lost Hope, so she may know the townsfolk.

"My buddy from the Marines," I tell her while feeding Clara a piece of lasagna as she claps her hands happily at me.

"Does your buddy have a name?" Lalah pops a perfectly arched eyebrow at me. The sass of this woman is strong enough to bring me to my knees.

"Carter. Tatum Carter."

She's taken aback at hearing his name, and I can see her brain working, connecting dots. *Does she know Carter? Is she involved with him?* A surge of red-hot jealousy burns in my gut at the thought.

It's not looking great for us staying with him if I feel the need to wring his fucking neck every time I set my eyes on him.

But for some reason, she's also looking at me now like she knows me. That's strange.

"Does he know you're coming?"

"Uhm... not exactly. This was more a spur-of-the-moment idea," I mumble, red creeping up my neck to my face.

"Tate's out of town until tomorrow. He went to visit his sister Sawyer in New York for the weekend," she informs me.

The little minx is testing me.

"You mean Selena in Chicago?" I retort with a smirk.

She rewards me with a full-wattage smile so bright that even Blake stops shoving food in his mouth to admire. You'd think I haven't fed the man in weeks with how fast he's chewing through the lasagna.

"Yes, I mean Selena in Chicago. You're welcome to stay here until Tatum comes back tomorrow. If the snowstorm stops and his flight is not canceled, that is," she sighs. "You're welcome to stay here until he comes back, whenever that is. Any friend of Tate's is a friend of mine."

I want to say I'm grateful for her hospitality, but all I feel is pure, blinding-white jealousy.

Chapter Twenty

Lalah

I'd like to say, looking at my unexpected guests, all I'm thinking is *There goes my weekend alone. Bye bye snowed-in solitude.* What I'm actually thinking is *Holy mother of smoking hotness,* and actively fighting my inner hussy who thinks it's a great idea for me to jump into his arms and kiss the bejesus out of those plump pink lips of his.

YES. I, Lalah, disliking strangers with fiery passion and actively hating being touched, I'm sitting here at my dining room table, watching the most handsome man I've ever seen in my life spoon-feeding lasagna to a two-year-old and daydreaming about having his babies.

And I don't even want to have children.

What the fuck is wrong with me? Never have I ever had such a visceral reaction to a man. My knees buckled when I first saw all six foot *three? four?* inches of him sprawled on the ground, a growly Astrum, ready to rip him to shreds, pressing his paws on his chest.

Cole wasn't afraid.

At least not afraid for his safety.

He was only concerned for the brave little girl jumping to his defense. I thought Drake was a big man, but holy cannoli does this Adonis take the cake.

I'm sure if he truly meant to harm me, he would have been able to hold Astrum back with one hand and wring my neck with the other.

Although three months have passed since my car crash, I am still fearful of strangers. But not for one second since I came across Cole have I felt one single twinge of fear. If anything, I have the same sense of safety Tatum gives me, if not more.

The only difference is, I'm quite certain I fell in insta-lust with Cole.

The minute my eyes met his light green orbs as he sprawled on the ground, my mind screamed *Mine!* at me. The strangest thing is, I felt the same wave of possessiveness for Eliza, Blake, and Clara, minus the butterflies taking flight in my stomach at the sight of them.

And of course, he then had to drop the bomb of all bombs.

He *is* Tatum's friend. I *did* wonder when Cole told me about his family if he was the one Tate only ever referred to as *Cap*.

There aren't many outsiders coming to Lost Hope unless it's ski season, and he definitely wasn't all that prepared for traveling through Winter Wonderland.

And of course, once he confirmed my suspicions, I had to make a fool of myself and force my hospitality down their throat. *Twice.*

We're all still eating, in complete silence, and I take this opportunity to study Blake instead. He looks to be much younger than Cole, in his early twenties, maybe? He does take after his brother with his tall frame, but he is more on the lean side, whereas Cole's body seems ready to explode out of his black Henley.

Where Cole's jet-black hair is curly but cut military short, Blake's is dark brown, long at the top of his head and short at the sides. They do share similar facial features, but Blake's eyes are silvery gray, the same shade as Eliza's, not the mesmerizing seafoam color Cole is sporting, framed by long black eyelashes.

With a full tummy, Clara goes right back to sleep in her big brother's arms. She shares the same eye color as Eliza and Blake. Tiny ringlets of blonde hair hallo her head where she's cradled by Cole's massive arm.

A wave of pain makes its way down my left arm. I try to massage it away as subtly as possible, but it keeps throbbing inside my bone. I'm sure I overdid it while riding the snowmobile, but as safe as I felt around Cole, he was still a stranger, and I couldn't exactly tell a stranger I'm not supposed to ride it yet and show physical vulnerability.

I also couldn't *not* help.

That suspicion of Cole being Tatum's *Cap* kept nagging at me, and my heart wouldn't let me turn my back to a child trapped in a snowed-in car.

Cole clears his throat and pins those hypnotic eyes of his on mine. "If you're still okay with letting us crash here, do you mind showing me to a room where I can lay this munchkin down?"

"Oh. Yes. Of course. If you give me five minutes, I'll clear the table and get those rooms ready for you. Do you need anything from the car? You'll be able to go out and get them but not come back in without me."

"I'll clear the table," Blake offers. "It's the least I can do to thank you for this great dinner. This was the best lasagna I had in my life."

I smile at him. "Thank you, Blake. I'll pass the compliments on to Ruth. She'll be happy to hear her food is appreciated." At their questioning stares, I continue explaining because this is what I do lately, explain myself to strangers. *Get a fucking grip, Lalah.*

"Ruth Lawson owns and cooks for Dine&Dash down in Lost Hope. We knew there was a potential snowstorm coming since yesterday, so she dropped me a couple of trays of food. You'll like it here. Everyone's very welcoming," I ramble.

It's not exactly a lie. Everyone was very welcoming to me, except for a couple of people, but I don't see them facing the same issues as I did.

"I'd like to put Clara to bed before retrieving our things if that's ok with you," Cole tells me.

I make a *follow me* gesture with my hand and lead the way up the stairs and to the bedrooms. Two guest rooms are ready to be used, and one of them actually has twin beds.

I didn't see the point, but Raven and Rhett Anderson insisted they'll want sleepovers and they'll want to share a room. Who am I to argue with a pair of fifteen-year-old twin menaces? A smart woman with a guest room with twin beds, that's who.

I reach the landing of the room the girls would sleep in, quietly open the door, and let Cole enter first. I turn on the light, making sure it's on a dim setting so Clara doesn't wake up.

"Do you need any more pillows for her? Maybe on the floor next to her bed in case she falls off?"

"Nah. She'll be fine. She usually sleeps in the same position throughout the night. She's a very good girl that way."

I nearly moan out loud at the way he says *good girl. Goddammit, Lalah. He was talking about his sister. HIS. BABY. SISTER. Down, girl.*

"Alright. I'll leave you to it. I need to change the sheets in one of the other bedrooms. Tatum usually stays in that one. Then you and Blake can choose between yourselves where to sleep."

A strange look passes over his face and his jaw clenches under his dark scruff at my mentioning Tate's sleeping arrangements. Hell, maybe I've started hallucinating. With how my hormones are acting out around this man, I'm sure I've imagined the relief I read in his eyes.

I spin on my heel and make my way to the bedroom at the end of the hallway, the one farthest away from mine. Grabbing a clean fitted sheet and clean linen, I proceed to strip the bed.

Tate has some clothes and personal stuff in the closet, but other than that, the room is in perfect order.

My left arm starts hurting more, and I already know I'll spend the night with the arm brace on and an ice compress. Serves me right for thinking I'm indestructible for a second there when riding the snowmobile with Cole all wrapped around me.

Three short months ago I found out exactly just how fragile I am.

The thought of a painkiller tempts me, but the ones Doctor Richards prescribed make me groggy. I might not have gotten one single bad vibe from the guys, and they may be friends of Tatum's, but I won't risk not being at full mental capacity, even if I know there's no way they can gain access to my bedroom.

Once I close the door behind me, no one can enter unless I willingly open it.

By the time I finish with the bed and carry the used bed linens to the laundry room, I'm cradling my left arm to my chest, I'm in so much pain.

When I clear the stairs from the basement into the hallway near the living room, Blake has Eliza snuggled to his chest.

"I'm going to put this sleepyhead to bed, too, and then go to sleep myself," he tells me.

"Of course. Directly at the top of the stairs is the room where the girls are sleeping in. To your right are two other bedrooms. You and Cole can decide who takes which bedroom. There are towels in the bathroom and things you may need. Feel free to use them."

"Thanks, Lalah. Your generosity is much appreciated. I'll see you in the morning. Good night," he tells me as he walks up the stairs with Eliza.

"Night, Blake." I wave spinning on my heel and heading to the foyer.

I put on a winter coat and make my way outside with Astrum. I'll wait here for him to go about his business and for Cole to come and get what they need from his car.

The snow seems to fall even harder, and my breath fogs the air. It is considerably colder than it was one hour ago when we returned.

"You'll turn into an icicle if you stay outside much longer." Cole's gravelly voice startles me. His heat blazes at my back, and it takes everything in me not to lean into him.

"Then let's get a move on," I quip.

He unlocks his car, opens the tarp covering the truck's bed, and pulls out a suitcase one-handed like it weighs nothing. My right-hand twitches with need to fan my face because *hawt*.

Since when have I started objectifying men to this degree?

Except, I'm not objectifying men.

Just this *man*.

He then opens the back passenger door and takes two girly backpacks out, hanging the shoulder straps onto the suitcase's handle.

"There's plenty of space in the garage if you want to move your truck there. This snow won't quit, and I don't know how well that tarp will protect your belongings once a healthy layer of snow deposits on top of it."

"You're right, thanks." He rounds the cab and jumps into the driver's seat. I pull onto the strap of one backpack and rest it on my right shoulder.

Stupidly, I reach for the other one with my left hand, and when I go to lift it, sharp pain seizes my arm, an anguished wail forces its way past my lips, and I drop the backpack into the snow.

Cole is at my side in seconds. How the hell did he hear that over the sounds of the truck's engine? He gently takes my arm in his massive hands and moves his thumbs slowly up and down on it, relaxing my muscles.

"What happened?" he asks, voice full of concern.

"N-nothing," I stammer and remove my arm from his grasp. His hands follow me as if wanting to touch me again, but he thinks better of it and fists them at his side. "I must've picked up the backpack with the wrist in an awkward position," I try to excuse myself.

"It's not nothing if you're hurt," he chastises me. "Leave the bags. I'll pick them up on our way in."

I nod my head and keep my arm to my chest, massaging my wrist gently. The garage door opens with a quick touch of my palm, and he backs the truck inside, turning the engine off.

Seconds later, he is once again next to me, and I have to lock my body tight to keep myself from moving as close to him as I possibly could get. He picks up the bags and makes his way to the front door.

"Astrum, introrsum," I singsong, knowing he'll be able to hear me wherever he is. Sure enough, less than thirty seconds later, a blur of fur and snow sprints inside through the front door.

Cole looks at me, impressed. My lips twitch at the corners. Yes, Astrum had his own K9 training and, even with the commands drilled into him during his service, he would only respond to me. But it bothered me that too many people were aware of what each command meant and were able to control him like that.

So I've worked with him tirelessly for the two and a half months we've been together to get him to forget his old commands, and created new ones for him in Latin.

Even if people know the meaning of each word, I use specific combinations that have nothing to do with the actual interpretation of the word. This strengthened our bond even more. It also helped a great deal growing my confidence in myself and my inner strength.

People look at him and see a beast or a pet. Astrum is a part of me. He is family, not just a pet and not just a guardian.

I firmly believe he has his own feelings, and he trusts me not to abuse the commands I give him; trusts me to protect and love him as fiercely as he protects and loves me.

He knew earlier today Eliza was no threat even after she made us both fall, and stayed on what he correctly assessed to be the bigger, *literally,* and badder, *also literally,* threat.

I gesture for Cole to wait for me while I check the alarm is armed and the house locked tight, then wave him up the stairs. At the head of the stairs, I stop him with a hand on his biceps. My fingers twitch at the feel of pure steel under them. *Dayum. Bad Lalah.*

"Sorry. I just wanted to show you…" I wave toward the wall to my right where a panel is located, "If you press this green button, a sliding glass door will seal off the hallways. If you're worried Clara might wake up in the middle of the night, this way she won't fall down the stairs."

One press of a button and the sliding see-through glass door swishes into the opposite wall with a soft click.

Cole bursts out in laughter. Oh boy, I could listen to that laughter for ages. Gravelly, raspy, a siren song to my soul. *VERY BAD LALAH.*

"W-what the h-hell is that?" he sputters in between chuckles.

Taking a step back, I look at the stickers on the door, and can't help but smile widely.

There's a bullseye in the middle of the door at thigh level with an arrow pointing at it, a message on the opposite end of the arrow "Astrum's first concussion".

"That's Astrum being impatient and nearly giving himself a concussion, slamming full force into the door. The vet I took him to – to make sure he didn't seriously hurt himself – told me it's best to have some stickers placed on the glass, so he'll know there's something there and won't slam into it again."

"And the rest?" he asks in a more serious voice, narrowing his eyes at Tatum's wall of shame.

There's another bullseye at my eye level, with a similar arrow pointing at it. "Lalah's second concussion." Yeah, the fucking door got to me too. Probably the only flaw this house has.

But, the door redeemed itself, so there's a third bullseye higher than mine. "Tatum's drunken concussion. Tequila is not your friend."

Oh yeah, he slammed face-first into the door after he drank himself stupid at my birthday party when Maevis was talking to one of the single guys from the fire station.

Serves him right for being a chickenshit.

"Mine's a lack of coffee. Not an actual concussion, just a tiny bump. The third one, now that's a thing of beauty. But I'll let Tate tell you the story. He'll probably threaten to break the glass into oblivion again, but those are his feelings for him to deal with."

He gives me a flat smile that doesn't reach his hypnotizing eyes and takes the wind completely out of my sails.

"I won't keep you any longer. Thank you again. Good night." He steps closer, bends at the waist, and presses his lips to my forehead, then promptly turns on his heel and slips inside his bedroom.

I think I just had a stroke.

My mouth opens and closes in shock, my legs begging me to unfreeze and follow him. Instead, I turn away and lock myself in my bedroom.

Soft tapping at my bedroom door rouses me from my restless sleep. I've tossed and turned all evening thinking about the four souls sleeping just beyond my bedroom door. One of them in particular, only it wasn't his soul I was thinking about. I managed to fall asleep just after midnight.

My eyes open and my ears peel. The soft tapping starts again. I search for my phone on my nightstand and fumble to unlock it to see the clock reading 02:38 am.

In my sleep-addled state, I climb off my bed and slowly pad my way to the door. Astrum is awake, but he remains at the foot of the bed, so he's not sensing any threats coming from whoever is just beyond this slab of wood. I press my palm to the reader and slowly open the door.

"Up, up," whisper-shouts a baby voice. I look down to see Clara's tangled blonde hair and her little face smiling up at me, arms in the air. "Up, up." I bend at the waist and pick her up. She immediately snuggles up to me and presses her face into the crook of my neck.

"What's wrong, sweet girl? Do you want me to take you back to bed?"

"No. Cuddle," she replies, not lifting her head from my shoulder but squeezing me tighter. I stand with her snuggled up to me at the entrance of my bedroom, unsure how to proceed.

If I take her back, she might start crying. If I get her in bed with me, and Cole wakes up in the morning and doesn't find her, he'll get worried.

Hell, she might wake up later and see herself next to a stranger and scream bloody murder. I'm actually questioning the sturdiness of my door, as I'm not sure it can withstand Cole's anger if he hears Clara crying from inside.

Eliza's sleepy face appears from their bedroom. "You have to take her to sleep with you. She won't go to sleep otherwise."

Clara perks up at the sound of her sister's voice and turns to her. "Eli, come, come," she says, making grabby hands at her sister. Eliza comes closer and tries to take Clara from me, but she quickly turns back to me, head on my shoulder, tiny arms wrapped around my neck.

"Sleep now. Eli, too," she commands in that sweet baby voice of hers.

Eliza looks at me with trepidation in her eyes, trying to gauge my reaction. I shrug and take a step back. "Come in if you are comfortable sleeping here with me. You're going to have to share with Astrum though, and the furry beast snores like a trucker."

She smiles then, hurries past me and, in one graceful move, jumps on the bed. Before I realize what's happening, she has the covers up to her chin and pats the empty side of the bed with one hand.

"Sleep now, pwease," Clara prompts me once again. *Ohh well, what's one broken door?* I can always replace it.

The door shuts with a soft click as I make my way to the bed, too. I sit on the soft mattress and place Clara in the middle, between myself and Eliza.

Astrum, the nosy beast of Lost Hope and not one to miss out on cuddles, gets up from his place at the foot of the bed and belly crawls behind Eliza, forcing her closer to Clara.

I, too, get under the covers, with the little girl once again snuggled tightly next to me. Her sister takes my hand and places it on the top of her head, beckoning me to play with her hair. I stroke her head slowly, and a few minutes later I have two sleeping girls in my arms and a furry, snoring furnace.

Life could be much, much worse than this. My eyes close and let their rhythmic, soft breathing lull me back to sleep.

Chapter Twenty-One

Cole

I'm not sure what rouses me from my sleep. I tossed and turned half the night, thinking of Lalah and all the things I wanted to do to her.

Then I'd remember Tatum and how he spends enough time in her home to lay claim on one of her guest bedrooms. And every single time my stomach tightened in knots, and my blood boiled with unrestrained jealousy.

The affection and protectiveness of him shone in her big, beautiful eyes whenever his name came up in conversation last night, but I don't have enough information to get a clear read on their relationship.

I'm also struggling to come to terms with the way I feel about her. This is not just pure, unaltered lust. I mean, fuck yeah, I'm attracted to her.

But there's also something else, something deeper than just physical attraction.

The first time I made eye contact with her, even though it was too dark for me to tell the color of her eyes, I felt a cord connecting me to Lalah.

When my palm touched hers as she was helping me off the ground, I could swear a tether clicked into place inside of me, my mind screaming *Mine!* over and over.

Never felt this way before for any other woman. Not when I met them, not when we spent time together, and not when we inevitably parted ways. *Never.*

I'm not a manwhore. I don't jump from bed to bed or woman to woman, but I'm not the committed relationship type, either.

Walking to the bathroom for my morning needs, I'm surprised to feel the heated floors. Hell, this entire house is done to exceptional standards.

I'm not sure what Lalah does for a living, but her home must've cost a pretty penny since I'm fairly certain it's not a rental.

I sense her in every nook and cranny of what I've seen of the house, and the security system seems to be designed around her. The curiosity eats at me. Not that what she does for a living is important. I simply want to know everything about her.

What makes her tick, what makes her smile, what makes her laugh. I want to know absolutely everything.

And I really fucking want to know what her relationship with Tatum is.

She's a stranger, for all intents and purposes, but a stranger who feels very much *mine*.

After a quick shower, I grab a pair of sweatpants and a Henley from the suitcase and put them on. Checking my phone, the screen shows it's barely after seven in the morning, so I'm hoping the girls are still sleeping.

I make my way out of the bedroom and decide to check on them before trying my luck in finding a cup of coffee, just to ensure they are not awake and in need of anything.

The door to their room is halfway open, and I pop my head in. The beds are unmade, but they're nowhere to be seen. With a deep breath, I try to calm the inkling of panic making its way through my bloodstream.

I look in the bathroom attached to the room but find it empty. The glass panel at the top of the stairs is still there. Maybe they went looking for Blake or me and ended up in his bedroom.

It wouldn't be uncommon.

There were many nights in the past three months when one of us woke up to find them cuddled against us, usually after a nightmare one of them had.

Listening at Blake's door, I cannot make out any sounds. I swear each room seems to be soundproofed. I open the door as quietly as possible and walk in.

Sprawled on his stomach, my brother is still asleep and very much alone in the bedroom.

I think it's safe to say I'm panicking now.

"Blake, wake the fuck up!" I bark at him. He startles and jumps to a seated position, his silver eyes dazed from sleep throwing daggers at me.

"What the fuck, man? This ain't boot camp," he whines, wiping a palm over his face, trying to chase away the last of his sleep.

"I can't find the girls," I tell him, pacing back and forth at the foot of his bed.

"Say what?" He blinks up at me, his face a mask of confusion and pillow creases.

"Get that fucking brain online, right fucking now. I can't find the girls," I bark again.

"Have you checked downstairs?" he asks in a slow cadence like I'm the one struggling to understand simple sentences. "Maybe they woke up and went there."

"I didn't check downstairs, you dick. The hallway door is still closed. They wouldn't be able to open it by themselves since the control panel is high on the wall. And I figured if they woke up and Lalah let them downstairs, there would've been no need to have the stairs blocked," I explain to my brother, barely holding back my rising panic.

"So you're telling me they're not in the room you slept in, not in their room either, and clearly they're not here." He starts making bell sounds. "Ding, ding. There it is. There's one more bedroom on this floor."

"Fuck. But how? I saw it last night when we went to bed. Hers is locked. They wouldn't be able to enter the master without her unlocking it. Unless..." I can't believe I went there.

Blake, apparently, can't believe it either.

"Nope. Don't say it. Don't even think it. If you say it and it's not true, you're going to be the biggest asshole on five continents. And if you say it and it's true, then we failed as brothers. She seems like a genuinely good person, Cole. I feel it in my gut."

"I know. I may have some questions about her, but didn't get so much as a whiff of bad vibe from her last night."

"Alright, I guess we'll go a-knocking."

We both rush out of the bedroom and toward the only closed door in the hallway. I knock on the black wood. "Lalah? Are you awake?"

No response.

Like the idiot I am, I press my ear to her door to try and listen for any sounds, because *of course* someone who soundproofed their guest rooms would've forgotten to soundproof the master.

I knock harder, my knuckles thumping on the sleek, black wood of her door. "Lalah?"

A soft click lets me know the door just unlocked. I knock once again, for good measure. "Can we come in, please?" but there's no sound coming from her bedroom, and the door remains closed.

Since all sorts of gruesome scenarios are crossing my mind, I decide my need to ensure the girls are safe is greater than my respecting her privacy. So I press on the doorknob, twisting it, and enter the room.

Her bedroom is still dark, and her windows are all opaque, but there is a soft night light on the opposite side of the massive room. My gaze moves toward the bed, where Astrum looms over her, with - *what the fuck* - a tablet in his mouth.

The dots connect when the screen glows with the outline of a palm. It's a fucking palm reader. The dog got her to open the door in her sleep.

I inch my way closer to the bed, gesturing behind my back for Blake to stay where he is.

Astrum ignores me and jumps on the floor, the panel still between his teeth. He hits a portion of the wall with his paw that has the windows go from complete opaqueness to slight transparency, allowing some daylight in.

I look back to the bed, and my whole body warms and relaxes. Lalah is still asleep, her face serene, pink lips slightly parted, raven black hair everywhere.

Clara is lying half on her chest, half on the bed, thumb in mouth, with Lalah's hand on her back, protecting her from rolling away.

Eliza is sleeping on the other side, leg thrown over the covers and over Lalah's knees, a brace-covered arm around my sister's shoulders.

Brace-covered arm? Did she hurt herself more than she let on last night with the bag? And then Tatum's words slam in my head, my whole body freezing on the spot.

We're on the porch in front of the house having a cold beer when he sits up from the front steps, phone in hand. "Sorry Cap, give me five minutes to call my friend. It's about dinner time back home, and I want to make sure she's doing okay. I know I came here to support you, but I gotta look after her too."

"Sure man. Is she alright? Do you need to go back earlier than next week?" I offer, even though I really need him here. My head is spinning with all that it's left to do and with learning how to move from being a brother who was mostly away to a parental figure for two confused, grieving little girls.

"No. I'm fine to stay, seriously. She's, uhm, been in a car crash herself just last week. She's as good as she can be, but has had a monster concussion and a broken arm that has to stay casted for three months. She's the one who had dinner sent for us the other night," he tells me with a somber face, and I can see the terror in his eyes.

His friend's car crash was much worse than what he lets on, and she's lucky to be alive. I can practically smell the relief coming off from him.

Fuck! Lalah is Tatum's friend who had him worried out of his mind. Lalah is the one who sent us dinner. And I'm fairly certain she's the one who sent the flowers too. There's a strange tingling in my blood as I recall the comfort her words gave me during one of the darkest days of my life.

This woman was just days from a horrible incident in her life, but she still took time to care for strangers going through their own tragedy.

And then, without even knowing who they were, she helped and rescued them. *Fuck my life*, she most likely sprained her arm on the snowmobile last night, hence why she was massaging it at the dinner table, and why she dropped the bag.

And now she's sleep-cuddling my sisters who most likely sought her out during the night.

Yeah, my mind is furiously shouting *Mine! Mine!* and not aimed at my girls.

Blake was right. If I voiced that unkind thought earlier, I would have felt like the king of assholes. I'm ashamed of myself for even thinking about it.

Clara starts wiggling on top of Lalah, and her hand tightens on my sister's back. She's still sleeping, but she's alert enough to look after the restless toddler.

Sleepy, gray eyes are watching me, and a smile forms around the thumb still in my baby sister's mouth.

I better get this little troublemaker out before she wakes everyone up.

Taking another step closer to the bed, I halt at Astrum's low growl. He's not advancing toward me, but he is keeping a close eye. Good. I like to know she is protected.

I extend my arms to Clara and wiggle my fingers in a *Come to me* gesture.

She lifts herself to a sitting position from where she was sprawled out on Lalah's chest and puts her arms in the air in the universal toddler-demand of *Pick me up before I scream the place down.*

Lalah moves her hand quickly and splays her palm on my sister's tummy.

"Careful, sweet girl, you'll roll right off," she tells her in a soft, sleep-laden voice. Clara wiggles more under her palm in response.

"Up, Coley, up!" she chirps in her cheery baby voice.

Lalah suddenly opens her eyes. I don't know if it's because she was still sleeping deeply, even with all her awareness of Clara, but I register the flash of horror and fear in her eyes, followed by pure fierceness.

And then she moves quicker than I've seen anyone moving, pushing Clara behind her and getting to her knees in one swift move, hands fisted in front of her face.

"Astrum, obsideo!" she barks.

And for the second time in less than twenty-four hours, I find myself flat on my back with a growling beast threatening to rip my throat out, my whole family as a witness, and Blake laughing like a hyena. Fucking great. At least he has the good sense of staying in the doorway.

"Lalah, babe, it's Cole," I tell her in a low, soothing voice.

I could pin Astrum, but it wouldn't be without me getting bit or without scaring Lalah even more. So I choose to ignore him and focus on her instead. And what a sight she is.

I actually get a chance to admire her body now since she's only wearing a tank top and a pair of sleeping shorts.

Her long hair falls down her shoulders in a mess of tousled waves covering her breasts enough so I can't see the shape of them through her white, thin top, with the ends touching her belly button. I drag my eyes across the expanse of her round hips, imagining how good it would feel to have my hands gripping them tightly.

I lower my scrutiny of her to her thick thighs, and I swear I could die a happy man with them wrapped around my head.

My eyes fly back to her face just in time to see the moment my words register, and she relaxes, slumping into a sitting position on the back of her calves, her hands falling at her side.

"How did you get in here?" she asks me suspiciously, and my eyes are glued to where her pulse flutters erratically in her neck.

Clearing my throat while mentally negotiating with my cock to stop tenting my sweats, I point a finger at the beast still growling in my face.

"Astrum." Yeah, buddy, I am very much happy to throw you under the bus. I really need to keep firm on my feet around him. This is twice he took me by surprise and got me down.

She looks toward the panel on her nightstand, sees the slobber the beast left behind, and shakes her head at him. "What did you do, you silly mutt? Laxo."

He immediately gets off me, jumps on the bed and in her lap. He keeps his snout at her neck, too, but lovingly, not one sharp fang in sight, darting his bushy tail back and forth.

"He got the door open for me. I was knocking earlier, in a panic, because I couldn't find the girls."

"Oh God. I'm so sorry," she cries. "You must have been out of your mind worried. This little troublemaker," she points at Clara who's found her way in between Lalah and Astrum, "came to visit me last night. Our little chat in the hallway must have woken up Eliza, and we girls had a sleepover. I should have considered leaving a note or something."

"Great, now we're all awake and accounted for, can I have some coffee, please?" retorts Blake from the doorway.

Both because he really wants coffee and because he doesn't want her to feel bad for taking care of our sisters the best way she knew how.

"Yeah!" She laughs, a touch of pink painting her cheeks. "Just give me ten minutes to shower, and I'll meet you guys downstairs."

She picks Clara up from her lap, giving her a hug and a kiss on the top of her head. "Ok, sweet girl. Go with your brother, and I'll see you down for breakfast." And then she's passed onto me. Her chubby hands clap me on the face, and she plants a big wet kiss on my nose.

"Thanks, baby girl. That's just what I needed this morning." I smile down at her and let her waddle-run to Blake.

"Thank you for the sleepover, Lalah," Eliza says, giving her a side hug and leaning her head on Lalah's shoulder before walking my way for a full-on snuggle around my waist. "Morning, Coley."

And then there were two.

Lalah gets up from the bed and moves toward me. Well, toward her bathroom most likely, but I'm in the way. I catch her left hand softly and extend her braced arm to me, pressing her palm to my abs.

She inhales sharply and looks me directly in the eyes. *Good girl.* I can actually see her eyes are hazel instead of rich brown, as I thought last night.

They're luminous, with a dark green outer ring, followed by a soft mossy-green mixed with amber flakes, which transitions into a darker chocolate-brown color around her pupils. I lift my other hand and gently cup her jaw, keeping her eyes on mine.

"You lied to me," I murmur, and her breath hitches but she doesn't pull away from me. "You said it was nothing when I asked if you hurt yourself last night. How sore's your arm this morning? And, for the love of God, please don't lie to me."

"Not as sore as it was last night. But still bothering me, if you insist on honesty. I'll keep the brace on today, and it should be good by tomorrow morning."

I nod my head and bend my knees, planting a lingering kiss on her temple, letting the smell of her flowery shampoo fill my lungs. "Thank you. I'll see you downstairs."

I release her and head out of her room. Just before exiting, I look at her over my shoulder. She's still standing where I left her, fingers pressed to the same place my lips were seconds ago, a dreamy look on her face. I can't help the smile forcing my lips to curve up.

Good fucking morning to me indeed.

Chapter Twenty-Two

L'alah

That's twice now he's kissed me... well, not on my lips where I need him the most, but still. I touch my temple with shaky fingers, right where he put that sinful mouth of his on me. Minutes later I'm still dumbstruck in the middle of my bedroom.

I honestly don't understand what is happening. When I met Callum, I was in my last year of high school, and he was my first boyfriend.

I found him handsome and cute, but it took me a while to get comfortable enough with him to let him kiss me, hug me, or even hold my hand. It took more than a year of us being together for me to trust him enough to sleep with him.

Sure, I was attracted to him. He was always respectful and behaved like a gentleman when we started dating, taking me out to dinner, to the movies, and opening doors for me.

I, of course, was impressed. This twenty-one-year-old man found me, thrown-away Alana, interesting enough to date and pay attention to.

When I started college, one year into our relationship, he asked me to move in with him. I jumped at the opportunity to move out of my mom's house. Perhaps I should have seen the red flag on my part when I was more excited about being away from my family than to be living with him.

The physical abuse might have ended with my parents' divorce, but the emotional manipulation, the gaslighting, the guilt trips, and forced competitiveness between my brother and me, were as strong as ever.

Hell, those behaviors continued even after I moved out.

Living with him, being with him, I thought I was supported and loved, but looking back, it wasn't quite that. I wanted to work through college.

Callum disagreed, saying he earns enough to support both of us, and I should focus on my studies. But every discussion around my expenses ended in a fight, and with me giving in to him.

I was also expected to manage the chores around the house – cooking, cleaning, laundry – like a good little housewife. The man was working long hours, after all, to provide for us, and I was just studying.

Things changed after I graduated from college and got a job. With my income – another source of contention since I was working fewer hours than him but earning more – I rented a nicer apartment for us and put a stop to the housewife routine.

I took care of the rent and bills for the following three years to pay him back for supporting me through college, which didn't really cost him anything as I went on a full scholarship.

The household chores were to be split since we were both living in the apartment. This seemed to make him happy for a short while, but then the conversations started again.

He confessed he only agreed to our little arrangement because he thought I couldn't afford to pay for everything, and I'd ask for his help.

Only, I've always been a hard worker, and advanced fairly quickly. Each promotion came with a hefty raise. I also knew, at the end of the day, I was truly the only one I could rely on.

Maybe that's when things soured between us. Looking back, it seems for the last four years of being together we were more roommates with benefits than in a romantic relationship.

But I was still safe, still cared for, and no one was putting their hands on me maliciously. There was no shouting, regardless of the disagreements, no name-calling either. Compared to the relationship my parents had, and what I was told over and over I deserved, my relationship with Callum was a success in my eyes.

There was no concern when the spark fizzled out and died since it was never that strong to begin with. I was happy with a partnership, or so I thought.

We had extensive conversations about what would happen if we fell out of love with each other and in love with someone else. All I ever asked of him

– if at any point he was unhappy and wanting to move on from us – was to tell me and for us to part respectfully. I actually begged him more than once not to cheat on me.

Well, we all know how it worked out for me.

Maddox was a different situation altogether. Yes, I found him ridiculously handsome, and yes, I was attracted to him. But I've seen ridiculously handsome men before. Was attracted to them too, and never once tempted to go out with them or have sex with them.

It all boils down to one thing – that night, I was pissed the fuck off.

I simmered in the kind of anger that makes you feel invincible, untouchable, downright bulletproof. It was what made me throw caution out the window and my clothes on his hotel room floor. And the attraction died as quickly as it ignited when I woke up in his arms hours later.

No regrets plagued me, but my skin was crawling under his touch and I couldn't get out of there fast enough.

Which brings us back to how Cole makes me feel. Around him I'm enthralled, enticed, longing, craving. Every time he's in my vicinity, I want to crawl into his arms, nuzzle my face in his chest, and purr like a fucking kitten. I just want to hold on to him and never let go.

I glare at the love-stricken reflection in the bathroom mirror and gently slap my cheeks. My eyes are bright and excited. *Who is this woman staring back at me?* "Come on, Lalah. Head in the game!"

I round the corner to the kitchen and take in the sight in front of me. Cole flips sizzling bacon in the grilling pan, his back to me, so I take a second to admire his wide, strong shoulders, supported by ropes and ropes of muscle on his back, barely kept contained by his navy-blue Henley.

His round ass looks firm enough in his black sweats to bounce a quarter or several off those sexy globes. Images of him moving on top of me, my greedy hands pressing down on all that raw strength, trying to get him as close as humanly possible, fill my head.

"There she is! We made ourselves at home." Blake startles me out of my daydreaming, pushing a cup of coffee in front of my eyes.

Cole turns his head over his shoulder, curious eyes roaming over me, and winks. Fucking winks at me. Yup. Busted. *Very bad Lalah.* A flush makes its way up my neck and settles in my cheeks at being caught ogling him.

"Thanks, Blake," I mumble, making my way to the breakfast nook to sit with the girls. My hands cup my steaming coffee and my lips gently blow on the surface. I lower my mouth to the rim and gobble a sip, which I promptly spit back into the cup. My tongue smacks the roof my mouth trying to dispell the taste of burnt, bitter rubber.

"Fuck, that's vile!"

"Told ya!" snickers Cole to Blake at the same time Clara's giggles fill the kitchen, and Eliza shouts gleefully.

"Swear jar. That's five dollars, just so you know!"

I can't help but laugh, too. "My apologies. How about I go swap this deadly poison for actual coffee, and once I'm fully awake, I'll pay up with interest."

"Deal!" She shakes my hand and goes back to reading one of the fairytale books I'm sure I had in the living room.

So I enjoy reading fairy tales. Sue me.

I make my way to my La Spaziale coffee maker and steam some milk for my latte. Cole bumps my shoulder with his, trying to gain my attention, and fuck if my thighs aren't clenching just from that innocent touch.

"Scrambled eggs and bacon okay?" he asks in that raspy voice of his with a direct line to my... "Lalah?" he smirks like he can read all my dirty thoughts.

"Yes, please," I squeak, quickly averting my eyes. "Anyone else interested in actual coffee or are y'all happy with the poison?"

"Hey. I take offense to that. Not everyone knows how to operate a spaceship," Blake smarts at me. I just pop an eyebrow in response.

"So, no coffee?"

"Coffee, please!" the men reply in unison, to my amusement.

"Any preferences?"

"Black, two sugars," comes from Cole.

"I'll take whatever you made for yourself," adds Blake. "I can smell it from here, and yuuummm."

I set to make their coffees, pushing Cole's near his cooking station, and grabbing the other two so I can make my way back to Eliza, when he leans down, once again presses his lips to my temple and whispers in my hair, "Thank you, baby."

It lasts less than two seconds, but it's enough for me to flush crimson red and my insides to clench and swoon. *Yes, I'm Lalah the swooning hussy now.*

Taking Blake's latte to him, I sit next to Eliza. She wraps her arm around mine, resting her head on my shoulder. My heart bursts with pride that this little girl trusts me and feels comfortable being around me. I can't help the sigh of contentment escaping my chest.

Blake's eyes bore into me, and when I turn to face him, he throws me a cocky smile. *Is that approval on his face?* He breaks eye contact and takes a sip of his latte, smacking his lips in appreciation. "Man, now that's the good stuff."

I smile to myself, happy just to look around and see these people making themselves at home in my kitchen. They're the picture of pure family bliss despite their recent hardships. A sense of raw longing hits me so suddenly the need to double over consumes me.

I want this for myself.

The family breakfast, the belonging, the acceptance, the love.

And I want it all with them.

Clara's tiny hands tug at my *I like books more than I like people* sweatshirt, pulling my attention to her. "Up, up!" she demands.

My left arm stretches to grab her around the waist and pull her into my lap, when Cole's warmth touches my back. His fingers encircle my forearm, pulling it toward my chest, as he lowers a plate of yellow, fluffy eggs and crispy bacon in front of me.

For one blissful moment, my back and his chest touch everywhere, and I lose the fight with myself and lean into him. He gently caresses my arm once, twice, then picks up Clara, spinning her around and blowing raspberries on her tummy, the sound of her giggles and squeals of joy bouncing off the kitchen walls.

He makes several more trips to the stove, returning with heaping plates for everyone and a basket full of toast, before taking a seat at my side with Clara on his lap.

His knees spread wide to accommodate her, and I nearly choke on my eggs when his outer thigh presses firmly to mine. I could move my leg to allow him more room, but I won't.

The physical connection to him both relaxes and grounds me, so I'm allowing myself this tiny indulgence.

"The phones still don't work," I tell them. "But Wi-Fi does. You're welcome to it. There's a QR code on the panel next to the TV. Just scan it for access."

I unlock my phone and tap the app controlling the windows, making them fully transparent. As if rehearsed, all five of us exclaim, "Woooow!"

Chapter Twenty-Three

Lalah

Everything as far as we can see is covered in a thick layer of frozen, sparkly water crystals, and snow continues to fall from the sky. The evergreen tops are shaking and bending in the wind, throwing snow haphazardly all around them.

"I guess we're stuck inside today." My eyes cautiously dart at Cole. "Tate's flight is most likely going to be canceled. No airline will dare fly in this blizzard." Something akin to relief crosses his face. I'm sure he is worried for his friend's well-being.

"Can we build a snowman?" Eliza claps excitedly.

"We can try," Cole agrees. "But will have to wait for the wind to settle down some, otherwise it will blow the snowman away." Eliza gives him a beaming smile and returns her attention to her plate.

Cole places his palm on my thigh and gives it a squeeze. I have to bite my lip to stop the moan fighting to escape me. Heat and tingles radiate through my body, concentrated where his hand still touches my leg. "Are you ok with us being here until he returns?"

"Y-yes, of course!" I choke out. "I'm just sorry your holiday here is delayed by the weather and T's absence."

"We're not on holiday." Blake frowns, his dark eyebrows scrunching together.

"You are aware of our circumstances," Cole says softly. "We decided as a family to have a fresh start, and since Tatum is one of my best friends, we chose to have our fresh start here. I was hoping we could stay with him for a week or two until I find something to rent or buy," he explains.

My lips curve in a soft smile, because I know he'll do anything to see his family happy again. It takes a certain type of man to assume responsibility for two children who are not even related to him.

And if I'm relieved at finding out they are here to stay, well, I'm not opening that can of worms right now.

"There's just the smallest of snags in that plan of yours," I tell him.

"What's that?"

"Tatum lives in a one-bedroom apartment. He converted the empty office spaces above his shop."

"Shit," he exhales, removing his palm from my thigh and dragging it across his face, prompting Clara to do the same.

"Two dollars," quips Eliza.

His pretty eyes roll but shoves his hand in the pocket of his sweats and picks two one-dollar bills from the wallet, passing them to the little swindler-in-the-making.

Much to my relief, his hand goes back to my thigh. There's just something special for my always-thrown-aside soul when Cole keeps such a possessive grip on me.

I'm as independent and feminist as they come, but I'm also smart enough not to deny myself small doses of happiness.

And if they come from a possessive grip on my thigh, then so be it.

"Here's an idea," I tell them all business-like. "A friend of mine has a three-bedroom house she rents out. She usually prefers long terms, but she's a bleeding heart and will work with you. Let me give her a call and see what she says."

His fingers again squeeze my leg, and I keep mine crossed Maevis won't read the lust in my face when I call her.

"That'd be great. Thanks, Lalah!"

"I'll clean up the kitchen. What do you say, girls? Wanna give your favorite brother a hand?" Blake says, pushing back from the table.

"Do you mind if we go to the enclosed porch for the call? I can let Astrum out and puff my vape while talking to Mae unless the fake smoke bothers you?"

"Nah, you're fine." He stands and picks up our coffees. "Do we need a jacket or something?" I shake my head and show him the sliding doors just off the kitchen.

"Astrum, spatior!" I singsong to him and quickly get out of the way for the furry blur to run outside.

The wind continues to blow the flurries in a mad dance, and I end up wearing most of them by the time I close the door behind Astrum. He doesn't seem to be bothered by the cold as he sprints in wide circles all over the backyard.

Plopping down on one of the sofas, I pull a fuzzy blanket in my lap, and inhale the minty sweet taste of the vape. The temperature in the enclosed porch is kept at seventy, but being surrounded by snow always makes me feel colder than I actually am.

"Is that an observatory?" Cole asks, standing with his back to me, looking out the window.

"Mhm. For my telescope."

"That's amazing. I bet you get an incredible view of the sky during clear nights," he muses.

"The best." The sound of a video call comes from my phone. "Speak of the deviless," I say with a smile, righting the phone so she can see my face.

"Morning, hun. How's the bakery going?" I greet Mae when her flushed face and tired eyes appear on my screen.

"Morning. It's insane. I've been working since four in the morning. Gosh, Lalah, thank God I live just upstairs. This snow is out of this world." She exhales heavily. "How are you, Elsa, all alone up in your frozen mountain?" she snickers at her own joke.

Everyone's a comedian these days.

"About that..." I start to say, but she interrupts me.

"Tatum called me earlier, all pissy his flight was delayed. He was huffing and puffing about you not picking up. I told him about the reception being down. He asked me to tell you to video call him."

"And yet he asked you to pass the message on instead of calling me directly," I quip with a wry smile, wiggling my eyebrows up and down.

Cole clears his throat and when I look at him, he seems lighter somehow and there's amusement twinkling in his green eyes. He walks toward me, moving like a lion hunting his prey.

I'm transfixed.

I hear nothing.

I see nothing.

Just him strutting closer and closer, his amused smile growing wider and wider until he drops next to me on the sofa.

I watch him, mouth agape, rearranging the blanket to cover both of us, and when he throws an arm around my shoulders, pulling me to his side, I swear my brain short-circuits and my body sags into him.

"Hooooly fuuucking hoootness," Maevis' screech wakes me up from my lust-induced trance. Fuck my life! I completely forgot I was on the phone with her. "Lucy, 'splaining, now."

On the tiny thumbnail now showing both of us my face is beet red and his is sporting a cat-that-ate-the-canary smirk. I so want to kiss that smirk off his face.

Maevis's eyes ping-pong from him to me and back again. Better open my mouth and explain before she jumps to the wrong conclusion.

"Mae!" There's a warning in my voice. "This is Cole Hayes, Tatum's friend. They served together," I tell her, knowing she, too, will connect the dots as I did last night.

She doesn't disappoint and, like the strong, independent woman she is, she wipes the drool off her chin - *I know, girl. Same.* - and her face takes a serious look.

"Thank you for your service, Cole. And I'm so sorry for your loss. I trust you and your family are doing well?"

Cole inclines his head at her in thanks, his arm tightening around my shoulders. I slip my palm into his, intertwining our fingers, and squeeze once, letting him know I'm here for him.

"We're as good as can be expected, given the circumstances. Actually, we've been quite well since yesterday. Lalah here has been taking excellent care of us." He then looks at me, a touch of possessiveness in his eyes, rewarding me with a dazzling smile. *Fuck me stupid.*

"You're definitely in excellent hands with her," she retorts and winks at him. Fucking dares to wink at him. I know she's done it in good fun and maybe to rile me up a bit.

I also know her heart is set on Tatum despite fighting her feelings for him.

But I still find myself narrowing my eyes and trying to suppress the growl rising in my chest. I fucking want to growl at her like an animal so that she backs away from my man. Cole's hand rubs soothing circles on my leg, pulling me even closer to him.

The irrational, jealous bitch in me puts down her weapons, satisfied with his claim.

"Cole and his family are moving to Lost Hope," I say now that I'm calm and settled again. "And he is looking to rent a house until he finds something to buy." He nods, confirming my words. "And I thought your house would be perfect for the four of them."

"Ohh, I'd love to have you, but my current tenants are there until just after New Year's. I don't know of anyone else renting right now. With winter fast approaching, everything's been booked. Especially since Skiing Season officially starts in a month. I could ask around and see if I hear anything." Her amber eyes flash, her shoulder covered in pink cotton rising and dropping in a careless shrug. "Or you could just stay at Lalah's until January. God knows she has plenty of room. Then, if you still want to move, my house is yours for however long you need it."

I throw a sharp look at her words. The meddling pixie just smiles at me. "I meant if you've found nothing to buy until then," she corrects, but I can smell the bullshit from here.

Cole sighs and stiffens. *Does he not want to stay here?* "Thank you. I'll keep your offer in mind. I'm afraid we have to let you go now. It seems Lalah and I have some things to discuss," he tells her, but his green orbs are fixed on me.

Without averting his eyes from mine or waiting for her to reply, Cole takes my phone and hangs up, then cups my face with his palm, running his thumb lovingly on my skin. Is it just me, or is he actively touching me whenever he's near?

"I'm sorry you've been put on the spot." He breathes, voice low and serious. "I'm sure once the snow clears, we can find a place in Billings."

Well, that's for sure not what I want to hear.

"I'm not. On the spot, I mean. Mae is right. There's plenty of room here for all of us. I didn't offer because I first assumed you were just visiting, and then thought you'd like to be on your own, not sharing a house with a stranger," I ramble since my brain lost all power for coherent speech under his hypnotizing gaze.

He frowns at my words and his jaw ticks.

"You don't feel like a stranger to me," he murmurs, his face coming closer to mine.

Oh fuck, he's going to kiss me, and I'll let him.

My pulse takes flight, and my lungs fail to inflate.

I'm fairly certain he can hear my heart hammering its way out of my chest, ready to jump into the palm of his hands.

The sliding door connected to the kitchen swishes open, and Blake steps onto the porch. "We're all done in here," he announces, with Clara toddling after him.

"I help," she giggles.

I jump off the sofa like I've been electrocuted, happy for the reprieve.

I want him to kiss me.

I want him desperately.

But I don't think I'd survive being kissed by this man, going by how erratically my heart beats in my chest and how weak my knees are.

"Good news!" I squeak, my voice three octaves higher than usual. "You guys are staying here with me for a while. Let's bring your stuff out of the car and get you settled properly." I clap my hands like a moron, making my way to the door to let Astrum in.

Cole passes by me and whispers, a touch of lust in his voice, "What almost happened there? Just delayed, babe. We're not done here."

I barely keep my knees from collapsing.

I'm fucked.

Chapter Twenty-Four

Cole

I was literally seconds away from kissing her. From tasting that pouty mouth of hers. "You have great fucking timing," I snarl at Blake.

I pick up Clara and kiss her rosy cheeks. "Of course you helped, baby girl. You are the greatest helper I've ever seen."

She smiles at me, that happy, carefree smile only a toddler can so freely give, and places her head on my shoulder.

Blake follows me to the kitchen. "What did Lalah mean we're staying with her for a while?"

"Seems everything around is already rented out. Winter season looks to be very busy around these parts. Anyway, she called Maevis, her friend, and the house she rents out is occupied until January. So Maevis and Lalah concluded there's plenty of space here for us all to stay until then or until I find something to buy for us."

"Hell yeah!" he grins, but then his expression turns somber. "And what about what I walked into?"

"You walked into nothing. And why the face? I thought you liked her."

"I do like her. But have you considered the implications of what something between the two of you might look like? Cole, you don't do relationships. You don't do serious commitments with women. I'll be seriously pissed if you hurt her. She seems to be an amazing person. Opened her house to us without blinking an eye. I understand the appeal, but..."

"But nothing. She's... different. I'm not jumping headfirst into anything here. I actually want to get to know her. I want to talk to her, be around her. It's fucking strange, man," I trail off, shoving my fingers through my short hair.

"And we'll be in the same space for over two months. I'm not going to force anything or make her uncomfortable if that's what you're worried about. But I'm also not going to pass up the opportunity to have something with her if it presents itself."

"You're still struggling to adapt," he argues.

I'm getting frustrated, but he's not wrong. And I like that he's protective of her. She gives the impression she keeps people at arm's length, and I don't dislike the fact there are people out there willing to fight being at her side, looking out for her.

Looks like my brother is one of them.

"I'm talking to the psychologist twice a week. The transition from that regimented way of living and high-adrenaline environment to being a parental figure for two little girls is difficult as fuck, brother. But I'm not dismissing the issue. I'm working on it. I never did relationships because I knew I'd be with the Marines until my last day. I never wanted to repeat history. That's not the case anymore."

He gives me a serious look, but the admiration in his silver eyes warms my heart. I hope he can see the determination in mine to make this life as good as possible for our family.

And if our family would grow by one more person, now, that wouldn't be the worst thing.

"Alright. I trust you, and I trust your judgment. And if you are absolutely serious about pursuing her, good luck, man." Blake smirks mischievously. "I hope it works out for you. As worried as I am about you hurting her, I'm also worried about her hurting you. I may be young, but I'm not blind. She's built a fortress around her. Figuratively and literally. Now let's go grab those bags and invade Lalah's home Hayes style." He claps me on the shoulder and leaves me staring out the window.

Soft cotton scrapes at my face as I wipe my forehead with the bottom of my Henley and exhale heavily. My eyes drink in Lalah sprawling out on the floor at the foot of Clara's bed, Astrum lying on his belly on top of her thighs.

"Unpacking is hard work," she huffs. "I never want to do it again in my life."

"I didn't even realize how much shit we packed and brought with us," I apologize to her.

"Well, considering half of what you packed were toys..." Blake laughs from his own sprawled position on Eliza's bed.

Clara jumps up and down on her mattress, happy to see the princess sheets, and I keep a cautious eye on her as she gets closer and closer to the edge of the bed.

"She's going to fall off, isn't she?" I mumble to myself.

"She's going to fall asleep sooner rather than later. Let's go feed me, I mean her, and then we can all just take a nap," Blake pleads, giving Lalah a helping hand off the floor.

"Mac and cheese in front of the TV good with everyone?" she asks on her way out, a chorus of "Yes, please," accompanying her down the stairs.

Five full bellies later, I find myself on my back on her U-shaped sofa, legs stretched in front of me propped on the coffee table, watching the fire dance in the electric fireplace. Eliza and Clara are already asleep cuddled together under a blanket on a recliner.

Blake is also snoring on the other end of the couch, with Lalah between us curled under a blanket, head resting on the back of the sofa. I watch as she blinks slower and slower, and I know she, too, is close to falling asleep.

My arm sneaks around her shoulders and pulls her into my side. She startles and tries to push away.

"Wha..?" she starts.

"Shhh," I whisper with a finger on my lips. "Just trying to get you comfortable. Come 'ere." She softens and lies her head on my chest, knees curled on my thighs. I run soothing circles on her hips and lower back with my palm, and sure enough, she quickly falls asleep, her breathing even, and her body completely relaxed into me.

The surge of pride in my chest leaves me baffled. She trusts me enough to fall asleep on me.

I didn't know what I was missing out on.

During my time in the Marines, it was one deployment after another, one mission after another. Adrenaline at an all-time high, we slept when we could, with one eye open and ears peeled.

But right here, right now, with her soft body curled around mine, her soft breaths tickling my chest, I'm happier than I have ever been.

I'm excited to see where this connection takes us. I have to tread carefully, getting to know her, gaining her trust, but I'm willing to play all my cards.

I'm also aware of how delicate this situation is, and that there are a lot of potential complications in our path.

We're a package deal.

Where I go, the girls go.

So if Lalah is open to something between us, she'll have to be open to being a mother figure to the girls as well. And it's a lot to ask of someone.

I also need to ensure she doesn't think the only reason I'm interested in her is because of the girls. Before meeting Lalah, I was happy to raise them on my own. But I have to admit, having a woman in their lives would be so much better for them.

And for me.

It's also complicated with us living in the same house for the next few months. In an ideal world, I would've met her, dated her, got to know her. She would have the space she needed – hell, the space we both needed – to process all that's happening between us, but it's impossible when sharing a home.

I was so fucking relieved when realization hit that she wasn't interested in Tatum when she teased Maevis about her relationship with him. Of course, even with that worry out of the way, there's plenty of potential for downfall.

If things don't work out between us, there are too many people who could get hurt or put in an awkward position but fuck me, I've never been so captivated by someone before.

She feels like she belongs right here next to me, in my arms, in my family, in my life.

Like all my life, I walked around with a missing part of me, and then I met her, and I was whole again.

I realize how insane my thinking is. We met just yesterday. I run a palm over my face, trying to clear my head and squeeze her closer to me.

She sighs in her sleep and wiggles around, trying to settle into a more comfortable position. Shuffling my legs onto the sofa and resting on my side, my whole body spoons her, my front to her back.

When awake, Lalah has such a big presence. Soft but strong. Nurturing but dominating. Here in my arms, though, she's small and vulnerable. Wearing that fragility she protects so fiercely on her skin. She won't have to do that alone anymore if I have anything to say.

Outwardly, she's a star, pulling all of us into orbit around her to thrive under her brightness and warmth. But strip the lights and the shine, and she's a supernova. Enclosed in darkness and pain, she's imploding into herself, trying to keep everyone safe from her doom and gloom.

No more. Not with me here.

I let the peace of having her in my arms and the slow up and down movement of her chest as she breathes soothe me to sleep, as certainty settles into my heart.

I'm strong enough to contain the supernova and fuse her elements back together.

Whispered giggles wake me up from the best sleep of my life. Small fingers poke my sides.

"Umph!" I slowly raise on my forearm when a knee hits me in the stomach. My eyes blink open to see Clara trying to wiggle her way between Lalah and me.

Even in my sleep, I held her as close as possible, with my right arm under her head, her own hand intertwined with mine, and my left arm banded around her waist, palm spread open on her warm belly, under her sweatshirt.

"Coley, I cuddle too," whines Clara, and I relax my hold on Lalah.

She too wakes up, wiggling her peach-shaped ass as she moves, back arching like a cat, and I bite my tongue to contain the groan trying to escape my throat.

My lower half inches away from her, trying to avoid her feeling just what she does to me. Lalah turns and faces me, leaving enough space for Clara to wiggle herself completely under the blankets between us.

She smiles softly at my sister and tickles her belly. "Hey there, trouble-maker. Did you have a good nap?" she asks in a sleepy voice, and man her sleepy voice packs a fucking punch.

I need to get up from this fucking sofa.

I can't be this turned on with my baby sister sharing the same space as I am, but that's the effect the woman still tickling her has on me.

Clara moves around until she finds herself completely on top of Lalah, arms around her neck peppering kisses all over Lalah's face. The happiness in her chameleonic eyes at the affection Clara showers her in lights up the room.

Untangling my legs from Lalah's and standing from the sofa, I adjust myself as discreetly as possible. A look around the living room confirms it's just the three of us now.

The clock on my phone shows it's early evening already, which means we've slept for over three hours. I'm not surprised. Sleeping with her in my arms was the best sleep I've gotten in a long while.

"The sleeping beauties are awake," comes Blake's voice from the entrance to the dining room.

Chapter Twenty-Five

Cole

"How long have you been awake? Where's Eliza?" I ask.

"For an hour now. Eli is reading in her bedroom. She wanted to get that snowman done, but I remembered we can't get back in, so we stayed put."

"Oh, no," Lalah says dejected. "Let me fix that right now. If you're living here, you need to be able to come and go as you want."

She gets up from the sofa and goes to pick up her phone. "This is awkward, but I guess it's a conversation to be had. The security around the house is tight and, uhm, I'm not extremely fond of people in my space."

She looks at us, and I'm sure she sees identical frowns on our faces. If she's uncomfortable with us in her space, maybe I need to go back to my idea of renting something in Billings once the roads clear.

Except every bone in my body down right revolts at the thought of living anywhere without her.

"No," she blurts. "I don't mean you guys. I mean other people. There's only one person with access to the house, and that's Tatum. I don't have many visitors. Uhm, Maevis and Annalise - her sister-in-law - are frequent flyers here. Occasionally, Matt and Beth Anderson - they are like my adopted family." She gives us a shy smile.

Her sleepy face and the tiny crease on her cheek from my Henley make my knees weak. Her ponytail is askew, hanging off one shoulder, and her pink lips are swollen with sleep. I wouldn't mind waking up to her every single day.

She clears her throat, and I switch my attention back to her words rather than how she'd feel cuddled naked against me.

"But they always let me know when they are coming around. I've, uhm, had some issues with someone damaging my car and, my... car crash... someone ran me off the road. The police haven't been able to figure out who it was. We're not sure if it was on purpose or simply road rage. I just feel safer knowing my home is as secure as possible," she mumbles, and my blood runs cold thinking someone wants to harm this precious woman.

"You don't need to explain yourself to us, Lalah," I tell her in a calm voice that doesn't betray the tempest raging inside me at the thought of her getting hurt.

"I u-understand if you don't want to live here anymore. I would never put you or the girls in danger. Nothing else happened since my accident. But I spent most of my time here, or with Tatum when we're in Lost Hope, so few people had access to me. And no one has access *here*. No one can get in unless I want them to," she continues, as if I haven't said a word.

I put my hand on her shoulder and massage the back of her neck with my thumb. I couldn't keep my hands off her if I tried.

"Lalah, this is your home. You do what you need to do to feel comfortable and safe. I speak for both Blake and me when I say we are thrilled and grateful you allowed us in your sanctuary, and we don't plan on leaving anytime soon. We also don't plan on bringing anyone here. The only person we know is Tatum, and even as we get to know more people in town, this is simply not an issue."

"Alright then. Let me fix you being trapped inside without me." She offers me a weak smile, then taps quickly on her phone. "I'm going to need your phone numbers, please," she orders, and we both rattle the digits at her.

A couple of taps from her fingers and two chimes come from our phones with a request for software to be installed. I give her a questioning look. "Security system software. I don't plan on spying on you," she laughs.

I accept the installation request, and in seconds the app opens on my screen. "Alright, so basically the app shows the plan of the house and the yard. All the doors and gates that require access are marked in orange. Set up a pin number for yourselves. If you want a door to unlock you tap on the orange circle and add your pin. When the circle turns green, it's unlocked."

She sucks in a breath that gets my eyes glued to her chest and those firm, perky tits of hers, then continues, "The red circles, well, those are doors you don't have access to. There are only two; my bedroom and my office. My office needs to remain off limits because through my work I have confidential information." She lifts a dismissive shoulder that only manages to pique my curiosity.

But my mind is still fixated on the rounded peaks beneath her sweatshirt.

"My bedroom, well, it's my bedroom. Yours are unlocked right now, but you can set up a private lock for yourselves. The gray circles show all the rooms with disabled locks. Since I'm the main owner, you won't be able to set up any locks in any rooms without my approval. I've made you both owners of your own bedrooms and the girls'. You need either Bluetooth, mobile data, or Wi-Fi to connect to the security system. But keep in mind, you won't be able to get in without your phone."

She looks at us, trying to gauge if we are following the plethora of information she just dumped in our laps before continuing.

"I've also given you access to the cameras at the gate, so you'll be notified if anyone is there in case I'm not around. Other than that, I think you're all set."

We both look at her dumbfounded. That's some serious fucking security she has around here.

"Oh, this is also connected to the fire alarm. Obviously, everything here is electric, so there wouldn't be any open fires, except if you want to barbeque outside. If an electric fire happens, the house and the system are built in such a way the affected area is sealed off and the fire department is called automatically, so any other rooms are protected." She twirls her forefinger around, and I nod in appreciation for all the work and planning that have gone into her home.

"If you are in the affected room, you need to type your code on the panel next to the door. It will open for 10 seconds so you can exit, then seal again." She trails off, lost in thought as if trying to decide if there's anything else she needs to add.

"Uhm, oh... the *full lockdown* option. If activated, the house practically seals itself from the outside. Metal shutters everywhere since the house is mostly windows. It's more for protection against the weather than anything else. Storms, even a minor earthquake, things like that."

"Be honest," chides Blake with an awestruck face. "You're a spy, right?"

Lalah throws her head back and laughs heartily. "Nope. Sorry to disappoint. Just a *little* paranoid about safety."

Blake looks at her, then down at his phone. "Wait a second. This shows me the plan of the house. When we drove in last night, it seemed bigger from the outside. It was dark, and I was tired, so I didn't give it a good look. But in these plans, there's a massive room, like half-the-house massive."

Lalah grins at him, and the sight of her playful side does weird things to my heart. And my cock. "Ohh, that's just the best part of this house. For me, at least. Come on then, let me give you the grand tour."

She starts toward the stairs, but instead of climbing up, she stops at the bookshelf near them and presses down on a book, then places her hand on top of its cover.

"Oh, this already looks good," Blake gives a sharp whistle, rubbing his hands together. She winks at him over her shoulder, and I'm ready to give my man card up considering the butterflies taking flight in my stomach.

The shelf moves backward, then slides to the side, and we all enter the dark room. Lalah taps twice on her phone, and about a dozen lamps come to life in the massive space. Blake was right. This room *does* take up half the house.

Everywhere I look, there are shelves upon shelves of books, with various seating areas spread randomly throughout the entire floor; sofas, bean bags, chaise lounges, rocking chairs, and what looks like a round bar dead in the center of the room.

"Boys, welcome to my girl cave!" she grins at us, arms spread, eyes twinkling with happiness.

"My fucking God." Blake gapes at her. "This library is amazing." He walks backward to the exit and shouts, "Eliza, come see this," startling Clara in my arms.

She whimpers, and I glare at him. "Sorry, baby girl," he tells her sheepishly, kissing her forehead.

Eliza's feet pitter-patter down the stairs at full speed. "You called, master?" She glares at Blake, then looks toward where we stand and blinks. Then blinks again. Then once more for good measure, her gray eyes glazed over.

Her mouth opens, eyes widen, knees buckle, and her chest inflates to maximum capacity with a deep inhale.

"What is this place?" she whispers. "This is like, this is heaven."

My eyes search for Lalah's. Hers are misty and her smile bright. "If I knew you liked books so much, I would've shown you this room earlier. Although, I'm afraid I don't have many age-appropriate books." She frowns and bites her cheek. "No problem. We'll sit down and order all the books you want to read. I have a shelf begging to be filled." She beams at Eliza.

"For real? Are you serious?" Eliza jumps up and down. Honestly, my heart can't take much more. In the past three months, I haven't seen my sister as happy as she's been since we got here. It's like she is slowly, slowly returning to the amazing, joyous little girl she was before we lost our parents.

Lalah nods at her. "Of course. The more books, the better. Come, let me show you the bar." She holds out her hand to Eliza, and my sister launches at her, grabbing her hand with enthusiasm.

"Uhm, not to be a party pooper, but don't you think Eliza is a bit young to be excited about a bar?" Blake asks, and honestly, maybe I hit my head too hard in one of Astrum's takedowns because I, too, am wondering the same thing.

Lalah rolls her big eyes at him. "Not that kind of bar. I don't drink alcohol, so there's none in this house. Oh, that reminds me, if you guys want to have a drink, we need to go shopping as soon as the roads clear," she says as she walks to the center of the room, Eliza in tow.

I mentally file away that tidbit of information.

"So what sort of bar is this, then?" Blake asks as he follows them. Lalah turns toward him, arms spread out, gesturing at the structure.

"Why, a coffee, tea, and hot chocolate bar!" she laughs. "What's a proper library without the correct means of hydration?"

"I think I'm going to move in here," he retorts.

"Me too!" Eliza claps and spins around.

"Not tonight," I cut them off. "Tonight we're having dinner and discussing our live-in arrangement," I say in a chorus of "Boos" coming from my family.

Yes, Lalah included, both in the booing and in the family.

"Alright. I'm fresh out of frozen already-cooked food, but there should be plenty in the fridge to throw something together. Why don't you two," she points at me and Blake, "see what we can cook for tonight, and I'll stay with Eliza to show her how to enter and exit the library since I can't exactly leave it unlocked," she says, ushering us out.

I follow Blake to the kitchen and head for the fridge, placing Clara down on the floor. I need to buy a high-chair for her. As much as I love feeding my baby sister, she needs some independence, and the marble tiles in Lalah's kitchen are easy to clean.

"Honestly, what do you think she does for a living?" Blake asks. "You can't have a house like this without being loaded."

I glare at him. "None of your business. The last thing I want to do is ask and give her the impression we're after her money. Whatever her job is, she's done well for herself. After we eat, I'm going to talk to her about us paying rent, bills, and food costs."

Blake's eyebrows scrunch together in a frown as his eyes find mine. "I'll never regret coming with you here, but I really need to look for a job. I'm broke."

"You're fine. I have plenty saved. Enough to keep us going for six months until we put some roots down here and find jobs. I took Mom's and Alecs's life insurance and split it between the three of you, so if you really need money, you have some there. And by the time both girls are eighteen they'll have a nice nest egg," I remind him.

"I know, Cole. But I still want to have my own money."

"And you will. We just got here yesterday. Let the dust settle for a bit and take it from there. We're all in this together." I reassure him.

He nods and slaps my back. *Good, this conversation is shelved for now.* He is my brother, and I'll support him for as long as he needs, but I understand his wish to work and provide for himself.

If there's one thing our mom drilled into us, it's a solid work ethic.

"Alright, looks like we have just enough for a stir-fry. Clara might put up a fight, but vegetables hurt no one, as much as we'd like to think otherwise."

I grab the ingredients I need from the fridge and set to cook. We were never a family with traditional gender roles. Without any of our fathers in the picture, Mom had to be both father and mother. She made sure we both knew how to fend for ourselves, from cooking to cleaning. Hell, I even know how to bake cookies if needed.

"Lalalalalalalalalah!" cries Clara, her small feet slapping at the tiles.

"What's wrong, baby girl?" Lalah asks.

"Up, up," she demands. I remember Lalah's arm was still hurting today, so I turn toward Blake.

"Can you grab Clara?" Blake frowns at me, at the same time Lalah protests.

"What? No. Did I upset you somehow?" she asks. "Why wouldn't you let me play with her?"

My feet carry me toward her, so she can see my face and look me in the eyes. I can see how she would misinterpret this, and I want to make sure she understands what I'm saying. I stop in front of her and lift her chin with one finger.

"I have no problem with you playing with Clara as long as you don't pick her up. You're still wearing your brace, which means your arm still hurts. Why don't you girls relax in the living room? She can cuddle with you on the sofa, and there'll be no need for you to pick her up. Blake and I have dinner handled. We'll call you when all's done."

My words soften her. I swear, a second ago, she was ready to fight me. I really love the fire in this woman. It burns so hot, it sets everything in me ablaze.

"If you're sure, then yeah. Thanks, Cole," she says, taking me by surprise when she hugs me around the waist. "Come on, Eliza. Let's go have ourselves a girls' evening."

"Can we watch Christmas movies?" my sister asks excitedly.

"Of course we can! Last on the sofa has to make breakfast in the morning," Lalah cries and takes off running.

"You're cheaaaating," Eliza accuses and chases after Lalah.

This. This feeling right here. I hate that my mom and Alecs had to die for us to end up at her door. But I can't help thinking maybe they guided our steps to Lost Hope and to Lalah, so we can all heal and be whole again. *Together.*

There's only one kink in my forever plan with Lalah.

I see the way she treats my sisters, how her eyes light up with every step Eliza takes to open up to her, with every cuddle Clara asks of her. She loves children, and clearly, children love her. And that's the one thing I can't give her.

Children.

I can't bring myself to regret the choice I made sixteen years ago. Seeing another day was never guaranteed when I was in the Marines. I still stand by my decision.

But it will kill me if it's what would make a relationship between the two of us impossible.

Chapter Twenty-Six

Lalah

I don't know what to make of him. I napped in his arms on the sofa, and I've never slept better. My skin doesn't crawl when he touches me. If anything, I crave his touch in whatever form it comes.

I crave his nearness, his warmth, his strength.

Usually, men of bigger builds scare me the most. My father is not the tallest man, but he was always on the bulky side. The fact he could overpower me so easily has always terrified me. But it looks like slowly, slowly, I am overcoming this fear.

It started with Matt, who is easily the tallest man I know. Well built, too, with the long hours he spends on the job sites, lugging materials around. But Matt doesn't really touch me. At best, he gives me a half hug as a greeting or as a goodbye.

Maybe I wasn't as stealthy as I thought with my aversion to touch because even Beth is quite restrained around me, although I know her to be extremely affectionate.

Then there is, of course, Tatum, who apart from the first day we met when my nerves were frazzled from finding my car damaged and the encounter at the police station with Maddox, has never once scared me.

If anything, I found safety and comfort in his touch.

Or what I thought to be safety and comfort because what I feel with him pales in comparison with the soul-deep serenity Cole's touch brings me.

And maybe that particular comparison is not fair since I've never had an inkling of attraction toward Tatum. Yes, he is drop-dead gorgeous. But I've always had very sisterly feelings for him. I thought of him as a kindred spirit, one slightly broken, a bit bent, and massively resilient.

Just like me.

And Cole, well, let's just say I've had to change my panties several times since he and his family *invaded* my home. If I ever had to label someone as sex on a stick, he's that fucking someone for me.

And it's not just his body.

Everything about him is attractive to me.

His voice, his personality, that quiet authority, the undertones of cockiness, his love for his family, his sense of honor and duty, his gentleness.

I look at him, and I see my forever, and that's just fucking crazy. I've only just met the man. Only weeks ago I was swearing up and down to Maevis I was not ready to date or put myself out there, still healing, still learning to love myself.

And then, I saw the most gorgeous pair of pale green eyes and I was completely done.

Smitten.

Love struck.

The clink of forks on plates brings me back to the dining room table. Everyone seems to be finished with their dinner and Clara is playing with two forks on a plate.

"Thank you for cooking. It was delicious." I smile at both Cole and Blake.

"You're very welcome," Cole's gravelly voice hits me and my nipples tighten, sending delicious tingles to my core.

"Does anyone want any coffee?" I ask. It's my routine after dinner to have a decaffeinated latte; relaxing on the sofa in the enclosed porch, with my hot beverage and minty vape, reading a book, surrounded by fairy lights.

"I do," replies Eliza in a serious tone.

"Aren't ya too young for coffee, missy?" Blake narrows his eyes at her. "And since when have you started drinking coffee?"

"Lalah knows my choice of coffee, Blake. All avid readers have a coffee with their evening book," she smarts back, all prim and proper. God, this girl is a firecracker. She's going to keep her brothers on their toes, that's for sure. I wink at her.

"That's right. All avid readers have a coffee of choice. Any other takers?"

"Well, I guess if you're making one of those lattes of yours I can't really refuse now, can I?" he mumbles, deciding to drop Eliza's choice in drink.

"None for me, thank you," Cole replies, and I nearly jump out of my chair when his palm squeezes my thigh.

Of course, he is sitting next to me at the table.

My dining room table seats eight people and can extend to sixteen if needed. He had plenty of choice on where to sit, but he chose next to me.

I continue overthinking as I get up from the table and start clearing the plates. Cole stops me when his big hand engulfs mine and takes it off the plate I was reaching for.

"Blake, Eliza, and I can clear the table. You go make those drinks," he orders softly.

"But you cooked," I argue.

"And we can clean, too. Rest that arm of yours. Stop trying to push yourself."

"What happened to your arm?" Eliza asks, and I freeze.

I don't want to lie to her, but I also don't want to remind her of car accidents. She grew happier as the day progressed, and I would hate to remind her of the loss of her parents.

"I hurt it during summer," I answer vaguely. "Had to wear a cast for what felt like a very long time. Just had it removed the day before you guys arrived here. It's still a bit sensitive and weak."

"Then Cole is right," she decides in an authoritative voice. Like brother, like sister. "You need to rest your hand. How else is it going to be well enough to help me shelve all the books we're going to order?" she continues in the same voice. I can't help but snort a laugh.

"Yes, ma'am," I salute her with two fingers and make my way to my space-ship, ugh, coffee machine. Blake's definitely rubbing off on me.

We all make quick work of our assigned chores, and I put a fresh bowl of water out for Astrum, as well as a bowl of dry food so he can snack to his heart's content. During the day, I prefer to give him cooked food. His diet mostly consists of meat and, much to my shock, carrots.

Yeah, I basically live with an overgrown, aggressive bunny.

Suddenly, Blake chuckles, the rich vibration of his laugh filling the room. "Food puts this girl to sleep faster than anything. She'll probably wake up before the sun, but she's down for the count now."

"Dammit, that's twice in a row I've let her go to sleep without brushing her teeth, but if I wake her up now, she'll be cranky all night and all day tomorrow," Cole mumbles.

"I'll put her to bed." Blake picks Clara up from where she's sleeping, bottom up on the rug next to the dining room table.

"Maybe just move her to the sofa. I need to buy some baby monitors for her room. Don't want her to wake up and get scared if we're all downstairs. And I can't really hear her as everything seems soundproofed," Cole tells him, and Blake heads that way, Eliza close on his heels.

"I'm going to finish my fairytale book," she announces over her shoulder.

I wince. Yeah, all the rooms are soundproofed. I still have nightmares of the things I heard growing up and when living in the first apartment with Callum. Those walls were paper thin. Every time our neighbors had sex or had a fight, it felt like we were right there in the room with them.

"Sorry about that. There's nothing I can do to get the sound traveling, unfortunately."

"Don't worry about it. That's nothing a baby monitor can't fix," he reassures me.

He must read the doubt painted on my face as he comes next to me and slips his arm around my shoulders, tucking me into him. My knees buckle at seeing how perfectly we fit together. "Seriously, Lalah. Don't worry about it. I'm actually surprised at how childproof your house is. A baby monitor is nothing. I'm sure if I order one tonight, it'll be here by morning if the roads are cleared."

I rest my back against the kitchen counter and sip from my coffee. "Speaking of cleared roads and tomorrow. How do you guys feel about a trip into town?"

"Is there anything in particular you want to do?"

"I came to get her majesty's coffee," Blake interrupts. "What's this about a trip into town?"

Passing him the hot chocolate topped with marshmallows I made for Eliza, I note from the corner of my eye, Astrum waiting next to the door leading to the porch.

Blake laughs, relieved when he sees the hot chocolate. "Hold that thought about town. I'll be back."

"Astrum wants outside. Do you guys mind if we take this conversation on the porch?"

"Lead the way." Cole slowly slides his hand from my shoulders to my lower back, his splayed palm touching as much of my back as he can, guiding me to the door.

I let Astrum out and take the same seat as earlier this morning on the sofa, but he chooses a recliner in front of me. I stifle a frown, although I am surprised he didn't choose to sit next to me.

Blake follows soon after and takes a seat himself on the recliner next to Cole's. I can't help but think I'm being put on the spot.

Me versus them.

Which is absurd, but I can't help what I feel. I puff a couple of times from my minty vape and see Blake reach into the pocket of his sweats, retrieving one for himself and puffing at it. The second the scent hits me, I burst into laughter.

"Bubblegum? I took you for more of a beer-scented type," I tease.

"Nah. I'm confident enough in my manhood to handle a bubblegum vape," he retorts. "Alright. Tell me about this outing in town we're planning."

"My friend Maevis has a bakery in town, and I swear, she bakes the most delicious pastries, cakes, and cookies, and basically anything that can be baked, she's baking and elevating them to magic."

"So far, it sounds amazing. Is she single?" His palms rub together, his eyes sparkling with excitement. "I don't even care what she looks like. My stomach demands I marry her." He laughs while Cole just watches us going back and forth.

"You may have to fight Tatum for her, so good luck to you."

Blake puts his hands in front of him, palms up, in a defensive pose. "Yeah, I'm out then. Not even my stomach is brave enough to cross that man." He shudders exaggeratedly, making me laugh once more.

It surprises me how freely and openly I've laughed since I met them.

Not one fake smile, not one fake laugh.

"Well, during this past summer, an angel investor chose several businesses in town to invest in. Suga'High is one of them, so she closed shop for a couple of weeks and has completely redone her kitchen and the seating area. Her grand re-opening is tomorrow, and I really want to be there to support her. I also need to see *To be Read Cafe*. This is Mae's sister-in-law's bookstore and coffee shop. The business version of my library," I clarify, wiggling my eyebrows.

"She too got an investment, and she's been busting her ass trying to get everything together to open her doors after New Year. And I think it would be good to do some shopping too, so maybe we can get a list started for what we need?" I ramble.

As friendly as their demeanor is, they are still sitting opposite me. Two big, burly men. One relaxed and easygoing, the other sharp-eyed and brimming with intensity, ready to pounce at the slightest disturbance. It's unnerving being the sole focus of their laser-sharp gazes.

"And you want us to come with you?" asks Cole.

"Well, yeah, of course. The more the merrier, no? And it would be a wonderful opportunity to get to know the folks in town."

"Then count us in." His whole face lights up with the smile he throws my way. My palm presses to my belly, sure any minute butterflies and bats will take flight from under my sweatshirt. His smile only lasts seconds before he turns serious. "About grocery shopping. We still need to discuss the rent situation, bills, and food."

"What about them?" I ask, my forehead scrunching in confusion.

"Rent price, Lalah. We want to pay rent for our stay here and share the bills, food included, if it's what you want too."

"No rent." I frown at him. "I'm not opening my home to you guys for money. There's no mortgage, and I have the free rooms. Your money's no good here, and please, don't start arguing." I point my finger at him when he opens his beautiful mouth to do just that.

"We can go back and forth all night if you want, but you offering me rent money is more of an insult than anything else. I understand where you are coming from, and I appreciate you offering to pay, but no, thank you," I tell him in my no-nonsense tone, so he knows I mean business, and I won't be persuaded otherwise.

He looks at me for a long moment, then looks at Blake who nods his head in response, then back at me. This man is so freaking intense, I want to squirm in my seat, but I keep all my muscles locked tight, showing no weakness and not backing down.

"Alright. No rent. Then let me pay the bills," he starts negotiating with me, and I just arch an eyebrow at him.

He really thinks this is a democracy.

"No bills either since I don't have any."

"What do you mean you have no bills?" they both ask and I bite my bottom lip to stop from laughing.

"Exactly that, Cole. This house is self-sustaining. It runs entirely on electric energy from my solar farm. The water comes from a nearby river, and is then filtered, treated, and distributed to my home. Since I've donated a couple of the water treatment machines to Forrest Falls, wastewater and sewer fees are non-existent. My security system is free since I own the rights to it and as payment for maintenance and whatever services I may need, I've allowed the security company to use the software. No bills."

As I finish talking, they both look at me with identical gaping mouths and round eyes, eyebrows shooting through the roof. Of course, they must be thinking about what I do for work.

This is where I have to sort of lie, but again, my job is not something I disclose. No one in my life – except for Marcus – is aware of what I do.

"It's ok," I tell them. "Go ahead and ask." Best to get it out of the way and then move on with our lives.

Chapter Twenty-Seven

Lalah

"Are you sure you're not a spy?" Blake asks, the shock clear as day in his rounded eyes and the high pitch of his voice.

"Not a spy, Blake." I smile. "Look, I have some investments that worked out for me. I also have a job that sometimes requires me to travel, but since I moved here, I'm less inclined to do so."

"So a spy!" he insists.

"Seriously. Cross my heart. Not a spy, Blake. I'm more of an auditor if you will. The corporation I work with sends me to assess different businesses and report back to them. And I live by myself. Apart from books and coffee, I don't have other things to spend my money on. It allowed me my dream home and one hell of a security system," I explain and cross my arms. Because that's as far as I'm willing to go.

"Sooo, do those businesses know you are auditing them?" He watches me with a challenge in his eyes.

"Uhm... no?"

"SO. A. SPY. THEN." He over-enunciates every word as if willing them into reality.

"Alright, Blake. If that makes you feel better, then yes, I am a spy."

"I knew it." He jumps off his seat, fist pumping in the air.

Cole rolls his eyes at his antics, then turns his attention back to me.

And I turn my attention back to not squirming.

"We're not charity cases," he tells me in a firm voice.

"Never said you were. You wanted to pay rent and share bills. There's no rent since friends don't charge friends for staying at their house, and there are no bills since there are *literally* no bills. Fair, I don't know what your financial situation is, and," I lift my hand in the air, palm facing him, to stop him from saying anything, "I don't really need to know. You could be loaded, or you could be dirt poor. It's all the same to me, and my answer wouldn't change either way."

He seems to find my answer truthful, dropping the intensity levels and nodding at me, a small smile playing at the corners of his lips.

"OK then. What about food? And household essentials?"

"Maybe we can add a shopping list to the fridge and make a schedule? I prefer fresh food, so I normally go food shopping every two or three days. With my work hours being quite relaxed, I have plenty of time to cook. Takeaway occasionally works too, but I'm not great at food planning." I shrug.

"I can work with that for the time being. Blake and I will start looking for jobs next week. I'm not sure how long it's going to take for both of us to find a job, so it may impact any shopping schedule we come up with, but it can always be changed. What about cleaning?"

Of course, they want to be looking for jobs I mentally facepalm myself. I didn't even think of that.

"I have someone coming once a week to clean because, honestly, I'm too lazy to bother. If I spill something I will mop and vacuum clean, do laundry, and such, but Renee cleans the *common* areas so to say, and the guest bedrooms. Things like dusting, window washing, vacuum cleaning, cleaning the filters on the washing machine, tumble dryer, the works. She does them. She's a lovely woman, working two jobs to support her son," I clarify.

"Not your bedroom?" he challenges, his gaze searching my eyes, and I get the feeling he's not interested in who cleans the master.

"Outsiders aren't allowed in my bedroom. The only people to have seen it are Tatum and you guys." Cole frowns at my mention of Tatum in my bedroom, and the need to explain rushes out of me. "He, uhm, helped me walk around and brought me food after the, uhm, after... back in July. Before he came to you."

Butterflies take flight in my stomach at the relief and anger dancing on his face. Cole looks ready to rip apart whoever dares *thinking* about hurting me, whereas Blake is simply confused.

"What actually happened to you?" he growls, his piercing green eyes boring into mine.

I take a full sip of coffee, debating what to say. I guess I already said some things to Cole, some he already knows from Tatum.

There's no reason for me to keep any secrets, and I am at least at a healthy point mentally where I can speak about it and not push myself into a panic attack.

"So, back in July, I was on my way to Billings when someone ran me off the road. Because I was going seventy miles an hour, when I hit the dirt, my car flipped several times before slamming into a tree."

I can't look at their faces right now, as I'm sure my tale will bring memories of their own tragedy, but they asked, so here we are. With my eyes averted to my latte, fingers fidgeting with the vape, I continue.

"I banged my head quite badly on the steering wheel and then on the window. For some godforsaken reason the airbags didn't deploy, so I lost consciousness for a while. Anyway, I woke up, called for help, and here we are. My forearm was fractured and I had a monster concussion, some stitches, and a big ol' bruise instead of a body. Hence why I needed help, and I wasn't in a great space mentally to trust many people," I finish, my eyes still on my coffee.

Maybe that's why I don't see Cole leaving his place on the recliner until he plops down next to me and pulls me in his lap. He moves me around so that I straddle him, and bands an arm around my waist, pulling me flush to his chest. His other arm fastens around my shoulders, palm cradling my neck, fingers tangled in my hair.

He hides his face in between my neck and shoulder, squeezing me tighter against him, his whole body shaking under mine. I rest my cheek on top of his head and run my hands up and down his back in a soothing motion.

I faintly hear Blake getting up to let Astrum back in, then leaving with my dog in tow. I let Cole have his moment. I know this hits very close to home for him.

I'm fine now, yes, and I try not to think of all the what-ifs, but I know how lucky I was to survive and escape essentially unscathed.

"Fuck!" he whispers and his warm breath caressing my skin leaves goosebumps in its wake. I hold him tighter in return. My whole body is a live wire, touching his so closely. My cells are buzzing, my blood dances in my veins, my heart is booming.

I kiss the top of his head, and he tips his head back slightly. So I kiss his forehead and let my lips linger there.

He takes a deep breath and tightens the fingers in my hair, angling my face so I can look directly into those gorgeous, mesmerizing green eyes of his.

"I'm going to kiss you now," he informs me.

I know that despite his words, he'll wait for me to consent, so I tip my head in a minuscule nod.

My nod seems to be just what he is waiting for. In the next second, his soft, warm lips touch mine, and I'm freefalling. He gives me a second to adjust to the feeling of his mouth on mine, then gently bites my lower lip.

I can't contain the moan escaping my throat, and he swallows it from my lips, the tip of his tongue tracing them, seeking entrance, seeking to be a part of me.

Deepening the kiss, eager to feel him as close to me as possible, I curl my fingers in his hair and pull while my other hand grips the material of his Henley, trying to rip it apart so I can feel his skin, so I can feel his raw strength under my fingertips.

With a strangled growl, his mouth slants on mine and Cole continues to explore my mouth with his tongue slowly, methodically, one sweep at a time, knowing me, owning my every breath, my every whimper, my every need.

The house could burn to the ground around me, and I wouldn't notice. I wouldn't care. I'm completely lost in him, in his kiss, in his touch.

I don't have a past.

I don't have a present.

I don't have a future.

There's just me and him, and our mouths searching desperately for one another. I don't know how much time has passed. It could be minutes, or it could be hours when he slowly gentles the kiss.

Pecking once at my upper lip, twice at my lower, pressing his mouth to mine one more time before stopping. His forehead touches mine, chests heaving, holding on tightly to each other.

What was that? My mind is spinning, reeling, replaying the kiss over and over. *Fuck me.* That wasn't a kiss. It was Earth being knocked out of orbit because surely something as simple as a kiss isn't so... so life-changing.

Isn't everything I've been missing in life.

Isn't the lost piece to finally make me complete.

And deep down, I know that in twenty-four hours, I started falling in love with Cole Hayes.

Fuck, fuck, fuck.

My breaths get shallower, and a panic attack creeps in. As my heart races, I can feel the walls closing in on me, suffocating me.

And even through all the madness, my skin doesn't crawl. Doesn't beg me to get away. My panic attack has nothing to do with him and everything to do with me.

I'm unworthy. I don't like people. I'm a loner. I'm ice cold. I don't know how to show affection. I'm emotionally dumb. I'm never enough. I'm never good enough.

I'm unworthy.

I'm unworthy.

I'm unworthy.

I can't breathe.

Cole's warm hands cup both my cheeks, his thumbs pressing on my cheekbones, massaging them.

"Breathe, Supernova. Come on now, slow, deep breaths. Breathe with me." I try to focus on the way his chest moves as he inhales. I try to focus on his breath in my hair when he exhales. His nickname doesn't even register after the crushing force of my panic attack.

One in, hold for four seconds, one out, repeat.

"That's it, baby. Give me one more," he whispers to me, his lips touching mine, his lungs breathing life back into me.

One in, hold for four, one out, repeat.

"I know, baby, I know," he murmurs. "Come on. One more and you're good. One more and we can go to sleep," he commands me, and I obey, trusting him fully to get me to the other side of this hurricane.

One in, hold for four, one out, repeat.

My breathing calms, my heartbeat returns to normal, no longer trying to escape my chest. I rest my forehead on his, eyes closed tight. I'm ashamed to look at him. One kiss gave me a full blown panic attack. Anything that could've been there...

"NO!" he rasps, voice full of authority, alpha power bleeding out of his tone. "Don't go down that road. You have nothing to be ashamed of. Hell, if you didn't panic, I probably would have. The kiss we shared was out of this world. God... I've wanted to kiss you since the second I laid eyes on you, growling beast at my throat and all."

A soft smile curves my swollen lips, thankful he's trying to get me out of my head with humor. I was right this morning thinking I would most likely not survive him kissing me.

He stands up, and I scramble to wrap my legs around his waist, trying to hold on to him. His hand moves from my lower back to under my ass, cradling it, as he takes decisive strides toward the kitchen.

"Put me down, you caveman!" I squeak at him.

I'm not a small woman. Never once was I picked up like this by someone I was attracted to. Callum couldn't even flip me in bed from back to belly, never mind picking me up and walking around like it was any other day.

"Settle down. I told you I'm taking you to bed. I just..." he sighs deeply, "I just need to hold you for a little while longer."

I calm down at his words. If it's what he needs, then who am I to stop him from taking it? I mean, for god's sake, he's not even breathing any harder, so I settle my cheek on his shoulder, arms tight around his neck, ankles locked above his ass, and enjoy the free ride.

"Eliza's sleeping in your bed tonight," Blake's voice startles me, and heat creeps into my cheeks. God, I'm a grown-ass woman being carted around, clinging to Cole like a koala.

His scruff tangles my hair when he nods at Blake. "I've left the door to Clara's bedroom open, so I can hear her if she wakes up during the night. I'll see you guys in the morning. Don't do anything I wouldn't do," he teases and my face flames even more.

"That doesn't leave us with much then," Cole deadpans and moves up the stairs.

I wiggle again in his hold, wanting to be put down. "Don't. I'm not letting you go, so if you keep moving around, I'm not responsible if we both fall down the stairs. But even if we do, I AM NOT LETTING GO," he stresses.

He makes quick work of climbing the stairs, with Astrum at his heels, and moves toward my bedroom door. I remove one hand from around his neck and blindly feel around the wall for the panel.

A soft click lets me know I've been successful in my task, and Cole, koala bear in tow, enters my bedroom and deposits me at the foot of my bed.

He bends his knees so he can look into my eyes. "I'm sleeping in here with you tonight."

I shake my head in refusal, but he continues, "Just sleeping. You in my arms, just sleeping. I need to feel you next to me. Call it insanity, call it whatever you want. I came THIS close," he puts his thumb and forefinger close together to show me exactly how close, "to losing you. This close to never knowing you. You could've died, and I would've never met you. Never gotten to hold you. Never gotten to kiss you. I can't deal with it right now. I'm an asshole, I admit. I'm making your tragedy about me. But every time I blink, you're trapped in that car, scared, hurt, and alone," he confesses, his voice somehow deeper, a raw quality to it.

He lowers himself to his knees in between my parted thighs and hugs his arms around my waist, head on my chest. "Please, Lalah. Please! Let me hold you tonight. I need to convince myself you're fine. I need to convince myself you are still here. Please," his voice a gritted whisper on the last word.

I'm not going to try and put myself in his shoes. I don't need a second panic attack tonight since just the brief thought of never meeting Cole sends ice-cold chills down my spine.

My fingers slip through his hair, playing with the curly, short locks. "Alright. Yeah. You can sleep here tonight," I whisper back to him.

He kisses my belly with a murmured thank you and gets back on his feet.

"I'll go and change into my PJs," I say, heading toward the closet.

Picking up a pair of sleeping shorts and a tank top, which is my usual sleeping uniform, I quickly change into them, then slip my arm brace back on.

My arm is still tender, so I choose to be cautious rather than sorry, and after wearing it all day today, I'm used to feeling its coarseness on my skin.

I make my way back into the bedroom and see Cole's clothes folded on the bench at the foot of the bed. I look in his direction, and he is already in bed, sheets covering him up to his waist.

His strong torso is all on display. With only a dim night light on, the shadows playing on his chest and the valleys and hills of his abs make him seem cut from marble. A stoic predator, beckoning his prey to surrender to his brand of danger.

I slip under the soft cotton covers, and he wraps an arm around me, pulling me into him. I'm touching him everywhere. My cheek rests on his steel biceps, my back to his chest, my ass flush to his groin, his forearm around my waist, fingers spread open on my belly under my tank top, the back of my thighs on the front of his, knees bending together, calves entangled.

I don't know where he starts, and I begin.

Cole kisses my forehead, shifting behind me, hovering over me. His mouth peppers kisses down my temple, behind my ear, my neck, my jaw, and, finally, my mouth. Before I can part my lips to deepen the kiss, he brushes his lush lips softly onto mine and settles down on his pillow.

"Good night, Supernova," he whispers. "Sweet dreams."

There's a question on my lips as I briefly register this is the second time he called me a supernova, but his breaths even out on the back of my neck as he falls asleep.

The excitement of the day mixed with the adrenaline crash after my panic attack are getting the better of me. My eyelids are getting heavier and heavier, and I soon follow him into sleep, dreams of supernovae held together by stubborn bands of gravity playing on repeat in my slumber.

I wake up in a cocoon of warmth, surrounded by all the strength that is Cole. And I mean *all* of it, judging by the erection trying to find its way into my sleeping shorts.

If that's the morning wood he's packing, then I'm kind of concerned about how I'll be able to walk after if we ever get to a different manner of sleeping together. I thought Maddox was impressive, but yikes, that's a whole fucking python in Cole's boxers.

My arm stretches, trying to pick up my phone from the nightstand when a notification alerts me there's someone at the gates. Even if I silenced my phone, these notifications are always with sound, just not on the loudest of settings.

As I move, my ass presses more into Cole's very awake cock, and he grunts. My lower belly tightens at the sound, and my panties dampen.

My phone beeps twice in succession, which means someone opened the gates. *What the fuck?* I don't have time to bask in the glory of everything

Cole is in the morning as I unlock my phone and see Tatum's car driving in.

Oh shit.

I didn't call him yesterday. Didn't even tell him his friend was here. His friend who just slept a full night in my bed, hands wrapped around me, hard, thick cock poking into my back.

Ohhh, bad Lalah. Very, very bad Lalah.

Running down the stairs and to the entrance, I get there as soon as my front door opens. Tatum smiles his big smile at me and spreads his arms wide, asking for a hug.

I go to him because I'm happy to see my friend. I'm happy to see he is safe. I'm thrilled he is back.

I'm also really interested in knowing how he got a flight so soon when all of them were canceled yesterday.

But just before I reach him, my skin revolts. My skin, that was caressed, and stroked, and held all night long by Cole, rebels at the thought of letting another man touch me.

And I flinch.

Barely there.

More like a twitch.

But Tatum being Tatum notices.

His smile dims and anger flares to life in his eyes.

"Lalah, is everything okay?" asks Cole in a sleepy, gravelly voice from behind me. *Oh, no. This is bad. This is oh so bad.*

In one smooth move, Tatum pushes me behind him, and, blink and you miss it, in the next moment he has Cole pinned to the wall, hand wrapped around his throat, arm cocked ready to punch.

"What did you do to her, you motherfucker? Why is she flinching?" he shouts in Cole's face, jaw tight and face red.

Chapter Twenty-Eight

Cole

With my back pressed flush to the wall and Tatum's hand choking my neck, I can't help but wonder how the fuck I keep finding myself in these situations.

First with the canine beast trying to rip my head off, and now with a very human one determined to punch the daylights out of me.

And all around Lalah. Talk about impressing the woman. Not.

At least I had the good sense of getting dressed before coming to check on her. I would laugh if I didn't think he'd take it the wrong way and escalate the violence.

"What are you talking about, Tatum?" I grit through the vise he has around my throat.

He doesn't get the chance to respond when Lalah gets in his face, pulling at his arm to release me. I go from slightly amused to protective mode in two seconds flat, my body stiffening, ready to strike.

As mad as he is right now, I don't want him to do or say anything to hurt her.

"Tate, let him go. Please! He didn't do anything to me. Please!" She pleads and continues to pull at his arm, but he doesn't budge. If anything, his fingers tighten even harder around my throat.

I need to snap him out of his rage before this gets out of hand. He might be big and strong, but I am bigger and stronger.

As I'm considering how to move Lalah out of the way and get out of Tate's chokehold, a low growl and a sharp cry come simultaneously from the stairs.

My eyes dart toward the source of the sounds, and see Blake with a frantic Clara in his arms. Eliza is hidden behind him, and a pissed-off Astrum poised in front of them in a protective stance, slowly inching his way to where we're all tangled up at the entrance.

Neither Lalah nor Tatum are paying them any attention. Lalah is too focused on getting him to calm down, and he's too lost to his rage. It makes me wonder once more about the nature of his true feelings for her.

This is not the reaction of a friend.

This is exactly how I would react if I were in his shoes.

Astrum's front legs drop closer to the floor, and I realize I have five seconds to push Lalah out of the way before this human pile is broken apart by ninety pounds of beastly muscles.

So I drop my elbow into the crook of Tatum's, causing him to bend the arm holding me on the wall. In the same breath, I take a step toward him, moving Lalah behind me with my other arm.

It seems to be what Astrum is waiting for because in the next second, he's on Tatum, paws on his chest, teeth pressed to his neck, and fuck if it doesn't feel good to be an observer to Astrum's attack instead of being at the receiving end of it.

Lalah trembles behind me, and I bend my arm backward, hooking it around her waist and holding her close to me without taking my eyes off Tatum.

He seems to slowly snap out of his rage and blinks confused eyes at me, jaw ticking, a frown marring his red face.

Clara continues to whimper in Blake's arms at the bottom of the stairs, but at least my brother has enough sense not to come any closer.

"Everything's fine," I say in a calm voice, although I'm anything but calm right now when we were so close to hurting Lalah. "Blake, take the girls in the kitchen and get breakfast going," I order him so we can deal with this mess without scaring them any further.

"No!" Eliza cries. "I don't want to leave you alone, Coley. Please!"

Her voice snaps Lalah from her daze, and she slips away from me, glaring daggers at both of us over her shoulder. She nears Eliza, and my sister runs into her embrace, wrapping her skinny arms around Lalah's waist.

"Come on, sweet girl. Let's go get breakfast ready and let the cavemen sort their issues out. Everything's fine, I promise. Tate was just surprised to see Cole here, that's all," she says, ushering my sister toward the kitchen.

My eyes linger on the way her cotton shorts hug her ample ass and the exposed skin of her creamy thighs before narrowing to slits, and move to where Tate is sprawled out on the dark rug.

Once I am sure they're out of sight, I extend an arm to Tatum to help him off the floor. He slaps at my palm, trying to lift himself up, but Astrum growls menacingly at him.

I can't help the satisfaction growing in my chest to know that, right now, he is protecting me. When he jumped between me and Tatum, he chose to protect me then, too, since he could've just as easily subdued me.

Tatum buries his hand into the fur at the back of the bristling beast's neck and starts massaging the bulging muscles at his nape. "I'm calm, boy. I'm good. You can let go now," he soothes through gritted teeth.

Yeah, that lie won't fly with the beast.

Astrum looks at me with the corner of his eyes, and I give him a sharp nod to release Tatum, but he doesn't move. My friend tries getting up off the floor once more, and this time Astrum moves back, until he reaches my side and takes the same sitting position he took the other night with Lalah.

Pride blossoms in my chest at his display of trust. He is one hundred percent loyal to Lalah, and he has now extended his loyalty and trust to me.

Tatum straightens to his full height and narrows his eyes at me. "What are you doing here, man? And more importantly, what are you doing here with Lalah?"

I ignore his questions and decide to check on how calm he truly is. "You good now?"

He looks me directly in the eyes, tipping his head back to compensate for our height difference, and nods.

In the next blink, it's my hand wrapping around his throat and his back slamming against the glass wall. Astrum remains behind me, most likely sensing there's no real aggression in me.

"This is what I hope the first – and for your own fucking good – last time you lose your temper in front of Lalah. Five minutes ago, you were blind with rage, Carter!" I grit in his face, keeping my voice low to ensure I'm not overheard by our audience. I force air in my constricted lungs through clenched teeth before finishing my threat.

"I know exactly how your rage works, and while I'm fine with you being an asshole in her defense, you fucking lost it. THE. LAST. FUCKING. TIME!" I over-enunciate every word before releasing him and taking a step back.

He drags a hand over his face and takes a deep breath.

"Fuck!" he spits. "She fucking flinched when she went to hug me, and I saw red when you appeared behind her. She hasn't flinched around me since we first met. I thought you did something to scare her. I fucked up, man." He throws me an apologetic look.

"I know you'd never hurt any woman. I just, I fucking lost it. She's as much of a friend to me as you are. She's like a fucking sister to me and has been through hell and back," he explains.

I try to keep the shock off my face. *Why would she flinch around him? She was cautious, yes, the first night we met, but we did touch, and never once has she shied away from me.* I file that tidbit of information for later.

"You scared the fuck out of Eliza, so you better be prepared for some groveling," I say to him, so he knows he is forgiven but still in deep shit.

He takes another deep breath, and the redness in his face slowly recedes. "Alright. Think I can buy her forgiveness with a dozen cookies once I get to Suga'High?"

"Only if you also babysit her overnight when she gets high on sugar and tries to bring Lalah's home down."

He smiles at me, relieved I'll not push the issue any further. And I know I don't need to. He heard me loud and clear.

"Care to tell me why you're here? And since when?" he asks again.

"You better get your asses in here if you want to eat," Blake shouts from the kitchen, followed closely by Eliza's voice with her *Two dollars* threat, and I realize they haven't closed any doors when they left us alone.

"I'll fill you in after breakfast. Come on." I slap a hand on his shoulder and nudge him toward the kitchen.

Lalah glares at us as we enter, folding her arms under her breasts and cocking a hip.

Here we go.

"Got all that testosterone out?" she quips, that sexy glare of hers not losing any intensity. My lips twitch at the corners, wanting to lift in a smile.

She's so fucking cute right now with all her feistiness out to play. It makes me want to run to her and kiss all the fight out of her. And, at the same time, turn around and punch my best friend in the gut because this is not how I imagined my morning going.

No, I was supposed to wake up with her in my arms, kissing the sleep off of her. Fucking cockblocking asshole!

Tatum smiles sheepishly at her. "I'm sorry, baby girl, that was uncalled for!"

I bristle at his term of endearment. Somewhere deep, deep inside of me I understand there's nothing between them, he said it himself she's like a sister to him, but there's this primal urge inside to shout from the rooftops that she's mine while beating my fist against my chest.

Like a fucking caveman.

She doesn't soften at his apology. If anything, she looks at him incredulously as if to say, *That's the best you got?*

He gets it too because he walks closer to her and wraps her in a hug. *Ok T, for the sake of that pretty face of yours, better make it quick.*

"I really am sorry. You flinched away from me, and I saw red. I thought someone hurt you when I was away. You don't do it around me anymore, and then, I saw Cole behind you, and my mind jumped to the worst-case scenario."

He opens his mouth to say more, but Lalah slaps a palm on his chest and pushes him away.

"You overprotective, over the top, fucking asshole!" she whisper-shouts at him. "How could you think *that* of your best friend? And do you think anyone here could hurt me with Astrum around? If he felt I was in the tiniest bit of danger, he would've ripped his throat out before he could blink." Her red-tipped nail finds its way to the middle of his chest.

"I really hope you apologized, Tatum, because that was a really shitty move on your part. I appreciate you caring for me and wanting to protect me. And most of the time it's something I welcome, but right now you crossed a line. You scared the shit out of me, and what's worse, you scared Eliza and Clara," she huffs, her eyes reddening around the rims.

If she cries, I'll fucking hurt him, seventeen years of friendship be damned.

"Tatum, I was talking to you, pleading with you. You didn't hear me. You were completely overcome with rage," she continues in a broken tone.

I'm impressed with how open and honest she is with him, calling him out on his shit. If Tatum's earlier reaction didn't clue me in, the way she looks at him with fondness and love, face full of worry for his well-being, would have shown me they truly are a family.

Maybe not one tied by blood, not one tied by legalese, but a family by choice.

It warms my chest to see that while she is a loner, she has made strong enough connections with good, honorable people, and they look out for each other.

The way she defended me, both with her actions in the hallway and her words just now, the way she worried about my sisters, about how they've been impacted by Tatum's actions makes me both weak in the knees and hard as steel further north.

I may not have known her since Adam, and what I do know is her walls are hard to crack, but once she lets you in, you're in for life.

She'll care for you, fight for you, worry for you for as long as she breathes, and I vow to myself to do everything in my power to get her to accept that she is mine. My Supernova.

She might not know it yet, but she'll find out soon enough.

"I know," whispers Tatum, "I'm working on it, I promise. Cole's aware that since I found out about Amanda, and then got that bullet through my leg, I've had a hard time keeping my temper in check."

"How is that possible?" she asks, her beautiful amber-streaked green eyes rounding as they roam all over his face.

"You're always so even-tempered, so calm... The only time I've seen you angry was on the first day I woke up in the hospital."

"That's because I cling to my calm with everything in me. When my control breaks, what you saw earlier happens. I'm working on it. I've been talking to an anger management therapist ever since your accident," he explains. "But, baby girl, why did you flinch?"

She averts her eyes from his and seeks me. The longing in her gaze cuts me soul deep. I want to pump my fist when the dots connect in my head, and like in a cartoon, a lightbulb turns on above my head.

She flinched because she didn't want another man to touch her when she just woke up in *my* arms.

Tatum turns his head and follows her gaze to mine. I'm certain he'll read the same longing in my eyes as he just read in hers. I don't try to hide anything from him.

All my feelings for her are pouring out of my eyes and face. I'm an open book for him to read out all my desires, my cravings, my intentions, and my need for her.

His own *Eurika!* moment shines on his face. A spectrum of emotions runs through his eyes; confusion, reluctance, support, then happiness, and I take the win of my best friend accepting what will happen between his honorary sister and me.

He gives me a sharp chin nod and simply says, "I see."

He reaches out and takes Lalah's hand in his, squeezing once, then bends down and places a kiss on her forehead. I can practically feel in my chest her exhale of relief.

I don't know if she understood the depth of my new feelings for her as well as he did, but there's plenty of time for her to know.

And for my feelings to strengthen and cement.

Chapter Twenty-Nine

Cole

We're all loaded up in my truck on our way to Maevis' bakery, with Tatum following us in his car accompanied by Blake. We agreed earlier to meet at the bakery, with Tate in desperate need of a shower and a change of clothes.

I filled in Tatum on the whys and hows of our presence here, and he agreed the best thing for us was to continue living with Lalah until... *If I have it my way, we're just going to continue living with her.*

It's not that I'm trying to take advantage of her, but if we're moving out, I want Lalah to come with us, and there's no way she'll move out of that beautiful home of hers, which means if things go my way, we'll all live there together.

Maybe not Blake, since I'm sure once he finds a job and settles, he'll want his privacy, and living there, he won't be able to parade his women and men in and out of the house.

Yeah, my brother is bisexual.

He's also under the very incorrect impression I'm not aware of his sexual preferences, but there's not much in this life able to fly under my radar.

He hasn't come out to me yet, and I worry if there's anything I said or did that makes him hide that part of himself, or makes him think I would not support his choices.

I don't care who he dates, as long as he's happy, and the person is of age and consenting. All I ever want in life is for my family to be happy and healthy. Everything else comes and goes. So I decided to let him come out to me whenever he feels ready to do so.

Tatum also let it slip during breakfast he camped out overnight at the airport trying to catch the first available flight out of Chicago, simply because he promised Maevis he'd be there for her grand re-opening.

With that admission, I let go of any jealousy I felt for the relationship he has with Lalah. I can't believe I haven't seen it earlier. He's head over heels in love with Lalah's friend.

The mischievous twinkle in Lalah's eyes when he talked, before he realized his slip that made him seal his lips faster than an X-59, told me the little minx will try to play matchmaker.

That's when he also told us the streets have been plowed, so we're good to head to town.

She directs me to a parking lot closest to Main Street, and we all jump out, Lalah moving toward Clara's door to unbuckle her. My baby sister wraps her arms around Lalah's neck and her tiny legs around her waist, squealing with joy at finally being allowed to be outside.

Eliza slips her gloved hand in mine, and I reach out for Lalah's. I'll be damned if, by the end of today, there's anyone in town unaware she's mine.

Better to stake my claim early since I know she's stubborn enough to fight me tooth and nail on this connection we have, as was made glaringly clear after her panic attack last night.

As a group of three, plus a koala baby, we make our way to Suga'High. The closer we get, the stronger the smell of baked goods permeates the air, and even though we just ate, my stomach growls in anticipation.

Shit, if the cakes are half as good as they smell, I have a feeling we're all going to be frequent flyers here.

There's a queue at the entrance of the bakery at least thirty people deep. *That's going to be some wait.*

I look around to see if there's anywhere else we can go until the crowd thins, as I don't want the girls to spend too much time outside. It may have stopped snowing, but the temperatures are still below freezing. Lalah pulls at my hand to stop when we get behind the last person queueing.

"Let me give Maevis a quick call," she says. "I want to get the girls out of this blasted cold as soon as possible, and by the looks of this line, I'm sure Mae will need a helping hand." She pulls out her phone one-handed and quickly taps on her friend's contact, lifting the phone to her ear.

"Slow down, babe. I just wanted to let you know we're right outside," she pauses for a quick breath, listening to whatever Maevis is saying to her.

I can't really make out the words, but I can tell she's frantic.

"Of course I can help. Alright, we're coming inside right now and getting to work. See you in a minute, hun." She slips her phone back in her pocket and turns to me.

"Yup, she's overwhelmed. Let's get inside. You and the girls can have a seat at one of the tables, and I'll stay to help her for a while. You can walk around Main if you don't want to sit and wait for the crowd to thin out."

She talks a mile a minute, not letting me get a word in, and I can barely contain the chuckle in my throat at how adorable she is right now.

"But I don't know if you'll find anything open. It seems like the entirety of Lost Hope is queueing up here."

I look behind us and see she's right. It took less than five minutes for another ten people to get behind us.

She pulls at my hand, not waiting for an answer, and walks around the people sitting in line to be served, greeting everyone with a smile on her face and a *good morning* on her lips. I can practically hear Maevis's sigh of relief at seeing Lalah, even from fifty feet away.

Lalah continues to drag me until we reach the counter behind which Maevis is moving a hundred miles an hour, juggling between serving everyone and refilling her baked goods display.

Maevis stops in her tracks and smiles at us. "Give me a second, guys, please," she offers to the family waiting to treat themselves with some exquisite desserts.

"You can't imagine how happy I am to see you here. I didn't expect this place to be packed. We're nearly out of everything. Please, Lalah, do you mind manning the counter so I can go back to baking?" she pleads, puffing at a solitary strand of hair escaping the blue hairnet fixed on her head.

"Toss me an apron, will ya?" Lalah winks at her, then passes Clara into my arms with a kiss on her chubby cheek. "Look around and let me know what you guys want, and if you choose a table before they're all snatched up, I'll bring whatever you order there."

My eyes roam the meticulously arranged shelves, brimming full of flaky pastries, artfully decorated with drizzled, velvety sauces. On the other side of the counter, a closed-off glass display has an array of perfectly round cookies, in any combination my heart would desire.

The show stopper is the massive glass fridge, holding mouth-watering cakes and tarts decorated in an explosion of colors. I must admit, Maevis is one hell of a baker, and I haven't even tasted one of her concoctions yet.

"Whoa!" whispers Eliza next to me. "Coley, this is amazing. How will we ever choose?"

I almost snort at her look of wonder. This bakery is most definitely what dreams are made of, especially for a ten-year-old with only books and sugar on her mind.

"Hmmm," I say to her, rubbing my chin with my forefinger. "How about we play a game? I'll cover your eyes with my palm, and you point your finger anywhere. Whatever you point at, that's what we're starting with. You know we can always come back, don't you? And I'll make sure we buy something nice so we can enjoy ourselves at home," I promise her.

She beams at me mischievously, and I want to jump in joy. *Yeah, take my fucking man card away, see if I care.*

I'm full of pride knowing I put that smile on my little sister's face. I've seen more of her smiles and her playfulness in the last couple of days than I've seen in the last three months.

Her little heart broke when she lost her daddy and her mother figure. She's a smart cookie too, and I'm sure she was worried about what would happen to her and Clara.

And that worry no child should ever have is what keeps me going and stops me from regretting moving forward with the guardianship.

Losing my career with the Marines may be a huge personal disappointment on top of the loss of my mom, but having these two little girls opening up to me, warming up to me, giving me their trust and love so freely, makes up for that disappointment a thousand times over.

Sliding my hand over her eyes, her tiny face is completely obscured by my palm. "Alright, troublemaker. Go ahead and pick our poison," I tell her.

Clara claps excitedly in my arms, then throws out her tiny arm, copying her sister's every move, and, of course, both stop their fingers in completely opposite directions.

Luckily I'm a growing boy and can do some damage at the dining table if I put my mind to it.

"OK, ladies. Let's see what you chose. It looks like little Miss Clara really wants some chocolate chip cookies, and Miss Eliza has her heart set on a strawberry cheesecake. Well done, sugar monsters!" I praise them, waving Lalah over to us.

"Fancy seeing you here." I wink at her and watch a pretty pink blush color her cheeks. *This fucking woman!* I sigh mentally.

She always keeps me on my toes with her commanding attitude when needed and her tantalizing blush when she lets her emotions fly free on her gorgeous face.

"We've decided to gorge ourselves with cheesecakes and cookies," I tell her.

"Looks like you're in luck then since there's plenty of both. Have a seat, and I'll be right with you." She rewards me with a smile that rivals Maevis's sweetest cakes.

We choose one of the empty booths by the front windows, all three of us sitting on the same side. Eliza, plastered to the window, wastes no time pulling out her fairytale book while Clara bounces on her knees between us.

I take my time admiring all the work Maevis put into her bakery. Her artistry doesn't stop with her creations in the kitchen but it also blends into the way she has decorated the bakery.

Close-up photos of sugary treats adorn the peach-colored walls behind the counter and on each side of the spacious room.

The front of the bakery is made almost entirely out of glass, except for the two pillars framing the entrance. Halloween-themed stickers of sweet delights are placed on the windows, much to the elation of every child passing by.

Three booths in different shades of green sit in a row in front of the left-side window. On the right, where we're seated, there are three booths in different shades of yellow.

A dozen tables are spread throughout the rest of the pastel-tiled space, with the counter brimming with sweet treats taking center stage, shelves of cookies and flaky pastries on one side, a glass display of colorful cakes on the other.

It's clear from the explosion of color everywhere, Maevis designed her bakery with children in mind since this would attract their attention so easily.

With the fusion of colors inside, you'd expect the space to be an eyesore, but amazingly everything blends together and simply looks joyful.

The best of all is the smell of freshly baked goods. All I have to do is close my eyes and take a deep breath, and I'm instantly transported back to my childhood home on base.

My mom fretting around with a red apron tied around her waist, waiting for Dad to get home, house cleaned and polished within an inch of its life, and a delicious smell of powdery sugar, cinnamon, and vanilla wafting from the kitchen.

All I have to do is take a deep breath and all my best childhood memories are coming to the forefront of my mind.

"You're new in town," a feminine voice purrs at me. I blink myself back to the present and look at the blonde helping herself to the seat in front of me.

Chapter Thirty

Cole

Her makeup is expertly done, full lips painted a deep red color tip in a predatory smile, her blue eyes framed by long fake eyelashes drink me in.

From where she sits directly across from me, her lower body is hidden under the table, leaving her half-exposed breasts on display. Clad in a form-fitting lacy crimson blouse, this woman seems completely out of place in the casual family-oriented bakery.

As are the flirty eyes she makes at me, considering my baby sisters are sitting right fucking here.

I'm not blind. Objectively she is a beautiful woman, but the desperation reeking off her is completely unappealing, even if I had eyes for anyone other than my hazel-eyed supernova.

"That seat is taken," Eliza says flatly, not even bothering to lift her eyes from the book she's reading.

"Oh. Is your mommy coming?" The unknown woman asks in a saccharine tone, head slightly tilted toward Eliza, fake concern dripping out of her mouth.

I lean back in my seat and cross my arms over my chest. I'm ready to shoo her away. She overstayed her welcome the minute she decided to approach our table. When Eliza replies in an equally saccharine tone, it shocks the hell out of me.

"My mommy is dead. Do you want to be my mommy?" She now looks at the shell-shocked woman with round gray eyes, a shy smile, innocent face tipped to the side.

"Uh, I'm sorry to hear that. I'm sure your daddy here misses her very much," the woman babbles, throwing me helpless looks.

I choke on a laugh because my little sister is sharpening her claws, and I'm more than happy to let her.

This woman is either oblivious or down-right blind. I haven't said a word to her since she sat down, and instead of taking the hint and moving along, she's now engaging my sister in conversation.

Most likely thinking Eliza's the easiest way to reach me.

I've seen plenty of women like her, and never once have I been stupid enough to tangle myself in that hot mess. They appear classy, a faint air of superiority floating around their head, convinced there's no man alive to ever refuse them.

Drop your guard for one second, they dig their claws deep into you, and before you know it, you're at their beck and call. Or so she likes to think.

No man worth his salt would fall for the cheap charade she's putting on.

"My daddy's dead, too," Eliza says. All pretenses of friendliness and innocence are gone, and I get a glimpse of what I'll have on my hands in four short years when she becomes a teenager.

Confusion crosses the woman's face; there and gone in a blink, the fake smile still etched on her lips. She's at a loss for words but still unwilling to give up and move on, her eyes shifting from Eliza back to me, curiosity spilling out of them.

"The seat is still taken," Eliza continues, unperturbed by the loss of her attention.

"Sorry it took so long, guys. It took me a while to figure out the cash register." Lalah's voice comes from directly beside me.

I can't help the smile overtaking my face when the subtle scent of jasmine and roses hits me, chasing away the smell of desperation and overly sweet perfume the stranger across from me exudes.

The blonde takes advantage of my diverted attention and her arm reaches across the table, taking my hand in hers, slowly racking her nails on my chest.

Lalah's eyes widen in disbelief and her face blanches. I rip my hand from the woman's grasp and stand to my full height, glaring at her.

"As my sister said, the seat is taken," I grit through clenched teeth. My arm curls around Lalah's waist and I pull her stiff body to mine, bending my knees to plant a kiss on the corner of her mouth. She tries to push away from me, but my arm tightens around her, not giving her a chance to escape.

"I don't know who the fuck she is, but trust me, she was not welcomed at our table," I whisper in her ear.

I'll be damned if I let her think even for one second that as soon as she's turned her eyes away from me, I'm looking elsewhere.

How could I when all I see lately is her?

"Of course, the town whore sank her claws into you," the woman spits.

"What did you just say?" My jaw clenches, my teeth grinding together at her hateful words.

The nerve on this fucking woman is out of this world.

"You waltz in here, sit at our table even though it's clear your presence is unwanted, and open your mouth to offend my woman?" I thunder.

"Maddison!" Lalah sighs. "You want to buy something, the counter is in the opposite direction. If not, go spew your hate somewhere else."

"Don't pretend to be all high and mighty, Lalah," she retorts, her eyes glaring daggers at the woman in my arms. "What? You couldn't fool Maddox, and now you've chosen your next victim?" The woman moves her eyes back to me.

"Don't let her dupe you. She's a desperate, lying bitch going after every man crossing her path."

Lalah stiffens in my arms even more, and I've had just about enough of this witch of a woman. "That so? What'd she do to you? Claim your corner of the street?" I sneer.

Her red lips open in disbelief as she huffs at me, red-tipped finger pointing at my chest.

"Don't say I didn't warn you! Did she tell you she moved here because she was stalking our chief deputy after he fucked her and dumped her?" she sneers right back at me, a glint of victory in her eyes.

Blind-hot jealousy scorches its way through my veins and into my heart, my body turns to stone with the overwhelming need to rip apart every man she's been involved with.

Lalah senses the rigid muscles in my body tightening around her shoulders and pulls even harder to get away from me.

"Maddison!" A man's rough voice thunders from behind the wretched woman.

Lalah takes advantage of the distraction he provided and rips away from me, scurrying off toward the counter. *Motherfucker!* I fist my hands at my side, doing my best to control my reactions.

I can't run after her and leave my baby sisters alone at the booth, and I can't rip this vile woman to shreds as much as she deserves it.

"What the hell do you think you're doing?" the male continues, voice hard. I take him in, his body positioned directly behind the blonde witch.

He runs his fingers through his longer at the top, cut short on the sides, light brown hair, narrowing his ice-blue eyes at the woman looking paler by the second; his displeasure is written as clear as day across his ticking jaw. He is nearly as tall as I am, his uniformed body just slightly leaner than mine.

"Madd, I-I," she stammers. "I was just protecting you and warning the newcomer of the desperate ways of that woman."

He turns toward me, his eyes assessing me from head to toe, a frown creasing his forehead. He deliberates his next move for two quick seconds before reaching out with his right arm for a handshake.

"I sincerely apologize for Maddison's behavior. She's absolutely out of place. I'm Maddox Lawson," he tells me.

I decide to play the civility card until I have a better understanding of the dynamic between him and Lalah, and clasp his hand with mine, squeezing tighter than the moment calls for.

Huh, looks like I'm not as civil as I thought I was.

He pumps my hand twice, no sign of discomfort or wince on his face, apart from a small crinkling at the corner of his eyes.

"Cole Hayes. I take it you're the chief deputy this woman mentioned earlier?" She scowls at my dismissive mention of her, but I'll be damned if I give her the satisfaction of addressing her by name.

His hand falls to his side, and he slides it into the pocket of his police-issued trousers. "Unfortunately," he mutters, glaring at her once again for good measure.

"Look man, I'm not going to speak for Lalah, just..." he exhales a heavy breath, tipping his head back and looking at the ceiling as if trying to find the answers written there. "Maddison has no idea what she's talking about," he pauses again, a faraway look in his eyes. "Fucking hell! She's going to break my nose again, isn't she?" he finishes, his face softening as if relieving a fond memory.

What the fuck is he talking about?

"That's seven dollars for the swear jar," Eliza quips, breaking the tension around us.

Lawson looks at the little swindler with amused eyes, slides his hand out of his pocket holding his wallet, and hands her a ten-dollar bill.

"Keep the change. I'm paying a swear in advance. You're steeper than my son. He only charges three dollars per swear." He smirks at her fondly, then turns back to me.

"I don't want this woman near me or my family, Lalah included," I tell him sternly. His eyebrows rise high on his forehead, and a look of understanding washes over his face. "Take this as my formal complaint against her for harassing me and my family."

"What are you talking about?" she screeches. "I just stopped to welcome you to town and warn you…"

"I'd stop right there if I were you," I dismiss her, my eyes still trained on Maddox. "As I said, I don't want her near me or my family."

"I can go wherever the fuck I want," she spits. "Do you even know who you're talking to?" her face reddens in anger, mouth twisted in an ugly sneer.

Did I just say ten minutes ago she is a beautiful woman?

Maddox grasps her arm gently, steering her to the exit. He gives me a chin lift in acknowledgement, letting me know he heard me loud and clear.

"Let's go, Maddison. You and I need to have a long talk. I'd fucking appreciate it if you didn't shout my personal business in the middle of the busiest shop on Main Street. In fact, I'd appreciate it if you didn't talk at all about my personal business." His voice trails off as the door shuts with a soft thud behind them.

I slump back in the seat and gently put my hand on Eliza's shoulder, giving her a small squeeze. "Are you ok, baby girl?" I'm sure it couldn't have been easy for her to sit here while the adults were being more immature than her.

"Coley, if you ever get a girlfriend like that lady, put me up in foster care," she tells me in a serious tone, eyes narrowed at me. "Better yet, ask Lalah to be your girlfriend so we can all live happily ever after like the characters in my favorite fairytale."

"That so?" I give her a chuckle. "Well, I better get to work then if I am to have any chance of convincing her to take us on."

She rewards me with a beautiful, ear-to-ear, toothy smile. "I trust you, Coley. If you don't know what to do, let me know, and I'll show you what books to read." She nods decisively at me.

"Mother of God, what's that tantalizing smell?" My brother's voice comes from near the entrance, and Clara starts clapping enthusiastically when she hears his voice.

"Bakey, pick me up!" she orders, arms fluttering in the air, reaching for him.

He plops down on the bench in front of us, scooting closer to the window, and bends over the table, plucking Clara from her seat. Her peals of laughter as he blows raspberries on her belly warm my heart.

"What is it you're learning from books, Cap?" Tatum smirks at me, his eyes scanning around for an empty chair. *Good luck with that.* These booths may be comfortable, but they are not wide enough to accommodate two men our size on the same bench.

"How to get a girlfriend," Eliza quips, nose still in that book.

"Read your fairytale, troublemaker!" I chastise, a smile on my face. "Or no more cakes for you."

She tilts her head to me, narrows her eyes in my direction, lifting her hand slowly, palm facing down, pointer and middle fingers making a V shape. She points her little fingers to her eyes, then even slower, rotates her wrist, pointing at mine, then back at hers.

"Don't mess up, big brother, or I'm taking *myself* into foster care," she deadpans, then buries her freckled, upturned nose back in the well-loved pages.

Tatum and Blake both watch me with an identical devilish smirk on their smug faces, eyebrows high in their hairlines.

Assholes.

"Didn't you come here to help your girl out?" I tell my best friend and nearly choke on air when the asshole's cheeks pink up, his smugness draining as if chased away by the blush.

Another one bites the dust.

"As for you, you overgrown teenager, stay here and treat your sisters with a cake. I have my own girl to chase down," I say, my eyes already on the counter where Maevis is back in charge, and Lalah's nowhere to be seen.

Chapter Thirty-One

L'alah

I can't stop my hands from shaking. Can't stop shaking, full stop. I can't believe the nerve of that fucking woman. *What on earth is her fucking problem?* I'm mortified down to the last cell in my body.

My mind plays her words on a never-ending loop in my head as I pace back and forth, puffing at my vape, craving a cigarette with every minty breath I take.

"Don't say I didn't warn you! Did she tell you she moved here because she was stalking our chief deputy after he fucked her and dumped her?"

One more lap around the bin area.

Five more puffs of my vape.

Ten more wishes to whatever deity is up there to open a black hole and let it swallow me whole.

Pace. Puff. Prayer. Repeat.

I'm a private person. I'm a private as fuck person. I have nothing to be ashamed of, regardless of what the blonde bimbo seems to think. But I hate, I absolutely fucking despise when my private life is dissected open in front of everyone.

I've been through this type of circus far too many times in my life; when I had to go to school sporting bruises I couldn't hide, purples, blacks, and yellows all over my body, and the *well-meaning* teachers and professors thought it best to question the bruises in front of the entire class.

At every social gathering I was forced to go with my parents, where inevitably Daddy Dearest would find a reason to criticize me loudly and publicly, then proudly state it was for my own good. He was educating me on the ways of life.

When Daddy Dearest stuck his dick in other women, then blamed me for his actions to whoever was there to listen. His favorite excuse being he caved under pressure as he simply couldn't cope with raising the out-of-control, stubborn demon he spawned. In case you're wondering, I'm the demon.

When Callum and his chosen aired our dirty laundry to all our mutual friends, justifying his cowardly behavior. He had to find love and comfort somewhere else because I was a cold, downright arctic bitch. Not a single bone in me good enough to be respected. And he had already wasted so many years at my side, with me dragging him down.

And when I finally, finally, think I'm getting my start-over-in-life chapter, an envious, pretty-package hollow-center of a woman comes and shouts in the middle of a full bakery that I fucked and stalked the chief deputy.

I don't even care what the good people of Lost Hope think.

Their opinion I could take or leave.

But the raging bitch had to say it in front of Cole, and what's worse, she had to say it in front of Cole with his little sisters present.

And the cherry on the fucked up cake of steaming bullshit, Maddox made his impeccable fucking entrance just in time to hear her little diatribe. *Fuck my life!*

My hands scrub nervously over my face, trying to suppress my tears from falling, trying to find the silver lining, the blessing in disguise in this living nightmare.

God, the way Cole stiffened next to me. One minute, he is defending me. The next, he's made of stone.

I guess this is on par with the story of my life, although it's unfair of me to have any expectations of him. Fuck knows the shit now going through his head.

Of course, I'm a slut. I let him kiss me like I'd die if he didn't breathe life into me with his tongue, and let him sleep in my bed all sprawled out in his arms like he was my personal body pillow, after knowing him for less than forty-eight hours.

Oh fuck, I'm definitely losing it now if I slut shame myself for going to sleep in the same bed as a man. I'm not a prude, if anything I'm all for equal opportunities.

As long as the partners are of age and consenting, everyone is free to do whatever they want and whoever they want as many times as they want.

He stiffened in my fucking arms. God, I wish I could scrub the last half hour from my brain.

I wish I had put a stop to Maddison's madness the first time I bumped into her on the street. But no, I had to play live-and-let-live-Lalah, and all I get for my troubles is a damaged car, a brush with death - since I can't shake the feeling she was somehow involved in my being run off the road, and now public humiliation.

God, I can't fucking breathe.

I drop to my haunches, hugging my knees to my chest, lowering my forehead atop my thighs, trying to hold myself together and stop the panic attack.

One breath in, hold for four seconds, one breath out. One in, hold for four, one out.

I repeat the breathing mantra in a desperate attempt to slow my racing heart and beg my lungs to fully open up.

A warm, calloused hand caresses the back of my neck before cupping it. Deft fingers tangle in my hair, rubbing circles on the soft skin below my ears. His warmth seeps into me when he crouches behind me.

His free hand bands around my knees. Tree-trunk thighs lock on each side of mine. His face nuzzles the crook of my neck, his lips peppering close-mouthed kisses right over my erratically fluttering pulse.

He holds me tight, squeezing me closer and closer to him until I don't know where he ends and I begin.

I soak in every single one of his breaths. I revel in his every caress, warmth spreading through my frozen limbs, chasing away the numbness with every sweep of his fingers.

He leans back and sits on the cold, snow-covered ground, pulling me even closer in his arms. His hand slips out of my hair in a gentle, affectionate move. His touch trails across my shoulder, following the patterns on my sweatshirt at the top of my chest.

He traces with the tip of his fingers the outline of yellow duckies printed above the *I don't give a duck* stitching above my breasts. His arm finally reaches the opposite shoulder and fastens tightly around me.

By sheer will and one hell of an embrace, he is holding together every broken, damaged, and fragmented piece of me, splinters and all.

"Although somewhere deep inside I'm aware I have no right to feel the way I feel," he whispers in a gruff voice, "I'm jealous as fuck that asshole got to be with you."

Sealing his words with an open-mouthed kiss on my neck, his cold lips curve in a smile against my now-flushed skin.

"There's nothing between me and him," I whisper back, my voice scratchy, my throat working overtime, trying to swallow all the tears I refuse to shed.

"I had an awful night, and I needed the distraction." I try again when I'm more in control of my voice. His palm moves and his index finger presses down on my lips, thwarting my attempts at explaining myself.

"Not now. Not here," he continues in his gravelly whisper, sending tendrils of warmth from the earlobe his lips brush against as he speaks, stoking an inferno deep down in my core.

"We're going to get up now. I'm going to turn you around and kiss you breathless. Once I'm good and ready to let you go, you'll take my hand and lead me back inside where you'll sit on my lap for everyone to see how fucking proud I am to be claimed by the most beautiful woman in this godforsaken town." He pauses, waiting to see if I'll rebuff his words.

When it doesn't happen, he carries on, "You'll eat the hazelnut coffee cake I got for you, and then we'll all go home. And tonight, when we go to bed, and I can hold you close to me again so you can't run off, you'll tell me what I need to know," Cole instructs, nose on my skin, inhaling my scent deep in his lungs.

"OK. Are you ready?" he rasps.

I barely nod my head in acceptance when he stands with his arms still banded around me.

Cole lets me drop to my feet, slowly sliding down his granite body. He presses closer to me when my ass reaches the mother of all bulges.

In a swift move, I'm spinning around. A strong arm encircles my waist, greedy fingers fist my hair, lush, hot mouth slants over mine. His warm tongue prods over my bottom lip, coaxing me, seeking entrance.

My hands find purchase on his shoulders, fastening around his neck, and I open my mouth to his teasing. Tasting the subtle hint of chocolate on his lips, my own tongue chases his, needy and desperate for his attention.

I can't tell if he kisses me for mere seconds or long-lasting hours.

What I can tell with certainty is I never want to let this man go.

And it's the most terrifying thing I've felt in my life.

He slows the kiss, teasing his mouth over mine in soft affectionate pecks trailing at the corner of my mouth. His lips follow the curve of my jaw and land on my temple.

A lingering pause on my forehead on the way to my other temple. A sweet press of lips down my jaw, stopping fully on the tip of my nose, as his arms squeeze me to his chest impossibly tighter.

I'm speechless, putty in his hands, a trembling mess of fears and hopes.

In thirty years of life, no one has ever made me feel this cherished.

No one has made me feel I can let go and let all my weaknesses bubble to the surface.

I open my eyes and take in his handsome face. His red lips swollen from my kisses tip in a soft smile, his nose pinked from the frozen air outside. Pale green eyes drink me in, desire, affection, and joy reflecting back at me.

He doesn't shy away from my perusal and lets me just exist in this moment. Lets me return the affection he so easily gives me. My fingers move of their own accord, frozen tips trailing on the scruff of his cheeks, smoothing over his cheekbones, and down to his lips.

He blows a hot breath on my fingers before tipping his head down and pressing a sweet, innocent kiss on the center of my palm.

"You're freezing," he chastises me. "Let's go have that cake, and then we can go home."

"Oh, no!" My face falls. "I promised Maevis I'd help, and instead I bailed on her when the bakery was busiest." I cringe, remembering how crowded the bakery was when Maddison opened her fucking mouth to air my laundry out for all to hear.

"None of that," he commands me in a sharp voice. "Don't go spiraling down on me again. No one cares, Lalah. And no one believes her either." He takes my hand and heads toward the back entrance.

"I don't care about what anyone else thinks, Cole," I confess to him in a small voice. As soon as my words hit him, he stops and turns toward me.

Doubt shining clearly in his green eyes.

"I mean it. Do I love that she announced my business to everyone around us? Fuck no," I continue in a stronger voice. "I care she spewed her bullshit to you. I care she said all that in front of your sisters."

"Then you have nothing to worry about," he cuts me off. "My sisters are fine. Clara doesn't understand what was said. Eliza may have a faint understanding, and she couldn't care less about Maddison. She may be young, but she can see through the bullshit as easily as we do. And I think I made my feelings about what went down clear," he murmurs against my forehead before pulling at my hand and leading me back inside.

As soon as I step foot inside the bakery, Clara notices me and climbs down from Blake's lap, toddling toward us.

"Lalalalalalah!" she squeals happily, planting her face on my legs, tiny arms wrapping around my calves. I bend to pick her up, being mindful of my left arm, and hoist her up on my hip.

I don't have time to brace myself before Eliza throws herself at me, forcing me to take a step back directly into Cole's chest. He steadies me with a possessive grip on my hip, and Eli wastes no time wrapping her own arms around me from my side, squeezing me tightly.

"I thought you left us," she whispers from where her face is buried in the fabric of my sweatshirt.

"Awww, family hug!" Blake saunters toward us, wrapping his arms around this already overfilled Hayes sandwich.

Peeking over his shoulder I see Maevis and Tatum approaching us. Her arm slips between my back and Cole's abdomen. Tate crowds her even closer, clasping his hands on the shoulders of the Hayes men.

Not five seconds later, Annalise throws her arms around me and Eliza, her husband Drake right behind her.

I can't hold them in anymore; traitorous, scorching, hot tears fall down my cheeks in small rivulets.

Cole kisses the side of my head and whispers, "I'm not the only one in your corner, babe."

More tears follow his whisper. Grateful, heartfelt, humbled tears of pure joy.

No, he's not the only one in my corner.

I'm not the only one in my corner, either.

Chapter Thirty-Two

Lalah

I'm all bundled up in a soft gray blanket, curled on the sofa, with a decaffeinated latte cradled in my palms. My eyes gaze at the large bowl dominating the center of the coffee table. Fiery materials resembling flames swirl and dance with abandon in their glass confines.

So this might have been an impulsive purchase for my enclosed porch.

Seated on a sleek, black, stony base, the ten inch tall glass bowl traps in its see-through enclosure long strips of fabric. A magic press of a button hidden on the side of the base makes the strips float.

A tornado of whites, oranges, and reds, tirelessly swirls around the glass walls. I'm not really sure how the contraption works, but it definitely makes for a mesmerizing fake fire.

I take a small sip of the still-steaming latte. The sweet tones of vanilla mix with the bitterness of the decaffeinated beans on my tongue. With my eyes closed, I savor its comforting taste, soothing my frazzled nerves.

After dinner, Cole kissed the tip of my nose and placed the cup of decaf in my hands. And then told me we'll have the conversation we started earlier today once he puts the girls to bed. He has done every single thing he promised he would when he comforted me outside of Maevis's bakery.

Well, he promised to have the conversation when *we're* in bed, so I can't run away from him, but I admit, I'm a coward. I can't have that talk lying in his arms. I'll be too exposed, too vulnerable.

What's curious is that I do want to share with him, and I want him to share his innermost pain with me too. We barely know each other, yet he feels mine.

I've never been as comfortable around any other person in my entire life. The hurt woman in me rings some faint alarm bells at the back of my mind, demanding caution.

When I saw Maddison sitting at his table, jealousy soared through me. I wouldn't have gotten to the table any faster if I teleported. And when she reached for his hand, touching his chest, my whole body shuddered in protest, possessiveness surging in my heart.

The realization I had then made me stiffen.

I was with Callum for eight years. Shared nearly all my firsts with him. Thought I was going to grow old with him and when I saw him fucking another woman in my bed, I simply shut down.

I was upset but not raging.

I felt betrayed, but not an ounce of regret we ended.

All it took was seeing another woman touch Cole for a brief second. One second and I was ready to burn the bakery to the ground if it meant getting him away from her.

Is the intensity of my feelings for him that has me hiding like a coward under the blanket. Throwing myself into the furious tempest of emotions he evokes in me is a coin toss.

Heads - I get my happily ever after.

Tails - He rips my heart out of my chest and incinerates it.

I know he thinks he wants me. Hell, I felt the proof of his desire when he kissed the life out of me earlier today.

But in all my coin tosses so far, Lady Luck has always used a double-tailed coin.

"There you are!"

Cole enters the porch, twisting the cap off a non-alcoholic beer, and drops it on the table. A satisfied groan escapes his chest when he plops down on the opposite end of the sofa. With his back against the plush armrest, he's the definition of cool and collected.

One long leg is stretched out in front of him, his sock-clad foot tickling my side. The other bends at the knee, stretching his sweatpants over his hips. The beer-holding arm dangling in between his legs is the only barrier between my eyes and what's hidden underneath the soft cotton.

The porch is cloaked in darkness, with only a faint strip of light coming from the kitchen door. The soft orange glow emanating from my little fake fire flickers around, half obscuring his face in dancing shadows.

As much as I hate not being able to see those pale emeralds of his, it makes it easier for me to talk.

And talk I do. Between sips of lukewarm latte and puffs of minty vape, I tell him everything. I leave all my pain down at his feet. The contempt I have toward my parents. The worst of the bruises my father left not only on my body but on my soul too. The unworthiness clouding my mind; the self-hate for not being good enough for my so-called family.

A cloud of minty fog engulfs me in my retelling of how I met Callum. My eagerness to leave my childhood home. It all dissipates into the darkness as I go over the plans Callum and I made for our future.

My eyes no longer tear when I think of my friends deserting me after I caught him cheating. The last of my cold coffee touches my tongue with the truth of how deep his betrayal was and how I met Maddox the same night.

"I know it doesn't portray me in the best light," I sigh, my voice weak after speaking for what felt like hours.

"But with the anger burning in my veins, it could have been anyone that night. I needed to kill the loneliness in me. I was desperate to feel something other than rage and betrayal. My skin was crawling from his touch since the adrenaline had long left my body when I woke up the next morning. And I left. There's nothing between Maddox and I. Never was, never will be. I don't know what Maddison's problem is, but I will not put up with her shit anymore." I trail off, eyes on my lap, my shaky fingers twisting and twirling at the now-empty vape.

I don't dare look into his eyes. I don't want to see those beautiful green orbs darkening in disappointment or disgust. I'm too tired right now, too drained with everything I purged out of me as I laid my soul bare in front of Cole.

Fabric rustles around me before the sofa dips closer to me. His forearm gently slides onto my lap, and his long, steady fingers intertwine with my trembling ones.

I blink my eyes open and take in the art etched on his skin.

I wasn't aware he had tattoos.

I think this is the first time I am actually seeing his bare forearm. Yes, he slept next to me last night wearing only a pair of boxers, but my bedroom was dark. To be completely honest, I was also distracted by his naked chest and the hard ridges of his abdomen the whole time.

I trace with a hesitant finger the edges of his tattoo and the silvery waning gibbous moon just below his elbow. A soft caress admires the looming dark peaks of mountains in the background, the dark green of blurred evergreens.

My red-tipped nail contours the majestic white wolf, his head thrown back in a mighty howl, the sharp claws of his front paws wrapped around Cole's wrist. I turn his forearm gently so I can see if the drawing continues on his inner forearm.

"Semper Fidelis, always loyal," I whisper as I follow each artfully looped letter branded permanently into him in dark ink. Directly underneath his motto, a faint dog tag frames *C.H. 01/96.*

"Colton Hayes, January 1996," his rough voice wraps around me. "He was my father, a Marine himself. We lost him that year in January. I got the tattoo after basic training in his honor," he explains.

"Why the wolf? Is it for your dad, too?" I ask, curiosity eating at my insides.

"No. During basic, the guys in my squad kept teasing me about being the leader of the pack. It went further when I refused to date anyone seriously. They started calling me a lone wolf." He chuckles, and I can hear the self-deprecation in his tone. I lift a questioning eyebrow at him.

His face is soft, with no trace of the disappointment I expected to see in his eyes. Just a fond look as he recounts his early days in the military.

"Retract your claws, babe. Tonight is about you. I will tell you everything you want to know about me. Just not tonight." He leans closer and kisses my forehead. Just a peck, a brief touch. Enough to settle the knots in my stomach.

"Back to my tattoo... About four years ago I met with a friend of mine who was discharged at the same time as Tatum. Jake loves his tattoos. I'm actually wondering if there are any uninked patches of skin on him. Since there wasn't much left at that time." He gives me a boyish crooked smile, and my stomach exchanges knots for butterflies.

"I didn't plan on getting another one. But as I watched the artist work on him, this image kept popping in my head, over and over. I got deployed soon after, but I couldn't erase the wolf from my mind. So as soon as I had my next leave, I got it done."

My heart starts fluttering. *What are the chances?*

"Do you have any tattoos?"

"I have two myself," I confirm. *How crazy is this?* Chances are high for multiple persons to have the same design or at least similar enough. High even to get them in the same year. My heart doesn't care about statistics though, instead flutters like crazy at the coincidence.

"Show me," he replies huskily.

With the tips of my fingers, I push the sleeve of my sweatshirt up my forearm until it reaches my elbow. He stares intently at the inked comet donning my inner forearm, nucleus pointing at my wrist, brilliant yellow tail spreading to the crook of my elbow. *Ad astra per aspera* in loopy, cursive black script overlaps the tail of the comet.

He replicates my earlier moves and traces the outline of my tattoo with the tip of his calloused finger, leaving goosebumps on my skin in its wake.

In the darkness of the night, with only sparks of light flickering around us, this mutual admiration of art, so personal to our wounded souls, is impossibly intimate.

"You have a thing for Latin. To the stars through adversities," he whispers. "And the second one?"

I lift my eyes to him from where they were fixed on the movement of his fingers. I want to see his reaction as he takes in my second tattoo, although its edges are curving around the sides of my arm, hinting at what my forearm hides.

I slowly rotate my arm in his grasp until my palm faces completely down. An array of emotions crosses his face, from curiosity to confusion and finally, awe.

His finger restarts its scorching journey on my skin, circling the waxing crescent moon just below my elbow. The eerie snowy peaks of mountains in the background with a mantle of dark starry patch of sky on their shoulders are treated just as gently.

The vibrant green of the pine forest surrounding a muted white clearing is an identical shade to the blazing green of his eyes.

After agonizing seconds, he finally reaches the moon-howling wolf with fur so dark it's tinted in blue, sharp claws wrapping around my wrists. The pad of his thumb stops at my pulse point, rubbing comforting circles.

Cole slides off the sofa, his knees hitting the plush carpet on the floor with a soft thud. He aligns his right arm with my left, our tattoos matching like a puzzle piece. Under a full moon on a starry sky, two wolves are embracing, howling their pairing to the moon.

Our fingers intertwine, my dainty ones completely engulfed by his. I move closer to the armrest, pulling him up next to me and resting my head on his shoulder as we stare at our complete puzzle.

"How? When? It fits perfectly. Like…" he trails off.

"Like the full design was ripped in two and we both got one half?" I reply in a soft voice, allowing the awe I felt myself to come to the surface. His cheek brushes the top of my head as he nods.

"I don't know. After I left East St. Louis, I started traveling. About six months into my new life, I stopped in DC on my way to Charlotte. And since I have a hard fast rule to do nothing but maximum laziness on my birthday, I enjoyed the lush Capitol life. I went for the cheesiest touristy things I could see." I laugh, although there was nothing funny about the state of my mind that year.

"Anyway, in one of my walks around the city, I came across this little gem of a tattoo studio and saw the design displayed in a frame. It called to me like a siren's song. Long story short, I treated myself with the tattoo for my birthday, and with the ink deep in my skin, I felt I regained a piece of me."

"Wait, so you got it four years ago? When's your birthday? And in DC? Do you remember the name of the studio?" He rapidly fires questions at me.

"Yes. August. Yes." I giggle louder and louder until, much to my utter mortification, a snort escapes my nose as I recall the studio's name.

"Oh God. I'm so sorry. But you'll understand..." I tell him between giggles. "Squirting Squid." I'm laughing as hard as the first time my eyes caught their proud neon purple display above the entrance door.

"No kiddin'! We both got the tattoos at the same time?!" He exhales sharply, turning toward me. The corded muscles of his arms cage me between the cushion at my back and the armrest. "In the same place?"

"What?" My laughter cuts off abruptly. "It was the twenty..." I trail off as his hungry mouth descends on mine.

Chapter Thirty-Three

Lalah

A moan rips from my throat at his unexpected possession.

His palms cup my face, tilting my head just so, his lips nipping at mine. All thought leaves my head, and my skin is on fire. He gives me his weight and my legs spread on instinct, making room for his hips to grind into me.

Desire burns through my veins as I cradle his trim waist between my thighs. My hands sneak under his shirt, touching his smooth skin, all that velvet encompassing deadly stone-like muscles rippling under my touch.

We're a mess of lust, lips, bites, and hands everywhere. My nipples harden in tight, needy peaks, my spine arching and reaching for him. His hot mouth trails from mine, and I can't stop the whimper escaping my throat at his loss.

He doesn't leave me wanting for long, rewarding my impatience with open-mouthed kisses down the sensitive, pebbling skin of my neck until he reaches the collar of my sweatshirt.

A frustrated groan escapes him at the sudden barrier between my bare skin and his mouth.

One of his hands releases my face, going at the back of his neck, peeling off his shirt in that smooth, sexy move only men can pull off.

I take in his wide, strong shoulders, the expanse of his chest, my eyes trailing down to those deliciously cut abs, and the peek-a-boo of his sculpted V hiding beneath the waistband of his sweats.

My eyes widen at the sight of his long, hard cock so clearly outlined by the dark material straining to keep it confined. I unconsciously lick my lips at the same time my fingers reach for his waistband.

His palms wrap around my wrist, stopping me in my tracks. A raspy moan is the sole warning I get. "Fuck, babe! Let me see you," he begs, and my eyes snap back to his. I'm drowning in the desire rising in the nearly black orbs. His pupils are blown open, with only a thin circle of jade surrounding them.

He pulls at my wrists, and I lean toward him as my sweatshirt is ripped away from me, my hair cascading down my back and over my breasts like a silk cloak.

He sits back on his heels, savoring my naked upper body. I lay back on the armrest of the sofa, a willing victim to his predatory perusal. I bite the inside of my cheek, fighting back the need to squirm or reach for him.

He strokes feather light touches over my collarbone, brushing away my hair, revealing me to him. "Fuuuck!" he rasps, his voice so low I can barely hear him over the pounding of my heart.

His fingers trail from my collarbone down between my breasts, lower and lower until his palm presses down on my soft belly. The tips of his fingers reach under the thin elastic holding my leggings up my hips.

His other arm braces atop of the armrest and he lowers back over me, staring into my eyes for one brief second.

I'm sure he sees in them the same burning desire I'm seeing in his.

I don't know where I want this to go, but I know with dead certainty I'll instantly combust if he stops touching me.

His hot lips touch one of my nipples, and my hips shoot off the sofa at the bolt of electricity traveling from my breast to my core.

I grind myself into his thick length, my ankles fastening at the small of his back pulling him closer.

"Look at you, so responsive to my touch." He praises me in a dark, lust-laden voice that only stokes my need for him.

"Oh, God! Cooole..." I moan his name into the darkness of the porch when his mouth sucks hard on my nipple, his teeth nipping at the tight peak, amplifying the electricity running through my veins.

His free hand moves from my belly to my neglected breast, covering it entirely, deft fingers pulling and plucking at my sensitive bud.

My hips grind harder against him, and he rewards me once again. This time with a savage thrust of his hard cock against my soft wet center while his lips release my nipple with a wet pop.

"Fuck, sweetness. The taste of you is driving me crazy," he grunts desperately.

His mouth seeks mine, devouring my every breath and every moan. I'm lost to him, a puppet at the will of her master. My hands are desperate to touch him. One fists in the curly short hair at his nape, holding on for dear life. The other presses down on his back, pushing him closer and closer to me.

I rotate my hips against him, trying to get his cock to rub against my needy bundle of nerves. He obliges, shifting just so, and starts thrusting in earnest against me, as if he could reach inside of me through the layers of clothing still separating us.

We're a tangle of moans, grunts, and desperation as we both chase our climax clinging to each other, drowning in the desire floating thick and heavy around us.

My clit throbs and my pussy walls start fluttering as I explode into nothingness. With his name on my lips, I'm disintegrating and forging myself back together through the power of the orgasm he just gave me. I fervently cling to him as I ride out the aftershocks of the best night of my life.

Cole continues to grind over my soaked, swollen center once, twice, three times before his hips still and his weight presses me deeper into the sofa.

A deep groan of pleasure releases from his lips into my mouth as he comes, his head dropping to the hollow of my neck. He prays my name over and over again in reverent whispers as he comes down from his own high.

I revel in his embrace when his arms band around me, his naked skin touching mine everywhere, both our hearts working overtime. They pump so hard I feel his heartbeat in my own chest.

"I can't believe you made me come in my pants like a fucking teenager," he chuckles softly into my neck. A smile curves my lips, lifting my rosy cheeks, as sudden shyness overtakes me.

Oh my fucking God! I dry-humped Cole in the middle of the night.

His lips brush my heated cheeks. "None of that," he chastises me. "It's you and I, babe! Please tell me you're not regretting this beautiful moment between us, the first of many to come," he shamelessly begs, the lusty daze all but vanishing from his eyes, worry filling his green orbs.

My hand moves of its own accord, caressing his jaw and I return his look, letting him see in my eyes how much I loved the expression of our passion. I've never felt as consumed by desire or blinded by the need for someone's touch.

I'm both scared and elated *he* is the one to gift me pure, unguarded oblivion.

"I could never regret you, Cole. I don't know what this extraordinary connection between the two of us is...." I peck at his lips to stop him from talking when his mouth parts ready to clarify and fix it all for me.

"And we'll not find out tonight. We've been talking all night. It's late. I'd like you to take me to bed, let me sleep in your arms like you're my favorite body pillow, and we'll take it from there," I plead with him, tiredness slowly creeping up my body, with each heartbeat chasing away the adrenaline he injected in my veins.

He nods at me, then lifts off the sofa, searching for our tops. When he finally finds them, he quickly dons his as he walks toward me with my own outstretched between his palms. He slides my sweatshirt down my body, cupping my ass as he pulls me to him.

"What kind of moron am I to help you put clothes on instead of removing them?" He teasingly lets out a sigh. "Go on to bed and wait for me there. I'll clean up here, make sure everything's locked, and deal with this mess before joining you," he gestures at the wet patch on the front of his sweats.

Standing on my tippy toes, I plant a kiss on his chin.

"Don't make me wait for too long," I throw over my shoulder as I make my way to the bedroom. The house is silent, and as I pass through the living room, the faint glow of an electronic clock lets me know we're nearing three in the morning.

Atop the stairs, I pad quietly toward the girls' room, peeking through the cracked door at their tiny sleeping forms, choking on a laugh at seeing Astrum being cuddled on both sides by Eliza and Clara, the three of them squeezed in a twin sized bed.

From vicious beast to cuddly teddy, how the mighty have fallen, I snicker to myself.

My bedroom is as dark as the rest of the house, and I don't bother with any lights. My eyes already feel sore after being awake for so long and the crying fit I had at the bakery. I quickly wash my face and my teeth in the bathroom sink with just the soft light of the mirror for guidance.

Taking off my clothes, I dump them unceremoniously in the laundry basket, while running a washcloth through water, then clean away the remnants of my desire wetting the top of my thighs.

I notice the door moving with the corner of my eye, a hand holding a T-shirt appearing through the opening. "Got you something to sleep in," he tells me with a yawn.

Looks like the long day caught up with us both.

I take the sunny yellow T-shirt from him and hold it in front of the mirror light so I can read what is printed on it.

"I'm great in bed. I can sleep for days," I snort a laugh at him. "That so? Well, come on then, let's take a closer look at those amazing skills of yours."

I shrug the T-shirt on, inhaling the scent of his cologne deep into my lungs, tasting the hints of dark roasted coffee and something that is uniquely Cole's on my tongue, and making my way toward the bed.

Much like last night, his naked chest welcomes me, bathed in the dim nightlight, the faint scratch marks I gifted him taking nothing away from his rugged beauty.

He lifts the cover on my side of the bed, and I allow myself a single second of freaking out since my mind already decided he has a side in my bed before sliding inside the cool sheets.

My cheek on his shoulder, arm laying flat on his chest, leg thrown over his abdomen, I whisper a faint, "Good night, meus bellator!" before succumbing to a deep sleep, knowing he's there to fight all my demons, to protect me.

Even from myself.

Chapter Thirty-Four

Lalah

I'm sprawled on a chair waiting for our lazy late-afternoon coffee. Maevis is sitting opposite me, bundled up in a pink cashmere scarf, knee bouncing up and down.

"Stop it!" Annalise, sitting to my right, says. "You're making me nervous."

"I can't help it. I'm so excited!" Mae squeals and claps her hands.

"So am I, and anxious, and panicking, and what was I thinking going for it?" Anna trails off, scrubbing her palms over her face.

"You were thinking this is your dream and in less than two months it'll become reality. You've got this." I chime in and push the bundle of ten pictures toward her. "I think these shelves would work best for that bohemian look you're going for."

She takes the pictures and studies them, one by one, her teeth sinking into her nude-colored bottom lip. I love her lipsticks. Every day she's wearing a different color, and every color tells us the mood she's in.

I wish I could pull off lipstick the way she does, but unfortunately, I'll end up looking like the Joker by the end of the day.

"I love them. Thanks, Lalah," she murmurs, eyes still studying the pictures in front of her.

"They did a really good job with my own library. I think it'll look great in the end, all the different carvings on the shelves, based on the genre. I can't wait for opening day."

"Neither can I. I'm going to put together a couple of recipes with To be Read Cafe in mind. You're gonna blow Lost Hope out of the park." Maevis smiles, the cogs in her brain working, mixing ingredients together.

"Alright, enough about me. There's only so much I can take before I explode with nerves. One day at a time. I reached my quota for today."

Mae straightens on the chair, palms pressed flat on the table. "Thanksgiving day. What's the plan?"

My eyes roll. We've been discussing Thanksgiving to death for the past week.

"How many of us?" I ask since the number keeps changing.

"Well, Drake and I will be there. Hopefully, they won't have a shift scheduled. I'm working my notice at Forrest Falls Care Home until mid-December, but I still have leave days left. I've put through a request for that weekend. The only wild card is Drake. And your Cole," she says, forefinger pointed at me.

My eyes narrow at her while my fingers thrum on the table. "Just Cole, he's not mine."

"Riiiiight, tell that to someone who'll believe you," Mae pokes her tongue at me.

"Seriously, we're... ugh, I don't know what we are. We live together, you're all aware of the circumstances, and we go on dates, and..." My mouth clamps shut as a teenager places my steaming hazelnut latte in front of me.

"Thanks, Audrey," The three of us say as one.

"Let me know if you need anything else." She smiles as she rushes back to the coffee station.

I curl my hands around the mug and take a sip of milky goodness. My eyes search for the girls, who are playing just behind Maevis, in the fun corner of the diner. Eliza is elbows deep in one of her fairytale books while Clara runs circles around her with a rainbow unicorn in hand, making neighing noises every once in a while.

Satisfied all is well and accounted for in the Hart-world, my focus goes back to the conversation at hand. "Cole has a shift ending on Thanksgiving, and then he's off for forty-eight hours."

"You're changing the subject." Annalise grins.

"I'm keeping to the subject at hand. Thanksgiving day. Isn't your husband making Cole's schedule?"

"They're on the same schedule. So let's hope nothing happens, and they can keep to it. They're eternally understaffed."

"He said as much. Cole was excited to use his skills and help the community. I'm happy he mentioned he had his EMT and firefighting certifications when enlisted – or whatever the military version of that is – when you were there."

"Believe me, Drake was over the moon to have him recruited. I know you've still not a hundred percent defrosted toward Drake, but he'll look over Cole and train him adequately."

The gist of it all is the fire station in Lost Hope is a sort of HQ for the small firehouses around the county. With the remote locations in the mountains, treacherous roads around, and a high risk of wildfires occurring, the local hub has specialized teams. Cole and Drake are part of the Wildland Firefighting Team.

"I don't know how you do it," I say, my voice somber. "How you're not going crazy with worry every time he walks out the door. Just thinking of Cole fighting a beast of a fire makes chills run up and down my spine."

Cole's whole life has been dedicated to serving and keeping people safe. Not just civilians but also his unit in the military, and it warms my heart to know he'll be able to find a semblance of the camaraderie he had in the Marines now with his firefighting team.

The training is intensive, especially since he'll have more responsibilities than just those specific to his specialized team. But there's this spark in his eyes, an excitement breathing more life into him, and I'm just happy being here, cheering him on. Even though I'm terrified for his safety to my very marrow.

"It's not for the faint of heart, that's for sure. I celebrate every moment with him and appreciate everything he does to keep people safe," she muses. "He was worried Cole wouldn't join though, after Tatum spilled the beans of your accident."

"I honestly thought Cole would plummet Drake to the ground, he was so furious." Mae rubs her forefinger and thumb on her chin. "Not that I blame him. I wanted to do it myself back in July."

"I think Drake's paid enough for his lapse in judgment. I've forgiven him. Measures are now taken to ensure all calls are being responded to, even if it's just to verify their legitimacy. I'm just happy I could convince Cole not to miss this opportunity because of me."

Both of them nod next to me, our eyes downcast to our drinks. That day back in July has affected all of us, not just me, and continues to have consequences.

"I'm going to knead up a storm of every kind of dough that can be frozen and baked at a later date without affecting quality. Two of my employees want a chance to earn extra cash, so they'll mind the bakery for the weekend, and Suga'High will be closed only for Thanksgiving Day."

"That sounds great, hun. You deserve a break." I smile her way.

"Tatum said his garage will run with minimum staff, again paid volunteers, and it's only open for emergencies." Mae informs us, and I can't hide the twinkle in my eyes at the blush painting her cheeks.

"Jackson Camden is on the list, too." I mention, letting Mae breathe before jumping on the M&T train.

"Doesn't he own JC's Pour?" Annalise asks, twirling a wavy caramel lock around her fingers.

"He does. I'm told he served for eight years with Cole and Tate in the Corps. I'm really excited to meet him since they speak very fondly of him."

"We've been to JC's." Annalise says, pointing a finger between her and Maevis. "The bar is really not what you expect. Very... seductive atmosphere, sultry even. The half-naked bartenders are just the cherry on the chocolate sundae." She winks mischievously at me.

"We definitely need to go then." I laugh.

"Maddox and Ryker," Maevis announces, her pen scratching over the paper where she's keeping a tally out of everyone joining us.

Much to Cole's and Tatum's grumblings, the chief deputy and his son are also going to join us. Drake pleaded and pleaded with me, Mae, and Annalise, and after some back and forth, we concluded he's welcome to come.

He has been nothing but polite and neighborly with me whenever we bump into each other in town since the day he became well acquainted with my cast-enclosed fist.

I won't be his best friend anytime soon, but I also don't harbor any ill feelings toward him. I just sincerely hope he has learned his lesson.

"That's all?" Annalise asks on a sip of her orange, mango, and cinnamon tea.

"Sawyer's joining us, too. I really look forward to getting to know her better. I've had more chats with Selena over video calls than with her, and she lives here."

"Sawyer is lovely. All the kids in Lost Hope love her."

"Clara is definitely a big fan," I say with a wide smile on my lips.

Clara is an amazing little girl, and we started taking her three days a week to the Daycare Center, so she gets to socialize with other children her age under Sawyer's amazing guidance.

Currently, the Daycare Center is funded through a collaboration between the local school and the city council, but the funds are not nearly enough for modern amenities and all the tools and toys children aged two to five need.

A little bird told me she is planning to take matters into her own hands and is pushing to open a private daycare through private funding.

I was open to investing before Clara ever landed in my life, but I'm more determined than ever to make Sawyer's dream a reality now.

I just need her to get her business proposal done and submitted to the Mayor. And I planned to use our little Thanksgiving get-together to nudge her in the right direction.

"So, who's taking one for the team and hosting all of us?" Mae asks. "We can use the bakery, but would have to lug all the food over there since I'm not tainting my ovens with turkey grease."

"We do need a big space. It's, what, thirteen of us?"

"Well, ten adults and three kids. I'm happy to volunteer my house."

"It's settled then." We all grin at each other.

My nose buries in my latte to hide the moisture in my eyes. Truth is, I do have a lot to be thankful for this year.

Especially all my friends in Lost Hope and my home invaders.

During the past month, the Hayes' have brought me into their fold and they're all holding on tight in their own way. Between Cole, Blake, and I, Eliza is being homeschooled until the start of second semester when she'll be enrolled at Lost Hope's Elementary School.

We spent the past month ensuring they had my address as their residence until they find something more permanent and get all the relevant documents in order.

One particularly displeasing conversation for me since I really don't want them to leave.

Ever.

I thought having people in my space would be claustrophobic and suffocating. Instead, it's like they were all made to be in my home.

They fit into my life as if when I was born, pieces of my soul ripped away and attached to each of their souls, and now they've been returned to me.

Blake's still trying to find a job and has been moping around for the past month as there are few jobs in the area where he could use his hard-earned diploma.

He studied Sales and Marketing in college and wants a job where he can put his skills to good use, but most of the jobs he has found so far require him to either relocate or work from home.

He's still holding out hope for something in Billings. Although not opposed to traveling from time to time if needed, he also doesn't want to be away from his family for too long.

I might know of a job for him, not quite sales and marketing, but a lot of those skills he gained are transferable. The only problem is, I would have to come clean to them on what I actually do for a living.

Guilt and feelings of extreme selfishness plague me. I'm not sure what I'm waiting for before opening up to them with this last piece of me, but I'm not ready for that yet.

As for Cole and I, we're living in a blissful gray area. We act like we are together, but every time he tries to initiate the dreaded define-the-relationship conversation, I dodge and avoid it like a professional running back.

I'm scared he will offer me the life of my dreams with added bonuses in Eliza, Clara, and Blake, then take it all away. I came to hate the word exclusive since it seems I end up being the only one adhering to said exclusivity.

So we continue sleeping in the same bed in each other's arms every night. We go on dates, just the two of us; we create new rituals just for us, like having a hot chocolate before bed where for an hour we talk about everything and nothing.

And not having sex.

Since I dodge and avoid the conversation of us, he withholds sex.

He is oh so generous with all the orgasms he dishes out, but refuses to let me touch him or put my mouth on him apart from those breathtaking kisses we share.

It's been killing me.

He didn't come right out and say it, but I'm fairly certain whenever glints of stubbornness flash in his eyes. He'll only give me what I want from him physically once I give him what he wants verbally.

So in limbo, we live.

Chapter Thirty-Five

Cole

With my elbows planted firmly on my knees, my face in an impassive mask, I take in my opponent. She's mimicking my posture, hazel eyes hard and unyielding. Her red-tipped fingernail presses on her bottom lip, and I barely stifle a groan.

"Queen takes Bishop at C3," she grins, her plump lips tipping upwards with arrogance. All I want to do is sink my teeth into her lips and my cock to the hilt into her.

But I won't. Not until she's open to us being more. Not until she's willing to sit down and have that conversation.

I lower my eyes to the marble chessboard separating us. The strategist in me assesses all potential moves ahead. I've been playing chess my whole life, and yet I find myself being bested by a novice.

Oh, she's good, I'll give her that, and in time she'll be great. What she's also good at is distraction, underhanded ploys. Like the spaghetti strap white top, she's wearing. With no fucking bra and those pert nipples of hers saluting me from under the thin cotton.

My palm rubs at my scruff, and I shuffle on my seat, trying to conceal the erection tenting my sweats. My fingers pinch the white king harder than necessary as I move it two squares closer to the rook.

"Closing ranks, meus bellator? A bit defensive, aren't you?" The little minx taunts, puffing those mouth-watering tits of hers in my face.

Goddammit.

"Seemed like kingside castling was needed with how much of a reckless wanderer your Queen is," I grunt, keeping my eyes fixed on the board since my body is primed and ready to jump her.

She snickers and then opens her sweet mouth and leaves me dumbstruck. "Why were you a manwhore?"

I sputter and my eyes spring to hers. There's no judgment in her beautiful face, just curiosity and a hint of cautiousness.

"I was never a manwhore, Supernova." I sigh and decide this is as good a moment as ever to spill my guts. "My mom, Romina, was fifteen when she gave birth to me, and my father, Colton, nearly eighteen. A shotgun wedding and his high school graduation later, they both decided the best thing for him was to enlist in the Marine Corps... Your move." I urge her.

If I'm reliving my past for her, might as well do it over chess. Her fingers move nimbly, clutching her knight, dropping a threat to my Queen. Bold little firecracker, bold and reckless.

"What happened after he enlisted?" she asks, her eyes not leaving mine, open and earnest.

"The enlisting guaranteed them a stable income and a house on base. When Dad was going through basic training, Mom was caring for me and studying to pass her GEDs."

"Your mom sounds like an amazing woman, determined, ambitious."

"She was. She had me young, yes, but they both wanted me and loved me since the moment they found out she was pregnant. They also loved each other fiercely. My dad was deployed, more often than not, but Mom always made sure I knew just how much he loved and missed me."

I look back at the board and capture her knight with my bishop. This move leaves my other rook unprotected, but I'm curious to see how she'll capitalize on it.

I lean back in my armchair and look out the window at the falling snow. "She would tell me stories about his adventures, his courage, his bravery, and his big, golden heart. To say I grew up hero-worshiping my father is an understatement. He may not have spent every breathing moment at our side, but we were a family. We were loved, and we were happy."

My eyes close on their own accord, and my heart seizes in my chest. Her warm weight presses on my thighs as she sits in my lap, arms wrapped around my neck. My forehead rests on hers as I continue my story.

"Our happy family ended on a cold, winter day when I was eight. On that day, two somber men dressed in military uniforms came to inform us that Colton Hayes had been killed in action. Ripped from the arms of his loving wife and son at only twenty-five. The anguished wails coming from my mom as she crumbled to her knees still send shivers down my spine, just thinking back to that day."

"Oh, Cole. I'm so, so sorry for your loss," she whispers, her fingers playing with the hairs at my nape while I'm lost to my childhood memories.

I was still loved. Once mom pulled herself out of the shock of losing dad and after going through the funeral and us moving from base with her parents, she doubled down in loving me enough for the both of them. She continued telling me stories of him, making sure I knew the great man my father was.

But where our home was filled with joy and anticipation for his return, grief and despair surrounded her after we lost him. As much as she tried to hide it from me, to shield me from her heartbreak, I could feel it like a living, breathing thing, the third member of our little family replacing dad.

We lived with my grandparents for a year after, and during that time, my mom worked a lot of hours and saved a pretty penny. That, combined with my father's benefits and insurance after his death, allowed her to buy a three-bedroom house. The same house I put on the market just weeks ago, back in Richmond.

"Right, where was I? When I was thirteen, my mom attended a bachelorette party in Atlantic City with some work friends. She never went out, never dated. She always said my dad was the love of her life and I was his spitting image but with her eyes."

"And what beautiful eyes you two share," she murmurs and kisses each of my eyelids while plastering herself closer to me.

"I was her best friend, and she was mine until the very last day of her life." I give her a sad smile, letting her see how much I miss the power that was Romina Hayes-Hart.

"Anyway," I continue, "She fell pregnant with Blake during that weekend. I wasn't quite sure what to make of a baby brother or that my mom didn't know the name of his father. But being the resourceful woman she was, she used it as a lesson in the birds' and the bees' conversation with me. And as a cautionary tale in alcohol consumption."

Lalah's tinkling laugh fills the library, the vibration of her chest rippling through mine.

"When she gave birth to the menace, and I met him for the first time, I loved him instantly. God forbid he ever knows that. He'll never let me forget it."

Lalah sighs as she nuzzles her face in the crook of my neck. She's all wrapped around me, fueling strength into me to keep going.

"I swore then and there to be the best big brother I could for him and a worthy role model. I gained my second best friend only hours after he was born."

"And you are, meus bellator, you are." Her lips mouth on the skin of my neck, causing my cock to stir once again in my sweats.

"I hope so. My mom was bursting with both pride and devastation when I informed her at my high school graduation that I decided to follow in my father's footsteps and enlist. I met Tatum there and Jackson, as you already know. I knew in my first year I'd be a lifer. The camaraderie and family I found there filled the parts of my heart that were empty since my father's passing."

"The Marines were your chosen family."

"They were. I also realized a long-term, committed relationship wasn't in the cards for me. I wouldn't... couldn't risk putting my family through the exact same thing we've been through. So I became Mr. Serial Monogamist. Date casually between deployments, one woman at a time."

Her tiny frame stiffens in my lap, and I push her chin up with two fingers so I can drown in her hazel eyes.

"You sure you want to hear it all?" I check.

A glint of determination washes over her eyes, and her chin pushes against my finger in a sharp nod. I kiss her forehead, rest my chin on the top of her head, and continue.

"They all knew whatever we had, came with an expiration date. I'm not an asshole. I cared for them and respected them, but couldn't allow anyone to consume my thoughts to the point where I'd be off my game. My team, my brothers, depended on me to keep a clear head and get us home safely through each deployment, through each mission."

"Semper Fidelis!" She exhales.

"Semper Fidelis. As life would have it, my mom and Blake's father reunited about three years ago. Alecs Hart, a high school history teacher, moved to Richmond from New Jersey after a messy divorce, with his seven-year-old daughter Eliza and one-month-old baby Clara."

"Whaaaat?" Lalah shrieks, pushing away from where she is nestled against me, palms cupping my jaw. "Blake and the girls are half-siblings?"

I grin and wink at her before nodding. "They are. Talk about serendipity. Alecs was married to Claire for twelve years before their divorce. She got addicted to opioids after she fell on ice and hurt her spine, leaving her with chronic back pain."

"God, that's awful. Drug addiction is no joke. The pain they all went through..."

"Yeah. Unfortunately, she escalated to heavier drugs, and Alecs had to divorce her when Claire was arrested for driving under the influence with Eliza in the backseat. She was also pregnant with Clara at the time. The judge ordered her to rehab. She'd commit for ninety days, get released, relapse, and repeat. It was nothing short of a miracle that Clara was not born addicted to drugs."

"Sweet baby Clara, a fighter from the womb."

I can't hide the prideful grin I have for my little sister. A fighter, indeed. "Despite her addiction, Claire did love her girls. She just loved drugs more. She gave birth to Clara and signed her rights away to Alecs. She decided her presence in the girls' lives would be more harmful to them than her absence."

"And that's how Alecs got to Richmond," Lalah concludes for me.

"Exactly. My mom bumped into him at a deli near the high school and recognized each other immediately from the night in Atlantic City. He admitted mom was the one who got away and regretted for a long time not exchanging names or phone numbers."

"Must've gotten the surprise of his life to meet Blake."

"Did he ever. He was both overjoyed and saddened to find out about my brother. He did legally recognize Blake as his son, but Blake refused to change his name to Hart. He kept his surname Hayes, as his way to honor my mom and me. Only for my mom to marry Alecs five months after they reunited and adopt Clara and Eliza."

"And now they're yours."

"And now they're mine. It was humorous for me to look at Alecs as a father figure since he was only ten years older than me, but I came to respect and love the man in the time I knew him. My mom was happy and loved until her very last moment of life, and he was a great part of that happiness."

Her sniffles make me stop, and I run my thumb on her cheek, drying the tears she's spilling for my family.

"Don't cry, Supernova. I can't bear your tears."

"I'm sorry," she sniffles once more. "It's breaking my heart you lost so much..."

"I did, and I didn't. My contract was finished, and I was up to renew it. When the lawyer told me my mom and Alecs trusted me to care for and to love the girls in case the unthinkable happened, it was a no brainer for me." I draw in a big breath, exhaling the sadness from my chest.

"The first three months after their deaths were difficult, with the collective grief of our loss, my struggles adapting to civilian life, and finding my footing as a parental figure to the troublemakers. But I vowed to myself they'll know every single day they are loved, and wanted, and protected. So I figured a fresh start would work best for us."

I lift her head from my chest to once again look into her eyes. "Our fresh start brought me to you. It wasn't just Tatum being in Lost Hope factoring in my decision. It was you, too. I figured the girls deserve to live in a place where a stranger cared enough to order flowers and dinner for other strangers in their time of need."

"Cole…" she starts, but I don't let her finish. My mouth is on her, my palm cups her breasts, and my fingers find their way inside her sleeping shorts.

Wet heat engulfs me, and I let Lalah's cries of pleasure heal all my hurts.

Chapter Thirty-Six

Lalah

"Good, this is a freaking disaster! What the hell was I thinking? I can't do this," I complain to the pale woman staring at me from my bathroom mirror. Out of all the stupid ideas I've had in my life, this is winning first place hands down.

I double over in pain over the vanity, the cramps in my tummy making my knees buckle. Periods are devil's work. All I want to do is crawl back into bed, a hot water bottle pressed to my lower abdomen, and hide from the world.

Instead, here I am awake at four in the morning trying to get enough food ready to feed an army. I finish with my morning routine, hobbling around and swearing up a storm under my breath. *Yeah, today's going to be pure hell.*

Cole's finishing up a twenty-four-hour shift, so he should get back home in about two hours. The plan is for him to get some sleep until mid-afternoon. Then he can have a cup of coffee and get ready before everyone else is due to arrive around four.

So that leaves me with about twelve hours of misery. I wish I could just leave. Get in my car, warm the seats on the hottest setting, and hide there. Alas, there are two excited little girls I don't want to disappoint.

I quickly down a coffee and start pulling things out of the fridge and pantry before I go over the menu in my head. The turkey should give me the least amount of trouble since it just needs to be stuffed and stuck in the oven, so I leave it for later.

Deciding to start with the pies so I can free my oven for the turkey, I stick a pair of headphones on my head as I go for my normal classical music playlist, select "Winter" and let the music distract me from my pain.

I set six pie dishes on the island, so when the pie crust is cool and ready, I can just start rolling it out and transfer it into the dishes. The sound of violins chasing a crescendo in my headphones stops me in my tracks.

My eyes close and my head tips back, feeling tears springing from under my lashes and falling down my cheeks. I wipe at my tears with a paper towel and let the music run through me.

Yeah, that's another lovely side effect. The heightened emotions starting the waterworks out of nowhere; a commercial about a happy dog? Here, have some tears. The sound of violins in concert? More tears. Can't open a jar of pickles to tame the out-of-the-blue craving? Rage with a side of tears.

I'd normally lock myself out in the library, surrounded by hot water bottles, and drown in as many hot chocolates as I can drink while I nap and cry until the worst has passed. But that's not a luxury I can afford anymore. Maybe the only disadvantage of the situationship I found myself in.

That's exactly how Cole finds me when he gets home. Elbow deep in apple pies, crying a river to the gods of violins. He gently takes my headphones off and cups my face in his palms, his thumbs racing to catch the unrelenting tears. *Fucking hell, this is embarrassing.*

"What happened, babe? Why are you crying?" He asks, brows scrunched in concern. I sniffle, trying to mentally find the leaky pipe and shut it closed. My shoulders lift in a sharp shrug and my face plants in his chest.

He slides one hand into my hair, cupping my neck, with the other one tenderly rubbing circles on my back. When I finally win my battle against my hormones and feel I have a proper handle on my emotions, I push gently away from him, and give him a shy smile, rolling my eyes.

"Nothing," I shrug again, then hurry to explain at the disbelief in his eyes. "I really mean nothing. It seems we have another guest to dinner tonight, and Auntie Flo gets the best of my emotions."

His face is a comical mix of relief and worry. Relief at understanding nothing out of the ordinary is hurting me right now. Worry, well, probably for his life. *He's a smart man, this one is.*

"Is there anything I can do to help?"

"Nah. I've got it handled." Lifting on my toes, I give him a soft peck on the lips. "Go get some sleep, and I'll see you when you wake up."

"Are you sure?" he asks, plastering me to his chest once again. "I don't mind helping you. I can sleep later or tonight."

I tilt my head and take his handsome face in. He's dead on his feet, so there's no way I'll ask him to stay and help, even if my knees are so weak from pain I can barely stand.

"Those pretty purple bags under your eyes disagree. Go to sleep. That's an order, Marine," I tell him playfully.

"Yes, ma'am." He grins at me. "I'd sleep better if you'd come to bed with me," he whispers in my ear, trailing kisses down my neck. I squirm in his arms and push away from him.

Fun fact, when in so much pain, getting turned on is the worst idea. Your body becomes overstimulated, your nerves skip the pleasure and go straight to intense pain.

It seems I don't hide the grimace on my face very well because his eyes narrow, glinting dangerously, daring me to lie to him. "You're in pain. And don't bother denying it. I wasn't asking."

I shrug again. There's nothing I can say to that. Yes, I'm in pain, but that's my burden as a woman to bear. Life doesn't pause or stop until I'm feeling all peachy again. If every woman would take a break every single month when this nastiness hits, the world would be pure chaos.

We grind our teeth, literally pull our big girl panties on, stuff our faces full of chocolate, and go about our day as usual. There aren't special concessions or sick days, since it's simply the way a woman's body works. Unfair as fuck, but the expectation everywhere is business as usual.

"Go to sleep, Cole. There's nothing either of us can do about it, and you're no good to me in the kitchen if you fall asleep with your face in my stuffing."

"Oh, how I wish I'd fall asleep with my face in your stuffing," he mumbles and bends down to kiss me. I burst out laughing and stop him with the heel of my palm on his forehead.

"Alright, pervert. Keep your face on the pillow instead. You need your beauty sleep." I scrunch my nose so he can see my displeasure at the marks his tiredness has left around those pale green eyes I can't get enough of.

He barks a laugh at me, kisses my forehead and the tip of my nose, then trudges his way to our bedroom. *Aye, our bedroom. I'm still reserving the right to my one second of freak out for that.*

I tap my phone for a rock music playlist, as cooking while crying is simply not an efficient way to go about my day, and start shoving pies in the oven. Luckily, my oven's big enough to have four pies baking at the same time.

I place the cooling rack on the breakfast nook since the girls will simply have oatmeal with bananas when they wake up, and they can eat in the dining room.

I get the ingredients for two biscuit chocolate pies because I've definitely earned them. They may not be traditional Thanksgiving desserts, but they are a tame-the-lady-dragon cheat. So it's a good thing I'm making them for myself only.

Not soon after I have them ready to be loaded into the oven, my phone vibrates on the countertop, alerting me to someone being at the gate.

The video feed shows Maevis's little SUV, so I get the gates to open and limp my way to my front door just in time to see her and Annalise getting out of the car.

My eyebrow lifts in question since I wasn't expecting them until late this afternoon, not at six thirty in the morning. "Aren'cha' just a tad early?"

"Nope. We're right on time. Let us in, would ya? It's freezing out here," Annalise quips, then slips inside past me.

"Morning, Lalah." Mae smiles at me, giving me a quick shoulder rub and a squeeze in passing.

"Seriously? What are you guys doing here?" I ask confused.

"We're the cavalry. We have been summoned, and we're ready to report for duty." Annalise grins at me.

"Mother of all pies, this smells amazing," Mae says as she enters the kitchen, beelining straight to the oven.

"Two apple and two pumpkin pies baking. Should be another thirty minutes until ready. There are two pecan and two chocolate pies on the counter still to be baked," I explain, waving my hand in the general direction of the pies.

"So, talk us through your system," Annalise demands.

"I thought you guys were coming in later and were bringing some side dishes. What exactly is it you're doing here, not that I don't love to see you?" I push the subject once more since no one has given me an actual answer.

"We're here to take over cooking from you and get your living and dining rooms decorated for this afternoon. We'll do our side dishes here, too, including my famous banana bread." Annalise winks at Mae over her shoulder, causing her sister-in-law to roll her eyes in response.

"She makes the most amazing banana bread I ever ate. Regardless of how many times I'm trying to recreate the recipe for Suga'High, I just can't get it right," Mae whines.

"Sorry lovey, I'm taking the secret with me to my grave." She smirks. "Once To be Read Cafe is open, we'll make a deal. You'll let me use your kitchen at the bakery so I can make it to sell at the cafe, and I'll bake extras for you as a special once a week."

Maevis narrows her eyes at Annalise, then seems to seriously consider her offer. "You've got yourself a deal."

"Now that's all settled in the land of the Barlowes, why are you taking over from me? I may not be a trained pastry chef like our Mae here, but I can pull Thanksgiving dinner." I glare, even though deep down I'm happy for the company.

My pain hasn't lessened since I woke up this morning, and with their help, I'll be able to get everything done much faster and have a laydown before everyone descends on my house.

"Don't shoot the hired help. We have been instructed to send you to bed wiiiith…" Mae says while rummaging in a massive tote bag and pulling out a plush purple hot water bottle, "the miracle cure," she finishes, thrusting it at me.

I fumble catching it and note it's actually hot.

"Get going then. We'll get everything ready or prepped, as can't really mash potatoes hours before dinner. We'll get the turkey in the oven around noon, then leave to pretty ourselves up. Just make sure to wake up around lunchtime and baste it."

My heart warms at their kindness. I'd protest, but I'm really close to collapsing, so with a heartfelt hug and a whispered thank you, I leave them to work their magic in the kitchen, and make my way to the bedroom before the waterworks start again.

I'm sure Cole's behind all this. It astounds me how observant he is, how attentive to my every need or want. After this evening is over, maybe it's time to be brave and take a leap of faith in his direction. I'm a thirty-year-old woman, and I need to start owning my shit.

Worst-case scenario: he breaks my heart.

I've picked myself up before, I can do it again, I think to myself, but I know if Cole does break me, it won't be as easy to pull myself back together since it's not just him I'll be losing.

Best-case scenario: I get everything I've ever wanted. Someone to love me for me. Someone who wants me. Someone to share my best and my worst days with. Someone who accepts me.

He's a risk worth taking.

My bedroom is dark, with only a soft glow on the floor so I can see my way to the bed. We've installed some red glowing lights on the baseboards, emitting enough light to see but not so much to disturb our sleep.

It was mostly done to accommodate the times Clara woke up in the middle of the night and wanted to cuddle with us. In my sleep-addled brain, I stubbed my little toes more times than I care for, as did Cole, so measures had to be taken.

Another change to my bedroom was him moving all his clothes into the empty second closet and Astrum permanently moving into the girls' bedroom.

I honestly think he prefers being with them now, maybe because he sees them as pups worthy of his protection or maybe because he knows I have Cole to chase away my nightmares.

I slip inside the sheets and shift around until my back hits the warm wall of sleeping muscles, and place the velvety hot water bottle under my tummy, sighing in relief. Cole's arm coils around my waist, pulling me under him as I rest on my belly, knees tucked in around my second source of heat.

He folds his entire body around me, cocooning me in his embrace, nose buried in my hair. "Took you long enough," he whispers, voice rough and sleepy. By his even breaths, I know he didn't actually wake up, so I keep myself as still as possible, and let his warmth lull me to sleep.

Chapter Thirty-Seven

Cole

The living room is in chaos with people milling about oohing and ahhing over Lalah's home. Two toddlers run around trying to get every adult's attention, luring them in one at a time, and the background music plays softly in all the downstairs spaces.

I keep throwing worried looks at Lalah, as she sits curled on one end of the couch with a pillow on her lap. I was surprised to see her wear a black knitted sweater-dress that looks painted onto her.

With a deep V collar and thigh-high heeled leather boots, she's every man's wet dream. Except she's mine. And she's out-of-this-world beautiful regardless if she's wearing a dress or her uniform of leggings and large, funny sweatshirts.

It knocks the wind out of me to see her wearing a form-fitting outfit. As my eyes travel up her chest, with a respectful pause on the perky breasts peeking from under the collar of her dress, I get my second surprise at seeing her red-painted lips.

Images of those lips wrapped around my cock, leaving red streaks on me as she bobs her head up and down my length keep popping in my head.

I constantly have to force myself to recite baseball stats in my head so I don't have to explain my slacks tenting in the middle of our Thanksgiving party.

I thought I left those days behind me with the discipline instilled during my days in the military, but it just shows how little I know. I was always in awe when Mom told me stories about the love she and my father had shared.

As I reached adulthood I believed more and more those were just that, simple stories, and her remembering their feelings for each other much more fondly with him gone.

But since I met Lalah, I actually understand what my mom was talking about.

She's all I think about, day or night.

She's all I see everywhere I look.

Her smokey eyes catch mine, and it fascinates me how her eyes keep changing color based on the most random things, like the way she dresses, or if she's had too much coffee or the brightness of the light in the room.

Best of all is reading the way she feels at any given moment. She has a great poker face, but her chameleonic eye color gives her away.

Deep jade-green when she's excited and happy. Dark swirls of velvety chocolate-brown when she's turned on. Moss-green when she is close to crying, or amber flecks sparkling to life when she's ready to rip me a new one, like the fire burning inside her sends fiery sparks to her irises.

I would love nothing more than to look into her eyes for the rest of my life.

Of course, I can't actually express my feelings and wants. Not because I don't want to. Because she won't let me. We've been playing a cat-and-mouse game for the past five weeks and I'm slowly, slowly reaching a breaking point.

I refuse to have sex with her until she agrees to be mine. I don't want her to think my feelings are muddled by sex. And with how strongly attraction crackles between us, another thing to avoid is her thinking sex is all I want from her.

She gives me a small smile that doesn't reach her eyes, and my alarm bells go off. The paleness of her face also speaks of her discomfort, regardless of how much she's tried to hide it with makeup.

She was in a significant amount of pain all day, even as she slept next to me. I've done my best to keep her warm as she kept squirming around and giving small moans of pain.

If it were up to me, I would've canceled the whole thing, but she was adamant she wanted to move forward with the original plan.

I also know she's not entirely comfortable having so many people in her space, as much as she wants them here. So I'm keeping a close eye on her.

She might not have agreed outright to be mine, but she is. And my job is to ensure she's happy and comfortable at all times.

I move behind the sofa and fist her sleek ponytail, forcing her head back, and I bend down at the waist, peppering her face in kisses, letting her giggles coax out my joy.

"Ewww, you guys are disgusting!" quips Eliza from where she's sitting next to Lalah. I turn my head in her direction at the same time Lalah does.

"That so?" I ask, and we both pounce on Eliza, tickling her and kissing her face, rewarded with peals of her delighted laughter and protests.

"Looks like you're as disgusting as we are then," I tell her and take a step back, so she can catch her breath, taking in her shining silvery eyes and her red face with slight lipstick marks, courtesy of Lalah.

I love seeing my little sisters happy. My mom showered both Blake and me with kisses and hugs. So I am not shying away either from these displays of affection toward the girls. If anything, with them it's even more important to make it known they are loved and they are wanted. Eliza, especially.

Clara doesn't remember her biological mom and most likely will never remember my mom and her dad either. But Eliza does.

And Eliza knows her mom willingly walked away from them.

It may have been out of love, but the intricacies of addiction are not something easily understood by a ten-year-old.

All she saw was her mom walking away, never to contact her again. Soon after, her father and stepmother died, leaving her too.

So I'm doing my damnedest every day to show her I love her, and I am beyond honored to be not just her older stepbrother but a paternal figure in her life.

I try every day to show up for my sisters. Not because I was appointed guardian and they are an obligation. But because I choose to be here. I choose them every single day and every single hour.

She throws her arms around Lalah's shoulders and hides her little face in the crook of her neck. Lalah rewards me with a genuine smile this time, and I wink at her, content I could make two of my girls happy and at ease.

My phone vibrates in my pocket. A quick peek confirms Jackson arrived, and I open the gates to allow him entry. I make my way to the front door and feel Lalah's hand wrap around my elbow.

"Jackson?" she asks. I confirm with a nod, and see her tapping one handed on her phone a message to Tatum.

I haven't spent quality time with him since four years ago. He came to the funerals, but no one was in the right frame of mind for a proper catch-up.

Jake's like Lalah in a sense. Loyal down to the last cell in his body but distrustful of the people around him, and prefers to keep to himself.

He's not one for keeping in touch more than a quick call on birthdays or for major holidays. But if I ever needed him, he's the type of man to drop everything and come to my aid.

Tatum joins us as I open the front door and take my former teammate in. Not a single hair on his head has changed since I've last seen him.

Dressed in his usual button-down black shirt under a black leather jacket and dark ripped jeans, he flashes us an amused smirk as his silver eyes assess his surroundings.

"Always expected you to retire to a wolf's den, Cap, not the fanciest fortress in the woods," he greets me with a half hug and a pat on my back.

"He's completed his transformation from beast to prince charming." Tatum jumps on the taunting, throwing his arm around Jake's other shoulder. *Nothing new here.*

"All right, boys. Settle down." Lalah smiles, her gaze bouncing to each of us. "Goddammit, be honest, is the level of hotness a requirement to join the Marines?" she winks.

A growl escapes my chest, and I move away from my friends, pulling her to my side in a flash. Objectively, I know the three of us are all good-looking men. I also know her interests lay in me and no one else, but I can't help the urge to stake my claim on her in front of everyone.

I watch Jake take Lalah in and narrow my eyes in his direction but realize soon enough he's trying to get a read on her, not leering at her. An awkward minute or two passes as they both look at one another, trying to take the other's measure, when Lalah relaxes at my side and steps in front of him, arm extended in his direction.

"It's so nice to meet you. I'm Lalah McAdams. Cole and Tatum have been singing your praises."

He shakes her hand, and I note she doesn't flinch at his touch. I'm so proud of her. She's been getting better and better at being around other people and allowing casual touches. It probably helps there are four of us living with her and we're all very generous with physical affection.

While she was more reserved with Blake and me at the beginning, she had no issues showering my sisters with affection.

Which means her fight-or-flight instincts kick in only around adults. In return, it makes me feel pure, unadulterated rage toward everyone in her life who failed her as a child.

"Nice to meet you too, Lalah. Jackson Camden, friends usually call me Jake or JC." He winks at her, the flirty asshole. "I'm very happy to put a face to the name I've heard so much of."

"How's that?" she asks, her eyes glinting with suspicion.

Definitely, nothing has changed about her love of privacy.

"Nothing bad," Jake quickly corrects. "Tatum has mentioned you quite a lot since you moved here. And Romeo here couldn't shut up about you when he called to invite me."

She gifts both of us with a backhanded slap on our abdomen. "Honestly, you men are worse than women when it comes to gossiping. Come on in, I'm half frozen." She gestures at the entrance, moving aside to let him pass.

"There's a bar next to that window," she points toward it, "and it's a help-yourself sort of situation because I'm a shit hostess and a firm believer of each to their own." She grins at him.

He barks a laugh and points at me. "I like her. Better keep a tight hold, or I might convince her I'm the better choice by the end of the night."

My first instinct is to get in his face, as much as the rational part of me is shouting he's only teasing. Before I can do something I'll probably regret later, Lalah steps into me.

She leers at him, and with the haughtiest look I've ever seen on a woman's face she tells him, "You really think you have a chance, pretty boy? Well then, let's see how well you fare against the dragon holding me captive. Gotta win this girl somehow. The McDreamy hair can only take you so far."

Jake snorts a laugh at me. "You growing scales nowadays, Cap?"

"Who said I was talking about him?" she asks, then sing-songs "Astrum, obsideo!"

Both Tatum and I start laughing as out of nowhere Astrum flies through the air, front paws pressing on Jake's chest, throwing him against the wall, razor-sharp fangs next to his crotch. *Shit!* I cringe. I'm definitely happy he chose my throat each time he went against me.

I don't want the snarling beast anywhere near my jewels with those knives he has for teeth.

"Jesus fucking Christ on a melted cheese cracker!" Jake shouts. "What the fuck?"

"Still think you're the better choice?" Lalah smiles serenely at him while Astrum is growling up a storm. He looks from her to the furry beast and, while we all know he'll easily be able to subdue Astrum now that the element of surprise is gone, he gives her a nod of respect.

He understands her little display of dominance is her way of telling him there's only one man here she has eyes for, and raises his hands in front of his chest, palms facing Lalah in a gesture of surrender.

"I think you're the better choice for him," he smirks and tries to move, but finds out fast enough Astrum isn't deterred.

"Glad we're on the same page. Astrum, cedo." And like the obedient little puppy he thinks he is, all aggression evaporates from him. He takes his seated place at her feet, tail thumping a million miles a minute.

Jake, still with his balls intact, straightens from the wall and slaps my shoulder. "Congratulations, brother! You're one lucky man. Since I've now met all family members, from the fur ones to the feral ones, I think I was promised a drink."

He winks at Lalah and flashes his signature half smirk, heading toward the makeshift bar in the living room, followed closely by Tatum.

"That one's trouble!" Lalah snorts out a laugh, wrinkling that adorable nose of hers in embarrassment. "It is ridiculously funny for me to see the dynamic of your trio though. Tatum the quiet, all grumpy and broody. Jake the tease, oozing mystery and charm. And then, there's you." She waves a hand toward me. "Cole the warrior, calm, unphased, radiating dominance all around you in a ten-mile radius."

"Cole the warrior?" I pin her with my eyes, letting her read there all the dirty, savage things I want to do to her with my dominance.

"You want me to get you to submit to me, Supernova?" I ask her, my voice dropping a couple of octaves, choked out by the desire raging inside of me.

She pushes on her tippy toes and brings her mouth close to mine. "Cole, meus bellator," she murmurs against my lips.

A lustful haze descends over her beautiful orbs before she blinks, and the desire is replaced by a mischievous glint.

She pats my chest with both her palms in a placating gesture. "Down, boy! I'm temporarily closed for business, remember?"

Like an ice bucket dumped on my head, the reminder of the pain she still must be in douses my arousal and I pull her to my chest, squeezing her tightly to me.

"Dinner time, everyone!" Maevis's voice sounds from the entrance to the dining room.

Chapter Thirty-Eight

Cole

The only ones not well on their way to a food coma are Clara and Ryker. Everyone else is spread on various seats in the living room, groaning and moaning. I'm sprawled on the sofa, with Lalah's legs thrown over mine, gently massaging her calves.

I fucking love those thigh-high boots of hers. My dick and I have numerous ideas for what we could do to a naked Lalah. Each one filthier than the last.

I can see her under my eyelids, writhing under me, with her leather-clad legs wrapped around my waist or my shoulders, those thin high heels pressed into my back.

My fist stifles a groan at the images floating around my mind. I really don't need to pop a boner with all these people milling around.

But if the conversation with Lalah doesn't happen sooner rather than later, I'm likely to die of frustration with a healthy side of blue balls.

Ryker's voice brings my focus back to the living room. "DADDY!" he squeals, running toward Maddox, a sippy cup held gingerly in front of him.

"LOOK, DADDY! I'm a good boy and I gots gwape juice!" he yells.

I watch in slow motion as his little excited legs trip over each other. The next thing I know, Ryker is belly down on the cream colored, fluffy rug Lalah has in front of the fireplace, purple juice spilled all over the pale fabric.

Everyone holds their breath for a second until an anguished wail escapes out of the little boy's chest, "Nooooo, Daddy! I maded a mess!" Mae hurries to the kitchen, most likely to bring him a new juice.

He slowly scrambles to his knees, little hands patting the purple puddle on the floor, big, fat tears rolling down his chubby cheeks. Maddox reaches him in three quick strides and heaves him up in his arms.

"It's OK, buddy! Are you hurt?" he asks his son, voice full of fatherly compassion. I may have my reservations regarding him, but he seems to be one hell of a father. I can't help but respect him for it.

Stained purple fingers grip at his white button-down, leaving tiny marks on the pristine fabric in their wake, but he doesn't seem to mind the mess one bit. He's one hundred percent focused on his son, eyes crinkled in concern, as he pats Ryker's little body, ensuring he didn't hurt himself in the fall.

"No, Daddy! I maded a mess." Sobs heave out of Ryker, his tear-stained face turning to Lalah, big, blue puppy eyes swimming with regret. "I sowwy, Lalah!"

She gives him a big wide smile and walks toward them, wiping at his tears and running her thumb affectionately down his cheeks. She leans in close to him as if sharing a secret meant for just the two of them.

"Wanna see a magic trick?" His sobs subside, and his head eagerly nods up and down, eyes rounded in wonder. "Come with me then!" She offers her hand to him, as he starts squirming in his father's hold to be put down.

Maddox gives Lalah a questioning look, but she's fully focused on Ryker, her genuinely amused smile not faltering once on her ruby-red lips.

I truly get his concern. When Clara made her first mess by throwing a handful of oatmeal at Blake, I expected Lalah to at least cringe at the oatmeal smeared on the floors and table since everything she owns seems to be expensive and of high quality.

Instead, she took a couple of banana slices and threw them at Clara, starting a food fight over breakfast and stopping my little sister from a full-blown temper tantrum.

Astrum was only too happy to lick the floors clean in the aftermath.

Lalah takes Ryker's hand and walks him to the kitchen. Armed with a bottle of white vinegar and a roll of paper towels clutched tightly in Ryker's chubby arms, they return soon after to where Maddox is picking up the sippy cup.

The three of them get down on their knees and start wiping the excess juice puddling on the carpet. Everyone else, myself included, watches in amusement as Clara stomps her little feet on the paper towels, never one to be left out of anything.

"OK, little wizard. Now let's take the magic potion and spray it all over the juice," she tells him, showing him how to spread the vinegar on the carpet.

Ryker claps excitedly when the purple fades from bright to a washed-out lilac.

"I'm telling you, kid. If you ever decide on becoming an abstract artist, I'll brag to everyone that I own your very first piece," she jokes and kisses his forehead, running her fingers through his soft curls.

Maddox helps her up and gives her a look full of gratitude. I don't miss the regret flashing in his eyes, so when he looks from her to me, I can't help the arrogant smirk coming to life on my face.

Yup, you fucked that one up. Your loss, my absolute fucking gain.

"I think this is our cue to get going," he tells the room. "This troublemaker has had enough excitement for one night." I get up from the sofa and join them, offering him my hand for a handshake. "Thanks for having us!"

"Thank you for joining. Clara loves spending time with Ryker. Don't forget the leftovers bag Mae put together," I remind him as Lalah picks Ryker up in a hug.

He nods at me before asking the room, "Does anyone need a ride into town?"

"I'll join you if you could drop me home, please." Sawyer claps her dress-covered knees with both palms and stands from the sofa. Tatum's sister is an interesting person, so different from her siblings.

Where Tatum and Selena are both assertive with a hard edge to them, Sawyer has a nurturing, gentle personality, and it shines out of her, from the way she dresses in soft, pastel colors and modest dresses to the way she treats everyone around her, especially children.

She joins us near the fireplace, giving Lalah a hug. "Thank you for the amazing dinner, Lalah."

"Can't really take credit for it. Mae and Anna deserve all the praise. I merely provided the props."

"Nonetheless, thank you. I had a great time. And thank you for the advice. You definitely gave me a lot to think about and the push I needed to set things into motion."

"You'll do great. Can't wait to see your idea come to life. It would help the community so much and benefit both the kiddos and their parents," Lalah responds, giving Sawyer's hand a gentle squeeze.

Maddox looks questioningly at me, and I lift my shoulders briefly in a shrug. I saw the two of them huddled in a corner just before dinner, engrossed in conversation, but I'm not sure what they were talking about.

We accompany them to the entrance once they say their goodbyes to everyone. Maddox guides her with a palm on the small of her back, and I can't help but laugh as we pass a grumbling Tatum.

We watch Maddox fastening in a happily chattering Ryker, then opening the passenger door of his truck, helping Sawyer climb in, when raised voices coming from near the garage have me turn my head in that direction.

Blake, with a hand wrapped around Jake's throat, holds him flush to the wall, shouting in his face. The slam of a car door turns his attention to us, and he quickly drops his hand, walking toward us.

"Your friend is a fucking asshole!" Blake mumbles darkly under his breath as he passes me, going directly for the stairs.

I wonder what all that is about since my brother is usually a happy-go-lucky kind of guy and it takes a lot to rile him up. His weird behavior isn't lost on Lalah either as she tips her head toward me, a questioning look shining in her eyes.

"I'm going to get going, too. Thank you for the hospitality," Jake says as he nears, giving me a half hug and a slap on the back.

"What was that about?" I narrow my eyes at him. It's none of my business really, but it is highly unusual for my brother to be this angry with someone he used to hero worship as a child.

Jake spent most of his free time either at my house or Tatum's, as he doesn't have a family of his own to visit. Blake has always liked both of them and saw them as older brothers. Until Jake fell off the face of Earth for a while there after being discharged.

I noticed their interactions were stunted during the funerals, but we were all shocked and dazed at the time, so I didn't make anything of it.

His face turns serious as he meets my eyes. "Not my story to tell, brother. And don't even try to intimidate the answers out of me. You want to know, you ask him," he tells me in his my-lips-are-sealed voice, and I know I won't be getting anything from him.

Lalah watches both of us intensely, and her face takes an understanding, knowing look, her lips tipping in smugness. It only increases my curiosity. But she can read me as well as I read her, and moves to give Jake a hug goodbye, effectively forcing me to drop the subject.

She whispers something in his ear, the sound too low for me to make out any words. Jake's face pales for a brief second, then the top of his clean shaved cheeks color in red. *What the fuck?!* He whispers back at her, her pretty head nodding here and there, and I've had enough.

I rip her out of his embrace, tuck her into my side under her peals of surprised laughter, and admire the look of pure adoration and mischief adorning her face. "What are you planning to do, Supernova?"

She rolls her sexy eyes at me, and all I want is to drape her over my knees and spank the sass out of her until her pretty pale skin turns fiery red under my palms. My lust is not lost to her either, and the naughty minx laughs even harder.

"Don't you worry, big boy. I promise not to use my powers for evil." She winks seductively at me, and in this moment I wish everyone else would leave, so I can have her all to myself and convince her once and for all to be mine.

As soon as December started, so did the snow. It's been snowing continuously for about three days now. Not as bad as the day we drove to Lost Hope, but enough to catch unaware residents and tourists alike.

Shifts at work have been gruesome. We've had no less than twenty car accidents. Luckily the injuries were all minor. The worst we've seen was a broken arm or a concussion, but enough of the drivers or the passengers had to be cut out of their cars.

I'm dragging my feet on the heated floors, just ready to hop in a shower and get in bed next to a warm, sleeping Lalah.

I take a peek at her in the middle of the bed and thank my lucky stars my sisters are not cuddled up to her. I love them to pieces, but sometimes I just need to come home from work and fall asleep holding my woman.

Seven fucking weeks of this back and forth and I'm slowly going crazy.

I wash as quickly as my tired muscles allow me, slip on a pair of boxers, and make my way back to her. I shuffle under the warm duvet and gather her in my arms, tucking her in on my side, letting her head rest on my chest and her leg bent over across the top of my thigh.

She moves around in my hold, trying to make herself comfortable, and blinks sleepy eyes at me. Her pink lips, pouty from sleep, smile up at me. "Hey. You're home. What time is it?" she whispers.

"Go back to sleep, babe," I urge her. "It's only six in the morning."

She clears her throat, sits up, folding her legs under her, and runs a hand through her hair, letting it fall like a curtain around her. "Uhm, I actually, uhm, I wanted to talk to you. I've been meaning to for days." She lifts her bare shoulders in a shrug, and dread coils in my chest.

It's never a good thing when a woman tells you *We need to talk.*

"Alright. I'm here," I say, trying to keep my voice even. I lift myself up, resting my back against the headboard. I can't help but cross my arms in a defensive position while my mind is running a million miles an hour, creating crazier and crazier scenarios.

It doesn't help that her fingers keep fidgeting in her lap and she refrains from touching me.

"So, uhm, there are a couple of things I haven't told you about me. And these things have been holding me back, along with all the issues you already know of."

Her worried gaze captures mine then, and, even in the darkness of the bedroom, I can see the fear in her eyes, the anxiety making her bottom lip tremble.

I hate not being able to look at her properly, so I reach on my nightstand and turn on the night light. Not bright enough to take away from the privacy of the moment, but sufficient to actually see her.

"And you want to go over them with me now?" I clarify because the hope she's willing to take a leap of faith with me and the dread of her breaking my heart are warring inside of me.

"Y-yeah. If that's ok. If you're too tired, we can do this later today?"

"I don't think I'll be able to sleep a wink not knowing what to expect, Lalah," I sigh.

"It's nothing bad," she hurries to say. "I mean, I don't think it is. It's not up to me to make that judgment. I didn't withhold this from you because I thought you'd judge me, I'm just so used to keeping that side of me hidden. Anyway, I have money," she whispers. "Loads of money."

I can't stop the laugh rumbling in my chest. "Babe, everyone looking at your home knows you're loaded. For fuck's sake, you have a heated road, which is most likely as expensive as your house."

She smiles shyly at me and then launches into telling me where her money came from and what she's actually doing for a living. I look at her in shock, at this amazing, generous woman. I'm seconds away from pouncing on her, but I know this is not what she needs from me now.

"Well, I knew you were well off. Just not the extent of it. But, love, I really don't care how much money you have in your account." Cupping her cheek with my palm, I pull her mouth to mine, kissing her in between each sentence.

"Your pocket size is irrelevant," Kiss. "It's you I want," Kiss. "Your intriguing mind," Kiss. "Your beautifully selfless heart," Kiss. "Your mile long list of issues," Kiss. "This sexy as fuck sassy mouth of yours," More kisses. "Your body entirely mine." I give her a last kiss and pull my mouth from hers when tears start running down her cheeks.

"I want you too, Cole. Everything you are, I want as mine. But there's one more thing," she says cautiously and straightens her spine.

"You are an amazing father figure to your sisters, and I absolutely love your family. I look at you and see you in the garden tossing up and down a little boy who's your spitting image. I look at you and see you being an overbearing, overprotective father to a beautiful daughter with pale green eyes and curly, dark hair. And I can't give you that."

She looks straight into my eyes, her heartbreak written all over her face. "Cole, I didn't want any children."

Well, fuck.

Chapter Thirty-Nine

Cole

"You gotta clarify that for me, Supernova. You didn't want any children in the past, and now you do?" I ask since once more her words bring both hope and doom. This is the one issue I thought may break us apart. I didn't want any children either, but now I have two of them.

Even if they are not mine by DNA, those two beautiful little girls are mine.

"You know very well how I grew up. I never wanted to bring a child into the world, convinced I'd either mistreat them the way my daddy dearest did to me or throw them aside, emotionally stunt them, the way my mother did," she draws in a deep breath before continuing.

"In my second year of college, Callum and I had a pregnancy scare. I freaked out because it definitely wasn't the right moment for me to have a baby. Callum freaked out even worse. And I realized as much as I like children, and as much as I love being around them, I'm not made to be someone's mother. And sure as hell I'm not made to be someone's mother and father..." She trails off, sneaking a look at me.

I remain quiet, listening, waiting for her to continue.

"I realized I didn't trust Callum enough to risk having a baby with him, and regardless if I ended up with him forever or not, I may not trust anyone enough to share a child together. So I had my tubes tied. It was not an easy thing to do by any stretch of the imagination, but I was determined." She stops abruptly, closing her eyes and sighing deeply before continuing, "Even if I wanted to have children, I can't have them now. I can't ever give you children, and you are too good of a man, too good of a father to be without yours."

"What about Clara and Eliza?" I ask her, trying to keep the shock off my face. Out of all the things she could've told me, her taking permanent measures not to have children would've never crossed my mind.

Her nose scrunches at me and an eyebrow arches on her still creased-from-sleep forehead. "What about Clara and Eliza, Cole?"

"We're a package deal. Where I go, they go," I clarify.

Is she being obtuse on purpose, trying to find the right words to let me down? Surely no woman would go as far as tying her tubes to ensure she'll never have children and then accept two girls who are not even mine.

"Not to be rude, but duh. Of course, you are a package deal. You and Blake are their entire world. Even if we tried and things didn't work out between us, they'll always have me in their corner, Cole. They may not be my sisters, but they are mine, too."

The fire in her eyes sparks back to life. She's willing to fight me for them even when we're still here, both in the same bed.

"So you're telling me we don't have a problem then? You have money and a big fucking heart, which I already knew. You don't want children, but you want Clara and Eliza. Am I on the same page so far?" She nods at me, and I catch her wrist in my hand to stop her fidgeting.

"What I'm hearing is you telling me you agree to be with me. Officially, exclusively, you agree I am your man. I'll be damned if at thirty-five I still use the term boyfriend." With the last word, I sit up on my knees, towering over her.

"Doubt is swimming in your eyes. You're thinking maybe one year from now, or five, or ten, I'll regret not having any children of my own. But you see, you and I are not that much different. I never wanted children, so I got a vasectomy."

I don't let the surprise fully take over her eyes when I pounce on her, my mouth seeking hers, my hands ripping her tank top off her torso, revealing those perky tits of hers I love so fucking much.

My lips trail hot, open-mouthed kisses down her throat and suck greedily at each of her tight, rosy nipples until she is writhing and moaning under me, her thighs rubbing on one another seeking friction.

My hands ghost down her rib cage and the curve of her hips, reaching the waistband of her sleeping shorts. I make quick work of ripping those off her and throwing them over my shoulder.

My cock throbs in my boxers, eager to come out and play, and I'm more than happy to oblige. I spread her thighs apart as far as they go and take my first fucking look at that pretty, pink pussy of hers, her arousal glistening in the soft light. I lick my lips, my cock jolting just at the simple thought of tasting her.

My hand caresses her soft thighs higher and higher until my fingers trace the outline of her pussy. She gasps at my touch, arching her back when I take my first proper feel of her warmth, my thumb petting her greedy clit in small tight circles.

A soft moan escapes her mouth, and I dive in, throwing her legs up my shoulders, mouth sucking her clit in, finger deep in her warm, wet channel. My blood races inside of me at the tight fit and the fluttering of her walls around my finger.

My mouth sucks and licks at her like I'm a man starved, her hips thrashing back and forth, chasing my mouth, chasing her pleasure. I throw an arm over her belly to keep her in place, and my tongue joins this game of chase.

I lick clean everything she has to offer, her tangy taste on my lips like the sweetest of nectars. "You're so fucking responsive to me..." I breathe over her, then dive back in, determined not to stop until she comes all over my face like the good girl she is.

Her head thrashes on the pillow, and her hands tangle trembling fingers in my hair, pushing my mouth where she wants it to be. I love that she's so open to me, so unafraid to take what's rightfully hers.

I thrust a second finger into her, stretching her, and I'm rewarded by a breathy moan. "Cole! Please, please," she begs oh so beautifully. My cock cannot take another second to feel her all wrapped around me.

Her walls start fluttering around my fingers, and wetness gushes past my knuckles and down her thighs. I kiss my way down to her core, licking clean all that she is and she so generously is gifting me. Her chest is heaving, and I'm almost sorry I'm missing the look in her eyes as she comes.

But the morning is long, and I don't plan to rest until she comes at least one more time on my cock.

I pepper kisses down her inner thighs, her skin sprouting goosebumps at my touch. "God, I love your mouth," she breathes. I stand next to the bed, wiping my mouth with the back of my hand, and smirk at her.

"If you love my mouth, you should see what I can do with my cock," I retort, my chest all puffed out, full to the brim with male pride at seeing my woman sprawled out on the bed, all flushed and sweaty in pleasure.

She exhales a joyous laugh, and my heart soars in my chest. This is what I want most for her. The freedom she feels right now, the happiness. I want her to feel like this every single day of our lives.

I shove my boxers down my legs and kick them somewhere behind me as I fist my dick. I give myself a couple of full strokes, root to tip, tip to root, lubricating the sensitive skin with my precome. Her eyes grow big and she stretches a hand toward me, her palm stopping me in my tracks.

"Holy mother of cocks, you have piercings?" she exhales as her fingers trail down my Jacob's ladder, making me shudder with every swipe she gives to every single one of my five piercings.

She scrambles to her knees, shuffling to the edge of the bed, one hand gripping my hip for balance.

"Fuck me, you're like a work of art."

She bends her neck and swallows the head of my cock, wet tongue swirling around it, her lips stretched out and puffy. With one hand I gather her hair, fisting it so that I have an unobstructed view of my beautiful woman, bobbing up and down my shaft, taking more and more of me, her hand jacking me off, following the rhythm her mouth sets.

Hollowed cheeks, lips sealed tight around me, drool at the corner of her mouth, tears blossoming under her eyes, she's never looked more fucking beautiful.

I keep myself as still as I can while enjoying the electricity coursing through my veins at the pressure her gorgeous mouth puts on me as she takes me in until the head of my cock hits the back of her throat.

Her throat spasms around me when she gags, and I try to pull back, even though my hips urge me forward. Her nails claw at my ass, keeping me in place, and she gives me a long hard suck, her mesmerizing hazel eyes pinned to mine.

My balls draw tight to my body, and the telltale tingle of my impending orgasm settles at the base of my spine.

I shake my head to wake myself from under her spell and move my hands under her arms lifting her to my chest, my mouth silencing her protesting whimpers. "Right now, the only place I'm coming in is that sweet cunt of yours," I warn her between kisses.

Laying her down in the middle of the bed, I move in between her legs. My cock jolts impatiently at the first contact with all the warmth exuding from her. I prop myself on my forearms, savoring her naked form underneath me, ready to receive me, and notch the throbbing head at her entrance, sliding home in one savage thrust.

I still once I reach the end of her, and bite my cheek to stop myself from coming too soon. She fits me like a fucking glove, all that wet, tight heat all around me making me lose my fucking mind.

Her palm cups my jaw, rubbing sweet circles on my stubbled skin, her eyes wide open, honest, cloudy with desire taking me in.

"Keep your eyes on me, baby," I whisper to her. "Let me see you go over the edge with me. Trust me with your vulnerability. Let me see you," I beg.

She gives me everything I ask for, willingly and with abandon. Every deep thrust inside of her is rewarded with a breathy moan.

I shift my hips, making sure she feels every single piercing as it rubs inside of her and when her thighs grip me tighter and tighter, her flesh trembling everywhere we touch, I know I've hit just the right spot. I speed up my movements, taking her with my whole body as she whimpers and cries out my name.

I lower my head for a kiss, breathing deeply into her mouth, my tongue battling with hers in tandem with my long, controlled thrusts. Her pussy clamps down on me so hard I can barely move inside of her.

"Cole, fuck!" She moans in my mouth. I move one hand between us, feeling her core fluttering with my fingertips, my thumb rubbing in wider circles at her clit.

When her belly quivers under my palm, I pinch her clit hard between two fingers and give her one long hard thrust, reaching so deep inside her I don't know where she ends, and I begin.

Her eyes glaze over with the force of her orgasm, puffy lips parted on a silent moan, her beautifully flushed body trembling under me, around me, surrendering her pleasure to me.

With my eyes boring down on hers, I let her see my body submitting to hers. I come with a guttural groan as ropes of hot cum spurt out of me. With my face pressed on the crook of her neck and one arm banded around her, keeping her as close to me as she can get, I move gently in shallow thrusts as my orgasm subsides, filling her to the brim with all of me.

Her arms coil around my neck, and she showers kisses on the side of my face, my neck, and my shoulders, her fingers massaging the back of my neck and my already relaxed shoulder blades.

My mind is a blank canvas, and all I see is her, all I feel is her. I knew I loved her weeks ago. The mind-blowing sex doesn't really change anything for me, except making it clear this woman has been made for me; from the tip of her dainty toes to the smallest hair on her head.

Now all I have to do is tell her, except I'm smart enough, even in my post-orgasmic state, to know what poor timing saying it now will be. So I force my words down my throat with a promise to myself to show her every day until I can actually voice my love to her.

Tightening my arm around her and keeping my hips stiff so my slowly softening cock doesn't slip out of her, I turn us around so I'm flat on my back in bed, and she's lying on top of me.

"You realize there's no getting rid of me now, don't you? You signed your life away to me. First with your words, then sealed the deal with that greedy pussy of yours."

Her quiet laugh vibrates in my chest as her small body shakes on top of mine. "I think it's best said you can't get rid of me now. You and your ladder have signed yourself away to me for life."

It's my turn to laugh now.

"Is that all you want me for? My ladder?" I tease her.

"Your hammer's not half bad either. A woman needs all her tools close to home." She plants a kiss on my chest, her breaths quickly evening out.

My hand moves up and down her back and a shit-eating grin spreads on my face. I couldn't drop the smile if my life depended on it.

Chapter Forty

Cole

B lake is in seventh heaven training under Lalah's careful supervision. We sat him down three days ago, and Lalah made him sign a never-ending folder of paperwork, NDA included.

She was worried he might take it personally or think she doesn't find him trustworthy, but my faith in my brother was rewarded when he reacted exactly as I expected him to.

He understands her love for privacy, and he respects her even more for not wanting or needing to take credit for all the good she is doing through Lege et Lacrima. She got him in touch with Marcus, who I had the *pleasure* of meeting via video call. The man is so ridiculously flirty he even got me to blush.

I do have to sacrifice some of my free time with her now that she's training him, but the pay is good, and the benefits are even better. His employment was set up by Marcus with Lalah making it clear to my brother she's not doing this out of charity.

She genuinely doesn't want to travel anymore and could really use someone she wholeheartedly trusts to carry on her work. She plans to give him intensive training until March and then set him free into the world.

Christmas is fast approaching too, less than two weeks away. I've decided the best time for me to tell her I love her is Christmas morning when we all open our presents together as a family to set our feelings out in the world.

She hasn't said it to me either, and while I long to hear those words coming from her pretty mouth, I know she does love me. Actions speak louder than words, and hers are screaming.

She's always making sure I rest as soon as I get home from the fire station. Always fusses over me when I leave for work, making sure I have everything I need, even popping into the firehouse to bring coffee and baked goods for the whole team. She listens to me, argues with me, cares for me, and best of all, she's spreading her love to my family, treating everyone as her own.

A pang of hurt twinges my heart when I occasionally think that we would've never met if we hadn't lost two important members of our family. But every time I look down at my tattoo, the one I share with her, I'm goddamned sure we're meant to be.

I'm thankful I hadn't met her when we got our tattoos, even if it happened on the exact same day. I wasn't ready for a relationship then, and I would've lost the person meant just for me. I'm also certain she wasn't ready for me either. She still had healing to do, she still had a lot to learn about herself.

And the end result is, right now, I'm the happiest I've ever been.

As I get lost in my thoughts of my mom and how proud she would be of us all, how much she would've loved Lalah, my phone rings from somewhere next to me.

I pat the sofa around to find it, then quickly answer when Tatum's name flashes on the screen and put him on speaker.

"Fucking finally, someone answered their fucking phone!" He thunders.

Eliza looks at me wide-eyed from her favorite place on the rocking chair next to the eight-foot Christmas tree. I make a shooing motion with my hand, as clearly Tatum's not in a reasonable mood right now, and even Eliza's swear jar swindling won't go well with him.

"What happened, man?"

"Where's Lalah? I tried calling her a thousand times."

"In her office, working. Now drop the fucking attitude and tell me what happened," I order, already sick of this pulling-teeth game.

"I need to talk to both of you. Should be there in five minutes," he informs me, then promptly hangs up.

I look at my phone dumbfounded but make my way toward Lalah's office and enter, finding both her and my brother debating over her desk.

"Sorry to interrupt. Tatum's on his way here. Blake, would you keep an eye on the girls? I think he wants to speak privately with Lalah and me."

He stands from where he is perched on the edge of the desk and walks out the door, throwing me a questioning look. I give him a slight lift of my shoulders because fucked if I know what has T's panties in a twist.

Lalah and I make our way to the enclosed porch after a quick stop in the kitchen for her beloved hazelnut latte. I don't know what's coming but, by Tate's tone, can't be anything good.

She sits on her favorite spot on the corner of the sofa, the minty scent of her vape floating in the air. Her phone rings this time, and she gives me a puzzled look.

"Mayor Brown," she mouths to me before greeting the caller. "Good evening, Mayor. How can I help?"

"Lalah, I am so terribly sorry," a frantic feminine voice comes from the phone she has put on speaker. "I don't know what got into her. I'm so, so sorry. I understand if you need to take legal action against me, but please, don't withdraw the investments Lege et Lacrima has made into the town. Our townsfolk have done nothing wrong."

Lalah throws me a worried, confused look. "Gretchen, I'm afraid I don't understand. What exactly happened?"

"Maddison. She broke into the safe in my office. She found out you were assessing the town on behalf of Lege et Lacrima, made a copy of our contract, and shared it on the town's social media page. By now everyone knows. I'm extremely sorry. Never expected her to do such a thing," she says, her voice breaking on the last sentence.

Lalah stiffens on the sofa, her eyes wide, panic bleeding out of them. I reach her side in three long strides, pulling her into my arms. "Why would Maddison break into your safe? What was she looking for?"

"Glam Up is bleeding money. She wanted me to cosign another loan for her, and when I refused, she asked me to put her in contact with Lege et Lacrima. I explained she was rejected in the first wave and the investors would not be persuaded into changing their minds. God, I am so embarrassed. This was the only condition you asked of me for helping the people in my town. I'm so sorry. Please, Lalah, please don't punish the whole town for my daughter's and my mistakes."

"So it's true then?" Tatum's voice thunders from the entrance to the porch.

Lalah looks at him, her face unreadable. One minute she is stiff in my arms, heart thundering, but now an icy calm exudes out of her, and I'm even more worried.

She asks for one minute from Tatum, a finger in the air, as she takes her phone off speaker and places it at her ear.

"Mayor Brown, I'm unsure yet of the implications of her actions. I will have to call my CFO and report everything you have told me. Please come see me tomorrow morning and I'll have some answers for you then."

She nods at her phone, as the frantic voice of the mayor still chimes through, quiet enough I cannot make any words. "That's fine. I'll see you tomorrow. But Mayor Brown, I have to tell you, your daughter has gone too far this time."

She drops the phone on the sofa and stands from my lap. Her face is a mask of cold, her fiery hazel eyes now pure steel in a hardened glint, the temperature around us drops below freezing levels under the ice of her glare. I don't recognize the person in front of me.

"Good evening, Tatum! By all means, come on in and yell at me some more," she deadpans.

He paces back and forth in front of the coffee table, his hands running through his hair, ripping the tie securing his man bun.

"I never wanted to hit a woman in my life, not even when I found Amanda cheating on me, but I swear to fucking God, if I put my hands on Maddison I'll..."

"You'll do nothing!" Lalah commands. "Sit down and tell me what got your balls in a twist."

He plops onto the rocking chair with a deep sigh, his knees nervously bouncing on the floor. He halts suddenly and looks at Lalah, a world of hurt bleeding from his eyes. "Are you planning to leave now?"

"Why would I leave, Tatum? Is Lost Hope gearing up to come after me with pitchforks?" she barks an incredulous laugh.

"I don't know. Maddison posted not only pictures, but some choice words about you, too. About how you only moved here to assess everyone and decide who is getting money based on your whims. She accused you publicly of refusing to have Lege et Lacrima invest in her business as revenge for her opening Maddox's eyes about you."

"For fuck's sake! I'm so fucking tired of hearing the same shit all over again," she yells, then turns to me.

Her face softens when her eyes bore into mine, ice slowly melting out of her veins. "Cole, would you call Maddox for me and ask him to come here? Tell him I'd like to file a complaint for harassment."

I nod at her, and pick up my phone, dialing Maddox's number. I'm glad she's taking this step. I've seen that woman harassing Lalah, and from what she has told me, it wasn't the first time, either. Pure selfishness has made her reveal Lalah's work, thinking she'd only hurt my woman.

"Lawson speaking," his gruff voice sounds in my phone. "Is Lalah ok? I read what the cursed woman put on social media. Fucking hell, I never realized her crush on me would take her this far," he mumbles.

"Get your ass here. You can feel sorry for yourself later. Lalah wants to file an official report against her," I bark at him.

"No shit? Yeah, I'll be there. Give me twenty. You'll probably need to call Richards, too," he tells me and hangs up.

I move behind Lalah and coil my arms around her until she rests her back against me. I know her first instinct right now is to do damage control, and she thinks she has to do it all by herself, but I won't let her push me away.

She hasn't been alone since the minute her dog laid me flat on the ground, and if I have it my way, she'll never be alone again.

I pull her closer to me when her body starts to tremble in my arms. "It'll be ok, babe," I whisper in her ear. "All you've done is help them. I know this violates your privacy, and her being so malicious makes everything worse, but you've done nothing wrong."

She turns around in my arms and hides her face in my chest. My hands move up and down her back in a soothing motion, while Tatum is throwing me helpless looks. As soon as she is calm, I'll rip into him.

He barged in, guns blazing, demanding explanations he has no right to. I should've realized the minute I saw the iciness in her eyes, she thought he was the first one to spew shit in her face.

I guide her to the sofa, and have her sit in my lap once more, throwing the blanket over her legs.

"Do you want me to leave?" Tatum asks.

"Are you going to yell at me some more?" she retorts in a small voice.

"I won't yell at you at all. I'm not upset with you, Lalah, I'm upset *for* you. Sure, I'm hurt you felt like you couldn't share this part of your life with me, but I also understand you wanting to keep your job out of our friendship."

"Thank you." She gives him a small smile. "It was not about you, nor was it about anyone in town. My job is private, and I wanted to keep it that way. My friendship with you, or anyone else in town, is not dependent on what I do for a living or what I choose to do with my money. I'm not going to apologize for doing what I honestly thought was right for me."

He walks toward us and crouches in front of her, gently taking her hand in his. "I told you before and I'll tell you again. I love you. You're my sister. All I want is to see you happy and healthy. And now we're closer than ever with you giving this dickhead a chance since he, too, is part of my family."

She squeezes his hand and gives him a wider smile this time. "Thank you, Tatum. I love you like a brother, too." She laughs, and I fume.

Motherfucker, she just said to him the words I want so badly to hear.

Chapter Forty-One

Lalah

Goddammit. If I put my hands on that fucking woman. I mumble under my breath, stressed out of my fucking mind. Last night seemed never ending.

After a long talk with Maddox and Sheriff Richards, I have finally filed a complaint against Maddison for harassment and have asked for a restraining order.

Neither of them are convinced there is sufficient evidence for one to be signed off by a judge, but I remain hopeful. And by that, I mean, I've tasked Marcus with finding me the most cutthroat lawyer to fight on my behalf.

If one is not signed, I'll report Maddison every time she comes near me and starts stirring shit. Despite all the shit she's pulled I've let her be, but she's never going to stop if I keep finding excuses for her behavior.

I managed to catch a hold of Marcus last night, which was lucky, seeing as New York is two hours ahead of Lost Hope, and it was pretty late in the evening.

He promised to pour over the contracts everyone has signed, to ensure there are no repercussions against the beneficiaries. He'll also search for the fastest exit strategy, just in case anyone wants to end their contract with Lege et Lacrima.

The contracts are made to benefit the businesses and the owners, not me. Unfortunately, it is stipulated that if the owners decide to sell or back out of the contract before one calendar year, they will have to return the money in full.

This clause was added to ensure no one got away with fraud, even after the thorough checks we've conducted. If they keep up business as usual and show consistent profit after one year, they are free to separate themselves from us.

My hand rubs vigorously over my face, trying to magic away the fatigue set deep in my bones. It's nearly lunchtime and I haven't slept in over twenty-four hours.

Cole had to leave for a shift this morning and Blake was keeping the girls entertained, with me elbows deep in phone calls and contracts, then busy with the Mayor, eager for updates.

No one else has called or messaged me, although Tatum assured me last night the whole town would be aware by the time he got here. I can't help the pang of guilt rising in my chest.

I should've taken a leap of faith and told my friends. Hell, I should've called them all last night, but I was in too much shock to think beyond damage control.

When I finally got into bed at Cole's insistence, not even that magic cock of his could take my mind off this mess enough so I could fall asleep.

He fucked me hard twice – so hard I can still feel the way he moved inside of me every time I shift my hips – but my mind still refused to shut down and let me sleep.

So I held him all night staring at the ceiling, making a pros and cons list in my head, looking for silver linings.

After debating the situation long after Cole left, I've concluded things are not as dire as they seemed last night.

There are only four major things on my cons list which I ended up writing down.

Maddison once again forcefully ripped control out of my hands. It's what hurts the most. Sure, I told Cole and Blake the truth, but I wasn't ready for everyone else to know. At least, she only knows about me being the assessor, not the pockets.

I won't be able to invest in about forty percent of the remaining business in town. Since the first wave announced back in August, I wasn't able to assess many more during my recovery. The only silver lining here is Sawyer's dream is already on the pre-approved list. That is, if she still wants to proceed, now she is aware I'm behind the assessments.

I can't decide what to do as far as Mayor Brown is concerned. While she didn't technically breach the NDA she signed, she took our contracts to her private residency without making sure those were adequately locked away. She had two major responsibilities in this deal of ours. First, to ensure my involvement was kept a secret. Second, to pass any investment requests and new business proposals requiring outside funding to me.

I don't want her to be punished for the deeds of her daughter, but this sets a precedent. If no actions are taken against her, then more and more people dealing with Lege et Lacrima will start breaking their NDAs.

There is a chance people would want to end their contracts. Which would be a silly move on their part, but is not outside of the realm of possibility. In the past five months since the investments were announced, all of them have used the sums they were granted for updates, improvements, or paying off mortgages and other business loans. They'll bankrupt themselves if they decide to end everything.

I realize as I go over every point, there are things I can do about each of them. I've started putting things in place by reporting Maddison. Now I pick up my phone and group message my closest friends in town.

> Hi all. I'm sure you've either heard or seen Maddison's social media post. I'd love it if you'd join me for a casual pizza dinner tonight and give me a chance to tell you my side of the story. Please be warned beforehand, if you decide to come, you have to sign the NDA attached. Hoping to see you all.

Me

If there's one thing I've learned during my time here, it's that sometimes people surprise you in the best way. I've chosen these people because there's something special about each of them and because I trust them, so it's time to put my money where my mouth is. Soon enough, the replies come in.

Attached - NDA signed. Unfortunately, I have a shift at the firehouse. Can Annalise fill me in?

Drake

Mine attached as well. I'll be there with bells and whistles. I also don't care what Maddison has to say. I've got your back, babe.

Annalise

I'm always down to see you. You don't have to ex-plain yourself. If the contract Maddison posted is real, you've helped this town more than you could know. Please take this message as a signature for the NDA. My online signature won't woooork. *frus-trated emoji*

Maevis

Shocked AF to be included. But if this is related to what we've already discussed last night, I can't sign the NDA, since everything you've told me has to be included in the official report.

Maddox

Must you always be an asshole, Lawson? Clearly, there's more she wants to share. For Lalah: I'm so proud of you, Supernova. See you tonight.

Meus Bellator

I'm surprised, too, Lawson was included. I'll be there, baby girl. You know I've got you.

Tatum

NDA signed and attached.

Maddox

I heard nothing here on the outskirts, so color me intrigued. Honored to be included. Won't be able to stay for more than one hour, though. I've a sick barman and I need to cover for him.

JC

Darling girl, Beth and I will be there. You are family, and will continue to be family regardless of what you have to share.

Matt

Thank you, guys. You're the best.

Me

I breathe just a bit easier knowing my friends are coming over tonight and there'll be no more secrets between us. I make sure to pre-order everyone's favorite pizza to be delivered later this evening, before moving back to the cons list.

For the last remaining items, I dial the Mayor, as I'll need her help. She answers on the third ring, her voice trembling with trepidation as she greets me.

"Lalah, I didn't expect to hear from you again today."

"Hi Gretchen, I'm sure you didn't. The CFO still hasn't gotten back to me yet with a solution to our predicament. I'm sorry I can't give you any updates on that. But that's not the reason why I'm calling."

"You'll tell me when you know. I'm truly sorry for my part in this. What can I help you with?"

"I'd like you to call a town meeting. I'd like to speak with everyone directly and explain the situation and consequences." I then proceed to explain the reasoning behind each item on my list as it's pertinent to her and the town.

"Maybe for tomorrow evening? I understand it's inconvenient, with it being a Saturday and all, but I believe the sooner we get this done, the better."

"Of course. Let me set everything up, and I'll see you tomorrow evening. Take care, Lalah."

"Thank you, Gretchen. Catch up soon!"

With my mind settled now that I have a plan in place, I move to the two-seater sofa in my office, drape a soft-knitted blanket over my shoulders, and let myself get some much-needed sleep.

The buzzing of my phone on the glass surface of the small side table rouses me from sleep. Eyes closed tight, I pat my way blindly to the phone and bring it in front of my face, daring to only half open one eye to peek at the screen.

Five messages from Cole blink at me. With a shaky finger, I swipe on the screen to read them. The clock on the phone shows me I've slept for about three hours, but with the way my body trembles in fatigue, I know that's not nearly enough for what I need.

My brain needs to get back online and fast, seeing as everyone is due to arrive in less than an hour.

Babe, I'm home. Can't find you anywhere.

Your car's still here. Where are you hiding, love?

Blake said he's last seen you in your office. The door's locked. Open up if you're in there.

Babe, I'm really starting to get worried. Where are you?

I swear to God, Lalah, if anything happened to you I'll rip this town to shreds. Don't do this to me, baby. Where are you?

Meus Bellator

I push my feet down on the floor and stand, one hand on the back of the sofa for stability. My body feels weak, weighed down with tiredness.

Scrubbing the sleep away from my eyes with my palm, I take slow measured steps toward the door. When I feel awake enough, I unlock the door and make my way toward the living room.

I really need to give both Blake and Cole access to the office. Obviously, Blake needs it now that he works for me, and I have nothing to hide from Cole. With everything happening lately, it has completely slipped my mind.

A hint of storm in the air alerts me to him stalking behind me, and as my body shifts toward him, he bends at the knees, puts a shoulder in my stomach, and, before I can blink, I'm airborne, draped over his back, a strong arm banded beneath my ass and face to face with his.

I playfully smack his rock-hard cheeks and start giggling. "Put me down, you brute!"

A hard palm lands on my ass, my skin stinging under my leggings. "Oh no, you don't! You don't get to call the shots right now. I nearly lost my fucking mind looking for you for the past half hour. You took ten goddamned years off my life," he says in a gruff voice, spanking me once more before hurrying up the stairs to our bedroom.

A jolt of arousal makes its way down my body. A pissed off Cole is a domineering Cole in bed, and wouldn't you know it, I love it when he orders me around while drowning my body in orgasms. It's like he has a direct link to all my pleasure centers. I'm also aware I trust him completely. I trust him to take care of my needs as much as I trust him to stop if anything he does to me becomes too much.

My back hits cool soft sheets, my body bouncing on the mattress as I land in the middle of the bed. Cole's face is thunderous, and while I feel guilty for falling asleep and worrying him, what I feel more is the desire for the unleashed animal in him to come out and play.

His green eyes are almost dark with lust and need to punish me, and my panties get wetter and wetter just thinking of the rough ministrations that are to come.

He rips off his body the black T-shirt straining to contain him, his washboard abs rippling when he straightens back to his full height. The outline of his hard cock pushes against the cotton of his sweatpants, and my mouth waters just thinking about having a taste of him.

Cole stalks closer to the bed, his knees hitting the edge. Long fingers encircle my ankles, dragging me to him. I lift myself on my elbows so I can get closer to him, my eyes defiant and hazed with desire.

His mouth gives way to an arrogant smirk, pure alphaness radiates off him seeping into my every cell, commanding me into submission, but I'm made of sterner stuff.

He bends at the waist, planting a veiny forearm next to my head, his mouth tickling my ear as he whispers roughly, "Take off your sweatshirt before I rip it off you."

I actually debate for a second letting him destroy it, but it's one of my favorites, so I'm quick to bare my naked breasts to him. "Such a good fucking girl," he rasps, his nose trailing on my naked skin.

"You fucking kill me with your penchant for not wearing a bra. Being around you all day, every day, knowing all I have to do is put my hand under your shirt, and I'll get to these tight, sweet nipples," Cole trails off as his mouth latches onto my breasts, biting and fervently sucking my nipples. I can't help the whimpers escaping my throat or my back arching, pushing more of me into his mouth.

He releases my tight bud with a wet pop, his hands trailing down my waist, fingers hooking into the waistband of my leggings, ripping them off me, leaving me completely naked in front of him. My legs widen in defiance, letting him see how wet I am for him, how my pussy is dripping, yearning for his touch.

"I want you," I whisper in a needy voice.

He sucks in a breath, his eyes leaving my bare pussy and meeting mine. Dark swirls of green take me in, his crooked smirk deepening. "And I wanted to know where you were, yet you left me to worry. Get on your hands and knees. Now!" he commands.

My stomach is quivering, and butterflies take flight in anticipation as I eagerly turn away from him, propping myself on my palms, knees widened in front of him, ass in the air.

"Goddamn, look at you. All spread out for me," he grunts, and his warm, calloused palm rubs the back of my thighs, his thumbs teasing my dripping entrance. I push my ass further into his palm, seeking his friction, desperate for more of him.

A sharp slapping sound reverberates through the bedroom at the same time my left cheek smarts under his ministrations.

"Fuck, your red ass is getting me so hard!" He praises, hand squeezing my hip before moving to treat my right cheek with the same stinging slap, getting me needier and needier for him as the tingling burn spreads through my skin.

I wiggle in his hold, panting, begging pleas escaping my mouth. "Cole, please, I need you now!" I cry out as he rubs his still-clothed cock between my thighs, the ridges of his piercings spurring me on.

Pure electricity is running through my veins at every slap of his palm on my heated ass, at every caress he rewards me with, at every kiss he presses lovingly on my spine. My core pulsates in greed, longing for him to fill me to the brim.

He doesn't leave me waiting for too long. With a last slap on my ass, he enters me in one long thrust, his thick cock stretching me, the twinge of pain mixed with pleasure just the catalyst I need for the coil of desire in my core to unleash.

My whole body shakes under him, and my knees give up. Cole snakes a strong forearm under my belly, keeping my ass up, as he strokes himself inside of me with short, shallow thrusts, prolonging the intensity of my orgasm.

"Fuck!" He groans in my ear. "You grip me so tight. Come on baby, give me more. I want everything from you!"

His other arm bands between my bouncing tits, his hand a collar of domination around my neck. My vision blurs as he lifts me up to his chest, his thrusts increasing in pace and strength. A chorus of moans and labored gasps leave my constricted throat as his finger strums my clit like the chords on his favorite guitar.

My core flutters once more around his unrelenting thrusts. His cock moves in and out of me with abandon as his mouth peppers open-mouthed wet kisses on the side of my head, the scruff on his face grazing my overheated skin.

The last of my defiance leaves me, my tiredness all but vanishes, and I completely give myself to him, my eyes closing in anticipation of the orgasm getting ready to burn its way through my body.

His fingers tighten around my neck, not enough to cut off my breath, but enough to tell me he, too, is close to coming.

"Eyes on me, Supernova. Keep your eyes on me. Let me see you soar, my love!" He pleads with me, his breath labored as the pace of his thrusts change from powerful and controlled to frantic jerks, his piercings digging into the wet flesh inside of me, pushing on just the right button to ignite my pleasure.

My eyes lock onto the green tempest showering me in love and unrestrained devotion as I detonate in a million pieces.

I come long and hard with his name on my lips, those three little words floating around in my mind fighting their way to the surface.

I push them down and squeeze my inner walls around him to distract myself, feeling the jerks of his monster cock inside of me.

A raspy, groaned moan floats in my ear, his hand moving from my throat to my chin, tilting my head just enough so he can devour my mouth with his, sucking on my tongue, biting my swollen lips as he lets himself go while planting his shaft in me to the root.

I sigh in his mouth as he empties everything he has in me, a deep peace settling in my chest at knowing he is just as lost in me as I am lost in him.

He lets us both fall to the bed, his weight pushing me into the soft mattress as he rests on top of me. Our chests move in tandem, one haggard breath after another, up and down, up and down, as we're both floating back to earth from orgasm heaven.

He grunts a deep exhale, and his body relaxes further as if he expelled every worry out of him now that he made sure with his body I'm here, and nothing happened to me.

Well, except for being well and truly dickmatized, that is.

A whimpered protest stains my lips as he slips out of me and lifts off the bed, his fingers caressing my upper thighs where our combined pleasure is dripping out of me.

"Fuck, babe, if I didn't just spend everything I had in me, just the sight of you full of us would get me going again." I stifle a laugh and give him a naughty wink over my shoulder.

"If I didn't have the body capacity of a wet noodle right now, I'd let you have your wicked way with me again."

"Stay there, Supernova. And no more enticing me. I believe you wanted people over for dinner?" he pops a questioning eyebrow at me, his eyes crinkling in amusement.

"I'd throw a pillow at you, but still haven't leveled up from a noodle to spaghetti yet."

The sound of his laughter as he moves toward the bathroom bounces from the walls.

I love you, I love you, I love you is on a loop in my head, my heart skipping a beat just at the simple thought of saying those words to him.

Yup, I'm still a little coward.

Chapter Forty-Two

Lalah

M y friends all stare at me from where they are seated at the dining room table. Empty pizza boxes are haphazardly strewn across the table from where we just finished eating before spilling the last part of my story to them.

Blake nudges me with his elbow, his eyes shining with laughter. "So, what you're saying is, my big brother here found himself a sugar mama, huh?"

I roll my eyes at his antics while Cole generously rewards him with a slap on the back of his head. The troublemaker starts laughing out loud before snorting out, "You wouldn't resort to violence if it weren't true."

I let him be while looking at each of my friends and Maddox. I guess I can reluctantly call him a friend too, although the reason he is in the know is mostly so Drake won't have to keep a secret from his best friend.

Selfishly, the more Maddox knows, the easier it will be to protect myself from Maddison's childish games. Jackson was vouched for by Cole and Tatum, and him knowing does no harm. His bar is doing incredibly well. He's definitely not hurting for money.

Tate claps his hands and gives me a pointed look. "I guess I know who's buying a round of drinks tonight."

"Uhm, didn't I just buy you pizza?" I remind him.

"But we can't toast with slices of pizza," Mae protests. Of course, she is going to side with him.

"We could've if there was any left."

"Smartass." He narrows his eyes at me. "I propose we all go to JC's, 'cause Jake has to take off soon anyway, for a round of drinks to celebrate Lalah looking out for our town. All in favor say, Aye!"

A chorus of Ayes come around the table over the scrape of two wooden chairs over black marble as Beth and Matt both stand.

"We're going to skip the bar celebrations. Our little devils cannot be trusted at home on their own for too long," Matt grumbles.

I stand, too, and throw an arm around Beth's shoulders and Matt's waist since I'd need at least three step stools to reach his shoulders.

"Thank you for coming. And thank you for staying."

"Baby girl, you're ours." He stops at Cole's growl, and I stifle a laugh. Matt turns his head to glare over his shoulder. "Settle down, lover boy. You and I are going to have words soon."

Cole smirks as he stalks toward us, and I gape at realizing he's nearly eye to eye with Matt's hulking frame. "I'll bring my bulletproof vest."

"Not even that's gonna save your ass if you ever hurt her."

"Believe me, sir, I'll rip my own heart out and feed it to Astrum before I ever hurt her."

"That's not gonna work for me since Astrum only eats cooked meat. Leave my dog out of your pissing contest, please." I wiggle myself between the two of them.

Cole kisses the side of my head, a smile curving his lips against my temple. "I wouldn't dream of it, Supernova."

We say goodbye to my adopted family in a concert of back-slappings and *take care of my girl or else* before returning to the dining room where my friends are still debating a trip to JC's.

I glare at Blake, who's cheering loudest of all. "Why are you so happy about going since one of us has to stay home with the girls?" I ask him. A quick wave of hurt dims his silvery eyes before he blinks it away and gives me a perfunctory smile.

"As if I'd step foot in that place anyway," he scoffs, then pushes off the table. "I'll go have a shower while you guys get ready to leave." He turns around waving goodbye at everyone before leaving the room, and I realize Blake has not once looked in Jake's direction.

"Well, I guess I'd better go get the bar ready for this rowdy lot." Jake stands and comes around the table to give me a hug. "Thanks for including me in your little circle of trust," he whispers to me.

I give his waist a squeeze and whisper, "He'll come around. Be patient." He nods sharply, and with a "See you soon" over his shoulder, he leaves too.

We all agree to meet at the bar, so no one would have to come back here to pick up their cars.

I'm the only one in need of changing clothes since my PJ shorts and Cole's sweatshirt I'm wearing are not bar-appropriate attire. Quickly donning a pair of white ripped jeans with a lacy black top, and putting my trusty studded motorcycle boots on solves that issue.

A quick swipe of mascara on my eyelashes, a dab of eyeliner contouring their base, and a brush swipe through my hair before throwing it into a sleek ponytail has me ready to go in five minutes flat.

We all jump into our cars, Annalise, Mae and Tatum riding together, as we head toward JC's. Luckily, the traffic is not too heavy at this late evening hour, so within twenty minutes we're all filing through the bar doors.

A sultry bass vibrates through the walls as we make our way inside. I cling to Cole's hand while we slalom around writhing, dancing bodies.

The place is packed to the brim, and despite my efforts to look around, I can't really tell what the inside looks like. All I can see as Cole ushers me to the large bar on the far wall is the ceiling made of mirrors reflecting the mass of bodies on the floor.

After what feels like forever, we reach the bar, where Jake pours drink after drink, a mysterious smile adorning his lips, his black button-down gone, his tattooed chest and arms front and center. My mouth hits the floor as I take in the work-of-art Jake is.

Never mind he's made of the same granite Cole and Tatum are, with well-defined muscles and washboard abs, although he seems to be on the leaner side of the scale.

I can't take my eyes off the tattoos starting on his neck and spreading over every inch of skin he's put on display, disappearing into his low-slung jeans.

His life story is inked on his skin, in dark swirls of blacks and grays, with bloops of colors here and there, chapter after chapter, for everyone to read.

"If you weren't still limping from me being inside you, I'd think you were drooling at the sight of my friend," Cole's amused voice sounds in my ear.

My head turns in his direction and I give him a half smile. "Shh. I'm reading!" He spins me around and presses a possessive, hard kiss on my mouth. A giggle escapes me at his display of jealousy, but I sober up quickly.

I don't want him to be jealous. I want him to be certain of me, certain of us. I love his possessiveness, as every display makes me feel wanted and seen, feelings I've severely lacked my whole life.

But I don't want his jealousy.

It's too much of an oily, nasty feeling that has no room between us.

I cup his face with my palm and lean my head back so I can look directly into his eyes. "There's no one else I want but you. There's no one else I see but you. If you believe anything, please believe this. I'm yours, and only yours and I have no wish or desire for anyone else. Not now, not ever."

He kisses me hard once more, his arms squeezing me so close to him I can feel his strong heartbeat in my chest. As we slow the kiss, breathless and weak in the knees, he whispers back to me, "You are mine, and I am only yours."

"Let the woman breathe, Cap!" Jake's voice comes from somewhere behind me. I laugh in Cole's chest and turn around to greet the tattooed troublemaker. He winks mischievously at me, then points to a booth.

My eyes follow his arm to the left side of the bar, where a reserved sign plastered to the thick pedestal supporting the burgundy round table top declares the table as ours. My hand lifts on its own accord to wave at the rest of our friends.

We make our way to them, and I slide over the buttery leather bench next to Tatum, followed closely by Cole.

"We were this close to asking Jake for a hose to spray you guys off each other," Tatum quips, holding his thumb and forefinger close together to stress his words.

"Phew," I tell him, pretending to wipe my forehead with the back of my hand. "We need to thank Jake then for saving us the time needed to attend your funeral."

He barks out a laugh at me. "When did you turn so vicious, baby girl? I thought love was supposed to make you all soft and cuddly, not porcupine prickly."

"Love does make me want to bake cupcakes and shit, but exclusively for Cole. The rest of you get to see the bushy tail of my broom." My eyelashes flutter at him as Cole sneaks an arm around my shoulders pulling me into him.

I turn my attention to the rest of the table as Tatum chokes on a laugh. "Alright, ladies and gentlemen. Name your poison. Apparently, drinks are on me tonight!" I say to them, met with a chorus of *Hell Yeah*.

With the list of drinks in hand I walk to the bar where there's already a line at least three deep. I beeline straight for Jake's area, hoping he'll have a waiter or a waitress help me. It's been a hot minute since I last worked as a server and my skills weren't exactly great even then.

As I take my place in the line, I try to look around me. I'm not exactly a bar-going kind of girl, but from what I've seen so far, Jake's bar is an eclectic mix with mirrored walls and ceilings giving the impression the space is a lot bigger than it actually is. Fine leather booths and a wide, dark-wood bar spread across the whole width of the building on the far wall.

The bar itself is an absolute piece of art, strung by high wooden columns, each one a story of carvings. The bar top is sleek, black marble glistening under the dim lights.

On the opposite side are a dozen or so standing round tables with mirrored pedestals and matte table tops, each adorned with a glass capsule containing either a flickering electric candle or a cryopreserved flower.

I move one spot closer to Jake when someone bumps into me.

Arms reaching in their direction, trying to steady them, I'm surprised to see Maddison's friend, Emma.

"Meet me in the bathroom, please. As soon as you can," she tells me, then bends down pretending to pick something off the floor. I try to keep my face as neutral as possible and subtly nod in her direction.

Sliding my phone from the pocket in my jeans, I quickly type a message to Cole to join me at the bar in five minutes, asking him to bring Maevis along. I don't look in his direction, but as I go to shove my phone back in my pocket, I notice the thumbs-up emoji he sent in response.

As soon as another person is served and just one more person is in front of me, Cole wraps his arm around my waist.

"You summoned us, Supernova?" he quips in my ear.

I turn to him and place my arms around his neck, peppering kisses on his jaw. He bends at the knees to help me reach up to him since he's a freaking giant and my boots are not made for ballet moves, such as standing on the tip of my toes.

"Maddison's friend wants to talk to me. I'm taking Mae and going to meet her in the bathroom. If I'm not back in ten minutes, come find me," I whisper to him while giving the impression that I'm trying to climb him like a monkey.

If he is troubled by my words, I can't read it on his face. He could win poker tournaments with his stoicism. His eyes are a completely different story. So open for me I can practically read every thought going through his mind.

I give him a brief kiss on the mouth to let him know all's good, then turn to Mae and widen my eyes while my chin tilts toward the bathrooms.

She stares at me for a second, probably debating if I got drunk just by inhaling the vapors from all the drinks in the house tonight, but then she catches on.

"God, it's like my bladder is the size of a peanut. Cole, be a gentleman would you and order our drinks while Lalah and I make a quick stop to the Ladies," she says loud enough for anyone nearby to hear.

"It's like you women are pre-programmed to travel in packs when peeing at a bar. Do you want me to holler Annalise here for you, too?" He rolls his pretty eyes, a hint of annoyance on his face. *God, I fucking love this man.*

"I think the two of us will handle it this time, big boy," I retort. "But the night's still young. Maybe next time I'll invite you." I tease, wiggling my eyebrows up and down.

His eyes darken, and he licks his bottom lip as his gaze bores intensely into mine. "Don't go making empty promises on me, love."

I laugh and wink at him as Maevis drags me down the darkened corridor leading to the bathrooms. We find the one meant for women and I stop her in the doorway.

"Wait here, please. If I'm not out in five, get Cole," I instruct her.

"I don't know about this, Lalah. What's the plan here?" Maevis asks. This is why she's a great friend. She plays along without question, trusting I know what I'm doing.

"Mix'n'Match Emma wants to talk to me," I mouth and her chocolate eyes widen in shock.

"And you want to walk in there alone? She's best friends with the Wicked Witch of the West."

"Well, she could be friends with Hannibal Lecter, Dorothy. I still need to find out what she wants. And I need you to watch my careless ass and get Cole if I'm not back in five." I smirk at her.

"Best get going then. I already started counting."

I quickly thank her as I push the door open. I'm not surprised to see the cleanliness and dark sleekness of the tiles. A huge mirror adorns a full wall directly across the entrance, with five red sinks with dark veins slithering through the tiles.

On the opposite side of the bathroom are a dozen black stalls with red veins undulating through the wood. I may not be a bar girl, but I love the dark, mysterious vibe JC's Pour has.

The door to a stall opens and out comes Emma, a shy smile on her face. As with everyone in Lost Hope, she's a gorgeous woman. Her long red hair falls in soft curls down her shoulders, with wide chocolaty eyes peeking from under her bangs.

Her body is clad in a form-fitting silver dress that hits her mid-thigh, and with her sky-high heels, she towers over me. Despite our history, I don't sense any animosity coming from her.

"Thank you for meeting with me. I know it's unusual and you are taking a chance. I've been friends with Maddison my whole life. My father has been their personal lawyer since we were little, so she's always been in my life. I'm not trying to find any excuses, I'm just... I honestly don't know how to say this, so I'll just come out and show you," she tells me, a flush creeping up her neck settling in her cheeks.

"Alright. What do you want to show me?" I ask, moving closer to her. She takes her phone out from the clutch hanging from her wrist, taps twice, then turns it around to me. A video starts on the screen, showing Maddison cross-legged on a cream-colored sofa, a bottle of tequila in her hands.

Sitting next to her is an elegant woman with hair so blonde it looks nearly white, braided artfully over her shoulder, her slender fingers holding a glass of what looks like champagne.

"Press play," Emma says.

"I'm done with her. If the people in this town don't fucking open their eyes to what a fucking bitch she is..." Maddison's indignant voice comes from the speakers, her face scrunched in displeasure, tequila-holding hand gesturing wildly in the air.

"What the fuck do I need to do to get rid of her once and for all? Regardless of what I do, she just won't fucking leave," she cries to the blonde.

"What did you do, Maddison?" Emma's voice filters through next. From her tone of voice she wasn't drunk when the video was taken, but Maddi-

son definitely looks inebriated. The other woman has a stone-cold, impassive face, so I can't really tell how she was feeling.

I continue to watch the video, seeing the blond lift a perfectly shaped eyebrow at Emma. It's recorded from an awkward angle as if she was hiding the phone with her legs. The image keeps moving in and out of focus when the hand holding the phone trembles or shuffles.

"Everything I could think of, I did. I told Madd what kind of woman she is. He didn't take me seriously. Even after I got that kid to slash her tires and blamed it on her, he still had his doubts. He only fucking knew her for a night. What does she have? A golden pussy? God, I can't deal with this fucking slut."

"Maddison...." comes the haughty voice of the blonde.

"Don't you Maddison me, Amanda. You have no right to judge, since you're still pining after your dirty mechanic."

"I'm not pining after anyone. I just don't see why I should let him be happy without me." The blonde shrugs, taking a sip of her drink.

I pause the video and look at Emma.

"Imma come off hella judgemental, but seriously, these are your best friends?" I ask her incredulously. She waves me off, although the crimson painting her cheeks intensifies, and restarts the video.

"See? You keep a hold of your man, even if you threw his greasy ass to the curb. Why can't I fight for mine? Maddox is mine. This little emo Barbie comes strutting her fat ass up and down Main Street, and he only has eyes for her. She even ensnared your ex-husband, so you should be thanking me for running her off the road. God, I just wish she died then. This bitch went after Maddox and then had the audacity to deny me an investor. I nearly fucking fainted when I saw the contract in Mom's safe. Of course, it was her all along."

The image of the video turns black when Emma's shouting voice comes from the phone, *"Maddison, what the fuck did you do?"*

Chapter Forty-Three

Lalah

I fucking knew it.

"You're her friend. Why are you showing me this?" I ask her, my heart pounding so loudly I'm afraid it's trying to claw its way out of my chest.

"I *am* her friend. Hell, I don't know what I am right now. I took this video last night when we met at my place for drinks. I started getting suspicious of her as whenever she brought you up in conversation, she made strange comments here and there... I'm ashamed. I supported her all this time, no questions asked. But this is not right." She drops her head, looking at her phone, tapping the screen a couple of times before giving it back to me.

"Add your email address. Send it to yourself. You can delete it from *Sent* if you prefer I don't have your contact information."

I take her phone and do as she asks. As soon as mine pings, I immediately forward the video to Maddox, Sheriff Richards, and my lawyer, Paola Townsend, with a clear message *I better get that restraining order signed and delivered in the next hour.*

My fingers grasp her wrist and squeeze her hand in gratitude. "Thank you, Emma. Sincerely, thank you. I appreciate it more than you could ever understand. And you choosing to do the right thing instead of siding with your friend speaks volumes of who you are inside. Choose better friends." She nods, then slips past me out of the bathroom.

I give her a head start, my feet shuffling to one of the sinks. Placing my wrists under cool water, I hope it will calm my racing heart. A sob rips off my chest, waves of adrenaline and relief undulating through my body.

I grip the edge of the sink to keep myself upright and let the tears fall down my face. I'm happy to finally know with certainty who was behind the nightmare.

I'm also angry as fuck all this happened because Maddison is an entitled bitch who can't cope with being told *No*.

My fingers clean up my face as best as they can, but my eyes are still red-rimmed. Nothing I can do to improve that. I make my way out of the bathroom, where Maevis is still waiting.

"I was just about to come inside and get you. Emma just walked past me, didn't even spare me a look."

"Yeah. Emma just dropped a bomb in my lap. It's all good though. I'll fill you guys in once we're all back to the table."

She slips her arm around my waist as if she senses I need the extra support right now. And I do. My mind is a mess. Even though I suspected Maddison, I still hoped bashing and bad-mouthing me was the worst she'd do.

It's silly of me, really, how I'm still surprised there are people so inherently malicious to harm others without regrets.

Our friends throw us curious looks as we near the booth, except for Maddox since he was on the email list. Cole stands from his seat and walks straight to me, enveloping me in his arms. *My safe place. My home.* My whole body relaxes into his hold. I didn't even realize how tense I was until I got back to him.

"I said nothing to no one, and I advise you not to, either. I can't do much right now, seeing I drank and am off duty, but Richards messaged me, and he's on his way. Maddison's also here, so I'm keeping an eye out, just in case she wants to stir some more drama. Can't fucking believe she'd go this far," Maddox grits through clenched teeth, frustration and shame washing over his face.

I turn to him and offer a weak smile. "You can't take her actions on you, though. I know the Mayor will be devastated. I feel sorry for her. She's throwing away her life for absolutely nothing. I'm not saying I would understand her reaction if there was anything between the two of us, but she's fucked her whole life up for nothing."

He rubs his palm over his face and nods at me, returning to his seat. I pull Cole toward the table and choose to sit in his lap instead, so I can easily and quietly get him up to speed.

A blonde waitress dressed in a smart uniform, with a white button-down shirt, tie, and black slacks comes to our table, dropping off a second round. I crinkle my brow in surprise when she places a pinkish-orange drink in front of me before leaving.

"Did you order alcohol for me?" I ask Cole. His eyes narrow in confusion as he shakes his head. Everyone around the table has their own drinks, so I just decide to move the cocktail aside. I'll let her know when she comes back she might have delivered this to the wrong table.

My mood has soured, and truthfully I'd rather just leave, but the petty side of me demands I see Maddison cuffed and escorted out of here.

A catchy rock song plays, and I decide to distract myself with some dancing. I pull Cole onto the dance floor and let myself be carried away by the beat for a few minutes. Music has always been a part of me, although I can't carry a tune to save my life. Nails on a chalkboard sound better than me.

Cole and Blake were close to suffocating laughing the first time they heard me singing while I was making breakfast. Didn't even realize they were there, I was lost in my own concert, headphones secured on my head. I don't enjoy hearing myself sing either, but I do love belting out tunes, so I noise-cancel myself with headphones.

I close my eyes and imagine myself back in the safety of my home, between the three mirrored walls of my gym. My shoulders shimmy and my hips sway. My back is pressed to Cole's chest, his own hips following mine.

Soft guitar notes float around me when a new song starts. My heart hammers in my chest, and lust coils between my thighs as Kekko Silvestre croons of desperate, anguished love, lowlights, and whispered promises.

Cole senses the change in my movements as my hips undulate closer, seeking him, my breathing changing from labored to wanton, and he spins me around in his arms.

He bends his neck, hot lips kissing my shoulder, then rests his cheek on mine. One palm finds its way deep in my hair, and the other beckons me closer to him, fingers spread atop my ass under the hem of my jeans. His steel cock pokes at my belly, and I'm seconds away from mauling him right here on the dance floor.

Hypnotized by the beats of my favorite song, I whisper in his ear, "Stay here with me because I'm crazy about you," just as his gravelly voice triggers my weak point when he rasps in perfect Italian the same lyrics back at me.

There's no gasp out of my parted lips when his mouth plunders mine and steals my breath away. His teeth sink into my bottom lip as he continues singing to me the magic of Modà's "Sono Già Solo" sultry lyrics.

I'm putty in his strong hands. Clay for his masterful fingers to break apart and mold into his perfect storm.

The song ends in the same wailing guitar notes begging his soulmate to return and Cole and I part, although our gazes are fused together.

I may be too much of a coward to say those three pesky words, but the fervent desperation of this song matches word for word everything I feel for him.

As the song hits the last note, we're both turned on, sweaty and breathing harder. I fan my face with my palm, then gesture to let him know I'm thirsty. He nods and points to the bar, then heads toward Jake as I return to our friends.

"Get it, girl!" Annalise hollers at me, her hands fanning her face. "I got hot just watching the two of you. Too bad Drake is working tonight!"

My cheeks pink up, and I'll blame the temperature in here if anyone's asking. "Is the bar always this busy? I'm so thirsty." I ask no one, looking around the table for the can of Coke Zero I had before we went dancing.

It'll be lukewarm, but I can't wait for Cole to come back. My throat is parched. I notice the pink cocktail is gone. Wouldn't have helped anyway since I prefer not to drink alcohol.

The same waitress returns and places a tall glass in front of me, the liquid inside green at the bottom and blue at the top. I stop her with a hand on her forearm. "Is this alcoholic?"

"I'm not sure. A guy at the bar ordering a bunch of drinks asked me to bring this to you." I thank her and put the drink to my nose to smell it. Cole wouldn't order anything I don't want to drink, but errors are made when preparing them on busy nights, so I'd rather be certain.

There's no whiff of alcohol coming from it, just a sugary blueberry scent, so I decide to take my chances and get a sip out of the pretty indigo straw.

The paper straw doesn't touch my lips when a hand rips the drink from mine and downs the whole thing in one go before sliding the glass onto the table. I look from the now-empty drink to Emma, blinking in confusion at her.

"Uhm, I would've bought you a drink if you were this thirsty," I say and narrow my eyes as she just stands there with a dazed look on her face.

"Oh fuck, what have I done?" she mouths, her face rapidly draining of color. She drops onto the bench next to me and looks at me with wide eyes.

"Emma, are you ok? Are you feeling sick?" I ask, concerned about her strange behavior. *What the fuck just happened?*

"I'm fine. I'm just freaked out. I don't know. I'm going crazy," she rambles, her eyes darting around unfocused.

"Can someone get her a bottle of water, please?" I request. I can't really go myself since she's blocking me in. My palm rubs over her forearm and I ask again, "Are you sure everything is fine? Why did you take the drink?"

"I... uhm... I think I saw Maddi put something into your drink. I'm not sure. She and Amanda bumped into the waitress when she was coming here. And she dropped a couple of drinks. They followed her back to the bar, and I saw Maddi take something out of her purse and drop it into that glass," she clarifies, and I note in horror her speech slurs at the end, and her pupils are blown wide.

"And your solution was to drink it yourself?" I shriek at her. She gives me a lazy smile, her cheeks getting rosier and rosier by the second. My shriek must've caught the attention of my friends, who so far were engrossed in conversation.

"Is she ok?" Maevis asks over my shoulder.

"Fucked if I know. I think we should call an ambulance or something. I don't know if she's just drunk out of her mind or the last drink was spiked," I tell Mae since Emma doesn't seem capable of forming any more words. "She thinks Maddison spiked my drink."

"What the fuck?" Cole and Maddox thunder at the same time.

"How long ago?" Cole asks me in a business-like tone, dropping a bottle of water and an unopened can of Coke Zero on the table.

"I don't know, about ten minutes," I inform him and quickly recap the events for everyone.

"Fuck!" exhales Cole. "She looks like she's high, not just drunk," he clarifies, as he pokes and prods at Emma's eyes. "Someone call 911. NOW!"

"ETA five minutes," Annalise tells him. "Let's take her outside."

I look around and see we're one man short. "Where's Tatum?" It dawns on me he hasn't been back at the table since before Cole and I went dancing. In fact, I haven't seen him the whole night except for when we got here.

Maevis gives me a look full of hurt as she answers. "He went to the gents when I was waiting for you. Amanda followed. He never came back."

Cole picks Emma up and heads toward the door, with Maddox clearing the way, so I make a mental note to bring this up later with her. We follow them outside, and I take my jacket off and drape it over Emma. The temperature is quite low, and she's only wearing a thin short dress.

I pace in the parking lot waiting for the ambulance, guilt racking my body. *It's my own goddamned fault. I never should have let her take the fucking drink from me. Should have realized something wasn't right. Cole would never order a cocktail for me.*

Should've and would've scenarios keep berating me as I walk from one side of the lot to the other until the ambulance finally arrives after what feels like hours. I jog to where Emma is placed on a stretcher and shoved into the ambulance as Cole explains her situation to the paramedics.

"Where are you guys taking her? We want to go with. We can't just leave her alone," I demand.

"Forrest Falls General since it's better equipped than Lost Hope for emergencies like this. Does anyone know her full name?"

"Emma. Emma Denvers." I tell him quietly. "Thank you for everything. Will see you there soon."

He nods at me, jumps in next to Emma, then slams the rear doors closed. I turn pleading eyes to Cole to get the car so we can follow the ambulance, but Maddox stops me.

"If someone drives me there, I'll go stay with her. You need to wait here for Richards. He should arrive any minute. He messaged me before Emma fainted to say he had the arrest warrant signed and was on his way."

My mouth opens to protest, but Cole pulls me to him and quickly sides with Maddox. "He's right, love. Let him stay with Emma, and we can join him once Maddison's dealt with."

Defeated, I nod my surrender and burrow tighter into his chest for warmth. I'm not sure where my jacket is right now, and I need the comfort of his presence.

Maddox and Annalise say a quick goodbye and head to his car while Maevis stays with us. Soon after they leave, the sheriff's cruiser speeds into the parking lot, blue, white, and red lights painting the night sky.

"Evening all. Miss McAdams, I have the arrest warrant signed. Your lawyer has been in contact with me, too, and told me you are determined to press charges against Miss Brown. Is that correct?"

"Evening, Sheriff Richards. That is correct. I'd also like to press charges against her for spiking my drink tonight, unsure with what, but it will be determined soon enough. Emma Denvers drank it," I say and inform him of tonight's events.

"My deputies and I will go inside to look for Maddison. I'd like you to follow us to the station to give a formal recount of the events," he instructs us before entering the bar.

I really hope all this madness ends tonight.

Chapter Forty-Four

Lalah

My protest of rushing to Emma's side falls on deaf ears. Again.

The guilt suffocates me. Without really knowing me, she went against her friend and then had a drink meant to harm me. If anything happens to her, I don't know what I'll do.

We may not be friends, but I never wanted anyone to be hurt, especially not because of me.

Cole cuts through my protests and quickly agrees with the sheriff before I push the issue further.

He spins me around so I face him, pulling the lapels of his coat around my back with one hand and cupping my jaw with the other, tilting my head so he can look into my eyes.

"I know you're worried, love. Let's deal with the closest fire, and I promise you, I'll get you to the hospital as soon as possible." He seals his promise with a tender kiss on my forehead.

"I'll head inside and try to find Tatum. Should I tell Jake what we're up to?" Maevis offers.

"Are you sure you want to find Tatum?" I check with her. I'm not sure what his deal is, but I don't want Maevis to get hurt. They've been so much more affectionate since Thanksgiving when he drove her home.

I don't know what happened between them, since both have been sealed tighter than an Egyptian tomb, but it looked like there was some sort of progress in their push-and-pull game. If Tatum really is with his ex-wife right now, Maevis will be crushed.

"Yeah, I'm not looking too hard. I'll talk to Jake and keep an eye out, then come meet you. We all drove here in Tate's truck."

I hand her my card so she can close our tab since she's going in. "Alright, babe. Could you check if we left any of our things back at the table, please?"

She plucks the black rectangle out of my hand, then hurries inside. I coil my arms around Cole's waist and sigh deeply in his chest.

"This entire night has gone to hell. It's just one thing after another after another. Fuck!" I sob, overwhelmed with worry for Emma, disappointment in Tatum, and stress over the consequences of tonight.

"Breathe, babe!" Cole encourages me, rubbing his palm on my back. "Emma's fine. It didn't take long for the ambulance to get here. They have her, I promise."

"You don't know that for sure. She had the drink and ten minutes later she was passed out. Who the hell knows what was in it? It had to be a concentrated dose for her to just pass out like that." I voice my fears out loud, my stomach flipping in dread.

"WHAT IS THE MEANING OF THIS? DO YOU KNOW WHO MY MOTHER IS, SHERIFF?" Maddison's shrill voice breaks the silence of the night.

"Maddison Brown, you have the right to remain silent. Anything you say can and will be used against you in a court of law." Sheriff Richards ignores her screams and starts reading her rights.

I turn around in Cole's arms, watching the sheriff guide a cuffed Maddison to his cruiser, surrounded by deputies as patrons of the bar all spill outside watching in curiosity. She turns her head toward me and pure venomous hatred pours from her ice-cold eyes, her mouth pursing in disgust as she looks at me.

"You fucking bitch. This is all your fucking fault. Why can't you just fucking disappear, you disgusting whore?" she screams as the sheriff gets her in the backseat of the cruiser with a hand over her head, slamming the door shut on her curses.

"I'll see you all back at the station," Richards tells us as he too climbs in the car and drives off.

I call Mayor Brown as a courtesy on our way to the police station. Her cried-out face, red-blotted from relentless tears, keeps popping up in my mind. Another reason for me to feel guilty. Sheriff Richards got Maddison booked in, and she'll have to spend the weekend in jail since it's a Friday night.

On Monday, she'll have her initial appearance before a judge where her charges will be formally presented, and the judge will decide whether or not to grant her bail.

I'm sure Gretchen will find a good lawyer for her, although I doubt Emma's father will represent her.

My lawyer is on the first flight to Billings because, regardless of how strong my guilt toward Mayor Brown is, I'd feel guiltier not doing everything I can to have a deranged person locked up.

Not just for my safety.

But for the safety of any other person she may fixate on next.

Ms. Townsend and Sheriff Richards will also get in touch with each of my friends to get their testimony, and Jake has offered to make available the video recordings from the bar.

After three long and tiring hours, we're finally making our way through the hospital doors, looking for Maddox. He kept us updated on how Emma was faring through the past hours. Once they reached the hospital, he got a hold of Emma's family and remained at their side until we finished at the police station.

We reach the floor where Emma is being held in the ICU. According to Maddox, she's had her stomach pumped and is getting intravenous fluids while being monitored. She seized a couple of times on the way to the hospital and a couple more while the doctors were trying to stabilize her.

She woke up once but was still extremely confused. An emergency blood test was requested so the correct antidote could be administered. They found out the drink was laced with a dose so high of methamphetamines Emma overdosed. Her parents consented for the blood test results to be shared with the sheriff as evidence since the drink was meant for me.

I usher Cole and Maevis in the direction of the waiting room while I stop by the nurse's station and get the attention of the nurse typing furiously at the computer, the clack-clack of the keyboard reverberating through the quietness of the hallway.

"Good evening. Could you please tell me the name of the physician looking after Emma Denvers?" I ask her.

She lifts her tired eyes from the screen and looks at me. "Are you a relative of Miss Denvers?"

"Uhm, no," I stammer, and as she opens her mouth to refuse me, I press my palm to my chest and rush out. "I'm not after private information. I'd like to request a private room for her and pay for anything her insurance won't cover. That's all. I don't need to know any details."

Her eyes assess me up and down as if she's trying to see in the depths of my soul, before nodding her head once.

"If you write down your contact details, I'll have someone from our Billings department contact you first thing on Monday," she says, pushing a piece of paper and a pen in my direction.

I scribble my details onto the flimsy paper and return it to her. "Could I also request this be done anonymously, please?"

"Of course. I'll leave a note for them."

"Thank you so much." I wave at her as I walk toward the waiting room. My heart beats furiously in my chest. I'm unsure if I should just walk in. What if her parents are blaming me for getting her to the brink of death? Not that I would hold it against them.

If it weren't for me, she wouldn't be in this situation. I provoked Maddison. I kept quiet and never confronted her directly.

My hands start shaking so I slide them in the pockets of my jeans, taking deep breaths, trying to find a sliver of courage to push through the door.

After five minutes of trying to convince myself to step in, the door opens and an older gentleman in his sixties, dressed haphazardly in a pair of slacks and a wrinkled jumper, comes out and steps in front of me.

His ginger hair is peppered with silver, his chocolate eyes sunken with dark bags underneath and concerned wrinkles at the corners.

"Ah, you must be Alana McAdams. I'm Lark Denvers, Emma's father," he says in a tired, shaky voice.

My breath freezes in my chest as guilt hits me full force in the stomach like a sucker punch. "Mr. Denvers!" I breathe in a whisper. "I'm so sorry for getting Emma hurt. I'll leave if you don't want me here," I rush out.

"There's no need, Miss McAdams. Chief Deputy Lawson apprised us of what happened tonight. It hurts me terribly to know someone I considered a daughter would do such despicable things. Emma has been stabilized and will be kept for observation, but her doctor is optimistic she is out of the woods, barring any complications. Go on inside. I'm sure she'll like to see you once she wakes up. Her mother has been allowed to stay in the room with her until then."

My eyes well up at his kind words. "You should be really proud of her," I tell him. "You raised an incredible woman. She helped me twice tonight, going against her best friend simply because she believed it was the right thing to do. I don't know her very well, as our interactions have been limited so far, but I'll never forget what she's done for me. I'll forever be in her debt."

He pats my hand and urges me in. "I'm going to get some coffee for everyone. Would you like some?"

"I'm ok, thank you. Do you need a helping hand?"

"That's alright. I just need to be by myself for a while. I'll see you soon."

He leaves through the dimly lit corridor I came from. Reassured by his words, I make my way inside the private waiting room, and I'm greeted by a sea of eyes all trained on me.

I beeline to where Cole is sitting and drop in the chair next to his. He pulls me closer, nestling my head on his chest, my eyes closing against my will.

After what feels like only seconds, I wake up with a start and slowly blink my eyes open. The waiting room is now bathed in daylight, and I notice only Emma's parents, Cole, and I remain here. I straighten my back, rotating my sore neck from side to side, trying to ease my stiff muscles.

"Morning, love," Cole murmurs gruffly, the raspiness of his voice telling me he also fell asleep on the uncomfortable plastic chairs.

"Emma? Do you have any updates?" I ask as the events of the night rush back to me.

An older, blonde, carbon copy of Emma turns on her heel to face me and gives me a weak smile. The paleness of her cheeks only accentuates the purple bags around her green bloodshot eyes. An air of sadness and worry surrounds her as she wraps her arms around her waist, keeping the pastel pink cardigan she's wearing tight around herself.

"Lalah, I'm Emmeline Denvers," she says but makes no move to close the distance. "I just returned from her room. She's doing a lot better than last night but will have to remain admitted until tomorrow. She's still weak and confused. The doctors want to ensure there are no complications before releasing her. They also want her to speak to a mental health therapist," she rushes out as tears fall down her cheeks.

"Do you think I could see her?" I tentatively ask.

"Of course. Just don't overwhelm her with details. She knows what happened up to when she took the drink from you, but nothing else. Emma doesn't know about Maddison's arrest yet."

I nod at her and give Cole's hand a squeeze, trying to draw from his strength. He plants a kiss on the top of my head in encouragement.

"I'll go grab us coffee and some sandwiches, and I'll see you back here soon."

He stands, stretching his back. He must be sorer than I am, considering I was sleeping in his arms and the chairs are much too small for his tall frame.

"Annalise left your jacket. Emma was still wearing it when the EMTs took her to the hospital," he throws over his shoulder as he makes his way out of the waiting room.

"Where's everyone else?" I ask curiously since I was expecting to see more people here.

"Either at the police station to give their statements or I sent them home," Emmeline informs me. "I pleaded with your boyfriend to take you home as well, but he was adamant you want to be here. There was no reason for everyone to stay once we knew Emma was doing better. It's more important that wretched woman be put in prison where she belongs," she wails.

I quickly stand and wrap my hands around her, running my palms on her back, trying to give her a modicum of comfort. I'm also confused as fuck. I thought the Denvers and Browns were close friends.

"I told Emma and Lark over and over again that Maddison is bad news. I saw the calculated look in her eyes, the way she manipulated Emma to do her bidding. The Browns may be stand-up people, but there's not an ounce of goodness in their daughter," she cries, moving away from me, wiping her tears with the back of her hand. "You go on now and see my daughter. I'm sorry for my outburst."

"There's no need to apologize, Mrs. Denvers. I cannot imagine what you must be feeling at seeing your daughter hurt. All I can offer in comfort is to assure you I won't be dropping the charges against Maddison and I won't rest until she pays for her actions."

A glint of fierceness and determination passes over her teary eyes and she gives me a sharp nod of approval.

Emma is right across the hallway from the waiting area, where she's been moved to the private room I requested last night. I knock gently on the door, hoping I won't wake her up if she fell asleep since her mom left her, and enter the room quietly, my eyes flying directly to the bed.

Her tall, curvy frame looks small and dainty as she lays under the white, crisp sheets of the hospital bed. Her eyes still have a confused glaze to them, the rich chocolate of her irises now dull. Her full lips barely lift at the corner as she sees me. I wave shyly at her. *How do I approach a woman who nearly died taking a drink meant for me?*

"I'm so sorry, Lalah," she whisper-cries, the sound raspy and dry as opposed to the melodic voice she spoke in merely seven hours ago. "I should've stopped Maddison before it got this far. I'm her best friend. I know her better than everyone. I'm so sorry."

I take her hand in both of mine, noting the coolness of her skin. My eyes roam over her face, taking in the drastic changes. Where last night her makeup was flawless, now it stains her ghost-pale skin, dark clumps of mascara, and eyeliner smeared around her eyes.

"You have nothing to apologize for. Maddison's actions are on her and her alone. I am the one who's sorry you got hurt. You brave, incredible woman, don't fucking do it again," I order her.

A weak chuckle escapes her throat. "A hundred percent do not recommend it. I feel like shit run over. I bet I look like it too," she whispers in a self-deprecating tone.

"Nah. You look like a strong woman who's been through hell and back." I look around the room for some wet wipes, and when I see none, with a quiet "Be right back!" over my shoulder, I scurry to the small attached bathroom.

Wetting a towel with warm water, I return to her bedside, softly cleaning and drying her face. "There you go. Like new." I wink at her.

"Thank you for staying. My dad told me you and that hunk of man attached to your hip have been here all night. The rest of your friends too, until my mom made them leave."

"It's the least we could do. We're here for you. All of us."

"It's funny, you know. I grew up in Lost Hope and I know each of them, and while everyone was always very nice to me, we were never friends. Not even with Tatum when he was married to Amanda. I was friends with Maddison since childhood, as I told you, but she was always closer to Amanda. She didn't grow up in our neighborhood but was always very ambitious and two-faced," Emma trails off, her eyes fixed somewhere behind me.

"The perfect girlfriend for Tatum when with him, an entitled bully when he wasn't around. I was just happy to be included in their circle and not subjected to their maliciousness." She sighs deeply, a sad frown marring her pale features, brown eyes trained on the fidgety hands in her lap.

"I'm not making excuses for myself, you know. My mom always warned me against her, but she was my friend. I didn't want to believe she would be this cold and uncaring. I just wish I had opened my eyes to her mad ways sooner. Maybe I could've prevented last night from happening."

"Stop, Emma. Stop blaming yourself. We all have a blind spot where the people we love are concerned. Hell, we have a blind spot even with strangers. We're wired to see the best in people, otherwise we'd walk through life alone and afraid of everyone. You stepped up when it mattered the most, even going as far as putting yourself in harm's way. You've done more than anyone ever expected. You've done more than others would have," I tell her, conviction coating each of my words.

"Then you need to stop blaming yourself, too." She lifts her head, her dull brown eyes boring into mine, small sparks of fire returning to her.

"She had no right to fixate on you. Regardless of your relationship with Maddox, she has no claim to him. He refused her at every turn, even before you moved to Lost Hope. But, I guess, for her narcissistic ways it was easier to blame you than to admit to herself Maddox is simply not interested. She's always been self-involved, and to my shame, it was a trait I admired. Her confidence, her queen-of-town attitude, I wanted some of that for myself," she finishes with a yawn.

"Alright. You've got yourself a deal. We both stop blaming ourselves, and you focus on getting better." I soothe her, ready to let her sleep.

"Thank you for coming to see me. You should go home now, but maybe, once I'm back on my feet, we can catch up?" she asks me, her vulnerability reigning on her face.

"You better believe it. Can't get rid of me now, even if you want to," I assure her as she finally lets herself fall back asleep.

Chapter Forty-Five

Cole

"**M**aevis! Calm down, girl. I can't understand a word you're saying." I hear Lalah from where I'm lying down on the sofa. I'm tired as fuck, and it's barely midday.

My whole body aches after the shift at the firehouse and the night sleeping on the hardest plastic chair in the hospital.

Still in disbelief over last night, I'm worried as fuck about Lalah. She assured me she was fine when we left the hospital, but there's a numbness to her, a cold detachment, and I don't know yet how to bridge it.

As soon as we got home, she took her phone and started planning with her lawyer. Once she finished with her lawyer, the Mayor called, apologizing for her daughter and pleading to Lalah to drop the charges. But my girl was adamant she won't be changing her mind.

Despite the disappointment dripping out of the Mayor's voice, she eventually understood her daughter went too far. She hurt too many people for her actions to simply be forgiven and forgotten. She asked instead to have the town meeting canceled, to which Lalah was quick to agree.

After the whole ordeal, I don't think she even remembered the meeting and, in her own words, she'll *cancel all the damn contracts herself if she has to if the townsfolk have a problem with how they received the money.*

"You know you're always welcome here, Mae. Do you want me to come and pick you up? You shouldn't be driving with how distressed you are."

Her worried voice makes me stand abruptly, my knees and back cracking as I stretch out to my full six-four frame. *Ain't a spring chicken anymore.*

"OK. Yeah, I'll come your way. Give me an hour."

She tosses her phone on the coffee table and lets herself fall back to the sofa with a groaned "Umph" before leveling me with a glare so cold my insides freeze. "Have you heard from Tatum today?" she throws at me, eyes narrowed in suspicion.

"I didn't. In fact, last I saw him was at the table last night before you messaged me to join you at the bar," I respond cautiously, running over the events of last night in my mind.

Lalah huffs and lazily stretches her arms to her phone, making a grabby sign with her fingers. I throw her a grin to go with her phone. A few taps of her fingers and the sound of Tatum's voicemail fills the living room. "Fuck," she mutters.

"Care to fill me in?" I ask, my worry now extended to my best friend. I wish I could turn back time to when I had Lalah in my arms just last afternoon, fucking myself into her, before everything went to shit.

"Maevis says Tatum left with Amanda yesterday. Got a message from him sometime last night when we were at the hospital. She called him a couple of times since, but it goes directly to voicemail for her, too."

She taps some more on her screen before turning it to me. My eyes nearly bulge out of my head as I take in Tatum's face, scratch marks on his shoulders and Amanda's head on his bare chest, lipstick smudged, arrogant grin shining.

"*Know your place, 'Cupcake','*" Lalah scoffs as she repeats out loud the message I'm reading.

"What the hell? No, babe," I tell her adamantly. "Absolutely not. I don't believe for a second Tatum went with her willingly, and I absolutely don't believe he slept with her. He can't fucking stand her. And she's married now. He's always careful when picking up women they're not married or in committed relationships. If you believe anything about him, believe this," I plead with her and see her face soften, the spark of war in her eyes dimming before flooding with concern.

"If Maddison had drugs to spike my drink…" she trails off, slender fingers tapping her chin. Her face drains of color and she jumps to her feet. "COLE! We *have* to find him now. Fuck, I'm such a horrible fucking friend."

I'm in her space in two strides of my long legs. "Can you stop blaming yourself for every single thing going wrong?" I demand of her, my palms cupping her chin, forcing her eyes to mine. She'll make herself sick with all the guilt and blame she's burdened with.

"We were all there. Whatever happened between Amanda and Tatum has absolutely nothing to do with you. I love that you care about everyone so deeply, but Supernova, you can't blame yourself for every poor decision we make."

"But..." she starts protesting.

"No buts. He wanted to go to JC's last night. You didn't make him go. It's his fishing pond, anyway. He knows everyone in that bar. He's an ex-Marine, for God's sake. He knows his mind."

I grab her shoulders, trying to keep her grounded to me.

"So, here's how we're doing this. You'll get your beautiful self bundled up, and I'll drop you off at Mae's, then go look for his sorry ass." I seal my promise with a starved kiss. That detachment in her eyes is killing me, and my lips are trying to reach her the only way they know how.

A pit of unrest swirls in my gut and the fear I'm about to lose her floods my veins with the same strength and desperation my tongue plunders her mouth. Not even her responsiveness to my kiss is soothing enough to quell my fears.

I send a prayer to whatever deity is out there willing to hear me nothing else happens because I'm sure Lalah is one breeze away from closing herself off again.

Pouring all my love into the kiss as my tongue greedily explores her mouth, my lips beg her to stay with me, to allow me to carry her over the dark times.

We got to know each other well in the past two months.

I know her fears, her insecurities. I know how easily she thinks she's unworthy, how the expectation of being cast aside and walked over lives just beneath the surface of her skin.

I'm well aware I have a battle on my hands proving to her I'll never leave her. She'll never be overlooked again, not for one single day of the rest of her life.

I crush her to my chest as I slow the kiss, resting my forehead to hers and breathing in her sweet scent of jasmine, roses, and something else I can't quite pinpoint that's uniquely her, as I ready myself mentally for everything that is to come.

I must've called Tatum at least a hundred times in the past three hours. I went to his shop, his apartment, at both his parents' and his sister's places. He's nowhere to be found. To top it all, Lalah decided to spend the rest of the afternoon and night with an inconsolable Maevis.

Even though Lalah shared our suspicions with her, Maevis is dead set on keeping her distance from Tatum, and this will break his fucking heart.

Just last night, he told me he was ready to take their relationship to the next level and was just waiting to make his grand gesture over Christmas.

He didn't share many details with me, but I'm fucking certain something happened between them at Thanksgiving. There was a new hope, a spark inside of him I thought was dead and gone since he found out Amanda cheated on him.

It seems things are slowly falling apart for all of us, and the dread coating my insides continues to grow with every minute I cannot get a hold of him.

I tap my phone unlocking the gates, and to my surprise, his car is parked next to the garage. I don't even bother backing my truck in as I jump out and run for the entrance.

Quickly shoving my shoes away, I jog into the living room, but stop in my tracks as I stumble across my friend's slumped-over form. He is seated on the sofa, his elbows on his spread-apart knees, head down, complete dejection pouring out of him.

"I fucked up, Cap," he whispers. His head turns as he looks at me over his shoulder. My stomach recoils at his red-rimmed eyes and the tears falling down his face. *Bloody hell. If he's crying...*

I take a seat next to him and clap my hand over his shoulder. "What happened, brother?"

"I remember nothing from last night except going to the bathroom and the venomous bitch following me, trying to hit on me. I made for the door to return to the table. She plastered herself to it, blocking me in. When I found her cheating, I swore to myself I would never touch her again, so instead of pushing her away, I just sipped at the beer I took with me and ignored her rants. Next thing I know, I'm in a fucking hotel room, wearing only my boxers, fucking scratch marks on my shoulders and it's lunchtime." He gives me a look so tortured my chest constricts.

"We all tried calling you..." I tell him.

"Had no battery. Helped myself to your charger and turned it on five minutes ago. Maevis wants nothing to do with me..." His last words barely escape his clenched jaw. "FUCK!" he bellows, jumping to his feet, and starts pacing back and forth in front of the fireplace.

"Goddamned witch of a woman," he curses, shoving his hands through his hair and pulling harshly.

I can't hold his desperation against him. I don't even want to think what state I'll be in if Lalah ever tells me she wants nothing to do with me.

"She left me a fucking note on the pillow," he spits, his voice muffled by the palm he holds over his mouth. "Took care of your cupcake. Never say I never did anything for you." His derisive chuckle drops the room temperature by at least ten degrees. "She signed it, *Your loving wife.*"

"She's as delusional as Maddison is," I say matter-of-factly.

"Don't even get me started on that. Blake filled me in on what happened last night. How the fuck did she put drugs in my beer? It's the only explanation. I had one fucking beer from the ones you sent to the table."

"The fuck are you talking about?" My head whips in his direction so fast I almost dislocate my neck.

"Come on, man, work with me here. Lalah messaged. You took Maevis with you to the bar. The girls disappeared down the corridor to the bathrooms. I went, too. On the way there, a smartly dressed waitress carrying a tray of drinks asked me if she should drop my beer to the table or if I wanted to take it with me, then pointed at you. I took it and went on my merry way to the bathroom," he pleads with me to confirm the chain of events.

"Brother, the drinks I ordered I took back to the table myself. No one else touched them except for me and Jake. Everything was bottled and sealed, including the bourbon," I tell him cautiously as redness creeps up his throat to his forehead, a vein throbbing prominently.

I swear I can hear his teeth cracking with how viciously his jaw clenches. He's going to lose his shit and with good reason.

"Fuck. Lalah asked me if I ordered her an alcoholic drink, which of course, I didn't. I didn't give it a second thought, thinking maybe it was someone else's at our table. I'll have to ask her who gave her the drinks. Both of them."

"Call Jake. Call him now before I go to the bar myself and get answers out of that fucking waitress," he thunders.

"I think we need to get you to the hospital first. Depending on what your drink was laced with, they may still be able to find traces in your blood. I really fucking hope you press charges against her."

"And say what? My ex-wife might've drugged and raped me, and I have no fucking memory of it?" he rages at me, his words tearing through me like knives.

"If that's what happened then yes, Tatum. And you take a restraining order against her."

He collapses to his knees right in front of my eyes, his shoulders shaking with the power of the sobs wracking his chest.

"I'm a fucking Marine, a fucking man. How the hell could a slip of a woman get the best of me and put me in this position?" He shouts, his firmly clenched fist hitting his chest.

"Fuck, man. I wish I knew what to say. As much as I want, I can't rewind time. But we *can* make sure she doesn't fucking do it again or to anyone else. And hell, until we know for certain, we can hope she didn't take advantage of the state you were in. Jake could at least show us if you two left together. Come on. I'll drive you to the hospital."

He looks up at me, his blue eyes bereft of any hope, dejection marring his features.

"Do I keep this between us or is Lalah allowed to know?" I check with him as we climb into my truck. This may put me in a shit position with Lalah, but as much as I want to share everything with her, some things are just off limits, not mine to share.

"She can know. She just can't tell Maevis. I... she was clear she wants nothing to do with me. I'm not going to force her to listen to me, and fuck if I'll have her forgiveness just because she pities me," he mumbles, looking out the window.

I buckle in and type a quick message to Lalah to let her know I have Tatum and where we're going in case she comes home and doesn't find me there.

Chapter Forty-Six

Cole

We make the drive to the General Hospital in complete silence. I can't imagine what is going through his head right now. To be hurt and violated in this way is absolutely vile. My blood burns inside my veins, demanding justice for my brother.

To have someone you once swore to love and cherish for the rest of your life, who swore back the same oaths to you, first cheat on you, then resort to these kinds of actions, it's absolutely heartbreaking.

I make my way to the nurse's station and greet the lean, brown-haired man dressed in pale blue scrubs behind the desk. "Hi there. I'm Cole Hayes. My friend and I would like to speak to a doctor in private, if possible," I ask in as friendly of a voice as I can muster.

"Alright. Let me see if I can get anyone to see you," he says as he types on the black keyboard in front of him.

I turn around to face Tatum. He seems smaller somehow, with his head down and shoulders hunched inwards. I'm so angry on his behalf, at Amanda mostly, but also at Maevis.

He would've rallied around her if the situation was reversed. He would've supported and protected her while burning the world to the ground demanding justice on her behalf.

He needs Mae right now, and she's not here for him. I get she feels betrayed, but Mae should've known him better than this. I'm pissed at myself, too. When she said last night she'd last seen him with his bitch-of-an-ex-wife, I should've known something wasn't right.

The truth is, we all failed him last night in one way or another. We all let him down. It's how it goes when it comes to men. There's no second thought of men also needing protection, also needing someone to be vigilant for them and their safety.

And if the man happens to be tall and well-built, people think he's invincible.

"You should call Lawson and have this reported," I say to him quietly. Tatum flinches away from me as if I punched him.

"If I do it, by tomorrow morning everyone will know," he hisses at me.

"I won't pretend to understand what's going through your mind right now, but you're a Marine, Tatum. You see an injustice, you fight to resolve it. Not reporting a potential sexual assault and being drugged just increases the risk of it happening again. Never mind what it will do to you long term. How are you going to react when you see her again? Knowing the bitch, she might taunt you. You already have anger issues. Do you think this will help?"

"Fuck! This is so incredibly fucked up." He drops his head back, eyes squinting at the ceiling, hands propped on his hips.

"It is. But you're not alone. We'll get you through this." I clasp his shoulder just as a woman wearing a white lab coat and a stethoscope around her neck stops in front of us.

"Good evening, gentlemen. Mike there," she waves at the nurse behind us, "told me you'd like to have a private conversation. I'm Doctor Richards. We'll be in exam room five if you'd like to follow me."

"I know you," Tatum states matter-of-factly. "You looked after Lalah McAdams back in July. The sheriff's your brother."

I lift both my eyebrows in shock. Such a small fucking world we live in.

"Indeed. Excellent memory. How's Miss McAdams doing?"

"Thriving. She'll be even better once the person responsible for her car crash is permanently behind bars," I respond instead of Tatum. She gives me a brief smile as she ushers us behind a solid wooden door with no windows.

"Alright. Which one of you is my patient?" she asks.

"I am." Tate lifts his hand. "I uhm... I... fuck. Sorry. I can't get the words out," he sighs, defeated.

"Tatum needs to have a sexual assault forensic examination. A blood test, too," I inform her. I have to give it to the doc, her poker face is impeccable. Not even the slightest twitch on her face, not a single shocked blink.

"When did the sexual assault occur? And what are we looking for with the blood test?" she inquires, her voice maintaining her professional demeanor.

"Potentially last night," Tatum finally grits out. "I don't know if I've been sexually assaulted. I can't remember. Someone roofied me last night. Next thing I know, I'm almost naked in a hotel with my shoulders scratched. There's also a picture on my phone not taken by me, showing a woman with her head on my naked chest. Can't tell from the picture if she's naked too," he finishes and looks at me with vulnerability in his eyes as if asking for my approval. I nod my head at him and let pride shine through mine.

"You had an OD patient here last night. Emma Denvers. You may want to check for the same drugs in Tate's blood, as there's a high possibility the same was used on both."

She scribbles her notes, then ushers Tate onto a chair and takes his blood. Once she's done, she asks me to step outside while she pages one of the forensic nurses specialized in performing the SA examination.

I reassure Tatum I'll be waiting for him just outside the door and make my way out. Before I shut it behind me, his voice rings loud and clear through the room. "Cap, call Lawson for me, will you?"

Another long fucking night, and I am dead on my feet. Drake has been kind enough to switch some shifts around, so I can have another twenty-four hours off.

As soon as Lalah gets home, I plan to bury myself in her and then sleep until I have to go to work.

Once Tatum had all his tests completed, he was greeted by Lawson, decked fully in his chief deputy gear, and myself decked fully in my tiredness and guilt.

A fucking sight for sore eyes, the three of us were.

Doctor Richards and Maddox conferred alongside Tatum for another half an hour as I waited outside some more.

We managed to get back home somewhere around two in the morning. Maddox swore up and down he'll try to keep things as quiet as possible, but we all know how small towns work. We're being kept out of the investigation unless there's a need for us to know.

I kept Lalah informed via messages, and she immediately put Tatum in touch with Ms. Townsend, so she's now representing both of them. First thing he requested was a restraining order against his ex-wife.

The piece of paper wouldn't calm him down, though. Wouldn't change the caged way he feels inside. Since we got home five hours ago, I think he's showered about once an hour. He was also considering leaving at some point during the night.

His plan was to pack a duffel bag, fly to Chicago, and live with Selena for a while. He's been hit from all directions in the last twenty-four hours, and I'm not blaming him for wanting to put some distance between him and the place where he was hurt so deeply.

We're now seated at the breakfast nook, both with a cup of steaming coffee in front of us, engulfed in silence. I don't know what to tell him. I'm hurt and miserable, and so fucking angry on his behalf. His deep sigh draws my eyes from the window to him.

I take in his disheveled, still wet hair covering half of his face, his shoulders slumped forward like a shield in front of his heart, face set to stone, his still clenched jaw, and my own heart shrivels in my chest. We may not be brothers by blood, but we are brothers by choice.

If he is hurting, so am I.

"I don't think I can stay here. I know I should, so I can see the bitch go down. I should be here to ensure this doesn't happen to another unsuspecting fool, but it's not what I need. Distance, some fucking space, that's what I need," he grits through his teeth.

"Where else would you be?" Lalah's shocked voice comes from the entrance to the kitchen.

We were both so lost in our misery we didn't even notice her come in. She walks toward us, stopping in front of Tatum, and rests both hands on his shoulders. His eyes are still downcast.

"Look at me and tell me where else would you be!" She orders him.

Like the good soldier he is, his gaze snaps to hers, only to be greeted by a full-wattage smile on Lalah's lips, pearly whites, bells, and whistles.

"There's my brother. My brave, strong brother. Are we going somewhere?" she asks him, and I could fall on my knees in front of her declaring my eternal love when Tatum returns her smile.

"You're staying put. Cole would hunt me to the ends of Earth if I dared take you away from him."

"Damn right, I would."

"And where will you go, then? Where else will you be if not with your family? You're not going anywhere," she demands, feet stomping for good measure.

Despite the seriousness of the conversation, I can't help but be amused by how my pint-sized woman orders the big, bad Marine around.

"You do realize I have another sister I can live with?" he retorts, only for her to roll her eyes at him.

"Sure you do. I know, I *know* all you want right now is to lock yourself away from the world. But I won't let you. I refuse to let you. You have *nothing* to be ashamed of. *You* have no reason to hide away. Do you understand me?" she asks, her tiny palms cupping his jaw.

"Maybe not similar, but I've lived enough years thinking I earned whenever others put their hands maliciously on me, without my permission, without my consent, without being able to defend myself. I thought I deserved it. When others saw my bruises and questioned their existence, I lied to cover my shame." She blinks back tears, her chest expanding on a deep inhale. "We are not responsible for the actions of others. We are not what was done to us."

He buries his face in her neck and squeezes her close. I step to them and envelop them both in my arms. Tatum can be weak with us. He can be vulnerable and show his hurt. I'll be strong enough for all of us.

And Lalah, she's the glue holding us together.

"I chose her," he whispers with derision. "I fucking chose her. My parents told me I was too young to get married. My sisters despised her. I chose her above anyone else. That's my shame and my guilt. I brought her into my life, and even when she left, she made sure to stab one of her claws in my heart and still pulls at it whenever she feels like."

"So then I need to live in shame and guilt, too, for choosing someone who manipulated me emotionally and cheated on me?" she retorts.

He immediately pushes to his feet and points a finger in her face. "Fuck no! You were a fucking child."

"And you weren't?" she asks him in a don't-fuck-with-me-right-now tone. "And don't you fucking dare tell me you should've known better since you're a man, or I swear to Saturn and all his rings I'll clock you one in the nuts to see if they turn into ovaries."

We both snort out a laugh, turning rapidly into a grimace since we're both well aware she will act on her threat if she must. Lalah gives us a long look, then nods her head as if the matter is settled.

"So, move in with us for a while. You'll do therapy. We'll let Maddox do his investigation, and we'll take it from there."

"Maddox doesn't need me here for the investigation. And I need to step away from Lost Hope for a while. I've been going over everything in my head. The best thing for me right now is to focus on healing mentally. And to do that, I can't be here," he informs us, and I know by his determined tone and steely glint in his eyes he won't be persuaded otherwise.

"Where will you go, T? I'll be worried out of my mind without you here."

"Selena. I'll stay with her for a while. Get my head screwed back on properly. And we will obviously keep in touch. But I'm too angry right now, too disappointed, not just with the she-devil, but Maevis as well. I need some fucking space to just breathe..." He trails off at the heartbroken look on Lalah's face.

Her hazel eyes, more green than amber as they fill with tears, move from him to me, then back to him. She takes a deep breath as she steps closer to Tatum, her palms cupping his face once more. *What now?*

"I absolutely hate what I'm about to say. And I hate my next words are going to cause you more pain, but you need to know. Truthfully, I also resent her a bit right now. Maevis has decided she needs to step back for a while, too. She's going to Florida to spend the holidays with one of her aunties."

She stops when Tatum scrunches his eyes shut, disappointment in Maevis floating all around the kitchen.

"Seeing the picture triggered her. Badly. I'm not excusing her, just telling you her truth. I stayed with her yesterday and just returned from the airport. The picture brought her back to the life she shared with her ex-husband. I already told her it's a shitty move to compare the two of you, but trauma doesn't listen to reason. She believed there was a possibility you had nothing to do with the picture, but, in her head, you got drunk enough and willingly went with your ex. I couldn't share what actually had happened since you forbade it. Are you sure this is what you really want?"

"She put her mental health first, and I won't hold it against her. I, too, choose to put myself first. That means I don't want people around who have no faith in me. She didn't give me the benefit of the doubt. She saw the picture and told me 'Thanks for the heads up. Do not contact me again.' just like that. She gave up on us before we even started. I may be a victim of Amanda's evilness, but I'll be fucking damned if I play the victim card to gain her trust when her knowing me wasn't enough. Regardless of the blood test results and the goddamned prodding done to me, regardless of the consequences of the investigation Lawson is doing, Amanda won either way."

Chapter Forty-Seven

Lalah

"Faster!" I beg Cole with a moan, arching my back into him as his hips relentlessly drive into me from behind. His palm grips my thigh, moving my leg over his, his cock moving in and out of me at a frenzied pace.

My walls flutter and grip around him, wetness pooling out of me as he hits that special place only he's able to conquer.

"Fuck, baby! You're killing me. Come for me! Come now!" He grunts in my hair, the arm he has coiled under my side and over my breasts moving to grip my throat.

He turns my face just so and seals his lips over mine, his tongue plunging into my mouth in tandem with the movements of his cock inside of me.

My body obeys his order, as always, and my orgasm washes through me with the power of a hurricane. I lose all sense of time and all my thoughts scatter in sweet, pure oblivion.

He jerks inside of me once, twice, three times before he impales himself to the root and stills, my name a groaned chant of pleasure on his sinful lips as he, too, finds his completion.

"Good morning to me," I whisper to him with a satisfied giggle.

His arms wrap tighter around me as he tries to regain his breath. "I missed you a whole fucking lot. One more day and this week from hell is done," he murmurs in a blissed-out, gravelly voice.

I turn my torso around as much as I can without making him slip out of me and plant a kiss under his chin. "I miss you, too. I'm so used to sleeping next to you. I've been restless all week with you not being here during the night."

His chin tips down so his tired emerald eyes look directly into mine. "One more night, love, and then I'm all yours for five days before I start my normal shifts."

"I'll hold you to that." I shift and can't silence a whimper when he slips out of me this time. "I'll get a cloth for us to clean up. And you go to sleep now."

My feet pad on the plush carpet and heated tiles of the bathroom. I clean myself up and wet a washcloth with warm water, quickly returning to the bedroom. My lower belly quivers at the sight of Cole on his back, thick arm thrown over his eyes, sheets tangled around his muscular legs barely covering his groin.

My eyes scan every inch of naked skin on his chest, every ridge and dip of his abdomen, his trim waist, the little happy trail disappearing under soft cotton and sigh to myself. I can't get over how gorgeous this man is. I can't believe he is all mine. *For now!* My insecurities scream in my head.

I chase away the negativity with a wave of my hand and clean him with the same care and tenderness he always shows me. Although he just came less than ten minutes ago, his cock throbs and hardens again under my ministrations.

"You sure you don't want to come back to bed with me?" he mumbles, his voice already rough with sleep.

"I'd love to. But the girls are about to wake up and, with Blake in New York until tomorrow, I'd better get their breakfast ready. You Hayes are the hangry sort," I laugh, withdrawing my hand holding onto the washcloth and he groans in protest.

"You're half asleep already and just fucked me awake. Don't you go protesting at me."

"I made love to you," he grumbles, and butterflies take flight in my stomach. We're three days away from the New Year, and I still haven't told him I love him.

I wanted to do it on Christmas morning, but he, unfortunately, was last minute scheduled to work. "Slow, fast, dirty, vanilla, hard, caring, regardless of position and state of undress, I'll never just fuck you. It's always making love between you and me."

Before I can answer or blink, the arm over his face strikes, hooking over my neck and pulling me on his lap, forcing my knees to straddle him.

"You know that, don't you? This, you and I, it's not just sex. Not just convenience or proximity. You're mine. I'm yours." His wide-awake green eyes bore into mine, and there's no tiredness in them anymore, no lust, no physical desire.

His emerald eyes radiate love and affection, trust and loyalty, possessiveness and yearning, awe and worship. Mine redden with unshed tears in response.

He doesn't just say that I am his or he is mine. He makes me feel the words, like a palpable, living, breathing tether between the two of us. An unbreakable cord connecting his heart to mine.

"I wanted to wait for the perfect moment, the perfect opportunity, but fuck perfect. Every day I come home to you is perfect. Every morning I get to slide between these sheets and find you warm and sleepy in our bed is perfect. Every time you reach for me in your sleep or in a room full of people is perfect. I love you, Alana!"

His words hit me square in the chest, and I suck in a breath. The tears can't be contained anymore, and they flow freely down my cheeks.

"I love you too, Cole! Just three months ago I was certain I was meant to float through life alone and fearful, distrusting of others. And then you let yourself be knocked flat on the frozen ground by my dog and stole my heart in your fall," I confess in a teary voice.

"I'm not going to waste more time looking for perfect moments. Life is too short and unpredictable for me not to tell you I love you every chance I have."

Elation flies through me, my heart pounding under my breastbone trying to reach him. I completely close the distance between the two of us and wrap my arms around his neck.

Cole's lips find mine, soft and searching, the scruff on his jaw tickling my face. His teeth nip playfully at my bottom lip, and I part my lips, granting his probing tongue entrance. Where our kisses during sex are always frenzied, burning with fire and passion, his kiss now remains dulcet and loving.

Another declaration of love from the same lips only without words.

I sigh my happiness into his lungs, and he greedily takes all I'm willing to give, unaware I'm willing to give everything I am to him. I let myself soak in all his love and warmth as he slows the kiss, his forehead resting on mine. "Now, that's a fantastic morning for me, too."

With a steaming hazelnut latte in one hand and a minty vape in my other, I watch the white flurries dancing just outside the window.

We've had a white Christmas, and it looks like we'll have a white New Year's Eve too, as it hasn't stopped snowing in a week.

An unexpected Christmas gift for me was Maddison being denied bail after the prosecutor made it clear Miss Brown had made life-threatening attempts to harm me twice. Her being released on bail would only create more opportunities to actually succeed in her attempts.

She's facing a mile-long list of charges, from attempted murder to aggravated assault. But this is a problem for the New Year and the trial we'll be due to attend since she entered a *not-guilty* plea to all her charges.

Our first Christmas together was bittersweet, with Cole on shift. We spent a lazy day, all decked out in our best seasonal pjs, opening presents and admiring the snowflakes constantly falling from the sky, with Cole on a video call from the fire station.

Eliza finally got her snowman, and because the competition is alive and thriving in this family, we all put our best efforts forth and now we have a family of five snowmen and snowwomen guarding the front entrance.

We also had a snowdog for our little frozen family, but Astrum didn't take too kindly to the competition and clawed his ice lookalike to smithereens.

We spent the day after Christmas with the Andersons, Annalise, Drake, Sawyer, Maddox and Ryker, sledding in our backyard and skating on the pond. The kids had a great time, and I think we all enjoyed ourselves.

There was an undercurrent of worry our group was hit with too much on that cursed night weeks ago. That with Tatum and Maevis temporarily gone, we'd grow apart, or worse, resentful. But we all worked extra hard at keeping the judgment low and the acceptance high and so far we only seem to grow stronger.

A chirp from my phone alerts me to someone being just outside the gates. I frown as we are definitely not expecting anyone, especially so early in the morning.

I unlock my phone and the crease between my eyebrows deepens when I notice the cherry red SUV and my brother standing in front of the camera.

Why is Alan here?

I haven't spoken to my brother in years.

Right after Callum and I went our separate ways, my brother also started putting distance between the two of us. Sadly, we were never the closest. Our relationship comprised of envy and jealousy on my part. He was the golden boy who could do no wrong, and I was the fuck-up, the never good enough.

Although the distance he's put between us was disappointing, it was not surprising. To see him at my doorstep is beyond shocking. My heart rate speeds up, as worst-case scenarios fly through my head at lightning-speed.

With a deep breath, I tap on my screen and the gates unlock as I make my way to the entrance. I step outside just as Alan opens the passenger door of the SUV and a delicate brunette exits the car with his help.

I take in my brother and his five eleven lean build. A black trench coat covers him from neck to knees, black wool trousers peeking from under the open lapels of his coat, and shiny Italian dress shoes on his feet.

There's not much change in his appearance since I last saw him. He always liked to dress smartly, business like. He's my family's pride and joy, so he must look the part.

When he graduated from college with a degree in software engineering, even my parents put aside their differences to throw him a graduation party.

When I graduated from college, my mom didn't show up to my festivities since they overlapped with Alan's high school graduation.

Daddy dearest sent me a congratulatory text for disappointing my family by graduating *magna cum laude* instead of *summa cum laude*. How I could've done better, but I whored myself to Callum instead of paying attention to my studies.

The brunette clutching Alan's arm and teetering on high-heeled cream leather boots is new.

New to me, at least.

She's pretty in a trophy-wife kind of way. Her dark hair falls in soft waves around her delicate shoulders. Her pale-pink trench coat cinched tightly at the waist outlines her waif-like posture and large breasts.

"Alana!" He greets me. There's no smile on his face, his dark eyes hold no warmth toward me, just cold calculations.

Chapter Forty-Eight

Lalah

"**A**lan!" I retort in the same uninterested voice as his. "What brings you by?"

"Are you going to let us in? Sophia's cold. You never did learn manners."

I roll my eyes at his condescending words and attitude. The little brother trying to make himself big in front of his girlfriend act is also new, but I've been dealing with my family's shit my whole life. My skin is diamond-strong, impenetrable to their bullets.

"Of course. *Please*, do come in." I usher them in with a swipe of my arm toward the entrance and a saccharine smile plastered to my face.

They both start unbuttoning their coats and make to drop them in my arms. *What in the actual fuck?* I ignore their gesture and slide past them to the living room where I plop into the love seat next to the fireplace.

"Have a seat." I gesture toward the sofa, and because I'm not completely without manners, I add, "Would you like something to drink?"

Who I now know to be Sophia gingerly takes a seat in the middle of the sofa, crossing her legs at the knees as she pulls down the short hem of her pink knit sweater-dress. My brother, the overlord of everything, sits next to her, ankle resting on his knee as if I'm the guest here.

Some fucking things never change.

"No drinks." He makes a show of looking around the living room while his girlfriend continues to stay silent. I guess I'm not getting an introduction then. "What is it you do here?" he asks out of nowhere.

"Uhm, what?" I very eloquently clarify since I don't understand where he is coming from. He doesn't get to answer as Clara flies down the stairs and directly into my arms.

She's a tornado of messy curls and pillow creases on her face. "Morning, sweet girl! Did you sleep well?" I ask her, forgetting completely about Alan sitting in front of me, in the face of all the cuteness snuggled to my chest.

"Lalah, me hungwy," she whines in her adorable baby voice.

"You're hungry? Oh, no! Whatever are we going to do about that?" I feign surprise as I stand with her in my arms. Heading to the kitchen, I see Eliza using the wall to hide. "Whatcha doing there? You ready for breakfast, too?"

"Who're they?" she whispers, pointing at the sofa, reminding me of my beloved guests.

"That's my brother, Alan, and his girlfriend, Sophia. Come, love, let's get you fed," I urge her, as a tiny smile forms on her face and she waves at them.

"So you're a nanny?" Alan's voice comes from behind me, completely ignoring the girls. Even Eliza can hear the derision in his tone, and she spins on her heel, ready to put him in his place, my little defender.

But I'm not willing to subject the girls to our barbs, so I decide to just lie. I hate lying, but with my family, there's no point in stressing out the truth. They're going to see what they want to see.

"Yup. That's me. The nanny. As you can see, I have to feed the girls their breakfast. You're welcome to wait or you can come back later on."

"We'll wait. Are you allowed to have guests?" he asks, and I make the mistake of looking back at him. The fucking eyebrow lifting on his forehead drips in condescension.

I don't dignify his question with an answer as I usher the girls into the kitchen and have them seated at the breakfast nook.

"Alright, my lovelies. What's it going to be today? Cereal? Pancakes? Scrambled eggs?" I offer, trying to get Eliza's mind back to the matter at hand. It's written all over her face that she doesn't know what to make of Alan. *Same, baby girl. Same.*

"I don't like your brother. He's mean," Eliza whispers to me.

I give her a small smile and tap the tip of her nose with my finger. "You're not wrong, baby. He is a little sour."

"We'll just have cereal. It's not polite to leave guests waiting, even if they are mean," she decides, and I collect two bowls and their preferred chocolatey kind as Eli sets the milk on the table.

I help Clara guide the spoon to her mouth instead of anywhere else as my mind wanders back to the living room. Nothing good can come from this visit.

Alan's been here less than ten minutes and he's already being judgemental. Even though I haven't seen him in so long, I can't wait for him to leave. I can only imagine he got my address from our mother.

Back in July after my car crash, I had a moment of weakness where I called my mom to let her know of my accident, hoping she'd want to come and look after me for a while.

I was nothing more than a child wishing her mom would be here to cure her pains and fears. She, of course, flat-out refused me since I'm a grownup and should know better than getting behind the wheel if I'm not capable of driving.

I could never understand my family and their complete disregard and disinterest in my well-being.

I look at Clara and Eliza, and I know from the bottom of my heart I would lay my life down for them, and they're not mine in any sense of the word.

So it completely baffles me how the people who gave me life and have the same blood running through our veins, can be so cold and indifferent.

Both girls are quiet as if feeling the same trepidation, the same restlessness in the air brought in by my brother. They finish their breakfast in complete silence and both drop their bowls in the sink as we all make our way back to the living room.

Sophia, the real-life — *questionable* — doll, remains on the sofa, but my brother is in front of the window, looking out, standing proud and tall with his hands clasped together behind his back.

"Thanks for waiting," I say to no one, taking my seat next to the fireplace. Clara demands to be put down, and she toddles at her fastest speed toward her box of toys. At least I know she'll be occupied for the next half an hour. Eliza picks up one of her fairytale books and sits at my feet.

"Must the children stay here while we discuss?" Alan hisses.

"They must, Alan, seeing as it's my job to look after them."

"Why are you wasting your life babysitting, Alana? Our parents didn't pay for you to go to college for nothing."

"Our *parents* didn't pay for my college at all, brother dearest. Why are you here?"

"Of course, you keep on with the lies. Dad told me of all the money he sent you when you were in college."

"Lalah... I'm going to my room," Eliza mumbles in a small voice, and my stomach clenches. As usual, any conversation between Alan and I escalates quickly to raised voices. This is the last thing I want the girls to witness.

"Has no one taught you not to interrupt adults when they're talking?" My brother snaps at Eliza and I feel my blood igniting.

"Go on, baby girl!" I urge her with a kiss to her forehead. "I think my *little* brother has forgotten I am his *older* sister. Let me remind him." The smile on my face feels as brittle as dried-over paper, but with small eyes and ears around me, I need to keep my face as pleasant as I can.

I turn to my brother as soon as I hear Eliza running up the stairs. "You're forgetting your place. This is their home. You are a guest."

"I can't believe someone is insane enough to let you care for their children. If this is how you educate them, they must not love their children very much."

"Why are you here, Alan?" Naturally, he thinks the worst of me. Of course, he thinks I'm not good enough to care for children.

"Sophia and I are getting married. Mom wanted me to come and let you know."

"Congratulations. You could've called. Saved yourself the money for the trip."

"Mom thinks you should come to the wedding. Sophia and I disagree. Callum is my best man, Rebecca is Sophia's matron of honor. We don't want them to feel uncomfortable, and it's not like you've been there for me, not like Callum has. Rebecca is Sophia's best friend. You simply don't fit into our lives," he tells me in a matter-of-fact tone.

"You really should've called, Alan! Why did you come all the way here just to spit a whole bunch of nothing?"

"Call it brotherly curiosity," he says, his thin lips lifting in a crooked smirk. "You're good to no one, sister. Best decision Callum made was to kick the trash out. He's happier now than he'd ever been with you. We all are. If your employers really care about their children, they should let you go before you infect everything around you with your misery. Unless you're fucking your employer and that's why they keep you around."

I blink at him in disbelief. Then blink again. Alan's in my face, victorious smile contorting his face.

"Dad was right. You're simply a waste of space. Good for nothing little whore. Can't you see no one ever wants you? You're pathetic, a fucking disgrace, Alana."

I feel his words deep in my soul. Everyone is happier without me.

What kind of example do I give to Eliza and Clara?

I can't even keep my temper in check for ten minutes in front of them around my actual family.

I got Tatum and Emma hurt.

My father cheated on my mother because he couldn't bear being at home around me.

I'm not good for anyone.

I'm not good.

My head is swimming in memories. A jumble of voices floats around me, shouting at me, trying to get my attention.

"Pack your bags and leave. You can do whatever the fuck you want with her." My father's thunders like it did the night he kicked us out.

"Why must you be this way? Can't you see your parents divorced because you're out of control and no one can put up with you?" My grandfather's fights for attention.

"Who the fuck would want to tie their life to a soul-sucking bitch like you?" Callum's circles around me.

"Why can't you be more like your brother? What did I do wrong to have such a deranged child?" My mom's adds. *"Can't you do anything right, Alana? I raised you better than this. I should've just left you with your father since clearly you don't care about me."*

"You need to get the fuck out of this house. RIGHT NOW! If you return, I'll have you arrested for trespassing." Cole's voice sounds closer to me than all the others.

I try to return to the present, but the ghosts of my past are stronger, pulling me under the surface. I'm fading under the truth of their wickedness.

"I wish we'd never had you!"

"Why are you crying? Do you think crying is going to make me forgive what you've done?"

My hand goes to my cheek as the phantom pain of my father's slap stings my skin.

"Are you trying to defy me? Or you're just not sorry enough to cry? Answer me, you stupid girl. You think you can defy me?"

Warmth envelops me as calloused hands cup my face. My favorite pair of emerald green eyes appear in front of me, silencing the ghosts still fighting to make me disappear.

"Lalah, love, he's gone. Supernova, come back to me." Cole's concern penetrates through the stones hitting me, settling like armor on my skin.

Too bad his armor doesn't protect me from the lashes of hatred already inflicted.

It just serves to hide the knife buried in my chest.

Chapter Forty-Nine

Cole

I'm fucking terrified. Her beautiful hazel eyes, normally sparkling with fire and life, are now dim, extinguished. The fucking nerve on her asshole brother to come into her home and be a miserable prick to her.

Thankfully Eliza woke me up when she did, otherwise who the fuck knows how long he would've kept at it.

With a hand on each side of her waist, I pick her up and sit her in my lap. My arms band around her tightly of their own accord, trying to keep her broken pieces together.

I only heard the last part of their conversation, but if this is how she was treated growing up, it's no wonder she's always with one foot out the door, ready to bolt, mistrusting of everyone.

All the progress I've made gaining her trust over the past few months has just gone out the door with the pompous ass she calls a brother.

She sits listlessly in my lap. Her body's here with us, but her mind is far away. And I'm chilled to my soul seeing her like this. Eliza looks at us, eyes full of concern. She may be young, but she definitely knows how to read a room.

"I'm going to put Lalah to bed. She needs to rest," I inform my sister. "Are you okay watching over Clara for a minute or do you want to come upstairs with us?"

"We'll stay here. I'll send Astrum for you if we need you. Coley... is Lalah going to be ok? Her brother was very mean. You and Blake are never this mean to us..." Eliza trails off in a small voice.

"She'll be fine. Don't you worry, squirt. Let me get her in bed, then I'll come sit with you here, and get you guys some lunch."

Picking up Lalah, I climb the stairs two at a time. My concern grows more and more when I get her into bed, and she simply rolls on her side and closes her eyes.

She won't even meet mine and hasn't spoken a word in the past twenty minutes. I can't get out of my shift tonight, and with Lalah in this state, I can't expect her to look over my sisters.

Tucking her in, I place a kiss on her cold and clammy forehead. "I love you!" I whisper in her ear before going back downstairs to my sisters.

I'll get her through this.

I can't begin to understand what she is going through, but I swear on my life I'll get her through this if it's the last thing I do.

She's my endgame, my happily ever after, and I'll be damned if I let an entitled asshole ruin that for us. She told me about her family and the way she grew up, so I had an idea of everything she had to overcome, but it's one thing to hear about it and a completely different story witnessing her being treated so heinously.

My knee bounces up and down in frustration as I sit in the living room with my sisters. Both of them are distracted; Clara trying to catch the dancing flames in the electric fireplace, Eliza with her nose in a book, princess-pink headphones covering her ears. I pick up my phone and quickly find the name I need before connecting the call.

"Morning, Cole! Didn't expect to hear from you today." Annalise's calm voice floats from the speaker.

"Morning, Anna. I wish you didn't have to hear from me today," I sigh, trying to expel some of the dread running through my veins.

"What happened?" Her now serious tone cuts through the air.

"We've had an unexpected visitor this morning and Lalah's quite upset. It's not really my place to share the story, but I would appreciate it if you could come and spend the night here."

"Shit. Is she ok?" she whispers.

"Honestly?" I huff and spear my fingers through my hair, trying to quell my anxiety. "No. Fuck no. She's not fine. She's pretty upset and shaken up. I've put her to bed just now, so I'm hoping some rest will help, but fuck, Annalise, I don't know."

"Say no more. I'll be there. I'm assuming you want a pair of eyes on the girls too, in case Lalah's not bounced back by this evening?"

"Yeah. Blake's still out of town until tomorrow morning, but I should get home before he does."

"Alright. Drake usually leaves around 6 pm for the fire station, but I'll be at yours at five. Not everyone is lucky enough to live one block over from their workplace."

"Thanks, Annalise. You're a great friend. See you tonight."

"You ready to get home?" Drake clasps me on the shoulder.

"Just about. Goddamned night felt never-ending," I gruff back. The pit in my gut only got bigger since I left Lalah at home, a shell of a woman curled up on her side in our bed.

"Look after her, man. And have faith in her. Lalah's one of the strongest people I've ever met. Whatever it is, she'll come out the other side kicking and screaming."

I wish his words gave me hope, but they fall flat amidst the coil of dread in my gut. Lalah *is* the strongest person I know, but where just yesterday she was pure fire and life, there's a black hole of emptiness around her now.

The house is eerily quiet as I stomp my way to our bedroom. It kills me not knowing what I'll find. Last night it was Lalah sleepy and warm, eager for my arms. Today... I don't dare hoping a night made much of a difference.

My hand trembles on the knob of the door separating us. A soft click startles me, my body spinning toward the sound on instinct. A wide awake Annalise walks to me, an apologetic smile on her face.

"Sorry, I didn't mean to sneak up on you, thought it was Clara lurking around again."

My palm scrubs at my face, fingers tightening on the strands of hair atop of my head.

"You're fine. Just got home. Couldn't sleep?"

"I slept just fine, thank you. The girls were good to me. Worried for Lalah, though. Clara kept trying for her bedroom tonight, but I intercepted and got her back to bed. I figured Lalah could use some time for herself to just be."

"Thanks, Anna. I really appreciate you going out of your way to look after my girls. All three of my girls." I give her a sad smile.

"Thank me with a tea, and then I'll let you crash. I'm staying until you wake up or Blake gets home, in case the girls need me."

I look back with dread at the bedroom door. Nothing in my life scared me as much as that fucking door does. Not jumping headfirst into life-threatening missions in godforsaken places, not guns to my head, not the threat of sneaky missile strikes.

Not knowing if I'll be welcomed into my own bedroom at the side of the love of my life terrifies me like nothing else.

"Coffee sounds good," I mumble, ushering her down the stairs and toward the kitchen.

"She didn't come out last night. I knocked a couple of times, but not a peep. What happened, Cole?" Annalise inquires over the rim of her steaming, milky black tea. I sip at my own cup of decaffeinated coffee, a pang of longing stabbing me in the gut since I got the habit from Lalah.

"I wish I could tell you," I sigh, scratching at the scruff on my cheek. "I don't want to betray her confidence, her privacy. I also don't know much." My shoulders lift in a defeated shrug.

"We're not gossiping here, Cole. How can we help her if we don't know what ails her? I'm not asking because I'm burning to know the details. I'm asking so I know if I need to pour poison in your coffee or get her a bucket of ice cream."

"Down, girl." I crack the first smile in twenty hours. It does me a world of good to see how fiercely she is loved by her friends. If only she'd open those beautiful eyes of hers and see how she brightens the lives of everyone around her. How she single-handedly changed the course of my life. "Her brother was here yesterday."

I open my mouth to say more but clamp my lips shut at the sharp gasp coming from Annalise.

"Where were you?" Her forefinger points accusingly at me.

"Asleep. Eliza woke me up, and thank fuck she did. I don't know what was said between them, I only caught the tail end before I kicked the fucker out. Too fucking late, turns out, the damage was already done."

The asshole's words keep playing on repeat in my head. My hands fist at my sides with all the pent-up aggression coursing through my veins. I really should've punched the arrogance out of him before throwing him out.

"Dad was right. You're simply a waste of space. Good for nothing, little whore. Can't you see no one ever wants you? You're pathetic, a fucking disgrace, Alana."

The ding of a phone has us both turn our heads toward the living room. I shuffle my feet to the sofa and pick Lalah's phone up. It's like I conjured the fuckface just by mentioning him. I slide the screen unlocked and tap on the message.

> Just because you're fucking your employer doesn't make you any better. You'd think you would have learned your lesson and stopped whoring yourself out to others. But what else is to be expected from someone as desperate for attention as you? Our parents were fools to have you. A condom would have been cheaper.

Alan

My fingers tighten around the phone, and it takes everything in me not to throw it against a wall.

"What the hell?" Annalise shrills from over my shoulder. "Who says shit like that to their family, their own sister?" My chin tips in her direction. I'd rather carve my heart out of my chest with a rusty knife than hurt my sisters like that.

My fingers tap on the screen, deleting the text, and blocking his contact. I have half a mind to fly down to East St. Louis and teach him a lesson. Him and her entire miserable family. None of them are worthy of her, worthy of having this amazing woman in their pitiful lives.

"Par for what went down yesterday," I grit through clenched teeth.

"It's no wonder she's all holed up in the bedroom. Anyone with a modicum of heart would be hurt. Go to her, Cole. She needs you to be there. She needs you to show up every day for her until she gets strong enough to show up for herself." She points toward the stairs and seconds later I'm once again face to face with the damned door.

I twist the knob, my heart skipping a beat when the slab of wood pushes open. Relief softens the tension in my shoulder blades with the realization she hasn't locked it. I drop my clothes on the floor and slide inside cool sheets. My hands latch onto Lalah's waist, and I pull her to my chest.

She's a tight ball of limbs, and her body doesn't relax into mine as she usually does. If anything, it stiffens even further, but, as I close my eyes and will sleep to take me, I celebrate the small win of her not pushing away.

Eliza watches me from the corner of her eye, and I'm ready to explode out of my clothes like Hulk and smash everything in front of me to smithereens.

"Coley..." she whispers, crawling on the sofa until she reaches me, her small palm settling on my thigh. "Is Lalah upset with me?"

The hurt in her voice makes my head snap in her direction. "No, baby girl. She's sad, so we have to give her a bit of time to be sad, but it has nothing to do with you. She loves you, Eliza," I murmur back to my sister.

Two days of misery. Two days of me forcing Lalah out of bed each morning. Two days of watching her sit lifeless on the window seat of the living room, eyes trained on the snow outside.

Ohh, she pretends. She pretends for the girls, a fake smile on her lips that never reaches her eyes. She responds if Eliza or Clara engages her, but she's not involved. Not anymore.

Eliza blinks her round, silver eyes at me, the cautiousness in her gaze giving way to determination. She steels her small shoulders and slides from the sofa, her tiny feet padding on the floor as she walks purposefully toward Lalah.

Her palm stretches for Lalah's arm and pulls at the black hoodie my woman seems to disappear into. Muddy brown eyes turn to my sister, her face as pale as the snow outside.

"It's New Year's Eve tonight," Eliza says. Lalah barely tips her chin in acknowledgement. "I want us to go to the Community Center. There's a party."

Anxiety coils in my gut and I jump from the sofa, striding in their direction, towering over both of them. I want Lalah to feel better and I want to give her the space she needs to heal, but I have to protect my sister from a potential lash-out if she's pushing too hard too fast.

"We'll go to the party then," Lalah rasps, her words quiet, resigned. She pushes to her feet and, with an "I'll go get ready" over her shoulders, disappears up the stairs.

Eliza throws me a victorious smile before running up the stairs in Lalah's wake. I look after her dumbstruck, squashing down the hope stirring inside of me.

Lalah's phone vibrates in my pocket, and I slide it out. Dozens of texts show up on the group our friends created, each of them worried about her well-being.

Annalise advised me the other day to contact her therapist, which I did, and arranged for her to have a one-hour session daily. I don't know if she's talking to the therapist during that time or not, but I'm not going to give up trying to reach her.

A new message comes through, followed by another two in quick succession. My fingers tremble in anger as I tap on the messages, opening them.

> Alana, I can't believe you are so obstinate and ungrateful to refuse to attend your brother's wedding. He is your brother. What would people think when they don't see you there? All you have to do is put on a nice dress; I'm sure Sophia will help you pick a beautiful one since the ones you wear are not wedding appropriate, and sit at a table.

> Why are you so selfish? Alan told me you can't attend because you are babysitting. You'll never find a husband if you don't make something of yourself, Alana. You're thirty years old. You can't hold a proper job and can't look after yourself. Why did you waste money on college to babysit children? What do you know about educating and caring for children?

> Come to the wedding and be on your best behavior. That darling man Callum is Alan's best man and he has moved on. Just because you couldn't hold onto him doesn't mean you need to make a scene. Think of your family for once, Alana, instead of just yourself.

Mom

My hands shake as I read the messages. Of course, the nutless scoundrel lied. At least, I now know the reason he visited, although I'd bet my life he extended no such invitation to Lalah.

I hurry to delete the messages but refrain from blocking her. As soon as I get Lalah back, we'll talk about healthy boundaries when it comes to these... people. My mouth twists in a grimace since I can't even call them that with a straight face.

We are a family.

A healthy family, where we all support and respect one another, not the travesty she had growing up. I throw her phone on the sofa and rush to get myself and Clara ready for the party Mastermind Eliza is forcing us to attend.

Silence. That's the new state of our relationship. We dress next to each other in complete silence. The drive to the Community Center is made in deafening silence, only the girls' chatter in the backseat providing some background noise.

Uncertainty eats at me from the inside out. The party could help coax Lalah out of her shell if all her friends band around her, or it could push her further down. She can clam up into herself even more.

I peer at her from the corner of my eye as she stands ramrod straight next to me. Her arm brushes the sleeve of my blazer, but she refuses to touch me otherwise. The strobing lights in the main hall-turned-ball-room are blinding, the music deafening.

Dozens of people mingle on and around the dance floor while we lean against a cold wall, me a ball of desperation and dread, her empty and far away.

"Lalah, Cole, I'm so happy you could make it," Mayor Brown greets us with a kiss on the cheek. I nod in her direction while Lalah plasters an empty smile on her face.

She's as beautiful as ever. To an outsider's eye, in her black A-line dress, Lalah is the picture of exaggerated happiness and maximum health. In my eyes, she's all plastic smiles, red lips and dead-on-the-inside eyes. That's what the love of my life has reduced herself to.

"Gretchen, how are you holding up?" she asks, her lifeless eyes on the blonde woman.

A grimace tightens the mayor's lips before they relax. "I've been better. This past month has been... eventful," she answers carefully, her eyes darting between Lalah and me. "Anyway, I just wanted to come say hello. And to thank you personally, Lalah, for not pursuing any action against me.

Emmeline will do a great job replacing me as the liaison between Lege et Lacrima and Lost Hope."

"There's no need to thank me, Gretchen. I didn't do you any favors. If anything..."

"Thanks, Mayor!" I cut Lalah off before she starts apologizing for things she has no business apologizing for. "Happy New Year. If you'll excuse us, it's getting late, and we need to get the girls home," I say as I grasp her hand and pull her toward Blake.

My eyes blink open, my hand patting behind me on the nightstand, and sigh when my fingers connect with my phone silencing the alarm. Slowly extricating my arm from underneath Lalah, I raise myself on my forearm, peering down at her sleeping form.

I'm losing all hope of having her back. I have no wild expectations of her bouncing back to her fiery self, but she's so lost to her sadness there's not even a glimpse of the woman I desperately miss and love.

As much as she pretends with the others, she can't pretend with me. I know every one of her smiles, every one of her frowns.

Where just a week ago I could read every single one of her emotions and thoughts just by locking my gaze with hers, she's empty now. A shell. She simply exists around us.

I roll off the bed and silently make my way to the bathroom. I'm starting a day schedule at the LHFD for the next month until I finally complete my training, then move to the normal twenty-four-hour stint.

My cock stirs as hot water pours over me from the showerhead above. I haven't touched Lalah like she's mine in five days. We went from not being able to keep our hands to ourselves for more than five minutes to not even a shared look.

The only gestures remotely sexual are the good night and good morning kisses I give her every day.

She doesn't react to my touch, and I'm not a complete asshole to push her into something she's simply not in the right frame of mind to consent to.

So I just hold her as she sleeps and hope beyond hope she'll snap out of this haze of depression she's found herself in.

I can't help the worry bubbling in my gut. Today's the first day I have to leave Lalah alone. I know as soon as I'm out the door she'll lock herself up in the bedroom since the girls are the only reason she ever leaves the bed. With Blake close by, she thinks she's not needed.

She doesn't cuddle up to me anymore as she sleeps.

She doesn't talk to me.

She doesn't look at me.

I'm invisible to her.

Chapter Fifty

Cole

I suck in a breath of frozen air as I unlock my truck and jump inside. I activate the heating in my seat as I back out of the garage. The fifteen minutes drive to the fire station passes in a haze.

To be completely truthful, I can't even remember the drive, my mind being on the beautiful, broken woman I left sleeping in bed.

"Morning, Cole!" Drake greets me with a pat on the back. "I'm doing a coffee and breakfast run at the diner. Bless Ruth's soul for being open twenty-four-seven. Want anything?"

"Sure thing, Captain! I'll have my regular," I say and pass him a twenty-dollar note.

Removing my regular clothes, I hang them in the locker assigned to me, changing into my station uniform of long-sleeved navy polo t-shirt and pants, then check the rota for today's assignments. Not surprised to see I'm assigned to be Drake's shadow today and to cook lunch for us and dinner for the night shift.

I make my way to the hall that was transformed into a canteen, with a dozen or so tables spread around the space and a long counter next to the far wall, where all the cooking takes place.

It's not much different than a high school canteen, maybe just smaller in size. The day shift today will have fifteen firefighters, out of which five are volunteers, and two EMTs, myself included.

We have five engines at the station. Unfortunately, we've been severely understaffed for over five months or so, according to Drake. We're all trying our best and we're extremely grateful to all our volunteers, but most of the time we're just praying we don't get a serious emergency when we're not at full capacity.

Drake wastes no time returning with our breakfast, and I take a seat at one of the tables in the canteen with him. Russel and Rowan, the other two firefighters in our team, plop down on either side of me.

Russel is a tall, solid, black man nearing his fifties, but you wouldn't be able to tell looking at him. He has one of those permanently young, smiling faces. He's one of our most experienced colleagues and the go-to man when dealing with people in shock.

Rowan is a big Irishman in his thirties, with the accent to prove it. He's our Nozzle Operator and a wiz around the engine. His actual job is writing thrillers, and he is a volunteer at the fire station, but truth be told, he spends most of his time here. He might as well be a full-time employee.

We all seem to be in a shitty mood today, so we're just shoveling food into our mouths in silence. I can't taste the food with all the concern running through my veins, but I can't allow myself not to be at full strength. People depending on us need me to be at one hundred percent, and Lalah needs me to be at my best, too.

The vibration of my phone in my pocket takes me by surprise. I'm even more shocked to see Lalah's name flashing on the screen. My heart hammers in my chest. Hope takes flight inside of me that I am finally getting her back.

I quickly unlock my phone and tap on her message.

> I think it's time you contact Maevis. Her house should be free now. It's been fun, but I think we both need to be honest with each other and admit this is not going anywhere. I'm not fit to make anyone happy and carrying on with this farce until you come to your senses and move on to bigger and better things is just downright cruel. I'm sorry. It's for the best for everyone involved. Who were we kidding playing house like that?

Supernova

My heart fucking stops as I read her message and my blood turns to ice. Over my dead fucking body I'll let her end us. Over my dead fucking body I'll move out and leave her alone.

I mentally curse the remaining hours of shift separating me from her. Lalah and I are going to have words once I get home. I've let her be for the past five days. Let her grieve, let her wallow in pain, but I'm fucking done.

Me

I'm trying to stay busy so I don't obsess over how the love of my life is actively kicking me out of hers. I make my way to the kitchen at the back and check the industrial-size fridge to see if I have all I need for lunch and dinner, then start compiling a list with the missing ingredients.

The list goes to Rus who's doing the shopping run today, before I join Drake and Rowan, who are doing the maintenance of Engine 11, to which we're assigned.

Just as we're about to finish, the alarm starts, deafening shrills bouncing off the walls. We rush to get our turnout gear on before hopping into 11, sirens on, red lights flashing.

"Alright, guys!" The Chief's voice comes through our comms. "It's a big one. Five tank trucks loaded with gasoline crashed at the Pine Ski Resort outside of Forrest Falls. Big fucking spill all over the place. To make matters worse, one of them ignited on the spot and exploded. We have more than one dozen cabins on fire, as well as the east side of the main building."

Drake and I exchange glances. There's fear lurking in his dark eyes. Gasoline spills are a bitch to clean without igniting. With cabins and the main building on fire in the middle of the ski season, there's a high risk of casualties.

And we only have four engines.

"We're all hands on deck," the Chief continues. "Now, Engines 1 and 2, you deal with the tankers and spill. Your priority is to isolate them. We don't want another fucking explosion on our hands. Engines 3 and 11, you're on the main building. I'm currently reaching out to everyone and calling people in, so we'll have Engine 4 available, too. A temporary camp will be set up on the west side of the building. I'm doing a quick assessment, but I've already reached out to neighboring fire stations, including Billings. We need all the goddamned help we can get."

"Engine 11, two minutes out." Rowan's voice crackles through the radio.

I turn my head to the window and feel the blood draining from my face. Thick black smoke rises to the skies, with fire crackling and burning everywhere we look. There are at least ten ambulances parked on the west side of the main building, red and blue lights flashing in the carbon monoxide fog.

"Alright, gents. This is it." Drake's voice sounds in the cab. "Let's do what we do best and save us some lives. Stay safe, stay smart, and fucking stay alive! Let's tame this motherfucking beast," he commands, then kicks the door open and we follow him straight into the fiery pits of hell.

Everything hurts. My arms hurt. My back hurts. My fucking hair hurts. I don't even know how much time has passed since we got here.

The Chief has us working in four-hour stints followed by a couple of hours' breaks where we can eat and nap.

Two massive tents have been raised about two miles down the road from the resort. One for the first responders to eat and rest, and one for the injured to be triaged and patched up before they're sent to hospitals via an ambulance or air lifts.

I just woke up from a nap. Gulping two Tylenol and a hot coffee, I look around the tent. I saw Annalise organizing baked goods for the first responders when I took my last break.

There are a lot of Lost Hope residents here bringing food and blankets for us, looking after us so we can go back out there and do our best to put out the fire.

I can't stop the disappointment bubbling in my chest when I don't see Lalah anywhere. Obviously, I want her as far away from this hell as possible, but I know how much it would help me mentally to have her here caring for me and my colleagues. To have her here showing her support.

I pour a second coffee, drinking it just as fast as the first one and shove a muffin in my face. When I'm properly hydrated, I make my way back to the Chief's temporary camp with Drake.

"Barlowe, Hayes, we have another cabin engulfed on the far east side. I've sent Four there, but they could use the help. Dennison seems to think there are still people trapped inside. How on earth have people not evacuated yet? We've been here for over ten goddamned hours."

We quickly don our masks as we rush toward the cabin. It's one of the last ones standing here. Everything around us is a blazing hell of orange and black. Flames surrounding us, smoke choking the breath out of our lungs, charred wooden cabins, and crisped-out Earth.

"Chief sent us. Status report?" Drake asks Dennison.

"Two children trapped inside, up in the attic. Three adults on the ground floor. We've worked out a way in," he promptly informs us, then walks us through the steps of the plan his team came up with.

Following his instructions, we carefully make our way inside through the back door, where the flames are not as high. We can barely make out the walls as the fire engulfs everything around us.

"The adults are in a bedroom just off this hallway. Dennison and I will go search for them. We have to hurry up. It won't take more than two, maximum three minutes until this whole damn thing becomes unstable." Jensen's voice crackles through the comms.

Drake and I reach the stairs and climb them as quickly as the bulky gear allows us. The landing of the attic is full of smoke, creating some visibility issues, but the fire has not reached this level yet.

We barge through the door of the attic and turn on the torches on top of our heads. "Anyone here?" I call out since I barely see anything in the darkness made even thicker with smoke.

"If you are hiding, please come out. We're here to take you outside to your family," Drake shouts over the roaring crackling of the fire as we spread out and search every nook and cranny of the attic.

"Ground floor clear. All adults are outside. Team two, you have two minutes to clear the cabin," Dennison reports.

A flash of pink fuzzy material draws my attention to the bunk beds on the north wall. I crouch down and reach underneath the bottom bed with my gloved hand.

Even through the thickness of my gloves, I feel the tiny fingers trembling as they squeeze mine. I hold on to the small arm tightly and pull out the toddler hiding under the bed.

"Come, sweetheart. Let's go find your parents." Soothing her in the most calming voice I can muster, I quickly unzip my turnout coat and pull the girl to my chest, rising back up before re-zipping it. I make sure every part of her that can be covered is.

"Found one minor, female, around three years old. On my way out," I inform my colleagues.

"On my way out with one minor, male, around seven years old." Drake follows.

With my palm cradling the back of her head, I run down the stairs as fast as I can while making sure the wooden planks are still strong enough to take my weight, then fly out the door and into the freezing air of the night. I head straight to the ambulance parked fifty feet away from the cabin.

"You're alright, sweetheart. I'm going to unzip you now and pass you over to this really nice lady. She's going to look you over to make sure you're okay, and your parents are going to be right by your side," I murmur in an attempt to calm her down, as her little body still trembles like a leaf.

"Please!" a voice cries next to me as I drop the little girl with the paramedic. "My other daughter is still inside."

My eyes dart to the distraught woman supporting herself on the ambulance as if her legs cannot bear her weight. Dark streaks of dirt and soot are running down her face, with clear lines of pale skin where her tears fall undeterred.

"Where was she when you last saw her?" I ask, my voice rough and raspy from the smoke I keep inhaling.

"In the attic. She likes to hide in the wardrobe," she wails.

"Alright, ma'am. On my way back to her now." I spin on my heel and take off at a run.

I know I have limited time to go back up there and find the girl. The flames have now reached the roof, which means the stairs' integrity may be compromised, as well as the attic's floor.

Bursting into the now burning room, I run straight to the wardrobe. With the fire eating away at the walls, I can easily find my way around. I rip the doors open and sure enough, a little ball of arms and legs dressed in red PJs is shaking inside.

I quickly shield her with my coat and once again run down the stairs. I can practically see the exit ahead through the walls of destructive heat. On the second to last step, my boot goes straight through the weakened, charred wood and I tip forward. Somehow, I turn at the last minute and fall to the fiery floor on my back instead of crushing the little girl underneath me.

A thunder-like rumbling comes from upstairs, and before I realize it, the beam supporting the stairs comes tumbling down, landing directly on my fucking calves, effectively trapping me to the floor. *God fucking damn it!*

A sharp pain spears my legs and the fire is already trying to breach my gear. I can't fucking push the beam away and take my legs out, since the girl is still wrapped around inside my coat.

"Mayday, mayday, mayday!" I call through the radio. "10-66 - Trapped at the bottom of the stairs under a wooden bar with a minor, female, around five years old."

I'll be damned if this is how I go, with my woman a fucking wreck and me burning in a cabin in the middle of the woods, both of us miserable and unhappy.

Chapter Fifty-One

Lalah

> Cole, don't do this to me. We both know I'm bad news. My heart can't take it losing you and the girls later on. It's best if I cut myself out of the picture now before my darkness sucks the life out of you guys. You deserve to be happy. You deserve to be loved. I'm not good enough for you.

Me

I'm drowning in memories. I'm drowning in hateful and painful words and I can't seem to find my way to the surface. My body is numb. My soul is shattered into a million pieces. I knew I wasn't my family's favorite person, but my brother's words cut me to the bone.

Unwanted. Unloved. Unworthy.

Always unworthy. Always undeserving.

I frantically check my phone one more time as I've done every five minutes in the last ten hours. There's no new message from Cole since that resounding *No* of his graced my screen. There's no reply to my latest message.

I give up on it and move my finger to the power off button, then throw my phone under the pillows on Cole's side of the bed. Out of sight, out of mind.

My heart beats painfully in my chest, fluttering and skipping beats as if not knowing how to do its job properly anymore. My mind is a jumbled mess. I know I now need to convince him to leave. I believe he thinks he loves me.

Everyone I held close to my heart believed they loved me at some point or another. Everyone left me one by one, all disgusted with me, all hating me once they actually got to know me.

He will too.

It pains me even more that he refuses to see this now. If my own family, the people who gave me life and made the choice to bring me into this world can't love me, how can anyone else?

Maybe I should leave.

Just disappear into the night with a handful of clothes and lock myself in a remote cabin where I don't know anyone and no one knows me. Where I cannot taint anyone's light with my darkness.

Although I'm bound and determined to have him and his family leave, strangely I'm also hurt he hasn't replied to my messages. He should be home by now.

He should've been home two hours ago. Maybe he's down in Lost Hope, looking at Maevis's house and organizing their move.

A sharp pain in my chest makes me suck in a breath my lungs refuse to accept. I felt relieved today when he left for work.

Pretended to be asleep as he moved his body away from mine, taking my only source of warmth away. I continued pretending when his lips whispered his love in my ear.

A shiver works its way down my spine and goosebumps pepper my flesh, even if I'm still in bed, wrapped up in a heavy duvet. I've been cold since my brother's parting words stabbed me straight in the heart before Cole kicked him out.

The only moments of warmth I have are when he is holding me to his chest as he sleeps.

But I know I can't be selfish. I can't tie him to me and condemn him to a life of misery with me. I don't make anyone's day better. Can't bring happiness into anyone's life, and I love him far too much to deprive him of happiness.

He deserves everything good in life. He deserves someone strong at his side, someone who'll love him and the girls with all their might.

Someone who would spend the rest of their life showering him with joy and affection.

Someone to care for him and those two beautiful little souls.

Someone who isn't me. Someone who is enough.

Pathetic. Waste of space. Whore. Soul-sucking bitch.

My bedroom door hits the wall with a resounding bang, startling me out of my head and my heart pounds even harder against my ribcage. *Of course, I forgot to lock the fucking thing. I haven't locked my bedroom in months.*

Light floods the room, stabbing at my eyes, and I quickly press the heels of my palms to my eyelids, hissing in protest.

"I don't know what's hurting you, Lalah. But right now, my husband and the love of your life are out there on a goddamned mountain, fighting a monster of a fire and saving lives. My husband counts on *your* man to be one hundred percent focused, so they'll both get out of there alive and uninjured!" Annalise's firm voice fills the walls of my bedroom.

I remove my palms from my face and blink rapidly, trying to chase away the spots filling my vision.

"What are you talking about?" I rasp, my voice gritty and rough from days of scarcely being used.

As my vision clears, I take Annalise in. Her palms are planted on her hips, her legs firmly apart, face hard. Her green-hazel eyes narrow at me and her lips thin. She looks ready to kick my ass ten ways to Sunday.

"You'll get that cute butt of yours out of bed. Hop in the fastest fucking shower of your life, get dressed, and come with me. COLE NEEDS YOU!" She orders.

"What happened?" I ask, and my stomach somersaults with worry, especially at hearing her swearing. Adrenaline replaces the numbness coursing through my veins, concern for Cole blossoming in my chest.

"Massive fire at the Pine Ski Resort. They were called there this morning. It's bad, babe. And they need us. They need us to go there and care for them when they take their breaks. They need us to go there and feed them. They fucking need us to hold them if they cannot save everyone, and they break down. They need us to fucking hold them together so they can return to the pits of hell and save more lives," she tells me in a single breath, her chest heaving and her eyes reddening with tears.

Fuck me! What have I done? When Cole was out there trying to save lives, I was breaking up with him over text like the coward I am. Instead of him being focused on staying safe and coming back home in one piece, I burdened him with my drama.

"Pull yourself together. RIGHT FUCKING NOW! I need you, no, WE need you to slap yourself back into the badass bitch you usually are and be there for all of us. You can go back to moping tomorrow or when we know for sure our men are safe. Hell, I'll come with the biggest fucking bucket of ice cream I can get my hands on and stay here in bed with you for as long as you need. But RIGHT NOW you need to pull it together," she pleads.

"Alright!" I concede. "Give me ten!"

I take the fastest, hottest shower in the history of all showers. As the scorching water rains down on me, I shove all the shitty memories, all the hurtful words, and all my broken pieces into the darkest corner of my mind.

Get yourself together. There are people with actual problems right now who need your help. COLE NEEDS YOU! He needs YOU!

I quickly dry myself and shove my legs in the warmest pair of winter pants I have, pulling on a random T-shirt and a hoodie, as well as the first pair of winter boots I get my hands on.

"Let's go!" I tell Annalise, marching past her and down the stairs.

Three sad faces turn to me at the same time. I can read the worry for his brother's well-being in Blake's gray eyes. Even the girls are subdued and quiet.

My absence and numbness have contributed to the way they feel right now, and I nearly stumble off my feet under the wave of shame and guilt washing through my body.

"Lalah..." Eliza gasps and jumps to her feet as I near the sofa. She stares at me for the longest ten seconds of my life before jumping over the back of the couch directly into my arms. "I'm so happy to see you. I miss you so much." Her words come muffled with her face hidden in the crook of my neck.

"I missed you too, baby girl." I may be depressed, but I'm not a complete asshole. I'll never deny affection or the truth of my feelings to these little innocent souls.

My eyes connect with Blake's and something akin to relief passes over his face. "Welcome back!" he mouths at me. Despite the seriousness of the situation, my lips twitch at the corners, trying to form a smile.

"Where are you going?" Eliza asks me, the arms around my neck tightening. "You're not leaving us, are you?"

The way her voice quivers on her last question breaks my heart. *What the fuck am I doing? I nearly threw away my family for the words of someone I just happen to share blood with and nothing else.*

The weight of what I almost did hits me straight in the chest, dislodging the poisoned knife my so-called sibling stabbed in there with a fucking smirk on his face.

A sudden clarity settles over me, and I can't stop the sob crawling its way out of my throat.

THIS is my family.

These people right here.

Cole is my family.

No. Cole is my entire fucking life, and I nearly gave up on him because someone I've never been close to didn't want me at their wedding?

With a renewed sense of determination flowing through my veins, I take my first full breath of air in a week. It's not too late to fix what I broke.

I may be unwanted and discarded by those sharing my blood, but my real family, my chosen family, has been at my side through thick and thin, even if we've known each other for only a short time.

Giving Eliza a quick squeeze, I brush my lips on the top of her head. "No, sweet girl. I'm not leaving you. Not ever. I promise."

Her hand snakes in front of me, even as her face remains pressed to my shoulder. "Pinky promise? You can't break a pinky promise. It's the rule!" she mumbles, but hope shines in her voice.

I curl my own pinky finger around hers and squeeze, sealing the easiest promise I ever made in my life. "I solemnly pinky-promise I will never leave you."

"Hate to interrupt, but we really need to go," Annalise chimes in from somewhere behind me.

"You're going to see Cole?" Blake asks.

"I am," I nod at him.

"Good. He'll be really happy to see your face," he tells me with a smile, and I feel the tendril of relief sprouting roots inside of me. I know I hurt and disappointed them in the last few days, but I'll make it up to them.

And what's even more important?

They'll forgive me and not hold my weakness against me. Because they love me. I know that now. I feel it in every cell of my body.

"I really fucking hope so," I reply with a self-deprecating laugh. At my words, Eliza wiggles her way down my body, and I let her drop to her feet on the sofa.

She brings her tiny face next to mine, and in the most serious voice she can muster, she proudly informs me, "You promised to stay and I'm not going to charge you for the swear. Because I love you."

I can't help the laughter bubbling out of me. It feels good to laugh. Like a weight has been lifted off my shoulders, I feel lighter and stronger.

"Thanks, sweetheart. I don't think my wallet could take it if you charged me." I wink at her as I swoop Clara from the floor and shower her chubby face in kisses. "All right, troublemakers. I'll see you later. Don't give Blake too hard of a time."

I fidget in my seat the entire drive to the resort. Annalise keeps quiet and just focuses on navigating the treacherous bends and twists of the road as we make our way higher up the mountain in pitch darkness.

We're about ten minutes away when I notice the orange glow of the sky and the clouds of smoke and ash twirling in the air.

"How bad is it?" I whisper. She gives me a quick side glance, then shakes her head.

"Bad. The resort is half destroyed. They were fully booked too, so a lot of people around. When I was there three hours ago, about twenty people had serious injuries and burns. Most of them are affected by smoke inhalation. There was also a fatality, but the person died when the tank trucks crashed."

"Fucking hell. That's terrible!" I muse and try to swallow the lump lodged in my throat.

This is not the time for me to feel guilty for being a fucking bitch to Cole. This is the time I pull on my big girl panties and help with whatever I can. Once everything is done here, I'll apologize to Cole in ten thousand ways for the rest of my life.

Annalise throws the car in park as we reach the area where two massive tents are sprawled out on either side of the road leading to the resort. I exit the car at the same time she does and we make our way to the tent where first responders are coming in and out of.

"The one across the road is for triage and injuries. The one we're headed to is where everyone eats and rests before going back out there. It's also where people with minor injuries are helped by finding them accommodations until they can return home."

"Alright. Put me to work!" I clap my hands once when we reach a long table, pushed to the side of the tent, full of baked goods and coffee.

"Lalah!" a baritone voice calls for me. "Thank feck yer here!"

I turn around to greet whoever called me and come face to face with the soot dirtied face of Rowan. His turnout gear is more black than high viz, and he smells strongly of smoke and gasoline.

"Hi Rowan! How are you holding up?" I ask him.

"I'm fine. Don't you worry about me. It's Cole."

Chapter Fifty-Two

Lalah

I'm sure I didn't hear him right.

He's not trying to tell me something happened to Cole, is he? But the pit in my stomach and the weakness in my knees tell me I heard him just fine. My mouth opens to demand he takes me to my man, but my throat is so tight no sounds can escape.

"NO!" He shouts, his eyes widening and cheeks turning a fiery shade of red under all the ash. "Bloody hell. He's fine. The fecking twat went and got himself pinned under a wooden beam. Drake got his arse out in time. His calves are bruised to all hell, first-degree burns on the severe side, but he is fine."

My knees do give out, but in relief at his words. I extend a hand toward him, and he takes my arm to support my weight.

"You took twenty years of my life there, dude!" I exhale. "Can you take me to him, please?"

"Yeah, of course. He's just over the road, giving the paramedics a hard time. His stubborn arse wants to return to the field." His pale blue eyes roll so far in his head, for a second I'm worried they'll remain stuck there.

I follow him to the second tent, jogging to keep up with his long stride, and stop dead in my tracks as I take in Cole's massive frame sprawled out on a stretcher.

His beautiful face is painted with the same ash and soot as Rowan's, making his tired, pale green eyes look almost translucent. His jet-black short curls are messed about, sticking up in all directions, as he repeatedly spears his thick fingers through them.

"Goddammit, I said I am fine. I need to help my team and leave this bed free for someone who actually needs it," his gruff, raspy voice commands the nurse tending to him.

"Mr. Hayes, you're not going anywhere until I make sure your burns are properly treated. You're no help to anyone if they get infected or start hurting so badly you can't do your job. Now let me do mine, then allow you to do yours," the nurse chastises him in an authoritative voice.

My eyes roam over every inch of him, making sure he is really here, and apart from the injuries Rowan already told me about, nothing else happened to him.

His defined chest nearly rips the seams of his T-shirt apart as he sucks in a deep breath, most likely biting his tongue not to lash out at the nurse only trying to help him.

His fire station-issued sweats are cut off at the knees, leaving his reddened calves exposed to the ministrations of the exasperated woman.

"You'll stay here and follow every indication of this fine woman, you bloody eejit!" Rowan orders him. "If I have to tie you to this fecken gurney myself, I will."

Cole's head turns toward his colleague and I feel the punch his gaze packs in my belly when he notices me. His eyes widen and a mixture of hope, satisfaction, love, and disbelief washes over his face as his gaze roams over me from head to toe.

That's all my feet need to unlock themselves from the floor and fly toward him.

I fling myself to his chest and coil my arms around his nape, hiding my face in the crook of his neck. Tears spring in my eyes, and I do nothing to stop them, allowing them to fall freely down my chin and into his skin.

I can't stop the sobs of relief, either. I nearly lost him today. Twice. First of my own goddamned doing. The second to a fire from hell.

He palms the back of my head, burying his fingers deep in my hair with one hand while the other rests on my back, moving back and forth over my shoulder blades trying to comfort me. I truly don't deserve this amazing man. I know that. But fuck if I'm not living each day trying to rise to his greatness.

"Fuck, I can't believe you're here," he rasps in my ear, the choked up emotion twined in his tone. "Please don't cry, love. You're breaking my heart. Please, don't cry. You know I can't take your tears," he begs me.

I gulp a big breath, trying to lock back the floodgates and kiss up his neck to his jaw, and lastly those soft lips of his. His tongue parts mine and with a grunt of longing Cole finds his way inside my mouth. The kiss doesn't last nearly as long as I'd want it to before he rips his mouth from mine.

"This will get embarrassing really fast for me if we keep going," Cole whispers, resting his forehead on mine. "What are you doing here, Supernova?"

My eyes spring open and bore into his. He's not trying to stifle the hope shining brightly at me from his green orbs. Nor is he withholding the love and gratitude either. They're all battling for first place to the surface, all battling to reach me.

"Annalise came to get me. She told me what happened. I'm here to support you." Taking a deep breath, trying to gather the courage I need, I tell him, "I'm sorry, meus bellator. I'm so so sorry! I've put you through hell in the past week, and when you needed me most, I wasn't there for you."

Cole's grip on my hair tightens. He gently pulls at my locks, forcing my eyes to meet his.

"You have nothing to apologize for. You're here now. Right when I need you the most. You came."

"I do have to apologize. The text I sent..." I start, but he shushes me with his fingers on my lips.

"The text you sent is bullshit. Complete and utter bullshit. That was not you talking. It was your grief and your pain," he murmurs.

"Look at me!" Cole orders and when my eyes meet his once again, he continues. "I'm not moving out. We're not breaking up. If darkness is what you bring to the table, I'll buy all the fucking candles in this world, do you hear me? But I'm not leaving you. And you are abso-fucking-lutely not leaving me. It's you and me, Supernova. Forever and always."

My heart soars at his words, pumping inside my rib cage with such vigor I'm getting lightheaded. I move my shaking hands to his jaw, cupping his dirty face, my thumbs stroking lovingly on his dry skin.

"You're right. Forever and always. I'm a selfish bitch. Though part of me still thinks you're better off without me, I can't let you go. Could I live without you? Yeah, a miserable life, but I could. Truth is, I don't want a future without you in it." My chest deflates on a deep exhale depleting the last of my negativity.

"I choose you, Cole Hayes. And I'll continue to choose you every day of my life, even when I'm not able to choose myself. I love you, and I'll continue to love you for all the breaths left in my lungs, even when I'm not able to love myself."

His emerald-green irises sparkle under the layer of tears coating his eyes. A slow blink of those dark, long lashes allows them to spill down his cheekbones and into the stubble covering the lower half of his face.

"I'll love you hard enough for the both of us when it happens." Cole sucks in a watery breath, unapologetic in letting his emotions fly free for everyone to see. "You don't need to be a walking, talking ray of sunshine. I love every one of your moods. I love your doom and gloom as much as I love your smiles and laughs."

I can't contain the smile taking over my face. My cheeks hurt with the foreign movement, but my lips are undeterred.

"All right, love birds. I'm all done here. Mr. Hayes, I suggest you eat something and hydrate before going back out there. You'll be sore for a couple of weeks, so take ibuprofen as needed. Ideally, you'd keep your legs elevated, but I know I have no chance of sending you home right now. If your calves swell over the next few days, please go immediately to the emergency room. In the meantime, have your lovely lady here wash the affected area with cool water every four hours and apply new sterile bandages for as long as you're here."

I turn to the kind nurse tending to Cole, and despite my aversion to touching people, I give her a big hug in gratitude. I make a note to get the names of all the first responders that are on scene, from medical personnel to firefighters and police officers, and have Marcus send them a gift basket when all's said and done, as well as a big donation to all the firehouses coming to help.

Cole stands to his full height, and I love the way he towers over me. I always feel safe and protected when I'm in his presence, even when I'm too numb to see reason. "Thank you, Grace. I owe you one."

"You owe me nothing except staying alive," she replies primly and with a soft smile says her goodbyes before moving on to the next patient.

Cole changes his cut-off sweats for the turnout gear, leaving the bulky, gray-streaked coat unzipped. I guess they must train like hell to put their gear on because one minute he was shoving his pants off and the next he's all suited up.

I grab his hand and entwine my fingers through his. "You heard the good lady. Let's get you fed and hydrated." I pull at his hand as I lead him to the other tent.

Less than ten minutes later, with a belly full of an egg and bacon sandwich, two cups of coffee, two bottles of water, and a clingy koala hug, I send Cole back to do what he does best, save people.

Annalise and I work tirelessly for the next few hours. She helps out in the triage tent. I'm running from place to place, ensuring we have enough clean blankets and clothes for the first responders and we don't run out of water bottles.

"Lalah, I need your help!" Mayor Brown gets my attention with a hand on my shoulder. I take her in, her tired eyes are crinkled at the corners, her cheeks hollow, and lips thin.

She looks like she has aged at least ten years in the past month. Her clothes hang loose on her tall frame, and a pang of guilt works its way through my stomach. I'm sure she's having a hard time with Maddison's arrest and pending trial.

"Gretchen!" I greet her. "Of course. What can I do for you?"

With the fog I was living in just last week, I couldn't trust my recount of the New Year's party. But now I'm fully here, fully myself and, by the small smile she gives me, I realize there's no animosity in her eyes for me, no resentment. I'm the reason her daughter is in jail, but she doesn't blame me for her actions.

I let out a breath I didn't realize I was holding and turn fully in her direction.

"I hate asking this of you, but we're desperate. Is there any way you can contact your bosses at Lege and Lacrima and see if they can donate hotel rooms for the people vacationing here? We have about one hundred folks with no means of transport. Their cars were too close to the explosion, and all their belongings were destroyed." Her hands gesture wildly toward the charred cabins.

"We used all the funds we had for emergencies. There are families with nowhere to sleep. I've allocated as many as possible in homes provided by volunteers, but the resort was at full capacity. Around a thousand people, staff included, were staying here," she tells me in a rush.

"Sure I can. What are we looking at?"

"Hotel rooms to start with. Closest available are in Billings, so we'll need some buses to get them there. And maybe plane tickets or rental cars for them to get home once they've had a good night's sleep and calmed down from the horrors of today? There are also a handful of staff who live at the resort all year round. They're homeless now."

"Consider it done," I assure her. "A hotel room won't do for the staff. Let me give Marcus a call and see what can be arranged for them. In the meantime, can you provide a list with everyone's name, contact details, and what necessities they have, separating the staff from vacationers?"

Her eyes soften and she clasps one of my hands with both of hers. "Thank you so much. I'm so incredibly grateful for everything you're doing for us. I'll get that list to you as quickly as I can."

"There's no need to thank me, Gretchen. We're all living in this county. When one of us is in need, we rally together."

She nods in acceptance and leaves. I grab my phone in a rush, thankful I remembered bringing it with me, and power it on. I jog out of the tent and take a seat on the hood of Annalise's car to ensure I have a bit of privacy. Tapping on Marcus's name, I bring my phone to my ear.

"It's been a while since I've had a late-night phone call from you. I thought you'd been fully replaced by that sexy minion of yours," Marcus's warm voice greets me.

"Hands off my brother, you horn dog." I laugh at him.

"Can't help the raw magnetism I have inside. But worry not, my fair maiden, this hot stuff here is taken. Your brother's virtue remains intact! What can I do for you?"

"Here's what we're dealing with..." I start. Twenty minutes later, I make my way back to the tent, my throat sore after talking so much in a short time and inhaling the smoke permeating the air.

"There you are!" Gretchen once again greets me as soon as I enter the break area. "I have that list for you!"

"Sorry, Gretchen, I just had Marcus on the phone, and I can definitely confirm now Lege et Lacrima will be helping. If you could scan the list and send it to him, that'd be great. He'll get back to you with the temporary accommodations soon, and tomorrow he'll deal with permanent housing for the staff."

A sob escapes her lips, and she tries to cover it with a trembling hand, but there's no hiding the tears accumulating in her eyes. "Thank you. From the bottom of my heart, thank you."

I squeeze her shoulder and give her an understanding smile. "Don't mention it. Get everyone on the list together and let Marcus know the address."

A group of firefighters makes its way inside. I leave Mayor Brown with another squeeze of her shoulder as I direct them toward the cots where they can have some shut-eye, while pointing at the food and beverage area.

"We're almost done," a tall, blond man informs me.

They all look the same. Tired, bloodshot eyes, faces covered in dirt, ashes, and soot, wearing even dirtier turnout gear. The smell of smoke and gasoline is even stronger with them inside the tent.

"We put the fire out completely. Now it's just a matter of ensuring the spill has been isolated and contained, and there's no further risk of the gasoline reigniting."

"That's wonderful news," I congratulate him with a smile as I pass each of them a bottle of water.

"It's a freaking miracle we didn't lose more people. It's been a long while since we've had to deal with something of this magnitude," he remarks.

They all solemnly nod their heads. The material damage is substantial, but the worst injuries are third degree burns which will hopefully heal in time.

Another half an hour later, I spy Cole's curly hair at the entrance of the tent, and I quickly drop the sandwich I was holding and make my way to him.

As soon as I'm close enough, I fling myself in his arms, legs locked around his waist, hands buried in his hair, as I become his personal koala and start peppering kisses all over his face. Catcalls and whistles sound around me, coming from the men in his unit, and I couldn't care less who sees me greeting him.

I almost lost him today. More than once. It's the first time in the past week when I feel myself coming back to life and I'm bound and determined to enjoy every single moment I have with him.

"A man could get used to this," he smirks at me, his voice even rougher than normal. I'm sure all the smoke he inhaled has done a number on his vocal cords.

"A man should get used to this," I retort with a smile, smacking a big, wet kiss on his lips.

He immediately retaliates by catching my bottom lip between his teeth and biting down on the plump flesh. Not enough to draw blood, but enough to send a jolt of pain and pleasure to my core. His tongue soon follows, soothing the sting, and my thighs squeeze his waist even tighter.

"As much as I hate letting you go, we're ready to return to Lost Hope. I'm going back to the fire station for a quick briefing, then straight home to you."

"I'll warm the bed for you." I wink at him, relieved to know he can finally come home and he's out of danger.

"I look forward to meeting you there," he tells me as I slide down his body. With a pat to my ass, he makes his way back to the engine, Rowan and Russel in tow.

Chapter Fifty-Three

Cole

T his day has been both hell and heaven. The uncertainty of my future with Lalah hung over my head like a dark thunderstorm cloud, burning and suffocating me even more than the fire and thick smoke at the resort.

There are no words to explain the relief and happiness I felt seeing her in that dreary gray tent where medical personnel tended to any and all wounded. The absolute elation of having her back in my arms, having her openly loving me and believing in me, made me feel ten-feet tall.

She's not magically cured. Depression is a cruel bastard who sneaks in when you least expect it, but I'll do my damnedest to be her light in the dark from now on.

I don't know what pushed her back over the edge and into the land of the living, but I'm not a fool to question the greatest gift I have ever been given. I can't stop the cat-that-ate-the-canary smirk gracing my face just thinking that in a short hour, I'll be in bed with her in my arms.

"You're a goner!" Drake claps a meaty hand on my back. I groan a swear since everything in me is a big ol' bruise.

"Just missing the collar and leash," Rowan retorts from behind the wheel.

I just widen my smile, lips stretching ear-to-ear. Let them mock me. There's nothing they can say to dim my happiness.

"Give the man a break!" Rus grumbles. Leave it to him to be the voice of reason. "Don't tell me you're not happy to be done with this day from hell and go back to your women?"

"Speak for yourself, old man," the Irishman mumbles. "All that's waiting for me is a feckin' unfinished book and a bloody cat I swear is the twin sister of the AntiChrist."

"And that's the only way you get to pet a pussy lately," Drake razes him.

"Up your arse, Captain! At least I still own my balls. Yours have been chained tight by that hot wife of yours."

A growl comes out of Drake's chest, surprising the fuck out of me. He's normally such a laid-back guy. I honestly didn't think I'd ever like him after the part he played in Lalah's car crash, but he has proven to me in the past few months he is an honorable, decent man who simply made the wrong call at the wrong time.

Before we get to see a pissed-off Drake, I take my shot at Rowan. "Someone's going to come one of these days and knock you off that high leprechaun of yours. I can't wait to see the day you willingly hand your balls to her, pink bow and all."

There's no time for him to bite back as he slams the brakes of the engine and parks it in the allocated bay. We waste no time climbing down and moving toward the shower room. We all toss our gear in the laundry room just off the shared bathrooms, groans of relief echoing in unison between the tiled walls.

Although we're all responsible for our own equipment, we have spares just in case we may need to use them before we get to cleaning them. It doesn't happen often, but best to be prepared than sorry.

Right now, every single one of us is concerned with one thing and one thing only. Getting through the debrief and going home.

Warm water flows over me, soothing the tiredness in my muscles. We were damned lucky today. Things could have been worse, a hell of a lot worse.

As much as I want to go home and bury myself to the hilt in Lalah and not come up for air for a full week, I know I'm going to crash as soon as my head hits the pillow.

I've been running on pure adrenaline and coffee for the past sixteen hours. Not even sure what's going to happen with the shift I'm supposed to start in three hours.

My bed and Lalah are all I can think about as I dry myself off, happy to note the smoked up smell we all seem to have embedded in our skin has toned down a few notches.

Slowly, slowly, we all shuffle our tired feet to the canteen, and I'm surprised to see how full it is. Nearly all of us, from all shifts and units, are here. The Chief props himself up on the buffet counter, and I lean on the nearest wall since all the chairs are occupied.

"Gentlemen!" his voice rings out in the stuffed-to-the-brim space.

"Thank you for today! You are an example of bravery, collaboration, and teamwork. I'm so fucking proud of everything you achieved and the manner in which this fire department has conducted itself. Thank you to our volunteers who showed up today and to all our colleagues who answered our call and came to our aid. I've redone the rota for the next two weeks. Please see the Captains or Lieutenants for each of your units and then, for the love of God, go home and get some goddamned rest."

We all holler and clap at his words. I hurry to find Drake who passes me the new schedule. "Don't bother reading it now, man. You have the next two days off. Get some rest and make sure those burns are healing properly."

"Thanks, Drake. I'll see you all later," I throw over my shoulder hurrying out of the firehouse and into the truck.

The bedroom is dark with only a soft, red light glowing dimly, just enough for me to find my way to the bed, keeping all my toes in the process. I can barely make out Lalah's sleeping form under the covers.

My hands make quick work of shedding any stitch of clothing on me. With gentleness, I lift the covers and slip inside the soft cotton.

As soon as my arm touches hers, she seeks me. Her head rests on my chest, a smooth thigh thrown over my abdomen. My muscles stiffen as I feel only soft, creamy skin everywhere we touch.

Lalah prefers sleeping in a T-shirt, in case my little sisters find their way into our bed – again. And for the past week, she's been sleeping in a full set of pajamas. To feel her completely naked in my arms is pure fucking bliss.

I was certain when I left the fire station I'd fall asleep as soon as my head hit the pillow. Clearly, my cock is not tired enough, as it thickens and throbs with every breath she takes. My hand sneaks down her back and to her ass in a slow glide, my touch restrained and shy.

I haven't been allowed to feel her in a week. Although finding her naked in bed is her way of telling me she wants me, after the uncertainty and pain of last week, I'm not sure this is the green light I hope it is.

She shifts closer to me and starts rotating her hips in slow, tantalizing circles, her wet pussy rubbing on my thigh. I take a deep breath and gather my courage.

The hand on her ass makes its way lower and lower until my fingers connect to her drenched flesh. I caress soaked folds with my fingertips, up and down, round one way, then the other.

A whispered moan leaves her lips and lowers my inhibitions. I dip a finger into her entrance to my first knuckle and start gently pumping in and out of her. The gyrating motion of her hips picks up speed and soft gasps leave her pillowy, soft lips. My cock is standing at attention now, so hard I could break walls with it, leaking and throbbing, trying to reach her.

A deep groan leaves my throat when her soft palm caresses the tip of my dick, fingers wrapping around my length in an agonizingly slow up-and-down movement. She feathers her fingertips over each barbell on the underside of my cock, my pre-come lubing her path.

"I want to come on your fingers," she whispers on my chest, her lips licking and sucking my skin, grazing my nipple with her teeth, her hand working me faster and faster.

Her dainty fingers add more pressure to my already sensitive cock, twisting her wrist around me. This is going to end embarrassingly fast as that familiar tingle rises at the bottom of my spine, my balls heavy and aching, drawing up tight.

I speed up the thrust of my finger in response, adding a second one, curling both inside her tight channel in a come-here movement I know drives her crazy. Her soft gasps turn into tiny mewls of pleasure, and I want to puff up my chest in pride.

I'm the one making my woman wanton with desire.

I'm the one pleasuring her, bringing her to the edge of madness.

My Supernova is back.

"Cole, please!" she begs me so prettily, an edge of desperation to her moan. I know by the quiver in her voice she's ready to fall over the edge. My thumb finds her clit and applies pressure to it, strumming the pad of my finger over her little bundle of nerves.

A gush of wetness coats the fingers thrusting into her as she drips pure fucking nectar into my palm. I'm fucking gone for this woman. Every fiber of my being screams she is the only one for me.

I can't control myself any longer, my hips jerking uncontrolled, pumping my cock in and out of her palm in tandem with the fingers fucking her.

My mouth desperately seeks hers, and as soon as I feel her plump lips on mine, drinking in her moaned breaths, I slant my mouth over hers and kiss her with all my might.

My cock throbs harder and harder with each stroke of her palm over me. I almost shout in victory when her hips buck into my hand, the flutters of her pussy taking flight around my fingers, her walls clenching down on me as she comes.

"Yes, God, yes, Cole, yes!" she chants on my lips, and I continue to fuck her with my fingers through her orgasm, drinking in the sight of her trembling body lost to the pleasure I'm giving her.

The flutters of her pussy, the quiver of her belly, the pebbled hard nipples I didn't even get to taste, all push me over the edge. Ropes of cum paint my abdomen and the hand still jerking me off in gentler tugs.

"Fuuuuuck, babe! You're fucking amazing!" I grunt my pleasure out as I ride the last of the aftershocks.

We're both a panting, sweaty mess, the air in the bedroom thick with the heady scent of sex, but I can't find it in me to care. She's in my arms, as beautiful as ever with her flushed skin and post orgasmic haze clouding her eyes.

Her lips feather a kiss on my heaving chest, pushing up on an elbow, her silky hair cascading all over us.

"Oh my, look at the mess we've made," she purrs, "I better clean you up."

Before I gather the necessary strength to reply, she throws a leg over me, straddling the top of my thighs. Bending down at the waist, Lalah starts kissing my Adonis belt, her tongue lapping up the cum painting my skin, teasing my cock back to life with her hot, wet mouth.

My impatient fingers find their way to her sleek hair, wrapping the silky strands around my fist to keep them out of her face. "Shit, babe! You're set to kill me this morning!" I grunt as she takes my rapidly hardening cock to the back of her throat, bobbing her head up and down on my length. She hums softly when curses escape my clenched lips, the vibrations sending electric shocks through my dick, rippling over my whole body.

"But what a way to go," she says, releasing me with a wet pop, licking her swollen red lips. Her palms land on my abs, then caress their way up my chest as her dripping sex rests directly on my overexcited cock.

She drags her bare pussy up and down my length, moaning every time one of my piercings touches her clit. "God, I fucking love this magic cock of yours," she cries as her hips move faster and faster over me.

My hand unfists her hair, letting it drop like a dark silken curtain around us, enclosing us into our own bubble of love and lust.

One hand finds its way to her hip, gripping her tightly, relishing how the heated skin turns white under my touch. My other palm cups her breast, thumb and forefinger pinching and twisting her tight, rosy nipple.

"Fuck, yes, Cole, more!" she mewls and without warning lifts herself up, aligning the tip of my cock to her dripping entrance, and impales herself to the hilt on me. A blissed-out groan escapes my chest as her wet heat envelops me, her pussy clamping down on me so hard I couldn't move if I tried.

"Goddamn! Look how well you take me, Supernova. Look how beautifully you stretch yourself around me, all swollen, silken pussy. Fuck! Move, babe. Let me see you taking me for all I am."

She obeys me instantly like the good girl she is, lifting and dropping her hips faster and faster. I thrust up too, meeting her halfway, causing more of those mewling sounds I'm fucking gone for to spill from her lips.

She once again tightens around me, and I know she's close to coming when the once-controlled up-and-down bounces speed up in gyrating jerks. "Holy fuck, yes, Cole! Please, please, fuck me harder," she cries.

Her back arches, pushing those gorgeous tits of hers in my face. My hungry mouth latches onto her nipple, biting and teasing with punishing sucks. My hands hold her hips steady as I fuck myself from below into her.

Only her moans, my grunts, and skin slapping on skin are heard in the quiet of the night. Pure, ecstatic music to my ears.

My palms move to her back, gripping her ass cheeks tightly, lifting and dropping her on my cock. Her own hands find their way to my shoulders, sharp nails cutting into my skin.

The mixture of pain and pleasure sends me over the edge, my cock throbbing as I continue to fuck her through my orgasm in frenzied jerks. "Holy fucking hell, yes, ohh yes!" She cries out her own completion, the flutters and ripples of her pussy milking me of everything I have, prolonging my pleasure.

I can't think. I can't see. I can't hear anything. I'm lost to the ecstasy only this woman has ever been capable of giving me. I'm completely lost to her, and dammit all to hell if I ever want to be found.

She falls onto me, her chest heaving, my softening cock still buried inside her to the root. "That..." she puffs a stream of warm air onto my sex-heated skin. "Was out of this fucking world."

I can't contain the prideful chuckle rumbling out of my chest. Just yesterday, I was walking around with a thousand boulders weighing my heart down. Now, I'm high on two amazing orgasms and drunk on all the love and adoration I have for this woman.

"You are out of this fucking world," I whisper, holding her tighter to me. "I love you so fucking much, Alana. I missed you like crazy."

She lifts her head, her eyes sparkling as they lock onto mine. The soft floor light may not let me see her as clearly as I'd like, but there's no missing the affection, life, and happiness shining in them. "I love you too, meus bellator, even if you called me Alana," she giggles.

And I know I'd put out a million more fires like the one we've dealt with today if I get to come home every day to that sound coming out of her mouth.

For the rest of my life.

Chapter Fifty-Four

Cole

I bite my fist, attempting to stifle my amusement. If she sees me laughing now, I'm sure she'll find a slipper somewhere to throw at my head.

"Don't just stand there. Our girl is leaving for her first day of school," Lalah orders me as she wears out the soft, creamy rug in the living room with her pacing.

"Well aware, love. I'm the one driving." I smart back and realize it may be the wrong thing to say based on the evil side eye she throws at me. "What are you so worried about?"

"I just want her to have a great first day. Children are assholes at this age. I don't want her to feel any pressure starting in the middle of the school year. Maybe we should've let her finish this last semester at home."

"Babe!" I get her attention, as my hand shoots out and catches the thumb she's determined to chew clean off her hand. "Eliza will be fine. My sister, the ten-year-old-going-on-thirty, is a strong and smart girl. I trust her to come and tell us if she has any problems."

"Coley is right!" Eliza's voice comes from near the stairs. I spin on my heel to see her in all her uniformed glory, blonde hair braided and wrapped around her head like a princess crown.

"I gotta be honest, being the new kid is not the best feeling, but I know I have you guys. And better yet, I have Astrum. I'll just get him to pin down anyone who annoys me."

Lalah hurries to her, trembling palms on Eliza's cheeks as she gives her a watery smile. "Maybe sic me on them first before we bring out the secret weapon."

"Even better. You can be really scary, especially when Blake's annoying you." My sister snickers and it makes me proud to see her confidence shining.

"Alright, let's get going," I say, hoisting Clara up in my arms and ushering my girls through the door.

The entire drive to the elementary school, I get to hear the *Frozen* theme song. If I never hear this song again in my life, I'll die a happy man.

Just when I'm one chorus away from throwing myself out of the speeding car, the school comes into view, and I'm quick to turn the volume down.

"Nooo, Bubba!" Clara screeches her displeasure, but Eliza distracts her with ease, planting kisses all over Clara's chubby cheeks, making her laugh.

I exit the car, rounding the hood to open Lalah's door. I envelop her soft hand in mine, helping her out, before making my way to Eliza's side.

I treat her in the same manner I did Lalah. I figure, if I can't convince her to sign up for a convent or to not start dating until she's forty or I'm dead, I can at least show her how she deserves to be treated.

So when a little pimple-faced hormonal teenager knocks on my door to take her out, she'll accept nothing less than being treated like the princess she is.

She launches herself into Lalah's arms, backpack hanging off her tiny shoulders, the biggest smile brightening her face. I can see Lalah's eyes reddening, and I bite back a laugh.

Do I love the sight of her tears?

Abso-fucking-lutely not.

But it amuses me to no end that my strong, ball-busting woman is losing her ever-loving mind over my little sister going to school.

It also makes me feel all warm and fuzzy inside, seeing how she loves my family so much she's incredibly distraught for my sister's well-being. It's that big heart of hers she's shared with us from the moment we met, making me want to hold on tight for all eternity.

Clara is riding my shoulders like a queen presiding over her loyal subjects as we sign Eliza in at the reception.

A pocket-sized brunette greets us as soon as we clear the door of the classroom assigned to Eliza. Despite the cold weather outside, she's dressed in a cheery yellow dress with short sleeves, her legs bare from knee down. She seems to be quite young, no older than twenty-four or twenty-five, but her assessing dark blue eyes give her an aura of wisdom.

Half of the desks in the classroom are already filled with children, all happily chattering away. Three rows of wooden desks dominate the center of the classroom. Behind them, the wall is hidden by a huge notice board where a mixture of drawings and paintings are proudly displayed. Bookshelves filled with brightly colored book spines are set on either side of the board.

On the opposite wall is the teacher's desk front and center, with three whiteboards hung behind it. A myriad of flowers are drawn around the edges of one of the boards, followed by cats, dogs, and ponies on the middle one. Finally, the last board has cars, rockets, astronauts, and bikes drawn.

It's a warm and joyful environment, and I know Eliza will get a kick out of all the books and drawings around. Clara does if the happy squeals and the jiggly dance she's doing on my shoulders are any indication.

"Ah, this must be our new addition, Eliza Hart," the woman says, a gentle smile on her lips. My sister immediately takes to her, her face splitting on an ear-to-ear smile, teeth and gums on display. "It's so nice to meet you, sweetheart. I'm Miss Violet, and I'm thrilled to have you in my class."

I'm proud to see my sister boldly shaking her teacher's hand, like the adult she wishes herself to be. "It's nice to meet you, Miss Violet. I'm very excited about all the books you have here. We have an enormous library at home. Bigger than the one in *Beauty and the Beast*!" My sister gushes, a rosy blush coloring her cheeks.

"Whooa. That's incredible. I take it you love reading?" At my sister's nodding, Violet continues, "I'll tell you a secret. Every week, we choose something to read. On Fridays, we all sit and discuss the book, what we loved the most, what we disliked, just like in a book club."

Eliza turns excitedly to Lalah and pulls at her hand. "Wow. Did you hear that, Lalah? I get to be in my first book club here at school."

"Sure did!" Lalah replies enthusiastically, crouching in front of her. "You're going to love it, then come home and tell me all about it. Now, hurry up and find your seat and we'll see you later in the afternoon."

Eliza throws her hands around Lalah's neck and squeezes with all her might. "I'll miss you," she murmurs.

"We're all going to miss you too, baby girl. But don't you worry, we'll be just outside waiting for you. Go on now. Have the bestest day at school."

"Thanks, Lalah," she squeals excitedly, then runs over to me, hugging my legs.

"Thanks, Coley! I love you both," she informs us before turning into a blur in front of my eyes running to the third desk in the center row, where a sun-flower yellow plaque displaying her name is proudly placed.

I take the first step of introducing myself to the teacher. I appreciate her first concern was Eliza, not sucking up to us, unlike some teachers back in Richmond.

"Nice to meet you. I'm Cole Hayes, Eliza's brother and guardian, and this," I say, a hand extended in Lalah's direction "is Lalah McAdams, my girlfriend."

She shakes both of our hands, her gentle smile still firmly planted on her face. "Good to meet you, too. Do I contact you both in case I need to reach out?"

"Yes," Lalah confirms. "I'm most likely to be available, as Cole works weird hours with LHFD. We've also given contact details for Cole's brother at the reception."

"That's great to know. We'll be having a meeting in one month's time to discuss individual performance or anything pertinent to Eliza's progress. I send reports out to parents or guardians every Friday. Just to keep them in the loop, or get permission slips signed."

"Thank you, Violet. We'll leave you guys be. Have a good day."

"Do you feel like going for a coffee and a slice of apple pie at the diner?" I ask Lalah as we exit the schoolyard. I know she won't resist a pick-me-up to get her mind off Eliza.

Besides, I have a surprise for her.

"You're well versed in the way to this girl's heart!" She laughs. "I'll take the pie, please. A sugar rush is needed to chase away the sadness of leaving our girl behind."

"You know she's coming back, don't you?" I laugh and earn myself a backhanded slap on the arm.

"Stop mocking me. I've never done this before, you know? It's this weird feeling at the bottom of my stomach. A mixture of pride for Eliza being so brave and teeth-clenching dread. I want to bubble-wrap and keep her plastered to my side, where no one can hurt her. At home, I'm right there if she needs me. Here, it's completely out of my hands."

I wrap my arm around her shoulders and squeeze her to me. "And that's why I love you, my little control freak." I wink at her as her cheeks turn rosy and her eyes sparkle. We make our way toward the diner when I feel her shoulders stiffen under my arm.

"I wish Maevis and Tate were back. Something's missing without them. Texts and the occasional video call are not cutting it."

"And you're frustrated because you can't fuss over them. How much bubble wrap do I need to order, exactly?" I tease her.

"Oh, you infuriating man!" she cries out just as I open the door to Dine&Dash for her. Everyone turns their head around at her screech, and I love seeing that pretty rosy color of her cheeks turn a deep crimson. "I'll soo get you back for this," she threatens under her breath and stomps away to our usual booth as I follow, laughing.

I'm ready when she turns stone-still and sucks in a deep breath.

"You're back!" she whimpers, "Oh my god! YOU'RE BACK!"

Chapter Fifty-Five

Lalah

I launch myself into Tatum's arms and squeeze the life out of him. Face planted in the middle of his chest, I inhale deeply his comforting scent of pine wood and wilderness with just the smallest hint of motor oil. Tatum is my best friend as much as he is Cole's.

He catches me with an umph and wraps a steel arm around me, patting Cole's shoulder with his free hand. "Found your lost koala, brother! Didn't even have to call the number on the Have-You-Seen-Her poster."

I tilt my head back and fake frown at him. "Just for that, you're paying for my pie," I threaten, poking his side with a finger, then promptly turn on my heel and narrow my eyes at Cole. "You're paying for my coffee. Chop-chop before I get hangry."

Less than five minutes later, I'm staring at the still-warm apple pie, the tangy smell of red apples and sweet cinnamon filling my lungs. I smile at Tatum seated across from me, a cheery Clara pulling at his much shorter strands of hair.

"What did you do to your hair?" I blurt out.

"What? You don't like it?" He cocks an eyebrow at me.

I tap a finger to my chin, pretending to think. "Hmmm," I hum, and he throws a wrinkled napkin at me, making Clara laugh her sweet baby giggle I could listen to for hours.

"I do like it. It's just... a big change, I guess. I was used to your man-bun and tousled hair all over the place, and now that's all gone," I surmise, my eyes roaming over the almost completely shaved sides, longer at the top, sandy blond waves.

His soulful blue eyes turn to me, and I don't miss the hint of sadness in them nor the slight flash of defeat. "I needed a change," and his tone of voice tells me it wasn't big enough to heal what ails him.

He looks the same, although his frame seems smaller. I can tell he has lost some weight. His clothes are not as form-fitting as they used to be. It's also the way he carries himself like the weight of the world rests on his shoulders.

"You're back earlier than we thought you'd be." Cole changes the subject, most likely feeling the sadness floating in the air.

"Well, I didn't plan to return until the end of January, but I'm gone for less than a month and evil brothers come into town..." he trails off, his eyes once more seeking mine, checking on how I'm faring.

I can't deny the pang of pain shooting through my chest. It still hurts my blood-family dislikes me so much, but I'm done seeking their love and approval.

I'm just done with them.

I know Cole has blocked Alan, and I considered blocking my mother too, but I ended up leaving one line of communication open.

Despite her never being in my corner and always, always choosing someone else over me, when Daddy Dearest kicked us out, she took me in. She put a roof over my head. Provided food, clothes, and basic necessities, when it would have been easier to completely wash her hands of me.

So one line of communication remains open in case she ever needs my help. Any nasty, manipulative messages will be promptly ignored and deleted.

I went through all the stages of grief already. When acceptance hit, I saw the undeniable truth. Tatum is my brother, the only brother who matters. I nod at him, letting him know his mention of Alan doesn't bother me.

He rewards me with a wink, then looks at Cole, who's all spread out next to me. His arm rests on the back of the booth, his fingers playing with the collar of my blouse, tree-trunk thigh glued to mine.

"And you, putting out the pits of hell. Clearly, neither of you can be trusted to be left alone. So I'm back to keep you in line." Tate smirks his bad boy, half-crooked smile. I can practically hear the panties melting off all the women in the diner. A couple of men's too.

I decide it's also time for me to ask hard questions since he's avoided any and all talk of that night back in December. I clear my throat, trying to get rid of the nervousness. "Have you heard anything about the ex-bitch?"

A shutter of steel and ice falls over his face, his blue eyes turning dark in anger. "Like the other she-devil, she pleaded *not guilty*. She's been granted bail but can't come near me with the restraining order your lawyer slapped on her. She's also blaming her friend for spiking our drinks, denying she had anything to do with it. I guess we'll be going to trial. Unsure when that's happening though. And this is all I'm willing to discuss on the subject."

And I believe him. I can see in the clench of his jaw and his fisted palms that I'll get nothing more out of him. I'm not sure what he sees on my face, but his softens, getting downright mushy when Clara places her tiny hand on his cheek, rubbing his stubble adoringly.

She jumps to her feet on the red vinyl of the booth and plants a wet kiss on his forehead. "I make ouchie better," she declares.

"You sure do, sugar!" He kisses her right back, making her giggle again, then picks up a piece of her sticky blueberry pancake and feeds it to her.

No, he's not one hundred percent who he was before that awful, fucked-up night, but he'll get there. And I'll make sure Tatum is aware he has an incredible support system at his back and he is not alone. We'll get him to the other side.

We spend the rest of the breakfast laughing, Cole and Tate sharing stories of trouble they got into when they served together. It makes my heart extremely happy to see both of them genuinely laugh, with crinkly sparkly eyes and cheek-hurting smiles.

Tate sees us to the truck, the three of us trudging through the frozen snow coating the sidewalks. Not like he has another choice, with Clara hanging off him like he's her personal monkey bar.

People say toddlers don't fully understand the world around them and, any bad things, they'll be sure to forget. But I can see how much she missed him, just by how she sticks to his side, nuzzling her face to his neck.

He straps her in her car seat and messes up her corkscrew curls with his fingers. "I'll see you later, sugar. Be good to Lalah and Cole for me."

He turns to us and hugs Cole in that hand-shake-fist-bump-shoulder-rub thing guys seem to pull off so effortlessly. Once they separate, he picks me up, pulling me to his chest.

"I'm the only brother you'll ever need. And maybe that knucklehead, Blake. I've got you, baby girl. You listening?" he whispers in my ear, and I nod since my voice is all choked up in my throat from emotion. "Good! Now hop in before you freeze your ass off, and Cole hunts me for getting you cold."

"You'll come for dinner?" I ask as he gets ready to shut the door.

"Not tonight. Maybe on the weekend?"

At my nod, he continues. "I need to catch up at the shop. I could use some lasagna on Saturday to repair my brain after reading invoices all week."

"I told you there was no reason to worry," Cole teases me, his fingers playing around with mine. We're sitting in complete darkness in our bed, watching the snowflakes dance through the forest as they weave a frozen mantle over our front yard.

This is our quiet time. Our sixty minutes a day when it's just us two. Our hopes, dreams, and illusions are all whispered in the silence. Our fears, losses, and worries are all laid bare on the crisp sheets for us to heal.

He holds me together. I hold him tall and strong. He's my strength when I'm weak. I'm his beacon of hope. He nurtures my vulnerability. I absorb his disappointment.

We're both lost and found in these sixty minutes of ours.

Everyone's gone to bed, from a tired Clara, an overly school-crazed Eliza, and a very cranky Astrum. Not sure where Blake is spending tonight since he disappeared after dinner with a shit-eating grin and a "Don't wait up!" thrown over his shoulder.

"I know, I know," I concede, patting his firm abs. I do it again, just for the sake of touching those mouth-watering, pantie-melting valleys and hills.

"I'm so happy she had a great first day and made quick friends with Daisy."

"Eliza could befriend a bear if she set her mind to it. Sometimes her determination and smarts scare the hell out of me. She's only ten. I'm sprouting gray hairs just thinking of how she'll be as a teenager," he exaggeratedly shudders under me, making me laugh.

"She's definitely going places." I lift my head off his chest and look at him. From the scruffy underside of his jaw to his plump lips and straight nose, up to those emerald green eyes of his that had me mesmerized the very first second we met. "And I'm honored to know I'll be here, cheering her on."

He gives me a lazy, half smile, and then his face turns serious. "Speaking of being here, I know we've discussed this before, but hear me out."

He suddenly sits up from where he was resting on the pillow and pulls me into his lap, arranging my knees on each side of his rock-hard thighs. "I want to marry you."

My eyes widen in shock. Butterflies take flight in my belly. A stroke of dread paints my insides. My heart is ready to jump out of my chest and into his palms. *What the hell?*

But I don't get to say anything with his long fingers pressed to my lips.

"I can already see the protest on your face. I'm not done. I am well aware you don't believe in marriage and what it stands for. I'm also aware we've only been in each other's life for three months, give or take. But when you know, you know..."

He cups my face tilting my chin, making sure my eyes are on his. He keeps his expression serene and open, so I can read everything he feels in his hypnotizing emerald orbs.

"And I *know*. You, Supernova, are my endgame. I never felt the way I feel about you for anyone or anything else in my life. *I love you* is too dim of an expression compared to my feelings for you."

He takes a deep breath and gives me a quick peck on the lips, taking me by surprise with the sweetness of his gesture.

"I'm also asking for selfish reasons. Your family doesn't deserve you. Your father doesn't deserve you carrying his name. If you have to carry the name of a man, take mine. Choose the name of a man who'd lay down his life for you. A man who lights up just by seeing you walk into a room. A man who works hard every day to be worthy of you."

His thumbs start caressing my cheeks, catching the tears I can't stop from falling.

"I will adopt Clara and Eliza. Soon," he whispers now, a hint of worry in his eyes. My fingers shoot up to straighten the crinkling between his eyebrows.

"I thought that was a foregone conclusion," I croak through the lump in my throat.

"I want you to adopt them with me. You'll be the only mother Clara will remember. And Eliza needs the guidance of a strong, smart, loving woman. Eliza needs *your* guidance."

A sob escapes my lips. He thinks I'm good enough to help him guide his sisters. He finds me worthy of being by their side, supporting them, and loving them, as they grow, and stumble, and learn.

"I don't want to marry you because I want a mother for my sisters. But knowing you are the best mom they'll ever have, I want to be able to give them *you*."

"Cole..." I whisper. Emotion is choking me, and I struggle to force any sounds out of my mouth.

He doesn't realize what his words do to me. How his words mean the world to me. How he is healing me second by second.

"And I'll sign a prenup. I don't care about your money. Am I happy you can live a comfortable life? Am I proud of you for everything you are doing to help those around you? Fuck yes! But I have enough. I earn enough, so if you decide we move out of this beautiful home and donate all your money, we'll still live a decent, happy life."

"Cole..." I try again. "I'd be honored to marry you, and carry your name; carry your father's name. I'm absolutely humbled you want me to be Eliza and Clara's adoptive mom."

A deep breath fills my lungs as my palm finds purchase on his chest, my fingers caressing the spot directly over his heart. *My heart.*

"You bring me back to life, over and over again. You fight for me. Fight for my happiness. You tamed my demons, got them to dance to the gravel of your voice. You're my warrior, meus bellator."

"But?" he grits through clenched teeth, and I can feel him trembling under me.

"But nothing. I don't need marriage to know I belong to you and you belong to me. I don't need a framed piece of paper to love you, respect you, and care for you. I never dreamed of my wedding day, of a big puffy white dress or the wedding cake. BUT..."

"I have a feeling I'm going to like this but..." he murmurs as if afraid speaking out loud will break the magic building in our bedroom.

"But I can see myself marrying you, meus bellator," I finish with a blinding smile.

He's frozen for a second. Eyes big, lips parted, muscles stiff, fingers gripping my hips. He blinks slowly once, then twice.

"Are you saying what I think you're saying?"

"Are you asking me a question?"

"Lalah, would you make me the happiest man to walk the Earth and take me as your husband?"

"Cole, only if you make me the happiest woman on Earth and take me as your wife."

I barely get the last word out when he pounces. His mouth moves over mine, kissing me hard. Kissing me with everything in him. His lips mold to mine, over and over again, tasting and probing as a kaleidoscope of butterflies takes flight in my belly. I feel him everywhere.

His tongue coaxes my mouth open, then he invades, he plunders, he conquers. As if by this one single kiss we're married, connected, tied together forever.

I feel the touch of cool metal on my ring finger and Cole's mouth curving into a smile as he slows the kiss. I bring my hand up and admire the lustrous silver-white platinum band adorning my finger. A deep green emerald reigns over a cluster of five star-shaped diamonds.

"You're awfully sure of yourself, Mr. Hayes," I tease him.

"I'm awfully hopeful, future Mrs. Hayes," he retorts. "Do you like it? I figured you wouldn't go for a traditional princess-cut diamond."

"I love it, Cole!" I squeal, sincerity shining through my voice and eyes. "I get to look at my exquisite ring and see your eyes in it."

"And you get to carry us with you everywhere. One star for each one of us: me, Blake, Clara, Eliza, and last but not least, Astrum."

I'll never be alone anymore.

Epilogue

It's amazing what three determined women – Annalise, Mae, and Beth – and a reluctant one – me – can pull together in a month.

I stare at my image in the mirror. The ivory ankle-length dress clings to my body. With a sweetheart neckline low enough to expose the top of my breasts, my satiny wedding dress hugs my waist and the top of my hips, flowing down my legs in white, sleek ripples.

Silvery stars are embroidered on the bottom hem of the skirt and throughout the full-length sleeves. I don't have a lacy veil, nor a puffy princess dress, but Annalise and Maevis made sure I look like one.

I finally have my entire family with me.

One quick phone call after Cole's midnight proposal was all it took for Mae to pack her bags and return home. Together with Annalise and Beth, the three of them transformed the empty guest room into wedding central for a full-on month.

Cole and I both agreed to a small wedding with just our closest friends. Turns out, our closest friends and their families still make upwards of forty people.

My long black hair changed its blue highlights to silver strands, braided like a crown atop of my head, with the rest falling down my back in soft, silky curls. My makeup is as subtle as it could be done, but my eyes sparkle in swirls of green and amber, framed by black eyeliner and a smoky effect at the corners.

Everything about me screams laid-back bride, except for my lips, the only drop of color on me, slicked with dark red lipstick making them look ripe for kissing.

"I'm marrying Cole today!" I whisper to the bride in the mirror.

"I'm marrying Cole today!" I repeat this time louder, my voice confident and elated.

Happiness practically drips out of me.

I still don't believe in marriage. But I believe in us. I believe in the love and respect we have for each other. And above all, I believe in the future we are building together, brick by brick.

The soft click of the door as it locks startles me, and I quickly spin on my heel toward the sound. The skirt of my dress billows and swirls with the motion before settling back around my legs. I nearly choke on plain air at the sight in front of me.

Cole in casual clothes is a work of art. Cole in a three-piece dark suit with a green tie to match his eyes is downright sinful. His waistcoat hugs his trim waist and torso, making his shoulders appear even broader.

My very own Atlas carrying my world on his infallible shoulders.

The suit jacket frames his biceps and the custom-made cufflinks I gifted him earlier today are peeking from under the sleeves. The sparks of gold on the plated emerald surface glint under the brightness of the room.

He gave me an engagement ring matching his eyes.

I returned the favor with the cufflinks matching mine.

He gave me an engagement ring immortalizing our family in priceless diamonds.

I returned the favor with our initials entwined in the center of one delicate piece, leaving the other to carry proudly the initials of his brother and sisters.

"I can't believe I'm the lucky son of a bitch who gets to call you wife from now on," he rasps at me as his eyes coat in sparkling tears.

"I thought the groom was not supposed to see his bride-to-be before the ceremony." I joke, but my voice betrays the tempest of anticipation and love I feel inside.

"Who's foolish enough to keep me away from you?"

"It's supposed to be bad luck. Lady Luck has never been a big fan of mine."

In three long strides, he's in front of me, his arm around my waist, pulling me to him. His chin rests atop my head as he sways us gently from side to side. A melodic humm comes from his chest, and it's my turn to shed tears when the familiar tune of Sono Già Solo rips from his throat.

"I think Lady Luck has always favored you. Everything you've been through. Every step you took. Every decision you made. Everything has led *you* to *me*."

I lift my head from his chest admiring the man who's going to be my husband in less than fifteen minutes. He smells like all my hopes and dreams, all wrapped up in a tall, powerful frame of unconditional support and trust. He is *home*.

"Last night without you was pure fucking torture. Let's never do it again," he promises me as his lips touch mine. My eyes close of their own volition and my skin tingles under his touch.

His kiss is not ravenous nor demanding. His lips brush mine with adoration and awe, feeding the intensity between us with slow, lazy strokes of his tongue against mine.

His cock presses against my belly. Even through our clothes, he's impossibly hard, and thick, and long, and I push myself closer to him, my hands clenching the lapels of his suit jacket.

One second.

One second before our tender kiss turns into a fiery inferno. My panties dampen as a moan escapes my lips, and he greedily drinks it in, grunting against my mouth.

The palm resting at the small of my back grips my ass possessively as his mouth trails desperate kisses on the underside of my jaw and down my neck.

"Fuck!" he murmurs against my skin, bending at the knees and picking me up. My arms and legs automatically wrap around him, the long skirt of my dress bunching around my waist. "You look so goddamn beautiful! It pains me how much I want you."

"Then you better take me, *fiance*!" I purr at him, grinding myself on his cock through my soaked panties as he stumbles his way to the dresser and places me on the cold wooden surface.

His eyes flare and his chest heaves when my tongue darts out, licking at my bottom lip. "Unbuckle me!" he orders.

My hands shake in anticipation as they rip his belt apart. A flick of my thumb releases the button of his trousers, and I palm his length over the thick linen, my other lowering his zipper.

He shrugs the suit jacket off, dropping it on the floor unceremoniously. I waste no time diving my fingers into his black boxers taking him out. The barbells on the underside of his cock shine as the light from the overhead mini chandelier hits them, his angry red head already leaking his need for me.

I give into the temptation and bend down to place a kiss on the swollen tip, my tongue lightly teasing the velvet steel under my lips. He tugs my head back with a hand wrapped around my hair. The slight sting on my scalp makes me moan, but Cole's mouth silences me with a punishing kiss.

"Not today. Right now, all I want is you in this pretty white dress all wrapped up around me. I'm going to fuck you so hard, you'll feel me inside you as you pledge your life to mine," he growls at me, his fingers shoving aside the dainty satin of my thong.

"Yeeees, Cole, baby!" I scream as his hips shove my thighs apart and, in one powerful, unrestrained thrust he slides home. He stills inside of me for a heartbeat, then two, before releasing a deep sigh of relief.

"I'll argue with everyone who dares to disagree. Me inside you. You clenching every inch of me tight enough to cut off blood flow. This is what heaven feels like," he murmurs in my ear, before clasping both of my wrists in his large palm, securely holding them behind my back.

My spine arches, forcing my breasts toward him. Cole doesn't waste a second before diving his face between my tits, kissing and biting the exposed skin of my cleavage. With a tender kiss over my heart, he straightens to his full height, eyes locked on me as he glides in and out of my soaked channel in long, powerful strokes.

My ankles fasten around him, sharp heels finding purchase on his glutes, opening me up to him as he slowly withdraws until only the tip of his cock connects us before slamming into me over and over and over again.

My nipples are so achy and hard they could cut through the lace of my wedding dress. My moans and his grunts become louder and louder as he fucks me into oblivion.

I'm lost to the power of his movements, completely enthralled with the look of adoration on his face, so at odds with the savageness of his possession. I feel his thighs trembling under mine, and I clench around his length with all I have when he bottoms out, reaching my end and his beginning.

"Fuck! Holy shit," he growls, and his hand releases my wrists. I barely have time to plant my palms on the dresser's top before the rough pad of his thumb finds my clit and starts rubbing maddening circles over my sensitive flesh as he savagely rams into me.

Stars are bursting under my eyelids, and pure electricity runs through my veins. The tendrils of pleasure coil inside of me, starting in my belly and spreading further and further through my limbs with every drag of his piercings over that magical spot inside of me.

"Come for me, Supernova. Come for me one last time as my fiancée," he orders just as a knock sounds from the tablet's speakers next to the door.

We both freeze for a second, him deep inside me, me clinging to him for dear life. "Do you think they're gone?" I whisper as the knocking comes once again, but much more insistent.

I shift around Cole and mewl on his shoulder as one of those magical barbells hits my G spot, the familiar flutters of my belly moving to my pussy walls, spurring Cole on. His lips land on mine again, so frenzied, so hungry for me as if he's been starved for months and now the most decadent of steaks has been put in front of him.

A distanced voice comes from the tablet. "You guys are in soo much trouble. I know you're in there."

But I'm too far gone. He palms my breast roughly, kneading and squeezing, pinching my nipple between his thumb and his forefinger through the delicate lace of my dress, grinding his cock on my clit at the same time and I'm done for.

With a last conscious thought, I press my face to the crook of his neck to muffle my cries of pleasure as I become one with the stars. Like the supernova he calls me, I detonate around him in a burst of color and ecstasy. I'm floating through the universe as euphoric shocks wreck my body under his skillful hands.

I come down from my high what feels like hours later, to find Cole with his nose buried in my hair, his big palm running up and down my spine coaxing me back to the present with his warmth, his cock still pulsing his release inside of me.

I feel the heat of his cum as it drips out of me, coating the top of my thighs and his groin with the evidence of our joining. "Just thinking, next time I get to have you like this, my eternal ring will be on your finger. It'll be my name you'll wear. Next time I get to lose my mind inside of you, it will be the first time I worship you as *my wife.*"

He gently slips out of me, rearranging himself inside his underwear. Blink and miss it, he is back to the composed man I know and love, no trace of our frenzied lovemaking. Except for a lone lip-shaped crimson smudge sitting on the crisp white collar of his shirt.

His calloused palms massage the trembling muscles of my thighs, causing shivers to run up my spine. His deft fingers rearrange my underwear on me, and I squirm, protesting, still feeling the aftermath of our orgasms dripping out of me.

"No. Leave it. It makes my knees weak knowing the creamy skin of your thighs will be painted with me when you vow yourself as mine in front of our entire family and all our friends."

"I don't think I'll ever stop being shocked at that filthy mouth of yours." I laugh, my chest still heaving, my body trying to calm itself down from Cole's thorough possession.

"You have a lifetime to get used to it," he smirks.

"Seriously guys. Open up. You'll both be late to your own wedding." Annalise's voice comes from the tablet and my cheeks turn scarlet, knowing I'll have to open the door and she'll guess in two seconds flat what we were up to.

Cole's face turns smug with stupid alpha pride as he comes to the same conclusion. I slap his chest with the back of my hand when he picks me up by the waist and gently lowers me to the floor. I'm thankful for the extra seconds he holds on to me, because I'm not sure my knees are fully recovered yet.

"Drop the smirk. Everyone will know why you and I locked ourselves together in here."

"Let them. Everyone will witness me pledging my life to you in ten short minutes. So what if we started celebrating early?"

"For fuck's sake!" Anna's muffled groan comes from the door. "Seriously?"

Cole sweetly presses his lips to the tip of my nose before he hurries to the door, unlocking it. I'm not just marrying the hottest of men, I'm marrying a smart one too. Everyone knows when Annalise starts spewing profanities, you better do as she says or else...

She bursts through the door in a blur of red satin and luscious caramel curls and stabs a finger to Cole's chest.

"You were not supposed to be here," she accuses.

Her nose wrinkles when she puts two and two together and comes up with pre-marital-hot-sweaty-animal-sex. "For the love of God, you couldn't wait one more hour?"

Cole shrugs like he doesn't have a care in the world, a shit-eating grin on his face. "Have you seen my future wife? Even dead, you couldn't keep me away from her."

His pale-green gaze finds me, humor and love twinkling in them. "I'll see you on the other side. I'll be the one crying my eyes out and thanking every deity conspiring to get you to walk down the aisle to me."

This man fucking slays me. I don't even get the chance to respond before he's hurrying out the door with Annalise's "Charmer!" thrown at his back.

And what a back it is. I guess I finally understand Travolta because I hate to see him go, but love to watch him leave.

After a side of evil eye, coupled with a *Good for you, girl* mother of smirks from Anna, my dress is once more wedding ready, my lips have a fresh coat of lipstick on them, and my hair is put to rights.

"Well, look at you glowing with bridal happiness," she smarts. "Ten world-renowned makeup artists wouldn't be able to replicate it with all their magic pencils and fairy dust. Come on, let's get you hitched. Tatum and Matt are waiting for you."

As much of a feminist as I am, I'm bursting with pride to be escorted down the aisle by a handsome-as-fuck Tatum in a blue navy suit, clasping tightly onto my left hand.

My adoptive father figure, Matt, all spiffed up in his own blue navy suit, leads me from my right toward a smiling Cole. He didn't lie when he left the bedroom.

He really is the one with tears falling down his cheeks waiting for me in front of the makeshift flowery altar the guys put together the night before.

Snow is still falling all around us, but under the heated lamps and the love warming me from the inside out, I don't feel the cold. The happy faces of all my loved ones surround me with joy. This is how it feels to belong. This is home.

My four bridesmaids are waiting for me to take my place next to them, all in fiery-red dresses looking as if they've stepped out of a magazine. I chose to have Annalise, Maevis, Eliza, and Clara at my side. As for Cole, Tatum stands as his best man, with Jackson and Blake as groomsmen.

My breath catches in my lungs as I stop in front of Cole. The adoration in his eyes as he extends his hand to take mine makes my knees weak.

Matt pats him on the shoulder and leans in. "Take care of our girl!" and I bite a laugh at the threat in this voice.

"Always!" promises Cole, his eyes not leaving mine even for a second.

It's Tatum's turn to hug his best friend. "It's my greatest honor to give my sister away to you and stand by your sides as you celebrate your love. I love you both. And I'm grateful to know and have you in my life. You crazy kids keep the hope of happily-ever-after alive in me."

And then, finally, it's my turn. Cole's big hands clasp both of mine. His smile never leaves his face when he presses a kiss to each of my knuckles; or when the officiant walks us through our vows; definitely not when my trembling fingers push the black tungsten wedding ring onto his finger.

If anything, it grows exponentially, pearly whites shining at me, when it's his turn to slide a silvery platinum diamond-crowned wedding band on mine. He doesn't miss a second when the officiant finally gives him permission to kiss his brand-spanking new wife.

I'm the brand-spanking new wife! I squeal inside when his strong arms lift me off the floor, his mouth finds mine, and the world spins around us while we share our last first kiss as husband and wife under thunderous claps, catcalls, and wolfy whistles from all those here to celebrate us.

"I love you! I love you! I love you!" Cole repeats over and over again through kisses and laughter.

As the world spins, my dress billowing around us like a cape of lace and satin, my head thrown back in happiness, his arms supporting me as I fly, I realize it doesn't get any better than this.

I'm loved in so many ways. From the all-consuming love Cole is showering me in every day to the cuddles Astrum still demands from me whenever the girls aren't around...

I'm loved beyond words and measure.

I'm accepted as I am.

I'm deserving.

I'm worthy.

I'm home.

Whoever invented heels can go straight to hell and spend eternity on five inch stilettos. My feet hurt something fierce and, as much as I'd like to sprawl out on the sofa and take a breather, I can't.

It feels like every man in my house agreed to take me for a spin on the dance floor as soon as they see me sitting.

And by every man, I mean Cole.

A large piece of decadent, velvety hazelnut and chocolate cake is placed in front of me as Mae plops into a chair. I keep looking left and right for Cole, terrified he'll once again make me get up.

I'm determined to ditch the stilettos from hell, snow be damned. I'd rather risk losing my pinkie toe to frostbite than keep them on my feet one second longer.

Wordlessly, Mae pushes a fork at me before getting her own and showing a massive bite of cake in her mouth. I know she's frustrated. Both Tate and her have tried their absolute best not to let whatever is going on between them spoil our day, but the awkwardness in the air is thick.

As is the anguish whenever there's less than five feet between them.

I'm honestly minutes away from pulling these two fools by their ears and get them to kiss and make up. But I can't, because Tatum went through the worst time of his life and Mae ditched him without even hearing him out.

She groans as she shoves another massive forkful of cake in her mouth. I mean, I get it. She's baked us the most exquisite of cakes. Melt-in-your-mouth chocolate, crunchy rich hazelnut, coffee soaked sponge cloudy soft, she's gifted us the cake of my dreams.

Except, I mistook her groan for pleasure.

Her face pales, then quickly turns a greenish hue. Her round, dark eyes become even larger as they widen in panic. She quickly stands, a shaky hand pressed to her mouth, turns on her heel and runs to the back entrance of the house.

I *finally* ditch my heels under the table and chase after her. I catch the door to the downstairs toilet inches before it's locked in my face. Maevis is already on her knees, head shoved into the porcelain bowl, vomiting her soul out.

I bite the inside of my cheek so hard, I taste the metallic tinge of blood. I'm a sympathetic puker. Just the sounds or simply the knowledge of someone vomiting close to me, and I'm there on my knees to cheer them on.

Before I'm tempted to join her on the floor, I hear the toilet flush as she sits back on her calves, wiping her mouth with the back of her hand, tears streaming down her face.

I help her up and guide her to the sink. She rinses her mouth a couple of times with water, gulping mouthwash like it'll go out of style. I wet a washcloth with warm water and gently clean her face of tears.

"Are..." I open my mouth to ask, but she quickly shushes me.

"Not here."

Mae clasps my hand in hers and starts dragging me to the enclosed back porch, in the furthest corner, away from the party. She leans on the wall, one hand holding her tummy.

There's both heartbreak and elation in her eyes as she smiles at me. Understanding washes through me as I see her eyes dart to the backyard, where Tatum waltzes Eliza around on the dance floor.

"I didn't want to tell you this on your wedding day..." she whispers. "I really thought I could sneak away and drink some ginger ale whenever a wave of nausea hit."

"Say it, babe!" I demand, but I can't stop the smile from spreading over my face. Even though I have a pretty good idea of what's coming, I still brace myself.

"I'm pregnant!"

Curious about what happens next in Lost Hope?

Find out in book two, *Vanilla et Motricium Oleum,*

Tatum and Maevis's story.

June 2024.

Acknowledgements

What a whirlwind this first book has been. MY very first book. I'm writing the words and I still can't believe them. From the very first sentence to the very last, this book has been so deeply personal to me, I just want to take all those fragile parts of Lalah and hide them back inside of me.

I had a very wrong idea of what it meant to actually sit down and write a book from start to finish. I saw myself all smiles at my laptop, putting the daydream hunting me for weeks on paper and writing "The End" like the naive, innocent woman I was just a few short months ago. Instead, I had to face headstrong characters, who never wanted to do anything I asked (read beg) of them, and whose voices demanded to be heard.

Have to admit, Cole grumbled in my head for a full month as I spewed poetics at Tatum.

The best thing out of this whole journey has been the incredible community I found. I'm so incredibly thankful to each and every one of you.

Ana Maria, your support (read – putting up with my whining sessions) has been priceless for me. From Alpha&Beta reading to calming down my hysterical self in the middle of the night, Annalise definitely had a thing or two to learn from you. You can't imagine how happy I am I couldn't get rid of you fourteen years ago. You're stuck now, beib. There's no escape.

Claudia, thank you for taking the time to read and debate with me over every single worry I had for every single paragraph that bothered me. Always and forever, pisi.

Jamanda, I couldn't have kept my sanity without you, you super-talented-superwoman. You're my sounding board, the gatekeeper to my sanity. You're absolutely the best cheerleader, shiny pom-poms and all.

Chloe, on the very last step of this process, I can't believe I found you. Thanks for making me doubt I ever knew how to speak English. I hereby declare you my personal Thesaurus. I'm keeping you. Sorry, not sorry.

A huge thank you to my editor Katelyn, for putting up with my impatience and wayward commas. Cole's introductory chapter would not have happened without you, and boy was he deserving of it.

Siiri, thank you for creating my beautiful beautiful cover – and book and series logos. I fell in love with it the minute I saw it. I'm so so happy I found you, and that you've been blessed with enough patience to put up with my lack of knowledge and puppy enthusiasm. Not to mention the last minute speed read of Lege. You slayed through the last of my rogue typos and inconsistencies.

A special thanks goes to Mr. Right. Thank you, love, for only grumbling occasionally for always doing the dishes. You're the absolute best. PS: It's still your turn. I'm starting book two.

The biggest thank you goes to my readers. Thank you for taking a chance on my dream with every page you kept going. I hope you found little pieces of yourselves in Lege et Lacrima and I hope I've done them all justice. All my love <3

For the smallest contribution in the grand scheme of things, this mention goes to Coffee. Thanks for keeping me awake and not attacking my heart in the process (hopefully).

About the author

When she's not having a latte in her hands, Alina has a book or her Kindle. Her time is split equally between her very serious day job, her very fun time writing, and providing Mr. Right infallible arguments as to why it's not her turn doing the dishes.

With a deep love for written word, she woke up one day with characters screaming in her head to be put on paper. And that brings us up to date. Alina writes everything romance, fierce heroines, and steamy scenes that make her hide under a blanket and ask for more.

Alina lives in the UK, with her infinitely indulgent Mr. Right (and human dishwasher).

If you'd like to poke the bear and find out more about other novels she's currently writing, please join her private book cave here:

AC's Book Cave

Since procrastination is an effective punishment tool when her characters misbehave, if she's not waiting for a latte to be delivered, she can be found on:

Facebook – Alina Comsa Author

Instagram – @alinacomsaauthor

TikTok – @alinacomsaauthor

Email – malumcatincus@gmail.com

Don't be shy, get in touch. She promises to be on her best behaviour, whatever that means.

Also by Alina

Lost Hope Series

Lege et Lacrima

Vanilla et Motricium Oleum (June 2024)

Atramentum et Telum Pulvis (Coming soon)

Lux Solis, Fumus et Specula (Coming soon)

Ardor et Glacies (Coming soon)

Printed in Great Britain
by Amazon

41278542R00249